Fire And Steel

RIČARDAS JAGUPENKA

Chapter I

Lord Delos removed his house crest last, handing it to his squire. The boy, the son of one of Delos' vassals with enough magic to be worth training, scurried away to Delos' lines. He felt naked without the protection of his artifacts, but tradition demanded a duel be fought without the aid of enchantments. This farce was Lord Kol's idea, the aging Lord had prattled on about the waste of life and protecting his subjects. Delos had only agreed to save himself the bother of a prolonged campaign. Small boarder disputes had a nasty habit of dragging out and prolonged conflict could catch the eyes of the court.

Lord Kol shambled his way across no man's land with the aid of his son. Delos smirked; it would be good to put the old Lord out of his misery. Two decades ago, this would be a fair fight, but age had stripped the man of everything except his mind. Lord Kol stopped just outside of the marked ring where the duel would be fought. Delos tapped his foot as Lord Kol slowly removed his house crest and a series of rings.

"Lord Delos, I must ask again is there no way we can resolve this? I understand that you suffered an offense. I have offered just compensation for the lumber harvested. Those who stole from you were brought to trial." Lord Kol said his voice wavering and his eyes downcast.

"You offer soft justice and a pittance. Honor demands blood for such an offense. You should have let me burn that worthless hovel to the ground. Instead, you choose to sacrifice yourself for what? Your vassals, most are barely better than citizens." Delos replied with a snarl as he stared down the feeble Lord.

"Father, let me deal with this rabid cur. One day I will lead House Kol but that need not be today." Lord Kol's son said, his hands balled into fists as he met Delos' gaze. Delos shrugged. A hot-headed young man who had never seen real battle or an old fool well past his prime, neither would provide a real challenge.

"If there must be blood. It is my duty as Lord to shed it. Whether that means killing or dying has yet to be seen." Lord Kol said, his voice no longer wavering. Delos smiled, perhaps Lord Kol still had some fight in him.

"Whoever has a death wish may join me in the ring. I would like to sleep in my keep tonight and all this prattling is wasting time." Delos said, the ring flared with a yellow light as he entered.

With one last glance at his son Lord Kol stepped into the ring which began to pulse with orange light. Delos stared down his opponent as the ring flashed faster and faster. Neither man moved until the ring flashed a bright red. Delos moved first raising his right hand to the sky as he wove a pattern with his left.

"Skybound radiance!" He shouted. Dozens of crystal orbs materialized in the sky above the dueling ground. Lord Kol had only just begun to move as Delos brought his raised hand down. The sky exploded as the crystals turned to miniature suns and rays or scorching light shot forth to engulf Lord Kol. Delos smiled as the light faded, and Lord Kol remained standing. Liquid metal coated every inch of the old lord. Where the burning light had stuck the surface glowed red and bubbled.

Lord Kol dashed forward twisting tendrils of metal extending from his arms. Kol covered the distance between them in less than a second. Despite the surprising show of speed Delos' body thrummed with magic and he dodged between the tendrils with ease. With a gesture, spears of light rained down on the old lord. Unfazed Lord Kol continued his assault the tendrils frantically writhing through the air in a bid to find purchase on Delos.

Delos began to hum, and crystal armor grew over his body. With the armor in place Delos ignored the tendrils and focused on crushing Kol. As the tendrils lashed him the crystal armor cracked to dissipate the force of the blows. Despite Kol's efforts the crystal armor reformed itself faster than his magic could shatter it. Delos planted his feet and using both hands commanded a ceaseless volley of blazing light to fall on Kol.

Even without physical form the onslaught drove Kol to the ground. Delos stepped forward to deliver the killing blow only to find his feet caught in a pool of liquid metal. The metal oozed over his crystal armor pressing it inward. Even with battle magic enhancing his body beyond natural limits he could feel the crushing force overwhelming his defenses.

Delos scoffed as he was forced to change focus from attack to defense. His crystal armor glowed bright, and the oozing metal boiled away. The brief reprieve had given Kol time to regain his feet. Delos brough his hands together and the small crystals fused together at the center of the ring. As Kol dashed forward Delos unleashed a single enormous beam of light. Kol whipped himself into the air with the metal tendrils narrowly avoiding the killing blow.

The ground boiled as Delos shifted the beam to eradicate his foe. Kol's tendrils shot him forward and he landed in front of Delos with a thud that shook the ground. Delos was forced to jump back to avoid the slamming tendrils.

Even as Delos brought his hands forward, he felt Kol's magic fading. The old Lord had pushed his fragile body beyond what his magic could sustain. Delos could see the liquid metal beginning to slough off.

"That won't do." Delos mouthed to himself. The old fool did not deserve a noble death; Delos took hold of the faltering magic and commanded it to strike. He moved through the rain of blows he had directed at himself with contemptuous ease. When he reached Kol's lifeless body, now only held by the magic Delos had stolen, he grabbed the man's head in his crystal gauntlet.

"Pathetic," Delos snarled. His magic amplified his voice so all those gathered could hear. As he raised Kol into the air with his right hand, he commanded the large crystal sphere to split into four. Chains of light shot from the orbs and drew Kol into the sky. Delos turned his back on the forces of his defeated foe. Delos smiled as panicked shouts erupted from behind him. He paused before leaving the dueling ring. With a wave of his hand the chains of light tore Kol's limbs from his body which fell to the ground with a wet thud.

***

Delos found the confines of his study rather stuffy and cluttered. He rarely spent time there and had no inclination to waste time having it put in order. His ankle throbbed where Kol's magic had bound him. Lord Kol had surprised him albeit briefly and had it not be imperative to quash any thoughts of retribution Delos might have let the man die with honor. Once back at the Keep Delos had left orders that he was not to be disturbed and went to the study. Releasing the magic, he had used to hide his injuries had floored him. The injury would heal in time, but healing magic was not one of Delos' strengths.

Delos was pondering his triumphant return to court when he heard a soft knock on the door. Delos immediately reactivated the physical enhancement spell. The pain in his ankle was replaced with a throbbing behind his eyes. Delos stormed over to the door and slammed it open. Despite the pain his magic was ready to punish whatever servant had dared disturb him.

"Lord Delos. A messenger from court wishes to speak with you. He bears a message with the seal of house Ironsong." Adrus said without hesitation or fear. The house steward was a decade younger than Delos and held himself with calm arrogance. The man was indispensable, and he knew it. Delos prized competence and efficiency above all and if the price was tolerating a bit of arrogance, then Adrus was worth it.

"Show him in, have the cook prepare something for our guest." Delos growled as he made his way back to his seat.

A message from court could be just the opening Delos needed after his recent failures in Krais. He had wiped the mercenaries turned bandits from the face of the empire but the Promises damn cold had proven deadlier than expected. He had lost good men, and the court had held that against him despite the mission being accomplished. Rebuilding his status at court was of the utmost importance but he had put that on hold. Because when he had returned to his holding, he found Lord Kol stealing from him. A slight which required immediate reprisal.

Delos had just made it back to his seat when a young noble entered the study. The young man was dressed in a fine red tunic with bright yellow and white highlights and sleek dark trousers. The outfit was more than eye-catching and with his head pounding Delos hoped this meeting would be brief. Delos did not recognize the young man or his house crest, a falcon holding a sword.

"Lord Delos. It is an honor to meet you. I am Lord Tyrus Merrel." Tyrus said with a deep bow. Delos smiled at the show of respect and gestured for the young lord to sit.

Delos surveyed the young lord as he walked to the open chair. With magic flowing through his body Delos' ability to sense magic was as strong as it could be without casting mage sight. Lord Merrel was a below average mage as far as nobility was concerned, barely worthy of his noble title. The court was clearly showing its displeasure sending the young noble as a messenger. Whether that displeasure was at Delos or Merrel would have to be seen.

"It has been a long day, and I have celebrations to prepare for. Deliver your message and be quick about it." Delos scoffed. If the court did not see fit to send a proper messenger, then Delos would not act the proper host.

"Celebrations fantastic, I knew it was best to come prepared." Merrel said with a smile and rising excitedly handed the sealed scroll to Delos.

A cursory glance told Delos the seal was legitimate. The magic still strong despite the two-week journey from Arabas. He broke the seal, unfurled the scroll and began to read.

Lord Theodore Delos, the court sees fit to elevate your station. Without delay you are to assume the role of Governor of Expera. With the passing of Lord Skolis, the region is without proper leadership. The administration of the region has been lacking of late and it is the belief of the court that you are distinctly qualified to restore it. A contingent of arcanist from the Shin-Rai arcanum will be dispatched under Lord Marius Kelen to assist you in your work. You may augment your forces as you see fit. Proceed with all haste and go with the blessing of House Ironsong. — High Lord Relos Ironsong

Delos threw the scroll to the ground and incinerated it with a beam of blood red light. Lord Merrel squeaked and nearly fell from his chair as the scroll burned away. Delos had hoped the young lord was sensible enough to leave once his task was complete. Delos rose and stormed through the study, burning whatever he found as he tore the piles of papers and books apart. He only stopped when he felt blood dripping from his nose.

Expera was a failed experiment filled with worthless citizens. Its only saving grace was its abundance of magical materials from Alethia's promise. Expera was where the houses of the empire went to die. Delos may not have an heir yet, but he still had time for that, but it would prove impossible in that accursed region.

"I think it best if I go. I thank you for your hospitality, Lord Delos." Merrel said eyes down cast and hands fidgeting.

"No!" Delos bellowed, "You will stay. I have need of a messenger and as my people will be busy that duty falls to you."

"But… I… I really must insist…" Merrel stammered. Delos glared and the young Lord who cowered back into his seat.

"Remain here while I prepare the missive." Delos commanded. He looked around briefly noting a small fire growing in one of the stacks. "Actually, make yourself useful and put that out."

Delos stormed through the Keep as he put his thoughts together. He could not refuse an order from High Lord Ironsong and that meant he was going to the city of Khaldra. *It would be better to burn the entire city to the ground but that would be another failure. Perhaps with the proper application of force something can be made of that worthless piece of land.* Delos though darkly.

Chapter 2

As Peter Dennet made his way through the gathered crowd he felt odd. Normally the crowds were there for him. But not today. Today, the amphitheater of the Khaldra's market was bustling with a far too many nobles. A few of the more prominent citizens had gathered on the outer perimeter but none seemed keen to make their way to the front.

Dennet was hoping to find his one noble contact before the new governor began his address. As Dennet scanned the crowd he noted a few people glaring at him. Despite the fact his clothes were finer than many of those gathered, his status as just a citizen was apparent from the lack of a family crest. No doubt some in the crowd knew his face but they would not be as inclined to scorn him publicly. Dennet mostly ignored the larger clusters of nobles. Unable to locate his contact, Dennet turned to make his way back to the outer ring.

"Unfortunately for you, my brother is far too busy to attend," a woman's voice projected over the murmuring crowd, drawing him back to the front. A distinquished group of noblewomen were gathered around the speaker. A younger woman with long auburn hair, wearing a short, deep cut dress that

Dennet knew cost more than most citizens made in a month, of hard labor.

"Alexandra, always a pleasure," Dennet murmured to himself, a bit sarcastically, as he worked his way through a group of rather older men in long robes. Even as he approached her he weighed whether the aggravation was worth it. Dennet bowed to Alexandra as he joined the group. If anyone cared that it was far less the formality dictated, he didn't care.

"Why would you call him over here?" scoffed an older woman.

"Because, Lady Imir, as a citizen and a gentleman he knows how to prepare for long, rambling speeches," Alexandra said, stepping forward and reaching into the breast pocket of Dennet's suit. With a swift motion she pulled out the flask he kept there. Taking a sip, she smiled, and said, "You always keep the best for yourself."

"Of course, Lady Hyde. As we all can attest wealth has its privileges," Dennet said, trying his hardest to keep the condescension out of his voice. He knew he was far wealthier than anyone in this group, save Alexandra, and all of it earned through his own skill and intellect. The Hyde family might be a small and largely inconsequential branch of House Dimiris, but Alexandra's brother was a shrewd businessman and ruthlessly used every advantage.

"What would you know? You speak of things above your station," Lady Imir said.

Perhaps she is new to Khaldra, Dennet mused.

"Peter Dennet, leader of the Field Knights of Khaldra. At your service, Lady..." Dennet replied, smiling. Feigning dismay he continued, "Alexandra, I seem to have forgotten this distinguished lady's name."

"Lady Imir is a truly noble person from a prestigious family known for…" Alexandra replied flippantly, pausing to take another sip from Dennet's flask. "Dennet, it is impolite not to warn a lady about the strength of the wine you serve her."

Lady Imir, clearly having had enough humiliation, left in a huff.

Even if she was new to Khaldra, Alexandra's proclivity toward indulgence was well known. Returning the now mostly empty flask to Dennet, Alexandra smiled and called out to Lady Imir, "I do hope we will see you and your husband at the governor's party tonight. My brother mentioned wishing to speak to you about your family's trade routes through the Miralocke."

Lady Imir turned for a brief second at Alexandra remark. Her face caught between anger and reluctant acceptance. Once again she's reminded Dennet that though she was often vapid, Alexandra was a master of the game of nobility. No matter how abrasive she could be Alexandra had connections valued by any noble with half a brain.

Luckily, before any further tensions could be inflamed, the new governor took the stage.

The man's face was gaunt, and his eyes were cold. His hair was cropped short like his beard. His features were not particularly striking, but his eyes and demeanor carried a presence far beyond his mundane appearance. His clothes were neat, closer to a military cut than the more ostentatious clothing typical of upper nobility.

Dennet did not recognize the house crest he wore, but the crossed staff and dagger was far more subdued than the thorn blade of House Ironsong embroidered over his heart. Clearly whatever house the new governor was from had the support of House Ironsong. The most militant of the Great Houses taking a direct interest in Khaldra and the region of Expera was a worrying development for Dennet. The last governor had been from a lower house with limited ties to the Imperial court. His hands-off approach to governance had worked significantly to Dennet's advantage as he was establishing his first expedition teams. Not that it was enough to satisfy Dennet's ambitions.

Perhaps it wasn't the best idea to send both of his expedition leaders into the Promise so close to a shift in leadership, but Dennet had not anticipated such a significant change. A governor with direct support from House Ironsong was likely to take a hardline approach to dealing with the powerful citizen class of Khaldra.

"My name is Theodore Delos," the new governor said. "As of now I will be taking control of the entire region of Expera. The solutions implemented to deal with the unique problems of this region have been wholly inadequate."

The scorn he put on the word "solutions" left no room for doubt in Dennet's mind that things were going to get tough for the citizens of Khaldra. Not only were the words projected far beyond what would be normal, Dennet thought they might be carrying some small amount of compulsion. Dennet had no way to know if the power necessary, to add compulsion, came from Delos or one of his retinue. Either of those possibilities were distressing for different reasons, and both made Dennet regret his decision to send his expedition leaders out.

Delos continued, "It has come to the attention of the Great Houses that the conduct of the citizens of

Expera has been in direct challenge to the rule of the empire. Of greatest concern is the complete inability to resolve the death of multiple members of the nobility. Such attacks cannot go unpunished, and I will see the perpetrator brought to justice. All those who posses the means and motivation to commit such actions will be questioned. The proliferation of arms amongst the citizens is also of note to the Great Houses, and should I find that such arms pose a danger to the safety of the realm then that too shall be dealt with."

Dennet's hand went to the small pistol hidden in his coat. Firearms were a novelty in most of the empire but in Expera they were crucial for survival. The strange effect that its proximity to the Promise had on the birth rate and development of mages left the majority of those born in the region without the magical talent that served as the foundation of the empire.

Dennet would need to move up the timetable on a few things. He had expected to have at least a year before he made his move. No citizen had ever been recognized by the nobility a fact which irritated him greatly. Years of planning might all go to waste if he could not adjust.

"To accomplish these goals I have brought a full battalion of trained guards and a contingent of magi from the esteemed university of Shin-Rhi. To those loyal to the empire, I bring hope that the scourge of lawlessness will end. I bring a chance to better the people of Expera and advance the arcane knowledge of the empire. In the coming days I expect to meet with those deemed worthy."

With that, Delos turned around and left.

Whatever spell had been cast broke and many of the citizens on the outer ring of the crowd stood stunned. Dennet wondered whether the effect was more targeted or his awareness of it saved him from the brunt of the effect. He had made his fortune selling magical oddities recovered from the Promise, but the functional limits of magic had never been of interest to him. Considering his current plans, it might be time to learn, and quickly.

Dennet noted that Alexandra had resumed talking with her group, completely ignoring his presence. He did not blame her. Anyone could see where the winds were blowing, and playing the game of politics had always been her only redeeming quality. He had hoped to set up a meeting with her brother, but that would have to wait.

Leaving through the market just to the south was his best option. Walking calmly, Dennet pulled a pin from his coat. Dennet pretended to drop something to cover the act of placing the pin on his collar. With the insignia of a burning heart he felt more confident that he would not be stopped and questioned as he moved to leave. The crest was the symbol of House Silram, a minor house closely tied with the church of Televilus. Dennet knew wearing it was a major offense in the eyes of the empire, but the benefits of appearing official far outweighed the risk. The fact he was a well-known figure in Khaldra was an issue, but he had found that his face was forgettable enough that a change in demeanor usually sufficed to throw people off.

Dennet made it into the market without anyone taking a second glance. Quickly removing and pocketing the crest he headed toward the center of the market. People often say a rumor travels faster than a horse, and it amused Dennet to see how true that adage was. He watched the shift in both merchants and shoppers as the news of Governor Delos's grand plans spread through the heart of Khaldra. It was small things: the placement of certain items, the way a merchant walked through his stall, the time a customer spent looking over an item. The kinds of things that could be overlooked, but these were his people he had built his life in this city as a businessman and none of it escaped his notice.

"Busy day, Mr. Dennet. Very busy," a merchant called from a nearby stall. The singsong quality of a native of Sera-Met clear in their voice.

"Zal, it's been a while. I thought you were not planning on being back in the city for a few months at least," Dennet said, as he turned toward the merchant's stall. A shorter man of perhaps forty years wearing the layers of light overlapping fabric typical of a trader from Sera-Met stood in a sparsely filled stall. The few items in the stall seemed old and shabby in comparison to many of the other merchants' wares. Dennet was sure many of the items in the stall were just that, but some were far more than they seemed. Zal had always taken the phrase "buyer beware" quite seriously, selling a combination of useless junk and highly dangerous artifacts with equal regard for customer satisfaction. It was perhaps an inditement of Dennet's character to deal openly with him, but Zal's ability to acquire or distribute items of incredible value was an asset Dennet could not afford to lose.

"It is foolish to fight the winds of trade. I am no fool, Mr. Dennet, and so I follow where those winds blow," Zal replied, smiling broadly.

"It seems in following the winds, you may have found a storm," Dennet said, in a serious tone. Dennet was not sure whether the merchant's presence in the city was simply a coincidence or if he saw a chance to profit from the coming chaos.

"Perhaps, but where better to weather a storm than with an old friend? Often a wise man can find many opportunities in a storm, and I think I may have just the opportunity for you," Zal said, gesturing for Dennet to join him in the back of the stall.

He walked over to a small chest tucked under a table, which held a oversized cracked bowl. Zal picked up the chest and as he rose he bumped the table slightly and the bowl slid off and crashed against the ground, shattering.

"Are you planning to clean that up?" Dennet asked, walking over to assess the chest Zal held.

"No, it should fix itself in a few days," Zal replied, holding up the chest but not moving to lift the lid.

Dennet looked at him quizzically, shrugged, and opened the chest. Inside, a small scroll sat upon the felt lined interior. The paper did not appear particularly old and without unrolling it Dennet could not determine what made it special. He was, however, sure there was something exceptional about it, otherwise Zal would not have stored it so reverently.

"I thought you did not deal in books," Dennet said.

Zal stepped back and spit on the ground a gesture Dennet had seen a few times. It was common among the people of Sera-Met as a sign of warding against evil.

"No, no, no, not a book, a map. But certainly not a book. I am no fool to deal in such things," Zal stated.

Dennet knew Zal had some personal superstition around books, but it seemed it was a far stronger aversion than he had thought.

"I meant no offense, my friend. I've just never

seen you selling anything similar," Dennet said, lowering his voice and raising the pitch of his voice It would not do to offend a valuable business partner. Whatever distinction Zal was making in his superstitious mind was none of Dennet's concern.

"No offense was taken, and perhaps I am a fool, but any merchant would dream of such a prize as this. Indeed, dreams are where this map leads. Or at least to the Dreamer's Crown and all that it holds," he replied his voice growing softer and sharper. Dennet was not a religious man, but he knew of the Dreamer's Crown. One of the three gifts Televilus gave to Alethia in exchange for assistance in creating this world. Of the gods who played an active role, Alethia, the embodiment of primordial chaos whose promised lands lay just beyond Khaldra's borders was the one who Dennet was most familiar with. Zal did not pull the map away as Dennet reached for it. Unfurling the map revealed a swirling mess of lines that twisted in ways Dennet could not quite follow. Despite this one small symbol sat fixed near the center of the page.

"If this is really a map as you say and not some worthless piece of enchanted paper then you can name your price," Dennet said, placing the map back into the chest.

"It would be improper for me to place a price on such a thing. That is why I will be holding an auction once I have found enough interested parties," Zal said, smirking. Auctioning such an item was a dangerous game to play but Dennet knew Zal often took risks in the name of profit. "Of course, you are the first I have revealed this treasure to,"

Dennet doubted that Zal had acquired the map in Khaldra and would not have brought it to Khaldra without already having a few people lined up to buy it.

"An intriguing proposition. Once my expedition teams return, I'm sure Ill have more than sufficient resources to give anyone else a run for their money. Let me offer you a toast. To the chance at unimaginable fortune," Dennet said, reaching into his pocket to retrieve his flask. He paused, finding his pocket empty.

"It seems you are missing something, my friend. But that is good. It would not be proper for me to except a drink from you. This is my business and therefore my home, it is only right we drink my wine," Zal said, laughing. He put away the small chest and pulled a bottle off one of the tables. They drank and talked of small things for a time before Dennet left. It seemed he would be paying a visit to the Hydes sooner than expected. Whether it had been Alexandra's invitation or a convenient excuse Dennet would take the chance to speak with her brother on the events of the day.

Chapter 3

Not for the first time Dets eyed the softly glowing crystals in the streetlights. She knew the penalty for stealing them but just one would be so useful back on the farm. Technically she could buy one, but money was always tight, and she was still paying down the rifle she had slung over her back. She still owed three full majors on it. A bit less than half of the original total. Kel had done so much work on it since than that it felt like she had barely made a dent in the total. The fresh jerky in her bag attested to the usefulness of the rifle. Dets appreciated that Kel accepted small portions of her kills as payments toward her debt though it was obvious he valued information far more. He would always grill her on the conditions and distance of the kill shots and any issues that arose during her hunts. She didn't mind, though the amount of detail always seemed extravagant to her. The man was a perfectionist to the core both in the construction of his rifles and their use. She had never met anyone quite as capable with a rifle and his insights had been crucial in feeding her and her family. The street was oddly empty, especially just off the market square. Usually there were at least a few people for Dets to avoid when she came into Khaldra proper.

Despite the hour the light over Kel's shop was

on. The small sign on the door read Kel Rifle Company carved in simple script. The other signs were far more ornate, ranging from ornate wooden replicas of rifles to gilded lettering proclaiming the names of the owners. Considering the respect Kel had among the craftsmen on Gunpowder Street Dets always wondered why he did not have some way to distinguish his shop from his competitors. Opening the door, Dets entered. Immediately the smell of powder and oil hit her. The interior of the workshop was neat, with lines of rifles stored on a rack on one wall of the small entrance room. Tools and munitions lined the other in various crates and hangers. The far wall had another door marked with a warning sign reading: NO OPEN FLAMES, NO CIGARETTES, NO IDIOTS.

The door creaked open as Dets entered the workshop proper. Kel was at his workbench, a small glowing crystal illuminating the workspace and casting oddly shaped shadows over the rest of the room. The rifle on the bench had a strange contraption mounted on top.

"If you are here to place an order, come back tomorrow. If you are here to pick up an order, take what's yours and leave," Kel said, his voice cold and flat as it always got when he was working.

Dets ignored his tone and walked over to the workbench.

"So, what is that thing?" she said. She could see that whatever was affixed to the rifle was composed of metal and glass. It looked like two cones affixed in the middle with some kind of dial. As she finished her question Dets heard the distinctive click of a hammer being uncocked.

"One of these days your curiosity will get you

killed, Dets," Kel said, but his tone was warmer. He turned to face her with a slight smile on his worn face.

"Not if Nadia's kills me first," Dets replied.

"She'll be the death of both of us, I'm sure. As for this, it's an improved sight I've been working on. Unfortunately, I needed to contract out for some of the smaller components, so I haven't had a chance to test it yet," Kel said, laughing. "Take a look for yourself," He worked the action, presenting a clear chamber, and handed her the rifle. Dets immediately noted the extra weight of the augmented sight. Kel's personal rifle was already heavier than her own and the added weight made it somewhat unwieldy for her smaller frame. She raised the rifle and looked down the sight.

"Is there some trick to this? I can't see anything," she said, somewhat annoyed.

"Try looking at the barrels over there," Kel suggested, gesturing at the far side of the workshop.

Dets adjusted the rifle and tried again. In the glassy surface she saw more darkness but as she concentrated, she realized the darker patches were in a distinct shape: the letter G. Nearly the entirety of the surface was taken up by the letter painted in black on the brown wood. She swept the rifle along the barrel and could make out all the letters G-U-N-P-O-W-D-E-R. She lowered the rifle and looked over at the barrel. Even squinting the letters were too small to make out across the room.

"Wow that's amazing. But how do you know where the shot will land?" she asked, handing the rifle back to Kel.

"I've got a plan for that, but I wanted to see how it worked first," Kel said, "But I doubt you're here to check up on a project you couldn't have known about. How's the hunting been?"

Dets smiled as she pulled the jerky from her bag.

"Brilliant, just like me. I got her from nearly a hundred meters. Should last us at least a month. There's a lot of meat on a full-grown bear," she said, standing tall with a bright smile.

"Standing or prone? Was there wind? One shot. Was it luck or precision that brought it down…?" Kel began his routine of rapid-fire questions.

Though she had not expect praise it was still a bit hurtful that Kel immediately began his questions. Before Dets could reply the door to the back room opened.

"You can get your details later. I've got more interesting things to discuss with her," Nadie interrupted, trying futilely to run her fingers through her short black hair. She seemed half asleep as she walked over to join them. "Did you get a chance to test them out? I made a few more but it's hard to gauge the delay without test results. There were a few unfortunate mishaps, but I've still got my fingers, and the shop is still mostly stable, so I'll call it a success for now," she said, her voice going from sleepy to her normal overly excited tone. As she spoke she rested her hands on the workbench, leaving sooty stains on the wood surface and eliciting a scoff from Kel.

"Well, I never got a chance to test them while I was hunting, especially since I need something to bring home," Dets said. She regretted saying so as she watched Nadia's face sag. "But father needed a stump cleared, a really big one he's been struggling with for a while. Cleared most of it in one go. Nearly blew me off my feet as well. Might want to extend the timer a bit."

"Well, you are supposed to throw it. It kind of defeats the purpose if the target has time to run away. Not that a stump could run away. Well, I made up a few more so be sure to do some proper testing next time," Nadia replied, back to her normal chipper self. Even as she spoke Nadia swayed on her feet. "Kel, I thought you finished setting that up yesterday. I know you want the thing perfect, but practical tests are far more useful,"

"Nadia, when was the last time you slept?" Kel asked watching Nadia closely.

"Well, you said we needed more gunpowder to fill that special order, so I did that. I whipped up something for my current project then made some higher-grade powder for the new prototypes I wanted Dets to actually test. Once that was done I started on those, hoping to finish them after I got the results. So probably some time before all that," Nadia replied after thinking for a moment.

"Dennet picked up that order two days ago," Kel said, exasperatedly "Dets can you make sure she gets home before I have to rebuild my shop again,"

"I'm fine I put this together just before Dets showed up" Nadia said, pulling a sphere from one of her many pockets and placing it on the workbench. It rolled a bit before settling precariously close to the edge of the table. Both Dets and Kel jumped back. "Oh, don't be babies" Nadia said, picking the object up and lightly tossing it across the room in the general direction of the barrels. It landed and rolled short of the barrels. "See? Perfectly safe. Now this one would explode" She pulled a second spherical object from another pocket and held it up to them, a small green line ran around the object. "I color coded them blue for impact, green for timer There was a long pause as everyone looked between the two objects. "Okay maybe I need some sleep but in my defense, anyone could have made that mistake,"

"Dets, take her home now," Kel said, his voice cold and flat again. Nadia began walking toward the object she had tossed. "Leave it, Nadia,"

"But I need to know why it didn't work," Nadia said, flinching.

"It'll be on your bench tomorrow," Kel said.

Nadia started emptying her pockets onto the workbench pulling out multiple tools and another two spheres both with blue stripes. Kel rolled his eyes but remained silent. Once she was done Dets started heading for the door. Before opening it she turned to Kel.

"I'll get her home safe. Guess I'll have to come back to report," Dets said. She gave Kel a informal salute as she turned and left with Nadia following behind.

The walk to Nadia's place was short and Dets only had to redirect her once when she tried to wander off, murmuring something about looking for a test site. After Nadia went inside, hopefully to sleep, Dets considered making sure the door was locked but quickly thought better of it. Nadia was always tinkering and there was a reasonable chance trying the door would leave her a stain on the sidewalk. Dets rarely spent much time in Khaldra proper, but the city was beautiful at night. She had some time considering her conversation with Kel had been cut short, so she decided to wander a bit through the mostly empty streets.

It did not take long for her to get lost in the winding streets. She realized it was probably a mistake to wander outside of the few areas of the city she knew by heart. No one was around so she climbed a series of twining vines to the roof of a nearby building. Between the streetlight and the vantage point she had a great view of the city. The scale of it shocked her. Thousands of houses and shops pack close together spread out before her. The intimidating, squat fortress to the north was the governor's mansion and the bright spot near the center was probably the market square. With those landmarks Dets began heading west, jumping the gaps between houses, and climbing when she needed to. Most of the houses in Khaldra were no more than two stories so it was relatively easy going. The cool air and the slight breeze exhilarated her, and she began to run, taking larger jumps and dropping farther than she probably should. It reminded her of hunting, traversing the uneven landscape and climbing trees. She had just finished dropping down onto the roof of a bakery when the air grew significantly colder. There was a strange fog gathering a block over, which did not seem normal for the season. Dets' suspicions were confirmed when the fog cleared in an instant. Curious she jumped off the roof of the bakery after unslinging her rifle so she could roll on impact. She sprinted through an alley and climbed a drainage pipe to get a view of the area where the fog had disappeared.

Three figures were chasing a forth down the narrow road. Two of the three wore uniforms, Dets did not recognize but looked official, and carried side swords. The third was wearing a strange shimmering cloak unlike anything Dets had ever seen but did not carry any visible arms. The fleeing figure was wearing leather armor dyed black and had a cloth wrapped around their head. The cloth wrap was reminiscent of her father when he was a merchant guard in Sera-Met., however, the side sword and dagger they carried were more common among the nobility of the empire. On their back was a sheathed greatsword Dets thought was a bit overkill. The extra weight might not slow them down, but it certainly would prove a hindrance in a long pursuit.

Dets went prone and brought her rifle to bear on the situation. She knew she could hit a moving target at this distance with ease, but it felt wrong to aim at any of the figures. She was a hunter not a soldier. She knew she could alter the course of events, but she did not know anything about this situation. More than that she was not sure if she could pull the trigger knowing she was ending a person's life. She moved slowly to position herself where she could watch the situation unfold without being seen.

The fleeing figure turned on their pursuers drawing their sword and dagger, which surprised Dets. A few seconds later, a wall of blue tinted ice sprang up behind them. This was magic on a scale unlike anything Dets had seen before, having spent most of her life in Expera where magic was comparatively rare and when it was employed it was for small, mundane things. She vaguely remembered some of the amazing things she had seen as a child in Sera-Met but those had been far less spectacular. The two pursuers moved forward while the one in the cloak stopped. Even if they were a powerful mage, three on one were bad odds at least from Dets' perspective. She considered fleeing and letting the situation play out, but she felt committed to seeing this through even if she did not intervene.

The air grew cold as the combats drew closer before they clashed the cloaked figure raised their hand

and a spear of ice shot forward. If the fleeing figure was not the mage then they were as good as dead. The ice spear slipped between the two men in uniform and was met with a slashing strike from the pursued swordsman, who reduced it to dust. The uniformed men began to circle while the mage began gesturing in an intricate pattern. Unfazed, the swordsman rushed the man on their right. Knocking aside the man's hasty swing with their dagger they cut toward the man's head. The blow had to be stopped short as the other uniformed man rushed to strike moving faster than Dets would have thought. Enhancement magic was common in Sera-Met and Dets recognized it immediately. Dodging away, the swordsman cut the air in front of the enhanced man's chest. Oddly, the man stumbled nearly falling over seemingly unable to arrest his momentum a task that should have been trivial under the effect of enhancement magic. The swordsman did not waste the opportunity and lunged forward, running the man through. The second man, having recovered, threw a cut at the swordsman's back, which was stopped by the greatsword sheathed there. Dets could see blood leaking through the swordsman's armor, the sheathed sword having saved them but not stopping the blow entirely.

All of this played out in seconds and had distracted Dets from the mage. Shouting a word Dets could not identify, the mage called forth a massive wave of snow, which froze the ground as it moved. It flowed around the uniformed man and engulfed the swordsman. Dets could not see what the blast of swirling snow was doing to the swordsman but she assumed the conflict was over.

Moving back from the roof edge took her eyes

away but a scream drew her attention back to the scene. The swirling mass of snow remained but the swordsman was standing over the uniformed man, who had a dagger imbedded in their shoulder. The swordsman's armor was coated in a thin rime of frost, and a scarlet icicle had formed on their back. If any words were passed between the mage and the swordsman they were drowned out by the screams of the uniformed man.

The cloth around their head had come loose and Dets could see the swordsman's eyes, which glowed a bright purple. Dets tried to flatten herself against the roof to avoid those eyes. She felt relived as the swordsman seem totally focused on the mage ignoring even the wounded man at their feet. With a shout the swordsman charged the mage crushing the wounded man's face under their boot as they went. The mage raised his hand and a hundred ice razors sprang into being around them. With a gesture the mage sent them forth in a stream that snake forward to meet the charging swordsman. The swordsman's blade cut the air repeatedly as they passed through the stream of tiny ice blades. Dets could see the stream slowing as the blade cut the air, but it was not sufficient to stop the onslaught. Cuts sprang up all over their armor and the cloth was shredded hanging in ribbons over a blood stained face.

The swordsman, or perhaps swordswoman's face was definitely feminine and had many of the features of the few Imperial nobles she had seen. Their sandy blond hair was cut short in a haphazard way that reminded Dets of the haircuts her parent would give her brother. The purple glow from the swordswoman's eyes flared and the maelstrom of shards fell to the ground with the sound of breaking glass. The mage turned and ran, calling forth walls of ice behind them. The swordswoman followed and the ice walls simply disintegrated into snowy mist as they came within arm's length. The chase was short despite their wound the swordswoman was significantly faster and though the mages power astounded Dets it proved useless. The swordswoman's blade nearly severed the mages head and he fell forward blood spurting from his neck. The swordswoman wiped her sword on the shimmering cloak, and it dulled. They turned and retrieved their dagger from the whimpering body of the uniformed man. As the swordswoman departed, Dets kept her rifle trained on them, but her hands were shaking so badly she knew she couldn't make the shot even if she wanted.

Dets wondered whether she had done the right thing. Could she have saved the lives of the men dying on the cobbles below? Who was this person who had cut their way through two armed men backed by a powerful mage? Dets found herself so far out of her depth trying to assess the situation. She could tell her family but that might drag them into something terrible. Kel and Nadia were the closest thing she had to friends in the city proper but that was more a professional relationship than a personal one. The trip home was a blur of conflicting thoughts. The image of the swordswoman charging through the snaking ice blades their eyes glowing the armor stained with blood and the tatters of cloth ringing their neck flashed through her mind again and again.

Chapter 4

Dennet woke early, as normal. It was critical he met with Alex today, but expecting either of the Hydes to be awake before noon was foolish. Alexandra always had guests over late, enjoying the privileges of nobility. Alex took the opportunity presented at such gatherings to further his business interests. It was a model that had worked for the Hyde twins throughout their time in Khaldra, though Dennet personally found it tiring to deal with. He worked best in the morning, setting up the events of the day. When he was in Khaldra that usually consisted of taking in the news and arranging meetings. If he traveled with his expedition teams, mornings were spent striking camp and planning the route. It had been some time since he had led an expedition and though he insisted it was in furtherance of establishing his interests in Khaldra.

Alethia's promise terrified him. His teams rarely returned without losses. The twisting reality of the Promise made exploration a near suicidal endeavor. The unnatural treasures found within had been the foundation on which Khaldra was built. As well as how Dennet had made his fortune. Leading teams into the Promise, he had seen friends die simply walking the wrong way or consumed by things whose form belied description. These thing had left their mark on him, but if others wished to enter then he would provide them what aid he could. If that made him a profit all the better.

Dennet made his way to a small shop known for importing coffee from Arabas. Dennet found it to be a good place to gather information about events in Khaldra and the wider empire. The shop was empty when Dennet entered. Not entirely surprising considering the hour but Dennet had hope at least a few patrons would be present. It did allow him to take his usual seat, which hada good view of the entire shop. He always paid well to be left alone but never so well as to become a person of interest. Dennet knew he was a well know figure among the citizenry of Khaldra but in a city of over one hundred thousand people it was possible to remain relatively anonymous. As far as the staff was concerned he was just a somewhat private regular.

Dennet spent nearly two hours in the shop. In that time only two patrons visited. That was telling of the state of the city in and of itself. The two patrons came in together. Dennet recognized one of them: a jewelry merchant who was know as a competent and unbiased appraiser. Dennet had never delt with the man personally but had worked with some of his associates. The other was a lean woman with a shaved head a loose grey robes. A priestess from Al-Sai-El judging by her attire. Dennet, like most people in the empire, knew little about Al-Sai-El despite the trade that occurred between the empire and the island nation state. Dennet had encountered a few people from that mysterious land, but they seemed focused on whatever business had brought them to the Imperial continent.

Listening in for a time Dennet learned little of relevance to his current circumstances. It was somewhat amusing to hear the merchant attempt small talk with the priestess. Her vague answers always brought the conversation back to the subject of gold. From what Dennet overheard the priestess was attempting to purchase a rather absurd quantity of gold. To what purpose Dennet could only guess though some kind of religious ceremony was alluded to.

Dennet left somewhat disappointed, but at least he was able to enjoy his drink. He still had a few hours before it would be prudent to head to the Hyde manse. Heading to the market, Dennet noted that the guards Delos had spoken of had already been deployed throughout the city. Two full squads of guards blocking a stretch of a nearby street caught Dennet's attention. The guards seemed to be doing a decent job in keeping the area clear and obstructing any view of what was happening. A few of the building on the street had signs marking them as places of business. Dennet figured that any shopkeepers whose establishments were closed would still be in the area. If anyone knew why the street was closed it would be the people who worked there. It was simple enough to guess that they would be in a nearby pub, it was just a matter of finding that establishment. In short order Dennet found himself in front of a pub called the Skull and Duggery.

Not the kind of place Dennet would frequent but better than most of the places he had visited when he was starting out.

It might hurt his chances to stand out as much as he did, considering his tailored suit and shined shoes. Since it was unavoidable he decided to play with the cards he had been delt. He swaggered in and immediately announced he was buying a round for the house. All said and done it cost him a full two majors, but people rarely question good fortune. He took his cup of what the barkeep had called brandy but smelled more like barrel cleaner and headed to a table with a group of three conversing around it.

A bearded man wearing a leather apron and tool belt was speaking with a man and a woman wearing cloth aprons dusted with flour. One of the shops on the closed road had a sign advertising a cobbler though Dennet could not recall a sign for a bakery nor any any building with an inordinate number of chimneys.

"What brings you here stranger? Not that I mind none, seeing as I could use a drink," the man in the leather apron said, eyeing Dennet's approach.

"Peter Dennet, I was actually looking to pick up some new boots for some of my men, but it seems there has been some kind of incident and the road is closed," Dennet said.

"No offense to you, Mr. Dennet, but that sounds like bullshit to me," the man said, "If you got some interest in the 'appening round my shop just ask. Might be we can come to an arrangement,"

"That we might, Mister..." Dennet answered calmly. Placing a minor on the table. The card held a depiction of a heart pierced by three swords. Not a significant amount of money but enough to by a decent pair of boots.

"Kents. For that you'll get the story whole and true," Kents said, pocketing the minor.

"Now if I had known your story was worth something I'd have claimed it was my own," the male baker said, laughing. "But me and the misses don't need to hear you again, so I think we'll get back to work,"

With that they left leaving Dennet to take their place at the table.

"Good riddance to you. Now it might not be the longest tale, but a dry mouth can ruin any tale," Kents said, jovially waving his empty mug.

"Let's see how well you spin a tale before anything else," Dennet responded.

"That's fair, can't fault a man fer trying," Kents said, "So I had a big order in the works. Mrs. Elet's got seven boys you see, and growing boys are always needin'. new shoes. Now normally it wouldn't need to be a rush job but her husband wanted to take the oldest down to Vesrin in a few days. Now I could get a few pairs done right quick but being as they're good folk I decide to do a pair for all seven. So that's why I was sleepin' in my shop when them fancy guards came a knocking," Dennet realized this might take a while and resigned himself. He leaned back in his chair and let Kents continue. If Delos had sent so many guards to cover up an incident it was something worth knowing about.

It took the good part of an hour and another round for Kents to tell his tale. A tale Dennet could have relayed in a few minutes. Dennet's take away was that whatever had happened involved a mage and resulted in injury or death of at least two individuals. Conflicts between mages were not unheard of in Khladra but they were normally relegated to the halls of nobilities manses. Beyond that the intrusion of the guards had upset a considerable number of people and significantly disrupted their lives. Even in the best planned areas the streets of Khaldra were a mess often ending abruptly. The closing of a single road could double the time of even a short journey,. The new governor would not be garnering any good will amongst the populace . The fact so little information was available on the incident did worry Dennet. It spoke to a quick and competent reaction combined with a disregard for any inconvenience to the citizens of Khaldra. The only silver lining was the possibility of a powerful mage acting in opposition to Delos' plans.

Dennet had only recently become involved in the politics of the city. It was not his choice, but his wealth had placed him in a predominant role among the citizenry of Khaldra. Khaldra's unique location had led to a far more powerful class of citizens than any other city in the empire. That power had been significantly limited by the noble class. Significant taxes on trade in the mundane arcane items that improved the quality of life of all the people in the empire. Significant restrictions on exporting of the many technological wonders invented by the citizens of Khaldra. All of these things and the stigma placed on people born in the region were the tools by which the citizenry of Khaldra was controlled. Dennet had personally struggled against this as he made a name for himself. Whether it was personal ambition or empathy for those who still toiled to achieve even a fraction of his status,Dennet could not sit back and enjoy his newfound wealth.

Dennet made his way through the city to the Hydes' manse it was still early but Kents's story concerned him. He needed to get ahead of whatever crackdowns were coming and find out who was fighting with mages in the streets of Khaldra. If his expedition leader were here he would have the resources to deal with these problems but for now his strongest allywas Alex Hyde. It might be a mistake to trust the young noble but Dennet understood the need to take calculated risks. The manse was located in the outer district on the southwest side of the city about as far from the Promise as was possible within the city limits. The area was filled with houses of minor nobility who came to the city either for the economic opportunity or to avoid the scrutiny of the greater Imperial court. Dennet had always thought it was silly to build on this side of the city. The area was far rockier and more uneven than the north but fear of the influence of the Promise was enough to keep the nobility away. Dennet had been in Expera long enough to know that the influence of the Promise was not something so easily avoided.

The Hydes' manse occupied a fairly prominent location in the district, but it was smaller than most except for its extravagant ballroom, which occupied the majority of the property. The property was not gated like some of the others and its drive was far more welcoming with ornate topiaries and ponds lining the well paved road. Dennet waved to the groundskeeper whose name he should know he had been the one to recommend her when the Hydes had first arrived. Dennet hoped she did not resent the amount of work he had saddled her with. The constant stream of nobility who visited the Hydes required the grounds to be kept in pristine condition.

Dennet knocked on the door and waited. A few moments later he knocked again with no answer. Why the Hydes did not have a better mechanism to alert the staff of guests always confused him. He had a small, enchanted crystal near his door that would light another in his study when pressed. It had cost him a fair bit and the hassle of acquiring it had been considerable, but it was convenient and made an important statement.

Before he could knock a third time the door was cracked open.

Alexandra's pale green eyes peered through the crack before she opened the door.

"You picked a terrible time to stop by. I'm barely dressed unless that was what you were hoping for," Alexandra said, smiling. She was wearing a flowing night gown though Dennet noted her hair and makeup already done.

"Alexandra, if you thought you weren't presentable then you would not have answered the door," Dennet said, entering the foyer of the manse. It was not as ornate as the grounds nor the entrance to the ballroom, which was its own section of the house. The few tapestries adorning the space were primarily religious, depicting previous Sword Saints. Though this was probably a statement of political neutrality rather than religious fervor.

"I'm perfectly presentable, just not for uncouth, unannounced visitors," she replied, feigning exasperation.

"I wouldn't need to arrive unannounced if someone would respect others' property," Dennet said, meeting her gaze and speaking calmly but with a firm tone..

"Oh well, if you're just here for that…" she said, producing his flask from thin air. She handed him the flask then turned and began walking away.

"I was hoping to speak with your brother, if that is not too much of a burden," Dennet said, relaxing his posture and tone eyes glancing down at his feet,, before she could get to far. Dennet did not have time to play games, and he knew if he did not give her a win she would ask him to leave just to show she could.

"Well, since you asked so nicely, I think he's

meeting with someone in the study. I'm sure you know the way," she said without turning around.

It was a bit out of character for her to make it that easy but if she was playing some other game Dennet did not know what the goal was. Shrugging to himself, he headed for the study. On the way he noted an alcove with a fine sheet covering an oddly shaped object. He briefly considered checking what it was but reconsidered. Alex would not appreciate the intrusion and Dennet was not sure if he wanted to see what kind of surprise Alexandra might have for her many guests.

Opening the door to the study Dennet saw a short man rummaging through the bookcase. Dennet did not recognize the man. He was fairly well dress though somewhat disheveled, and his hair was a tangled mop on his head. As Dennet entered the man jumped, dropping the book he had been placing on the shelf.

"Oh, um, I was just…" he stammered, turning to face Dennet. "You're not Alex," He turned back to the bookshelf.

"Neither are you, sir," Dennet said, somewhat annoyed at the disrespect. It could be the case that this person was some important noble, but his state and mannerisms made that unlikely.

"It would be odd if I was, though it would probably help me navigate this sorting system. He's got Thomas Zifer's *A History of Empire* next to Martus Sinvarus's *Fundamental Enchanting*. I mean really it's bad enough that that book circulates, but … Ah now that's something worth reading" the man said, moving up a shelf and looking over a rather ordinary looking tome there. He took the book off the shelf and sat down in a fine if well usedrecliner.

"Do you know where he is?" Dennet asked

"No, I could, but I'm told that spying on people is rude. Honestly, it seems ruder to ask a question someone couldn't possibly answer," the man answered, opening the book to what Dennet could only guess was a random page.

"My name is Peter Dennet. I am a business associate of Alex's. May I ask to whom I'm speaking?" Dennet asked, hoping to get something useful out of the man.

"Oh, I knew I was forgetting something. I'm always doing that. It's always good to know who you're speaking to or at least who they're claiming to be. Not that I'm not accusing you of lying, Mr. Dennet. I do apologize if it comes across like that. Wait, what was the question again?" the man said, trailing off into thought.

Dennet was beginning to question Alex's choice in guest. =This man did not seem to have a solid grasp on the world around him. Dennet was going to repeat the question when the man continued. "You asked me my name. Well, technically you asked who I was but as neither of us have the time to actually answer that I'll just assume you were asking my name. I'm not sure why it would help you, but people do seem to want to know so many useless things. I'm Marcus Velen arcanist of the Shin-Ria Arcanum."

An arcanist well that explained the odd behavior. Arcanists studied the workings of magic on a fundamental level. A process requiring a flexibility of thought that often was to the detriment of the arcanist. Dennet had never met an arcanist in person but he had heard stories from the various merchants he dealt with regularly. That he was associated with the Shin-Ria Arcanum was distinctly worrying. Dennet resigned himself to waiting for Alex to return from whatever business had called him awayand sat down across the room from the arcanist.

"That's complete nonsense. You were doing so well but than that's a complete mischaracterization of spell formation!" Velen exclaimed, tearing a page out of the book he held. Dennet chose to ignore the outburst. For all he knew it was entirely justified.

"If you're done arguing with the dead. It seems we can begin, now that everyone has arrived," Alex said, entering silently during Velen's outburst. He was wearing a charcoal grey suit, neatly tailored, and a short brimmed wool hat. The crest of House Hyde, a crescent moon overlaying the sun. was pinned on his collar. It wasn't often Dennet saw him wearing the crest outside of official functions.

"The dead make poor conversation partners, at least when I've had the misfortune of speaking to them. Books, however, are far from dead," Velen said with a smile eyes focused on nothing in particular.

"Are you sure about this, Alex?" Dennet asked preempting whatever rant Velen was probably about to begin.

"Velen is mostly harmless, unless you're a book or at risk of dying of boredom. Beyond that he, like my family, are somewhat outcast from the court," Alex answered, pouring something from a decanter into three glasses. Dennet would not call the Hydes outcasts from court. Alexandra always seemed to know about the events transpiring outside of Expera and Alex's business connections were even greater than his own. Perhaps there was more to their arrival to Khaldra than he knew. A small house with two young successors was certainly in a poor position at court, but that alone would not make them outcasts. Dennet was curious but unless it effected the business at hand it would have to wait.

"Expera is a region of outcasts, at least as far as the empire is concerned. I am going to need more than that to trust someone I have never met," Dennet said, taking one of the glasses and sipping. Dennet noted Velen had made no move to take his glass or looked at either of them.

"Well, if my word is not enough for you then perhaps he can assuage your concerns," Alex said giving no indication he had taken offense.

Dennet was not sure how the arcanist could manage that. Alex did seem earnest in bringing them together toward a common goal, so Dennet would hear the man out. Dennet turned to the arcanist, who had resumed reading, seemingly unaware that he was the topic of conversation. Dennet watched the Velen closely for a time before coughing in an attempt to get the mans attention.

"Oh, I don't really know if we have the time to fully explain who any of us are but if its important I guess I can try," Velen said after turning the book to another random page.. "How to begin... how to begin. Well, I could start at the beginning but that assumes there is a beginning and I'm certainly uncertain if that is true. Perhaps it would be easier to just answer any questions you have but I'm doubtful that would work as you've demonstrated little skill in asking questions. Wait, was that rude? I'm terribly sorry. Well, not terribly. That doesn't make sense. How would being sorry be terrible?"

"Velen, just tell Peter why I asked you here," Alex interjected calmly. Velen looked from Alex to Dennet before his gaze wandered off to the bookshelves.

Dennet felt like this was a significant waste of time, but he trusted Alex enough to give it a shot. If Alex was ready to tolerate the absentminded arcanist then Velen must be useful for something.

"Of course, that should work. I'm here to assist in multiple capacities but primarily Alex has suggested there are several challenges he needs to overcome for which I am well suited. Wait, I don't think that explains anything. Well, maybe I should say…" Velen said, trailing off.

"Peter, I understand your reticence, but clearly he is not dangerous. Velen is probably the single most knowledgeable arcanist in the empire. This, combined with a distinct lack of social graces, has made him the target of several powerful houses either as an exploitable asset or an obstacle to be removed. With the new governor bringing far more Imperial mages to Khaldra I thought it might be best to have someone on hand who know their capabilities and weaknesses. In addition, you have mentioned needing a better appraiser for the oddities your teams bring back," Alex said, attempting to salvage the meeting.

Dennet watched Velen closely. If he was acting a part then he would put House Dimiris to shame. It irked Dennet that he couldn't get a solid read on the man, but Alex's suggestions had considerable merit. If he wished survive his bid to gain a true title he would need every advantage. He was confident in his own abilities but it would be foolish to turn down aid freely offered..

"To desperate times and strange bedfellows," Dennet said, raising his glass to Alex.

Velen took notice and moved toward the glass but hesitated.

"Probably best not to mix alcohol and alchemy, at least if I want to be able to walk anywhere," Velen said, smiling. Dennet could see and odd swirl of light in the mans eyes.

"Shall we get to business?" Alex said, placing his glass down and pulling a small notebook from his suit pocket. "The new governor has a lot more resources than the previous one and the mandate to use them liberally. Which means it's only a matter of time until they notice our operation."

"I've already acquired enough supplies to keep the men fed and housed but we need time to train and we are still considerably short on arms. Unless circumstance force us to act we can't rush ahead. The front is still solid I even have the appropriate paperwork for establishing a homestead," Dennet replied.

"I'm aware, but it's a thin ruse at best. There is a real possibility Delos will put a halt on any homestead operations while he is consolidating power. There is also the issue of scrying. If any of the governor's entourage are capable of it then it will be hard to hide any training," Alex said, glancing at Velen.

"Oh, sorry, I was not really following along," Velen said, distracted.

"Do you know if any of Delos's mages are capable of scrying and if there's a way around it?" Alex asked repeating the question without changing his tone.

"Well, yes and no to both parts. Scrying is basic ritual magic but it's unlikely anyone capable of evocative scrying would be present. So, they probably can perform ritual scrying, which is far more limited than evocative scrying, though it's possible to construct a sa-ren map, which would probably be far better than just having a seer. That would take a significant amount of time and effort so probably not a concern. In terms of preventing scrying, the problem is somewhat reversed. A seer can be block with basic precautions, but a scrying ritual would be harder to block, though it does require foreknowledge of the target and some kind of physical connector," Velen said, happily enjoying the chance to explain something he knew in detail.

"Precautions would be good, but I would rather keep them from looking in the first place. Something happened in the city last night involving mages that seemed to have gotten the governor's attention. Perhaps we can use that to our advantage. If their resources are focused elsewhere then with some work we might be able to buy enough time," Dennet said.

"There have been rumors circulating around the nobility regarding a house war or some kind of corrupted mage. I have multiple confirmed reports of minor nobles turning up dead throughout Expera, but no one has anything solid on the culprit, Until now there have not been any incidents in Khaldra" Alex replied his normally placid face showing the barest hint of concern.

"Delos mentioned that in his speech. If this recent incident is connected than we may have our distraction. The question is how do we make this situation Delos's top priority? Playing copycat would be too risky and might hurt our chances in the long run. Velen, do you have any tricks that could locate the culprit? Making contact with them might be our best chance to steer this in a beneficial direction?" Dennet asked glancing over at the arcanist with a hopeful smile.

"I'm not sure what you mean by tricks. An mysterious killer with unknown magic is quite intriguing, though I'm not exactly good with confrontation. I avoided the more aggressive books when I was at the Arcanum. I am curious why this culprit has not already been found. I can think of six, no eight ways to track someone given the circumstances , which means any mage worth the title would have tried one or two," Velen said, quickly. Dennet noticed he talked faster when he was nervous.

"I like the confidence. If you have eight ways to track someone and they've only tried one or two I'm sure we can sort this out quickly. Don't worry about any confrontaitons, I think I can arrange backupeven with my expedition teams out in the field," Dennet said, only somewhat jokingly.

"I didn't say... But if... Maybe I could...? It would be better if..." Velen stammered in response.

Dennet almost felt bad for pressing the man but if he was going to be of use to their cause then this was just the beginning of the challenges ahead.

"It will be fine, Velen, all we need you to do is find out who is behind the disturbances before the governor does. Then we can take it from there," Alex said, staring daggers at Dennet, who shrugged nonchalantly.

"I should be able to do that. If I can't, well then it will actually be worth doing. Yes, I do hope I can't. That would be interesting. I should get on it sooner. Would be better if I try... Well, actually maybe that would be better... or perhaps..." Velen said, standing up and heading for the door. He took a few steps then turned around, "Where exactly am I going? I've only been in the city a few hours."

"Start at a pub called the Skull and Duggery. You should be able to pick up the trail from there. Alex, perhaps your sister can show him how to get there?" Dennet said, hopeful that the strange arcanist might be able to get some answers.

"If we want our arcanist to remain in one piece best keep him away from Alexandra. I'm sure one of my staff can escort him," Alex said, laughing.

Arranging an escort did not take long. With the arcanist's departure Dennet and Alex sat down to discuss in detail their operation. Five hundred men, women, and children required a lot of food and materials. The fledgling town had begun as a front to train and recruit people dissatisfied with the state of leadership in Khaldra but it had taken on a life of its own. Dennet hand recruited an additional five hundred men who visited the settlement on a monthly basis to train under the guise of delivering supplies. The acquisition of nearly a thousand rifles and sufficient ammunition would take a significant amount of time. Maintaining the operation required both Dennet and Alex to expend a small fortune in majorsand tested the limits of their connections in the city. Though basic understanding of firearms was common amongst the citizens of Khaldra Dennet felt a more expert hand was needed to train the recruits. Alex had suggested a gunsmith by the name of Rickart Kel, who both had dealt with when arranging to acquire their armory. This had proven more challenging than either had thought. Rickart had proven to be stubborn preferring to practice his craft in peace rather than get involved in the messy politics of the city. Dennet had been forced to obfuscate the true nature of their plans for the time being. Dennet still hoped to recruit the man when the time was right.

Over the next few hours they discussed logistics and potential alterations to their original plans to fit the new timeline. Having exhausted their predictive abilities Dennet decided it best to retire for the evening. On his way out Dennet noticed that the arcanist had not returned and hoped the strange man had not gotten distracted.

Chapter 5

Two days in Khaldra and Delos had barely begun moving into his new keep. The squat fortress would be considered an eyesore in a proper Imperial city, but Delos had to admire its functionality. The keep had been designed to withstand the threats which emerged from the Promise rather than for any aesthetic value. If the sheer number of magical defenses was any indication none of the stories Delos had heard about the Promise on the weekslong journey had been exaggerated. Delos had retained Lord Merrel's services throughout the journey and the flamboyant nobleman had proven a font of knowledge on the region of Expera. The more he had learned about the region the less he wanted anything to do with this accursed city.

Delos waited impatiently in the bailey of the keep for Lord Kelen to return. The very night he had delivered his address to the people of the city. A squad of his personal guards had been killed in the streets, by an unknown assailant. It was to early to assume any relation to the string of assassinations that had plagued the region for months but if it was a coincidence, it beggared belief. He had ordered Lord Kelen to investigate the incident personally. A command that had agitated the young noble much to Delos' amusement. As the heir to house Kelen the young noble was not used to taking orders. It was a lesson Delos was happy to teach.

Marius Kelen approached with a trail of robe clad arcanists trailing him. His uniform was neat and well maintained the crest of house Kelen displayed prominently. If it was not for the mans long unruly hair, he would be the perfect image of the warrior noble. Though it irked him, Delos allowed such liberties for those who earned it.

"A pleasant morning for a stroll Lord Delos," Kelen said with a smile. The arcanists clustered together while the Lords conversed. Delos spared them a glance before responding. They were a sorry lot for arcanists, barely worthy of the title.

"While you were strolling about did you learn anything of value? I expect you to return with a prisoner or a corpse." Delos said turning his attention squarely on Kelen.

"Patients, it seems our quarry is more capable then expected." Kelen said meeting Delos' gaze with a slight smile.

"I expect results Lord Kelen not excuses. The three Lords slain in the past few months can perhaps be attributed to the incompetence of the local nobility. However, Lieutenant Ross was one of my personal guards and a trained battle mage. With his death the competence of our adversary was no longer in question. If that is all you learned, then perhaps I need to find someone more capable." Delos replied, doing his best to keep his anger at bay. Lord Kelen might be a powerful mage and technically a peer, but Delos was the Governor of this region now. Even if that had been more a punishment than a promotion, he would not tolerate insubordination.

"No need, though the assailant appears to possess considerable power they clearly know nothing about how to use it. Your man put up a good fight and wounded the assailant considerable. The arcanists were able to recover a sample of their blood. It will be a simple matter to track them down. Then we can recover whatever artifact they possess it." Kelen replied smiling broadly with a hungry look in his eyes.

"What makes you think they possess an artifact." Delos asked raising an eyebrow.

"Unless one of the High Lords or their heirs have taken up murder for entertainment the sheer amount of magic in the blood recovered could only come from an artifact." Kelen stated.

"Bring the sample here." Delos shouted to the ensembled arcanists. One of the arcanist broke from the group carefully carrying a small vial. "Hurry up girl."

"Of course, Lord Delos," the young arcanist said nearly breaking into a run in her haste. Her robes marked with an eye surrounded by glyphs marked her as a seer in training. A true seeker would have been a boon to this operation, but Kelen had only been allowed to conscript the most junior of arcanists. The order from the court had of course cited the need for the junior arcanists to receive practical experience under controlled conditions.

Delos snatched the vial from the arcanists hand. Even without casting he could feel the raw power present in the blood. Kelen had not been exaggerating. As Delos could not conceive of any of the upper nobility acting in such a manner the only explanation was an artifact. The Promise with its twisted reality was the most likely source but it was not unheard of for the works of insane arcanists from the distant past to surface throughout the empire.

"How long will it take you to find whoever this came from?" Delos asked, the words sounding more like a command than a question.

"That depends… Not that I won't be able to its just…" the arcanist replied her speaking quietly with her eyes downcast.

"Get it done." Delos said his tone clearly indicating or else. He handed the vial back to the arcanist and waved her away.

"Arcanist Rem is capable enough, but we will need to provide someone capable of dealing with the threat." Kelen interjected.

"I have just the man for the job." Delos said with a wicked smile.

Patrick Iresel was the third son of a minor house in Renmarsh. Delos had recruited him for his guards a few years ago. A powerful mage with little prospects for advancement in society Delos had expected to gain an exemplary captain for his house guard. Iresel had proven a failure as a leader, but his personal brand of cunning brutality had proven far more useful. It would be good to put the soldier to a task that suited his talents. His mind made up Delos lead Kelen and the arcanist around the bailey to where his men were training.

The previous governor had relied heavily on the local nobility to supply the guards that patrolled the city. One of Delos' first actions on arriving had been to correct that mistake. He might be nominally in control of the entire region, but it would take years to effectuate that control. Khaldra, however, was a smaller area and though its population was on par with his original holdings he felt confident in his ability to take total control in the short term. To that end, his troops had begun training with the local guards.

Though several members of the local nobility supplied the troops that policed the city the most prominent was Lord Regius Pell. The short and heavily scarred man was in Delos' opinion a model noble, deferential to his superiors and contemptuous of those below him. With Lord Pell' aid Delos hope to have his men begin regular patrols by tomorrow.

The impromptu training ground was simply a clear patch of ground where the keeps gardens had been just yesterday. It was a regrettable but necessary step in his plans to bring order to the region. Nearly all of the thousand men he had brought with him were present either listening to explanations from the local guards or running through various drills. It did not take long to find Iresel.

Inside a dueling ring Iresel was facing off against one of Lord Pell's guards. Delos considered ending the exchange, but Delos knew the value in such demonstrations from personal experience. Delos made his way over to the ring as the duel began the familiar red light pulsing rapidly. Kelen joined him with calm disinterest. Delos had yet to see Kelen fight but the young lord had a reputation as an aggressive duelist. House Kelen's unique style of magic focused on altering gravity. It was a complex skill and though not particularly flashy could be used to devastating effect, Delos gestured to where the arcanists waited awkwardly a dozen meters away conversing amongst themselves nervously. If the apprentice seer Rem would be guiding the group of hunters Delos felt she needed to understand the man who would be leading the operation.

Iresel stood still, giving no indication of casting as he waited for the guard to make the first move. The guard circled warily sword drawn in one hand and the other moving through a complex pattern. The guard's body was turned to obscure his casting while the sword provided a threat. Roots, arrowlike heads at their tips, erupted from the ground in front of Iresel and shot forward. Iresel remained still as a dozen roots embedded themselves in his chest hard enough to move the man back.

"Your backs wide open" Iresel said his seemingly coming from behind the guard. It was a poor ruse but the moments hesitation as the guard decided whether to turn his head was enough. Iresel whipped his hand forward and the roots exploded leaving arrow length shafts embedded as he rushed forward propelled by a series of explosions behind him. The guards kept his blade on line and met the threat. It spoke well of the man's training to stand his ground as the bloodied mage barreled towards him. Delos could see the ground around the guard boil as more roots emerged. Iresel was too fast the roots had barely emerged when Iresel struck out. His arm knocked aside the sword. The sleeve of Iresel's shirt parted and blood spurted forth from a deep laceration. The blow took the sword from the guard's grasp. As it spun through the air Iresel's other arm shot towards the guard. The guard jumped back hastily but with his balance compromised the explosion that erupted from Iresel's outstretched hand knocked the man from his feet and sent him flying towards. If the man left the ring the duel would end. It seemed Iresel had other plans. He gestured with his injured arm sending blood raining down in an arc across the dueling ground. Another explosion detonated behind the guard just before he would have exited the ring. Iresel stood waiting as the dazed guard struggled to rise. The guard's uniform was singed and covered in dust but no blood stained it. The real damage would be below the skin where the concussive force wreaked havoc. The guard managed to his knees under him before falling forward a trickle of blood coming from the man's mouth. Iresel strolled forward and raised his hand.

"The duel goes to Lord Iresel." The referee shouted, as the ring flashed green. Iresel turned to the referee with a look that spoke of violent intent.

"Enough." Delos commanded. If he was still in his holdings he would have let Iresel continue as he wished but Delos need all the men he could get to bring this city under control. "Iresel, if you are done playing with the locals I have work for you."

Iresel glared at the referee before turning towards Delos. He walked over, blood still spreading from the roots which sprouted from his chest. With magic enhancing his body Iresel could ignore his injuries, but this operation might take time. After Delos explained the task, he order Rem to escort Iresel to the keep's doctor. One look at her pallid face told Delos that she understood just what kind of man Iresel was.

With the assassin problem in Iresel's capable hands Delos turned his attention to the myriad other problems in Khaldra. He had ordered Lord Merrel to make contact with the local nobility a task the courtier seemed well suited to. There was still much about the city Delos had been unable to ascertain from stories alone. With Kelen in tow he made his way through the keep in search of Lord Merrel. The man was always scurrying off when he had complete whatever task Delos set for him. They found Merrel badgering the servants In the ostentatious ballroom the late governor had used to hold court. Delos had attended gathering in a dozen similar places throughout the empire. It was a necessary part of court life. He had avoided hosting such events on his lands due to the enormous costs with very little benefits over simple attendance. He would need to utilize the space now that he was governor.

"Ah, Lord Delos I see Lord Pell's men have already begun training the new guards." Merrel said bowing to Delos and Kelen in turn.

"Indeed, if you are wasting your time here, I assume you have already collected the information I requested." Delos replied.

"Of course, of course. There are a few matters I think will be of interest. It will take time for me to learn everything, but rest assured I am working on it. In fact, my presence here is to prepare this space so you can hold an event. Having the nobility of Khaldra in one place will be most helpful." Merrel said, speaking quickly without meeting Delos' gaze.

"An excellent idea. There are a few questions I would like to ask of the local nobility. By all accounts the defense of Khaldra are wholly inadequate if the stories regarding the Promise are to be believed." Kelen interjected. If Kelen wished to handle such arrangements alongside Merrel it would save Delos the headache.

"I may have an answer to that particular question. The local nobility rely, far to heavily on the local population to manage defense. One group was mentioned more frequently the any others. An organization called the Field Knights is led by a particularly affluent citizen. I have not had the time to dig deeper into the details but give me a few days." Merrel said.

"Make that your priority." Delos said his hand tightened into fists at his side. Citizen merchants were not uncommon in the empire, but they rarely had enough wealth to be worth noting. It was an affront to common sense for a citizen to lead men in defense of an imperial city. Delos had known the previous governor was lacks in his treatment of Khaldra's citizen class, but the extent of his incompetence was quickly growing clear to Delos.

"As you wish. Before that there is another matter which requires your attention. As you well know Khaldra's economy is heavily dependent on trade. This would not be a problem except that despite my best efforts I have been unable to locate a complete accounting of goods entering or leaving the city. After considerable effort I have come to the conclusion that not such accounting exists." Merrel replied.

"I should have burned this retched city to the ground when I arrived." Delos bellowed. It took a few moments to bring his temper under control small beams of light radiated from his clenched fist causing the servant to flee as the light charred various pieces of furniture that adorned the ballroom.

"Allow me to suggest an alternative for your consideration." Merrel said looking at Kelen for support. Delos breathed deep before he gestured for Merrel to continue. If the man's suggestion proved insufficient, Delos could always proceed in laying waste to the city. "The simplest method to create such a record would be to station guards at strategic locations throughout the city. As governor you have the right to inspect anyone entering or exiting the city. Not only would this provide the accounting that is sorely needed, it would also provide opportunities to deal with any parties that may take umbrage with your rule."

Kelen nodded in agreement as Merrel finished. Delos cursed himself for not seeing such an obvious solution. There would be grumblings from the local nobility and outright hostility from the citizens but those were problems he could deal with. He had been handed the impossible task of reshaping this region. Should he succeed, no one would question his methods.

Chapter 6

Kel awoke with his head resting on the hard wood of his workbench. His back was aching, but that was normal. It had been years since he could wake up at his bench and function like a real person. He checked his watch, a rather shabby copy of the intricate artifice produced elsewhere in the empire. It was, however, a copy he had made himself without the aid of magic. A process that had been as informative as it had been painstaking. It was nearing noon, which meant he had only slept for two hours or so. The events of the night before had kept him up far longer than he would have liked. He knew Nadia would be back in the workshop in the next hour or so. She wasn't the kind of person to waste a day even if she needed to rest. A trait that had been a blessing and a hinderance since she had started as his apprentice some fifteen years ago. She officially finished her apprenticeship ten years ago, but she preferred to work for him than start her own business. The thought of Nadia training apprentices always amused him, and he pitied anyone brave enough to try. Her apprenticeship had been far more eventful than his own.

His sleep deprived mind began to wander. So much had happened since his apprenticeship began thirty years ago. He forced himself to refocus on the present a task that seemed to grow harder as he aged.

He had managed to finish the adjustments to his rifle and all that was left was to sight it in and test out just how much of an improvement his new sight was. He could utilize the test range the Gunsmith Guild had built but he preferred the practical challenges of a true field test. He could check that Dets had made it home safely on his way back. He ate a small meal while he waited for his body to wake up. As Nadia had not returned by the time he had finished, he wrote a note and left it along with the explosive device on her workbench. The note written on a small scrap of paper read:

> Heading toward the Maras Plains—need
> a clear line of sight for testing. Should
> be back before tomorrow but no need
> to worry until this time tomorrow. We
> should be caught up on outstanding
> projects and I'm not expecting any new
> order today. Don't destroy the shop. —
> R.K.

Kel packed his backpack quickly. A small amount of jerky, an apple, a waterskin, several rounds of ammunition and a field glass. The last item to go in was a gun designed by Nadia with a short and very wide barrel. He doubted he would have need of it but life in Khaldra had taught him to be prepared for anything.

The Maras Plains were located to the north of the city. The land there was poor for farming, or at least for producing food safe for human consumption.

Though fertile it produced strange aberrations in the foliage that grew there. In the early days of Khaldra it took a contingent of mages and men wielding axes to remove the trees growing there. An action made necessary when the trees started entering the city and destroying buildings.

Kel had been too young at the time to remember those days, but his father had told many stories about the founding days of Khaldra. The destruction of the Maras Plains was far from the most interesting. As one of the first gunsmiths in Khaldra his father had played a key role in the survival of the fledgling city.

As he made his way through the city he noticed a far greater number of people staring at the rifle slung over his back. A man carrying a rifle should not be an uncommon sight especially in this area of the city.. Something had them more on edge than normal, and that would usually bring the community together, usually armed, and ready to face whatever new horror had emerged. Even the less fortunate citizens of Khaldra still had the pioneer mindset and would often travel armed when danger was in the air. The fact something seemed to be having the opposite effect worried Kel as he made his way out of the city. As a gunsmith he was often the first to know when a new threat had emerged but no one had mentioned anything in the past few days. His father would have asked around but Kel preferred to focus on his work if the problem could not be solved with a well placed bullet then it was none of his business.

The area just outside of the city to the north was almost entirely empty of civilization. Its proximity to the plains made it useless for farming. There were one or two small houses that Kel knew were home to

Purifiers. A self-proclaimed title for the few families who dedicated themselves to keeping the Maras Plains a barren waste. Generally, they were viewed with an odd mix of revulsion and accolade, which seemed to suit them fine. Kel had dealt with them a few times and found them to be good folk if a bit obsessive, but Kel could not bring himself to fault them for it.

In about two hours he had reached the unofficial border of the Maras Plains. The flat ground before him was dotted with charred patches and small piles of dirt where plants had ripped themselves from the ground long ago. Despite the barren and charred waste before him the air was clear and clean. There was little to no wind, which was a partial blessing. It would make zeroing the sight easier, but he would have welcomed the challenge. Setting up a range was a simple matter of pacing out two hundred meters. He placed down an apple on a charred stump as a target then walked a bit over two hundred thirty-five paces away.

Everything prepared, it was time to begin. He unslung his rifle and went prone. Looking down the sight, he centered the apple in the small cross he had etched in the center of the sight. He hoped the plan would work. Etching the glass was a bit risky. The uniquely formed glass had taken a significant amount of time and money to have made. He breathed in and held his breath, lightly squeezing the trigger. The shot was a bit low and to the left but its impact in the stump was a good sign and made the error easy to see. He pulled a small metal bar specially designed to adjust how the sight sat on his rifle. A small adjustment to the alignment, and he shot again. This time the shot zipped past the apple directly to the left. He made another adjustment and prepared to fire again. So far everything was working as intended, which was a good sign. It occurred to him that this was still not a good test. He could make this shot easily without the new sight. He decided to trust his adjustment and jumped to his feet. He took a quick step back and to the right, sighted quickly, and fired. The apple exploded as the round hit home.

Kel smiled to himself, the easy part was done now for a real test. He pulled a few other assorted objects he had brought for targetsand arrayed them in the general area around him. Then he started running counting his strides as he went. It was imprecise but there was rarely time for precision in an emergency. Once he felt he was sufficiently far away he quickly turned and fired at the first target he sighted on. The shot went high but from the small cloud of dust it was properly aligned. Firing again, steadier this time, the round hit home and punched a hole through the can, sending it tumbling. *Ten years ago, I could've hit that at a full run I must be slowing down in my old age. Unacceptable*, he thought. He began running again faster than before when he felt he was slowing, he tucked the rifle to his body, careful not to knock the scope. He dived into a shoulder roll, pivoting as he rose to his knees sighted and fired three shots in quick succession. Two out of the three shots hit their targets. The scope made the targets harder to identify at this range narrowing his field of vision significantly. It was a problem but seemed a fair tradeoff if the final tests were successful. Noting the distance at approximately three hundred meters, he began to pace out an additional seven hundred meters. Technically he had made shot at this range but only on larger targets. Kel took pride in the fact that even the best hunters in Khaldra would laugh at the thought of attempting such a shot.

Shooting at this range came with a significant number of factors to consider but Kel had accounted for many in the construction of his scope. As he got into position, he heard indistinct voices carrying over the plains. The scope proved extremely useful at finding the source of the voices. Kel noted four figures approximately two kilometers away in the general direction of Khaldra. Sound should not carry so far but whatever corrupt magic infested the place carried sound farther than would normally be possible. Having grown up in Khaldra Kel had learned to accept such things without question. He could not make out details but without the aid of the scope the figures' dark clothing would have blended into the charred ground around them. Even with the limited details he could make out, the figures seemed out of place. Their attire was unfamiliar and clearly did not match the typical clothes worn by the Purifiers. Few outside of the nobility wore robes or carried swords. Most in Khaldra carried knives or axes preferring utility over lethality

Kel nearly jumped when the figures abruptly turned and headed in his direction. Hiding was not an option. He was far enough away for now to remain undiscovered but the barren nature of the plains made concealment difficult if not impossible. Kel prefered not to deal with these strangers. Something felt off about the group there was little of value out on the plains and most avoided traversing the region unless absolutely necessary. As Kel watched it became apparent that the group was heading directly for him. This concerned Kel, the general unease he had felt leaving the city seemed like too much of a coincidence to ignore. He figured from his prone position it would be at least ten minutes before there was any chance the group spotted him.

He slowed his breathing to calm himself, getting twitchy with a rifle pointed at someone could end in disaster. As time passed Kel began to be able to make out the conversation going on in the group.

"Promises, Rem, where are we even going? This place is a mess." Kel could not make out who was speaking.

"Shut it Tel, I'm trying to concentrate. This is hard enough without you complaining. ..." Kel could not make out what the female voice said, but it seemed like a curse "I lost them again. What kind of gods damned protections does this bastard have." Kel was able to identify the female he assumed was Rem by the exasperated gesture she made.

"This is the third time you have lost them. If you can't do this then just say so. Delos won't accept failure but wasting time will only make things worse," a calm voice said, barely loud enough for Kel to hear.

"I'm the closest thing to a Seer this gods damned 'revitalization' project has. If you or anyone else thinks they can do better go right ahead. It'll save me the damn headache. Even with blood, setting the tracking spell is like holding down a damn eel and when I can get it set something cuts the connection. Whoever this bastard is they have more protections than a high lord," Rem said, clearly annoyed.

Kel should have been relieved that they were not tracking him, but a group of nobles on the hunt was not something he wanted to be anywhere near. The group had stopped just before where he had estimated he would become visible.

"Then find them. I'm not interested in traipsing through the ass end of the empire after some arrogant mage who got their hands on more power than they deserve. At least there is no need to hold back in this wasteland," the calm voice said, though the last part seemed as much a threat to the group as their target. The group seemed to have stopped to discuss, which could be a good thing, but it did leave Kel trapped until they moved on. He contemplated firing a warning shot and running for it. Kel did not know much about magic, but he doubted he was in the effective range of anything dangerous. Kel ran through a number of potential options as he watched the group. Rem pulled something from her pocket and began what Kel could only assume was a tracking spell. Kel knew there was significant power behind it, power enough to warp the air around Rem.Despite its potency magic always looked like a drunk mummers show to him. Moments later Rem stopped waving her hands around and the group to continue in his direction. Kel scowled as his finger found its way to the trigger. He stopped himself before making a rash decision. If an encounter was unavoidable it was best to try diplomacy first.

Kel figured his odds were better with a significant distance between them, though It was still a risk he did not have much choice. He rose, keeping his rifle aimed at the group. Their reactions were immediate. Three of the four halted. The figure Kel had identified as Rem nearly walked into one of the unknown figures.

"Identify yourself," the calm voice said, the sound seemed to come from directly in front of Kel.

"Rickart Kel, citizen of Khaldra. I think it would be best if we keep our distance…" Kel said, doing his best to project his voice to be heard over the significant distance. Not for the first time he wished he took after his father, who had what many called a sergeant's voice.

"I don't think you're in a position to make demands of us," the reply came. Kel noted one of the figures look toward Rem, who shook her head. Kel wondered at that, but more concerning was that the group began moving toward him.

"Probably not, but I'm trying my best to avoid a fight. I don't think I am the person you're looking for so I think it will be best for everyone if we go our separate ways peacefully," Kel said, slowly moving away and circling toward Khaldra.

He was used to talking down irate customers not groups of militant nobles on a hunt. He still was not entirely sure what the group was doing or where they came from. If they were local nobility he figured they would at least have some respect for a rifle pointed at them. Kel felt he was missing something important and hoped it would not cause things to spiral out of control. The group halted for a second and a whispered conversation between Rem and the figure Kel decided was the leader he had been speaking to began. It did not take long for the group's leader to turn back toward Kel.

"I shall grant your request but do not think yourself fortunate. The mission must come first but I will have time once this task is complete," the calm voice said, this time coming from behind Kel.

It was a horrible, disconcerting bit of magic and added significantly to the ominous threat. Kel circled slowly toward Khaldra keeping an eye on the group. After more whispered discussion the group began heading on a slightly altered course. It was slow going having to walk while keeping an eye on the group through the scope of his rifle. Curiosity had Kel scanning the horizon in the direction the group was heading trying to see if he could spot their target. He noticed a small clusterof rocks approximately fifty meters along the path the group was traveling. Kel figured it might be where the person they were hunting was hiding so he focused on it to see if he could spot any movement. With careful observation he noticed that the largest of the rocks seemed to be moving slightly. The rock seemed to shift up and down slightly in a rhythmic pattern.

"*Bratvensha,*" Kel muttered to himself. It was a common curse from Sera-Met he had picked up from Dets. He could never remember what it actually meant. He had a choice to make even if they were noble pricks they were moving toward danger they had no idea about. evimikwazi were not joke. Growing to over twelve feet in height and weighing over a ton these enourmous ambush predators use there powerful front claws to create burrows to hide and wait. Once their prey drew close the would strike. They were very rare and were only found in the northern part of the Sera-Met desert where it becomes the foothills of the Mistvale mountains, however, the anomalous nature of the Promise attracted many unique and strange creatures. If he tried to warn them he doubted they would heed his warning. More than likely they would treat him as a threat. The group did not seem to notice that he had stopped as they made their way drawing ever closer to where the evimikwazi waited. Kel knew just how fast evimikwazi were and he did not like his chances at hitting a target moving that fast over a kilometer away. Moreover, the rock-like exterior of the evimikwazi was not simply designed for concealment the plates would stop a bullet even at close range. It would take a clean hit to the head or heart to drop the thing before it could tear the group to pieces.

Kel began heading toward the group, trying to slightly close the gap without alerting them. It seemed to work, as no one turned to watch him. As the group drew to within ten meters of the rock formation they stopped briefly. Two of them broke off from the main group and began circling the formation. A good idea if their quarry was the only threat hiding within. Kel dropped his attempt at stealth and broke into a run.

"Run!" he shouted. It was a split-second decision he hoped he would not regret.

"Well, it seems you're keen to die, Mr. Kel," the leaders voice rang in Kel's ears loud enough to cause him to stumble. The man sounded pleased at the thought of killing. Kel cursed himself even as he ran to the aid of these murderous nobles.

The two who had broken off continued to circle, seemingly more concerned with their task than Kel's warning or any threat he might pose. That choice proved fatal. The evimikwazi pounced crossing the distance to one of the circling noble in a single bound. The figure was caught completely unaware as it brought its massive claws down nearly bisecting the figure. Its talons embedding themselves deeply into the stoney ground. The group reacted quickly, turning to face the massive creature that had erupted in their midst. Rem seemed torn between assisting and maintaining whatever spell she had cast. One glance from the leader kept her focused on her magic. That they had not fled immediately impressed Kel. If they had been father away from the creature perhaps they could have escape but over short distances evimikwazi were faster than a horse at full gallop. The figure who had circled in the other direction charged the evimikwazi faster than Kel thought possible. The figure's hands crackled with energy it looked like they were holding storm clouds.

The evimikwazi turned to meet the threat and silently setting itself with its forearm length claws splayed in front of it and standing on its hind legs. The figure dodged the evimikwazi's first swipe easily. Striking its body even as its talons swiped through empty air. There was a flash of light, nearly blinding Kel despite the distance. The strike sent the evimikwazi convulsing its massive front limbs flailing wildly. The figure was forced to focus on dodging but even with the incredible speed they had demonstrated prior, one claw glanced their shoulder, sending them sprawling to the ground. The evimikwazi shook off the shock and brought its claws down on the sprawled figure. A burst of red light exploded between the two sending the evimikwazi stumbling back, slightly singed but still ready to fight. The figure who had been knocked to the ground clothes were smoking but Kel could see that they were still moving. A series of explosions rocked the evimikwazi sending it farther from the prone figure. The leader seemed to disregard the plight of his subordinate as he pressed the attack. Kel watched the fallen man attempt to rise only to fall as the expolosions rocked their body. Kel turned his attention to the leader who was striding forward, gesturing toward the evimikwazi and unleashing explosions with each movement. Kel could not see the leaders face but Kel imagined the man smiling as he unleashed his magic on the evimikwazi.

The evimikwazi dug its hind legs in and stood its ground against the onslaught. Kel knew it was preparing to lunge at the leader. He leveled his rifle and sighted on the creature's head. The flashes of the explosions made things more difficult but from a steady position Kel was confident he could hit his mark. The leader seemed to grow frustrated with ineffectuality of his attacks and began gesturing for some larger spell. With the explosions stopped and the evimikwazi coiling to strike, Kel breathed out, steadying himself. With a crack barely audible over the ringing in his ears the rifle fired.

Kel did not check to see if he had hit his mark, instead he began running again. He knew he should be running away but he had committed himself to the fight and he would see this through. Still a few hundred meters away he watched, the evimikwazi as it lurched forward slowly and was met with a small orb of fire burning so bright Kel had to look away.

When he looked back the orb was gone and the evimikwazi had a massive hole burned through its chest. It slowly fell forward as its body finally gave out. Rather than moving to assist his fallen comrade the leader turned to face Kel. He could feel the man's glare and slowed to a walk. The leader raised his hands in a gesture similar to those he had used to fight the evimikwazi.

Chapter 7

Marcus Velen exited the grounds of the Hydes' manse accompanied by a young woman whose name he had already forgotten, much to his discomfort. She seemed far more enthused by the prospect of a day in town than he was. It did not help that Khaldra seemed devoid of the minor magical conveniences that filled most Imperial cities. The lack of distractions made traversing the city far more nerve racking than he would have thought. Khaldra was a far smaller city than Shin-Rai and lacked the numerous towers and other odd architecture that had become familiar to Velen. Few building in Khaldra were more than two or three stories tall. Despite this the narrow streets and crowds of people made the place seem far more alive than Shin-Rai. As they walked through the city the sheer number of people reminded Velen of his first days in the Arcanum before he gained access to the more secluded areas. Without any magic to occupy his mind he observed the people around him. It seemed an odd mix of eastern Imperials with a disproportionate number of people from Sera-Met and the Miralocke. There was a distinct lack of people from the Dracic Coast or Ilimat. It was certainly not representative of the demographics of the empire. Velen only a cursory knowledge of the social structure of the empire so his speculations centered on the effect the Promise had on magic in the region. He began running through a variety of theories he had developed.

"Mr. Velen, if you're done staring into space. I was—" the young woman said, snapping Velen out of his thoughts.

"Oh, sorry, far too many problems to deal with—hard to keep track," Velen said, interrupting her. "You are correct that we best be going Lord Hyde seemed keen for this particular puzzle to be solved."

He would need to wait till he had solved the puzzle Lord Hyde had given him to satisfy his own curiosity. It was odd to think of him as Lord Hyde, House Velen was more prominent and connected than House Hyde at least in the empire proper, but Marcus had largely been disowned by his family. He had been a prodigy in his youth but ran into a wall when his peers far outstripped him due to the strength of their internal sources. The weakness of his magic had almost barred him from the Arcanum but a combination of intellect and what remained of his family's good graces had opened the doors. His own struggles with magic were a big part of why he found Khladra's lack of magic so fascinating.

Velen realized he was losing his guide who easily navigated the crowded streets. He had to push his way through in order to catch up to her. It took him almost two blocks to catch up and at no point did his guide turn around to check on him. Velen spent most of the trip alternating between speculating on what people were doing and rushing to keep up with his guide who seemed determined to leave him behind. It did cross his mind that if she intended to leave him behind it would probably be trivially easy to do so. The thought was not particularly comforting as he struggled to keep pace. After an indeterminate time they arrived at the Skull and Duggery. It seemed like an unremarkable place though the craved image of a skeleton sweeping dust into its skull amused Velen. It was reminiscent of the many pubs that serviced the Arcanum, not that he had spent much time in any of those.

"Well, I'm off. I've got a few errands to run for myself. Good luck," Velen's guide said, turning to go.

"Oh, um, thank you. Am I supposed to pay you? I don't exactly have much money," Velen said, nervous at the thought of having to find his way back. He had not been paying much attention to the route they took to get here.

"Oh no, Alexandra said she would cover everything as long as I bring her back some pastries from the bakery she likes. If I remember correctly its just around the corner," she said, laughing as she walked away with a wave.

It was a relief that his expenses would be handled for him. He had always had problems dealing with money. Dealing with money had been the reason he was forced to leave the Arcanum. It was apparently inappropriate to fiddle with the magic in place on the currency of the realm or something like that. He did not really understand the problem. The enchantment on minors was relatively simple and did not differentiate between the numeric value. He had been interested in the enchantment initially and it was good practice for enchanting simple objects.

Velen entered the pub. He was not sure where to begin searching, but a relatively quiet place to sit would give him a chance to work some minor spells that might point him in the right direction. He sat down at an empty table and pulled a small pouch of sugar from his pocket. He poured some onto the table and used a small pen knife to shape the pile into a glyph. Pricking his finger and allowing a small drop of blood to fall in the center of the glyph completed the ritual. It was a basic spell he had learned from a book of Fae magic. It made the caster extremely easy to ignore and had served him well whenever he had to work in public areas.

He had been asked to find whoever was causing disturbances in Khaldra though what he was expected to do once he had found them was unclear. Without any tether to the person scrying would be useless so he either needed some way to find a tether or to come up with another approach. It was an interesting puzzle. He knew whoever was behind the disturbances was capable of dealing with mages. The simplest assumption he could make was that they were a fairly powerful mage themselves or in possession of an artifact with interesting properties. Normally, looking for sources of magic, even powerful ones, was futile in Imperial cites. There was simply too much potential interference. In Khaldra it might be possible but if they had managed to stay hidden so long it was likely a measure that had already failed. If he wanted to pinpoint a hidden source, he would need to be able to evaluate lentire swathes of the city at the same time.

Aberrations were far easier to spot in larger scale patterns. If he had the proper materials he could produce a cherub. With the right adjustments he could use the minor magic construct as a means of aerial surveillance.

Lost in his pondering Velen did not notice his

guide enter the pub. She spent a good bit of time looking around before going to the bartender. It was not until the conversation became somewhat heated that Velen noticed. He was surprised to see her again so soon unless he had lost track of time, which was certainly a possibility. He waited until the conversation died down and his guide moved to leave. Before she got to the door he stood up and waved her over. She quickly came over and sat down at the table.

"How? Where? " She asked, exasperated. Velen sheepishly gestured at the glyph on the table. "Is that supposed to mean something to me?"

"It's just a bit of magic. I did not want to be disturbed while I was planning. I honestly did not expect to see you again so soon. Unless of course it's been a while," Velen explained.

"Unhelpful but probably unimportant. Can anyone see or hear us?" she asked

"Well, they can but they won't. It gets complicated from there. Are you familiar with Imisaras's theory of cognition. Probably not. I guess it would be better to start with something…" Velen began.

"I'm not even going to try to determine what any of that meant. I think I might have found something useful," she interrupted. "I was not able to get any pastries because the bakery was dealing with a backlog due to a disturbance earlier. Inconvenient for me but I think it might be a better place to start than this dump." She continued glaring at the barkeep.

"Well, I could keep planning, I had some interesting ideas though I'm not entirely sure where I could get pumice. I guess its worth a look," Velen said, getting to his feet. He used his hand to wipe away some of the sugar breaking the glyph. He swayed as the feeling of drunkenness washed over him. It was an odd side effect and grew worse the longer the glyph remained intact. Velen found Fae magic useful and fascinating though the presence and nature of side effects made it a rarity among most mages.

The bakery was not far, and Velen managed to not get lost on the way. He did not even need to enter the shop to see the evidence of a duel between mages. It looked like most of the damage had been repaired and everything looked relatively normal, however Velen noted several patches of stone that had cracked due to the expansion of water. A common indicator of ice magic. Some of the banners seemed frayed despite the colors not being faded.

Velen sat down in the middle of the road and began focusing. Mage sight was one of the spells he could cast without the aid of a ritual. It was a common spell among artificers because it helped with visualizing how effective the enchantments were setting. When he opened his eyes, small threads of magic emanated off multiple surfaces. He focused on the ones near the broken stones, trying to get a feel for the caster. Reading the remnants of magic was difficult but with skill it provided significant information about the nature of the spell. It seemed at least one powerful mage familiar with thermodynamic magic had been present.

"You can't just sit in the road," the guide said pointedly. The sudden interruption broke his concentration. Velen was annoyed by the interruption, but it was probably best to listen to someone who knew the city better.

"Oh well, um, sorry. I'll need somewhere to take in the scene better," Velen said, slightly irriated by the interruption he rose to his feet slowly. . Looking around he did not immediately see anywhere that was out of the way but provided a good view. Until an idea popped into his head.

"Perfect, I know just the place," he said, and quickly walked over to the wall of a nearby building. He pulled a small pouch of melet sap, a common component used in crafting artifacts. For this particular instance Velen only needed its most basic property. When exposed to magic it went from a sticky sap to a hardened resin that could bind surfaces together, returning to sap once the magic faded. He had tried this concept before with a minor construct, but he was confident in its efficacy. Applying the sap to his hands and the front part of his shoes he began to scale the wall. Alternating directing magic to his hands and feet to affix them to the wall.

"Promises what are you doing," the guide shouted, drawing more attention to Velen.

He had not gotten particularly far but as he was focused on the success of his practical experiment he ignored her. He kept going as a crowd gathered below.

"Oi, you some kinda street performer?" someone in the growing crowd shouted. Velen was focused on his climb and ignored them as well. The building was not very tall, but it took a considerable amount of concentration to move. In essence he was casting cantrips in succession with fairly specific timing while straining his body to continue upward. He was not particularly in shape, probably due to all his time spent sitting and reading. Though only halfway up he was already sweating and his muscles were beginning to burn.

Breathing heavily, he heaved himself onto the roof. The feeling of sap on his hands was irritating but he welcomed the distraction from the pain in his arms. He had not considered how much physical exertion it would take to climb a building. Next time he would find a less strenuous method.

The easiest way to remove the melet sap was to use a spell that manipulated water. When exposed to that kind of magic the sap ran like liquid off of his hands and shoes. With a bit of manipulation he directed the liquid sap into a sphere in front of him. Dismissing the spell mostly solidified the sap into a ball that fell to the roof. The sound of clapping caught Velen's attention and he finally noted the gathered crowd staring at him from below.

"Um, does anyone know if there's an easier way down?" he asked.

Some in the crowd laughed as they dispersed. Velen noted that a few remained, eyeing him suspiciously.

He was not sure what to make of that, but it seemed he would need to figure out how to get down on his own. He cast mage sight again from the new viewpoint and surveyed the scene. It was more difficult, considering the amount of casting he had been doing in quick succession. He could feel the headache coming on as his brain created glyphs using a combination of visualization and its architecture. Surveying the scene, he could immediately tell there was a duel between mages in which at least two had died. There were a few oddities present that confused him. He could see traces from a two different casting styles, but they seemed to cut off abruptly in ways that did not match the usual traces. Much of the traces of ice magic seemed to have gaps in the traces that did seem intentional and there were no traces of defensive magic that would block it.

He also noted that there was the presence of significantly more magic than any of the spell traces could account for. There was more he could do to reconstruct the event, but it seemed more prudent to find something he could use for a scrying ritual. Despite the evidence of violence he could not see anything with enough connection to anyone involved to track. From the corner of his eye Velen spotted a trace of magic on the roof. It did not seem like a spell had been cast rather it was an alteration in the general field of magic indicative of some kind of protective artifact. It had not been a particularly powerful artifact and seemed unconnected from the conflict. Perhaps there had been a witness to the events below. If whoever had cleaned up the scene had not known about the observer than perhaps there would be something on the rooftop he could track.

It took a few minutes and some scrambling on his hands and knees to find a small number of fibers from whatever clothes the witness was wearing. The residual presence of magic clung to them, which was a good indicator of their origins. Velen hoped it would be a sufficient amount to track down this witness. He had a few plans that might work though most would require a good connection. He might be able to track them down based on the signature of the protection charm but that would take a lot more resources than he currently had.

"Are you done up there? I'm not waiting around here all day," His guide shouted from the street. Velen looked over the edge of the roof.

"I think so. I have a possible lead. Though it will require some more walking," Velen replied. He realized he had been so focused on finding something to track he had forgotten that he had not come up with a good plan to get down.

"Um, do you have any idea how I can get down?" he asked. Hoping he would not have to climb down. He was not sure if he could pull it off.

"That's your problem I'm not paid enough to go scaling buildings," came the reply.

Velen found it hard to switch his thinking to solve the more immediate problem. His focus was entirely on what method was best to track down the witness with his limited resources. The fact none of the components involved in tracking could be used to safely return to the ground made his current mental checklist fairly useless at present. If he was gonna be stuck up here he might as well work on formulating his tracking spell. Sitting down Velen pulled out a small spool of twine cut an arm's length portion and began working the fiber he had found into it. He was careful not to lose any and had to be careful not to use any magic that might disrupt the traces of the protective spell. It was a time-consuming process and delicate work that consumed his focus.

"How did you even make it to Khaldra?" his guide asked sarcastically the sound came from behind him and nearly disrupted the final steps of his preparations.

"I walked, well mostly I was in a boat for a bit in the Miralocke and I did ride in a cart for some of it," Velen answered, turning to see how his guide had made her way up. "I was going the wrong way at that time so I don't know if that counts. I also—"

"I'm gonna stop you there. If we are all done let's get out of here," she interrupted, gesturing to a trap door in the roof. The door was surrounded by straw.

"That's helpful. I wonder if it has any information

about whoever was up here. But I don't know if the straw might have dampened any sound. Probably not worth the time," Velen said, pocketing the length of twine and heading over.

"Are you going to start making sense at some point or am I just going to…? You know what? Never mind," she said, climbing down the ladder into whatever shop was below. It turned out to be a clothing store. The owner was waiting for them at the bottom of the ladder.

"If that's all you I need to get back to my customers," the man said.

"Thank you, House Hyde appreciates your discretion," the guide replied, taking a more polite tone than normal.

"Of course, Mrs. Sensel. We appreciate Lady Hyde's patronage greatly," the man said, bowing low. Hearing the name jogged Velen's memory. His guide's name was Eris Sensel. He really should work on remembering such things. When they left the clothiers shop Eris turned to him.

"I hope that was worth it. I'm gonna get an earful from Alexandra for promising to place an order from that dump," Eris said, her tone returning to her normal. Velen was not sure what the problem was. They had returned to the street without injury and nothing expensive had been broken.

"Well, it certainly was helpful assuming I can get this to work," he replied holding up the length of twine. "As to whether it was worth it technically that is to be seen. Unless you count the opportunity gained as a thing of value in and of itself. I'm inclined to press on. I'm sure it's a question that will resolve itself."

Velen held the twine between his hands and began singing. He always hated spells that required complex vocal components. Most grimoires translated the combination of pitch and syllables needed for a spell into chants or songs. A process that Velen found wasteful, but he had never had the time to break down the necessary components from those added to make it a more memorable tune. It was one of the few methods of doing magic for which he had to rely on rote memorization rather than deep understanding. It may also have had to do with his aversion to singing in public. As was often the case none of that mattered when there was a problem to solve and magic to do. The twine began to twitch between his hands. Once the motion became sufficiently frantic, he let go with his left hand and the end of the twine snapped forward, pointing the way to the target.

"Now we are following a string. Lord Velen you are the strangest mage I have ever met. At least this seems more practical than Alexandra's light shows," Eris said.

Velen was a bit shocked to hear himself called lord. It was a formality that was frequently dropped in most of the empire where mages where far more common. He considered asking about the light shows. Any details on the magic of the Hyde family were useful. He decided against it, not wanting to be too nosy.

They followed the twine through the winding streets of Khaldra for nearly two hours. Velen found it easier than the shorter journey to the scene. Following the tracking spell served as a good source of focus. The twine nearly pulled itself out of Velen's hand when they approached a specific shop.

"Well, I think I finally found where we are going," Velen said, smiling and waving his hands excietedly towards the door. He nearly lost hold of the twine in his excitement. Eris Rolled her eyes but moved towards the shop. The sign on the door read Kel Rifle Company, carved in simple script. Velen had a vague idea what a rifle was but only from some of the conversations he had during his trip to Khaldra after having entered the Expera region.

"I'll take the lead from here. I have no interest in being shot. Leave the talking to me and don't touch anything," Eris said, matter-of-factly.

They entered the store and found themselves in a small atrium. Velen was interested in the tools lining one wall. It was an odd assortment of blacksmith tools and some things he had only seen in an artificer's workshop. Nothing on the wall seemed inscribed with any glyphs, which was odd. The other wall was lined with what Velen assumed were rifles. A novel application of one of the first developed alchemical powders. Velen learned a bit about the creation of what was now called gunpowder during his lessons on the history of alchemy. He briefly considered picking one up but a glare from Eris stopped him.

"Read the sign," Eris said, gesturing at the door centered in the far wall.

"Which one?" Velen asked. There were two signs on the door. One seemed more of a permanent fixture. The other was a piece of paper nailed to the door.

Eris ignored his question, heading toward the door at the far side of the room. Velen decided to read both the signs just in case. The more permanent sign was three simple lines, no open flames, no cigarettes, no idiots. The paper had only one word on it: CLOSED written in letters that filled the page. The twine was still indicating that whoever they were looking for was in the building somewhere beyond that door and off to the left. Eris knocked on the door.

There was a loud bang as something heavy fell to the floor beyond the door. A short while later a young woman, her brown hair tied back, opened the door. She was perhaps seventeen maybe eighteen with a mix of features Velen could not identify. Beyond the door he could see the full extent of the workshop which comprised the majority of the building. At one of the workbenches sat another woman with short black hair working on something Velen could not see. Her attire, well worn and disheveled, reminded Velen of many of the first year arcanists.

"Do you need something? The shop is closed," the young woman said, looking over both Velen and Eris in a way he found far more threatening than her age suggested.

"Its okay, Dets. I was just finishing this up anyway," the woman at the bench said, turning around to face them. Her face was stained with soot but her eyes were bright and alert. She was older than Dets, perhaps in her thirties.

"We are sorry to bother you but there was an incident recently and we were hoping you might have some information that would be helpful to us," Eris said.

Dets took a step back and looked at the older woman.

"Oh well, I was hoping you had an interesting request, but I can't help you with that. If something happened around here recently I didn't notice. Too much work to do," the older woman said, turning back to the bench.

Dets continued walking backward toward a chair with a rifle slung over the back.

"We are not here to cause trouble. It really is important to Lord and Lady Hyde that we return with more information. If you don't know anything then we will be going," Eris said, putting emphasis on the titles. She warily watched Dets while gesturing to Velen to back up. Velen was too interested in whatever project was being worked on to notice. Magic might be Velen's only real interest, but he admired the dedication and ingenuity needed to craft devices to mimic the powers magic provided. Lost in thought Velen nearly walked into Eris while trying to get a better look at the workbench. As he recovered his balance he remembered why they were here.

"Oh, I guess I should make sure we are going the right way," Velen said, refocused on the task at hand he pulled out the twine and it nearly flew out of his hands toward Dets.

Eris glared at him while walking back to the exit. Velen followed the string and notice a small bracelet of shells on Dets's wrist. He recognized it immediately as a charm often used in the Miralocke for good fortune when fishing. It was a simple if effective bit of folk magic, which explained why he had not been able to identify it from the residual signature.

"Did you make that? It's quite interesting. I have not had much time to study the construction of artifacts with biological components," Velen asked, pointing at the bracelet. Dets held her arm to her chest, covering the bracelet with her other hand.

"My mom made it. What are you talking about?" Dets said, seeming more confused than scared.

"Now you've done it," Eris said quietly to herself.

"If I had to guess your mom grew up in the Miralocke and learned how to craft it there. If I remember correctly only the stronger mages in that region are taught how to craft artifacts like that bracelet. They're heavily relied upon by the Reefwalker clan on longer hunts to keep them safe. I would love to get a closer look at how she inlayed the spell without disrupting the natural properties of the shells," Velen answered.

He was somewhat confused when Dets pointed the rifle at him.

"I think its time for you to leave," Dets said, her voice trembling.

"Did I say something wrong? I don't remember there being a taboo about asking to see such artifacts. From what I read they are generally shown with pride as they are a status symbol. I will make a note not to ask in the future," Velen said, turning to go. Before he reached the egress door he turned around again.

"Wait, I was supposed to ask about what you saw last night. It's a bad habit whenever I find an interesting piece of magic," Velen said. Eris had already had the door open and was quickly moving to leave.

"Are you trying to get shot? Actually, don't answer that. I'm going to hide somewhere down the block. Good Luck," Eris said, nearly running as she left the building and headed down the street.

"Its okay, Dets, he seems mostly harmless for a mage. And if he causes problems I have just the thing," the woman at the workbench said, turning around briefly with a smile. The casual disregard for safety reminded Velen of his cousin Telor. The alchemist was one of the few members of Velen's family who still spoke with him though infrequently.

Dets lowered the rifle but only somewhat. "If you say so, Nadia. I wish Kel were here. He would have a better idea what to do," Dets said, glancing over at Nadia while still facing Velen.

Velen was not sure what was happening or who Kel was. It seemed that his personal safety was still and open question but he was no longer required to leave immediatly. If he could get his answers then it did not really matter. He would prefer not to be shot but that was a problem to deal with should it happen.

"I'm just trying to avoid having to clean up if you shot him. I don't know what he wants or why you don't want to tell him but whatever you do make it quick I need some help testing this," Nadia said, holding up a small metal box with the word front inscribed in it.

At that Dets lowered the rifle fully and slung it on the chair. She began walking over to Velen quickly.

"It could be good to talk to a mage about what I saw but it might take a bit. I'll leave you to your work Nadia. Mister...?" Dets said, heading for the door. Nadia made a vague sound of approval and waved without turning around.

Velen was curious about the purpose of the metal box, but it seemed he would not have time to inquire.

"Marcus Velen, Arcanist. I am sorry to bother you but the situation has caught my interest whatever magic was used left an odd signature and I can't put enough of it together to get a clear picture," Velen said, following Dets out on to the street.

Dets led him a few blocks to a small shop selling coffee. There were a considerable number of people in the shop, but Dets found them a table easily.

"Okay, Mr. Velen, I'll answer your question only because it keeps me from having to test whatever contraptions Nadia has put together this time," she said, having settled in.

Velen considered setting up the Fae glyph but thought better of it. Mostly he was hungry and had not had coffee since his first years in the Arcanum. Over the next hour or so Dets relayd the events of the previous night and tried her best to answer Velen's odd questions. Dets seemed to have an eye for detail and a willingness to listen when Velen explained some of the principles of magic critical to his inquiry. Even so the conversation left Velen with more questions than answers. The swordswoman was clearly using some kind of magic he had never encountered or even heard of in his considerable studies. It seemed to function like a counter spell but the method of action did not fit into any framework he could discern. Whoever this swordswoman was Velen wanted to meet them preferably with Lord Hyde present to keep her from cutting him to pieces.

"That's about everything, I think. If you have any more questions, ask someone else." Dets said with an air of finality. "Hopefully, Nadia is done testing and hasn't destroyed the shop.". Having finished her story Dets left in the direction of the workshop.

Velen sat for a few minutes more before realizing he had no idea how to get back to the Hydes' manse. While he was thinking through his options the waitress came to collect the bill. Velen had to remember where he had kept his meager fortune and while he was searching his pockets the waitress sat down.

"Well, apparently you're better at this than I thought," the waitress said.

Confused, Velen looked up.

Eris was sitting in front of him, her hair tied up

and wearing a server's uniform, which only added to Velen's confusion.

"House Hyde is an offshoot of House Dimiris. It's only natural. Now I think it's time for us to return. I think Lord Alex will want to hear your report and I have some explaining to do to Lady Alexandra."

Their trip back was largely uneventful excepting a small detour involving a cat, a shoe, and a diatribe on the proper use of eggs.

Chapter 8

"Well now, if y'all get off your asses we might be makin' it in time for lunch," Kinthross shouted to the expedition team.

It was a bit of a pointless gesture as at least half were up already packing up camp. Less than half a day out of the Promise it did not hurt to maintain discipline. Kinthross looked over his men, though technically only half were his men. Both expedition teams had merged about a week ago after Drake had gone off on his own to "check something out" as he had put it.

Kinthross was not too worried about whatever had caught the mad bastard's attention and Drake's team had integrated surprisingly easily, but moving so many through the Promise had proven to be a challenge even for him.

"Hey, Boss, everyone who's still asleep was on guard duty half the bloody night," Nico said in response.

"Now Nico, where did you get off to? Thought I had you looking into the status of the wounded," Kinthross replied, looking around for his second-in-command. Nico was a good second. She was young for a Field Knight, perhaps twenty-two if Kinthross had to guess. She was quick on her feet and had an uncanny knack for getting herself out of trouble. He finally thought to look up and spotted Nico sitting in the upper branches of a nearby tree. She nimbly hopped down through the branches despite the violin case strapped to her back.

"Brandish got me the reports. I figured I could catch some shuteye before we move out. Kari is still seeing things, but she can walk as long as we keep someone nearby to keep her on track. Darius seems to be in good shape. The burns will need to be checked on once where back but he's back to serviceable shape. Thomas's leg is still disappearing at random, so he'll need the stretcher. Brandish said he's got some of his people on that. Unless you need anything else I'm gonna see if Pot has got anything going," Nico said.

Kinthross ran through the list. With the two dead from his team and Kari wounded that brought him to twelve able-bodied knights himself included. Drake's team had just two wounded and with Darius on the mend Brandish was overseeing an additional thirteen. In terms of expeditions it had been about average for casualties. Of the thirty Field Knight who had entered the Promise twenty-seven were returning though two would probably never serve again. Kinthross did not count Drake as a true loss. The man was damn near impossible to kill and would probably show up in Khaldra in the coming weeks.

Kinthross looked over the camp, watching everyone bustle around striking tents and gathering gear. The one remaining wagon was ladened with whatever objects they could find that had not immediately killed anyone who got close. It was an odd assortment of rocks, crystals, small hastily potted trees. It was not much to look at but he knew it would fetch a considerable fortune once Dennet got around to selling it. As he surveyed the scene, Brandish approached him, Xec perched on his shoulder.

"Xec, 'ere," Kinthross called.

The crimson bird took flight, alighted on his shoulder, and eyed him expectantly. He pulled a small piece of jerky from his satchel and fed it to the bird. Xec had been with him since his time in the Miralocke and the had always brought him good luck.

"She's been eyeing something in the wagon since last night. It's got me a bit spooked. Anything that's got your luck charm acting strange is bad news," Brandish said, eyeing the wagon. Brandish was a short, heavily muscled man who had served on nearly as many expeditions as Kinthross. That made him one of the most veteran Field Knights, which made him worth listening to regarding anything from the Promise.

"Now, once we get to Khaldra that'll be Mr. Dennet's problem. If we made it this far it shouldn't be much of a problem. Put an extra guard on the wagon if it's got you bothered," Kinthross replied.

"Think I will at that. I'd be more comfortable if Drake were here. Bastard's always running off but he's worth ten men when we're in the shit," Brandish said, his hand going to the knife at his belt.

"That ain't much of a way to be talkin' 'bout your commander," Kinthross admonished.

Brandish scoffed. "Commander, you say. He leads right enough but its usually right into the worst of it. Can't complain on account of I'm always taking point. Saved our asses more times than I care to admit," Brandish retorted.

Kinthross smiled at that in wide toothy grin. The

Field Knights were an odd group, part explorers, part merchants, part paramilitary. It was clear that Brandish respected his commander in his own way.

"Think we'll leave that till Drake finds his way back. For now let's get these lazy bastards moving. As much as I love Pots's cooking I think we could all use a drink and a real meal," Kinthross said. The Field Knights might spend the majority of there time in the Promise but Khaldra was their home. The city provided a much-needed respite and that was something they all sorely needed.

"Aye, sir. I'll be glad to sleep somewhere sane," Brandish said, turning to go.

Kinthross watched him move through the group, dispensing advice and motivation in equal measure. The group was able to get moving within the hour. They moved with a speed and efficiency that the marshals of House Ironsong would envy. After a few hours of uneventful walking they came within sight of Khaldra. Kinthross called a halt just before they entered the city.

"Now let's form up to give them back home a show," Kinthross bellowed. It was a custom for the Field Knights to reenter Khaldra in a parade formation. If their approach was noted or expected many of the citizens of Khaldra would turn out to greet them as returning heroes. It was always good for moral especially when they had suffered heavy losses.

"Should I play us in, Boss?" Nico said, already taking her violin from its case.

"That be right good," Kinthross replied, taking his place at the head of the column.

Nico began to play a slow building tune timed to crescendo with there arrival in the city proper. Xec circled overhead her snow-white feathers blending seamlessly into the sky. The city was quiet for midday but the few people who saw them waved or ran to get family members. A subdued but warm welcome was unsurprising they were not supposed to return for a week or so. As they entered a small group of uniformed men eyed them. Their uniforms were far neater and more formal than the normal town guard.

"Halt! Identify yourselves!" one of them stepped forward and shouted.

Kinthross almost laughed at the man. Clearly they were new to the city.

"Kinthross Reefwalker, acting commander of the thirty-second expedition. Now you don't want to be what's standing between these hungry men a good meal," Kinthross replied. He was tired and did not have time to deal with whatever Nobles guards had taken it upon themselves to play officers. Judging by their reaction the group intended to stand in their way. Which meant they were new to the city. Most of the regular guards respected the Field Knights for their assistance in protecting the city when called on.

"By order of Governor Delos, all those entering the city will be detained and questioned," the man said, doing his best to speak with authority. Judging from the hesitancy in the man's voice Kinthross figured he could get the man to back off and save them all the hassle.

Kinthross knew that the noble who ruled Expera was granted the title governor, but he had never had a reason to learn their name. It was something of a personal failing but, the political intrigue between the clans had been the driving force behind him leaving the Miralocke. Dennet would not appreciate him causing a scene but he was ill equipped to deal with some minor noble with an oversized ego.

"Well, I'm not sure we got time to oblige," Kinthross responded, gesturing to Nico to lead the team into the city. Kinthross figured it would be better to get them moving and away before someone decided to deal with the obstacle. Diplomacy was rarely an option in the Promise and many of the Field Knights had rather loose opinions on what justified using force. Nico seemed to have the same idea and was already issuing stand-down orders using the hand signs they had developed to deal with areas where verbal communication was unwise.

"This is your chance to comply with a lawful order, have your men disarm and submit to inspection immediately" the man said struggling to meet Kinthross' gaze.

Despite Nico giving orders he could see some of the Knights reaching for weapons. Kinthross cursed under his breath. He might want to avoid a fight but some of the Knights had other ideas. He needed to get the guards to back down. Dennet could talk his way out of anything and leave everyone feeling like they walk away the winner. Dennet was not here which meant Kinthross needed to sort this out his own way. The best he could manage was to bluff his way through. Even with magic five against twenty-five was not a fight the guards were likely to win. He just needed to convince the guards that they had more to lose.

"Now, neither of us wants trouble but I'm not seeing how this plays out in your favor." Kinthross said smiling with confidence he did not feel. Odd were his team could handle the guards but the thought of any of the Knights dying over such a pointless squabble was an insult to the risks they took whenever they entered the Promise.

"I am well within my rights to kill you where you stand for such insolence. Perhaps you need a lesson in why citizens should respect the nobility." The man replied, the tremble in his voice made jest of the intended threat. Kinthross smiled the man was clearly shaken with a little more pressure this might end without anyone dead.

"Now, no bloods been shed just yet. I have enough road dust to get out of my clothes as it is. I don't need to the hassle of scrubbing out whatever stains that piss water you call blood will leave." Kinthross replied. Insults might not be the best example of diplomacy, but he figured the sheer audacity would make the guard think twice about engaging.

The man stood with his jaw hanging open for a moment. Then turned to the other unarmed guard and nodded. The other man began chanting.

As the chant grew in volume Kinthross knew his plan had failed. Whether it was because he had pushed to hard or simply the guards being overzealous it did not matter now. He did not have time to react as the air grew hot.

Nico rolled out of the way as a wall of fire burst forth blocking the road leading into the city. Any chance at a bloodless resolution went up in smoke as in the blink of an eye the three other guards drew their swords.

"Brandish, Zed, with me. Nico, get everyone to base," Kinthross shouted, pulling his harpoon from where it hung at his waist. He had never been much of a marksman and preferred the tools he had grown up using.

Zed, the best marksman in the group, already had his rifle trained on the guards.

Brandish unfurled the rope around his waist and had his grappling hook spinning ominously as he came to Kinthross's side.

Kinthross did not have time to see how Nico dealt with the situation, but he trusted her to figure something out. A wall of fire should not be a challenge compared to the things they encountered in the Promise. The three swordsman moved forward with inhuman speed, but Brandish was ready. His hook shot forward, striking one in the leg. The crack of bone was drowned out by the retort of Zed's rifle. The shot exploded in a flash of light as it stuck an invisible wall inches in front of the leader's head.

Kinthross dodged to the side to avoid the swordsman who had rushed him. The third swordsman passed him trying to close the gap with Zed, a plan that proved foolish as they were only able to make it halfway before Zed fired again, dropping them with a round to the head.

Kinthross might not be faster than his opponent, but he was larger, and his harpoon gave him considerable reach. He was not able to land a decisive blow, but he could keep the swordsman at bay.

Zed was forced to take cover as a concussive wave cracked the stone wall just to the left of him. Brandish was still facing off against his opponent who seemed unperturbed despite their injuries.

"Xec," Kinthross called.

At his call Xec dived, talons forward, at the swordsman facing him.

The swordsman reacted immediately, striking at

the new threat. The blow missed by a hair's breath and Xec's talons drove into the man's eyes.

Kinthross took the opportunity to drive his harpoon into the man's throat. He stepped in and kicked the man's body as he moved to withdraw the harpoon. The barbs tore the man's throat completely open, blood spurting from arteries as the corpse fell to the ground.

Kinthross looked over to see Brandish finishing their opponent as well. The grappling hook was caught in their opponent's leg and Brandish was stomping their head into the pavement.

Zed had stopped firing, which was concerning but Kinthross still had two opponents to deal with, both of whom seemed to be powerful mages. Kinthross began to advance on the leader of the group but was thrown back by the wall of force. Brandish pulled his grappling hook out of his opponent's leg but he was moving slowly blood beginning to seep through his shirt. Kinthross felt something grab his arms and legs holding him fast. The leader was gesturing in his direction and the chanting had stopped. Kinthross looked to the other mage who had begun to conjure a ball of fire and seemed intent on unleashing it at him.

A dark shape dropped from the roof behind the mages, landing silently. As the mage brought his hand forward, the fire crackling between them, there was a sharp crack. They traveled only a few feet forward before disappearing. The mage fell to the ground, a crimson rose just forming on his shirt right over his heart. The leader of the group released his hold on Kinthross and ran, sending a wave of force that knocked Kinthross, Brandish, and Nico off their feet.

"Should I follow him, Boss?" Nico said, springing to her feet.

"Nah, we made enough trouble as is. Let's get back to base before we are really in the shit," Kinthross said, looking around. Brandish was bandaging his side with a piece of cloth cut from his opponent's uniform. Zed staggered out from a nearby alley with blood running down his face using his rifle for support.

"Bastard smack me around a bit. Give me a bit to get my head on straight," Zed said, lowering himself against a nearby wall. Kinthross moved to help the man but Zed waved him off, gesturing to the crowd gathering. Kinthross was pleased that he could not see anyone from the expedition team in the crowd that had gathered to watch the commotion.

"Can't help you with the one who ran but if any more come poking around we'll set them off in the wrong direction," said an , older man from the crowd. He was nearly as tall as Kinthross but considerably heavier.

"Now we can handle ourselves, don't want none you to get in the shit over us," Kinthross replied.

"Least we can do. That place might be cursed but what y'all bring back has helped us more than any Imperial noble. Saved my boys life few years back," the man replied, and the crowd seem to mummer its agreement. Most of what was retrieved from the Promise was sold off to fund future expeditions, but Dennet always made a point to set some aside to assist the people of Khaldra.

"Sorry about the cistern. I'm sure we can cover the repairs," Nico said, staring at her hands which were fidgeting with the ends of her hair..

"Don't worry 'bout us Miss it was quite a show.

Never thought I'd see men never mind horses willing to run through a wall of fire. We'll get by till Mr. Dennet sends someone around," the man replied. Kinthross had wondered how Nico had gotten the team to safety.

"Brandish, Zed, are you good to travel?" Kinthross asked.

"I'll get by. I've gotten worse after pissin' in the wrong man's drink," Brandish said, with a coughing laugh.

Zed simply nodded and pushed himself up. Kinthross was concerned for the man but it would take more than that to drop a Field Knight. They would need to cover up the blood if they did not want more trouble on the way. Nico led the way to the hall altering their course whenever she spotted more guards. The sheer number of mages patrolling the streets was worrying, Something had clearly changed in Khaldra while they had been in the Promise.Avoiding the patrols was simple enough with a small group well versed in avoiding notice. Kinthross did not want a repeat of the disaster a the city boarder. They might have emerged largely unscathed but combat was never a sure thing. In a little under an hour they had arrived.

The Field Knights' Hall, located a few blocks from the market square, was an unassuming building located between a blacksmith's shop and a cooper's. Dennet originally bought the spacious building to house and sell the many strange items he had pulled from the Promise. As the expedition teams grew it became necessary to convert it into a barracks of sorts. Kinthross could not see any of the expedition team loitering about, which was good. It would not do to draw more attention to their base of operations.

Despite their reputation in Khaldra the location of the hall was not well known. Dennet worked to keep it that way as a test for any perspective new members.

They entered the hall through the side door located in the alley between the hall and the blacksmith's shop. The front door was boarded up,mostly to keep out young fools looking for adventure or a chance at wealth. The side door led into the main room of the hall, which was currently being converted from a bar to a medical ward. The work was fast and efficient. Tables were being moved out of the way and cots being brought from other rooms. It might seem excessive, but it was not uncommon for injuries to go unreported until they were back in Khaldra. Kinthross was about to send someone to get Dennet when Nico chimed in.

"Already done, Boss. Already sent someone to fetch the doc and Mister Dennet," Nico said, walking around the working knights to grab her violin case from a pile of gear in the corner.

"When did you find the time to do that?" Kinthross asked.

"Hard to say. Sometime between coming up with a plan to get everyone out and coming back to save your ass," Nico quipped.

Brandish and Zed sat down on cots neither seemed interested in conversation. Kinthross and Nico went to sit at the bar to wait until Dennet arrived.

Elias Shen arrived first, his medical bag barely closed and bulging with supplies. In any other part of the empire he would not be considered a true doctor but in Khaldra a lack of magic was simply a challenge to overcome rather than disqualifying. Kinthross always found Elias's attire a bit strange. Fine clothes seemed an impediment in the bloody surgeon's arts. It did not really matter the man was an exceptional doctor and years of treating the numerous and strange injuries accrued by the expeditions had honed his skills. Elias took a quick look around the room before heading over to Kinthross and Nico.

"Next time do send word before you arrive. I am quite busy. Without a list of injuries I may be completely unprepared to treat my patients adequately," Elias said.

"I'm sure you'll manage, Doc. Best to start with Zed and Brandish, Their injuries are fresh. We got three others with notable injuries but they're stable fer now," Kinthross said.

"Fresh injuries? How did you manage that?" Elias asked his eyebrow raising over the rim of his monocle quizzically.

"Bit of trouble getting into the city. I'm sure either of them will give you the rundown. Shouldn't be much trouble for you. Now Thomas might give you a bit of it when you get around to him," Kinthross replied. Elias stroked his mustache while staring intently.

"Best wash up and get to work. Is Anis around? She's getting competent as an assistant," Elias asked.

"She didn't make it," Kinthross said, somberly.

Anis had been his team's medic and a solid one at that. Always the first to run in to pull someone out of whatever horror had ensnared them. At least until one of those horrors turned its fangs on her.

"Best get to work then," Elias said, in the tone he used when treating the worst cases. Elias might not travel into the Promises with the expedition teams but he understood what being a Field Knight meant perhaps more than anyone who hadn't been in the Promise.

Nico began fidgeting with her violin case. "I'll

help you out. I know enough to not get in the way," she said, hoping off the stool to follow Elias.

Kinthross let her go. He could speak with Dennet on his own and it would be good for Nico to be working. Dwelling on their losses was his responsibility.

Dennet entered the hall without a word and immediately headed for Kinthross. He walked confidently through the crowd of Knights, putting the last touches on the conversion of the main room. Even after seven years it still surprised Kinthross to see Dennet in a suit. Kinthross remembered when Dennet had been the expedition leader it was hard to square the rough adventurer with the wealthy entrepreneur. The one thing that had remained the same was the man's confidence. Dennet acted as if the world owed him everything and if it disagreed then he would change the world.

"I see both teams are back early. I'm sure there is a story there but for now what were our losses?" Dennet asked.

"Might be best to start with recent events," Kinthross replied.

Dennet took a seat at the bar and poured himself a drink from one of the bottles on the counter.

Kinthross took that as a cue to continue. "We had some trouble getting into the city. The governor's new dogs seem a bit jumpy. Took care of it well enough but one ran off. Might be we hooked the wrong fish."

Dennet took a long drink before responding.

"How many dead?" Dennet asked.

"Just four on their end. Brandish and Zed took a beating, but Doc should be able to patch 'em up," Kinthross said.

"Could be worse I suppose. We'll need to keep

everyone off the streets until I can arrange transport," Dennet said calmly.

"Transport where?" Kinthross asked. Dennet was right about laying low but it would be hard to get everyone moving again so soon after an expedition.

"Not too far. A new homestead project to the west. I was going to send some of you there once you returned but if we have already drawn the new governors attention it will need to be everyone. It seems fate is trying to force my hand," Dennet replied. Kinthross could tell Dennet had some new scheme in the works but vague allusions made Kinthross job harder.

"Extermination jobs are nearly as bad as another expedition. Not sure we'll be up for that any time soon," Kinthross said, annoyed. He understood the need to get out of the city till things blew over, but even Field Knights had limits. Helping a homestead clear an area from whatever monsters had wandered out of the Promise was hard work. An extermination was the only reason he could think of to send them to a new homestead instead of to Senrena or Vesrin.

"Don't worry, you'll have time to rest. All you need to do is keep everyone out of trouble and ready to go when I say so," Dennet responded cryptically.

"Moving so soon ain't gonna be an easy sell. I'm gonna need more than that," Kinthross demanded.

"Unfortunately, that's all I'm going to say. It needs to be done and you're the man to do it," Dennet said, his tone flat and face impassive Kinthross wanted to argue but when Dennet gave orders he expected them to be fulfilled.

"I'll get it done," Kinthross said, matching Dennet's tone.

"I know you will, and I'll handle the rest," Dennet replied.

Kinthross would have to trust Dennet's plan. Anyone else and he would have walk away then and there, but Dennet knew his business. Dennet had proven himself both in the field and as a leader. He had built the Field Knights from the ground up and had led more expeditions than any member except Drake.

"We got twenty-three in service, maybe a few more depending on who Doc can set right. We pulled out a cartload, but I can't speak to what it'll be worth. Brandish took over Drake's team when he decided to disappear," Kinthross said, running through the basic details of the expedition.

Dennet listened while counting the wounded on cots. "So, we lost two. We'll need to send them off in the proper way," he said with a resigned tone and eyes downcast.

Kinthross was surprised the Field Knights' tradition to honor their dead was far from subtle. He eyed Dennet quizzically.

"Some things are too important to push off. I'll make what arrangements I can but to the Promise with anyone who gets in our way," Dennet said, his voice trembling. Dennet might be more businessman than adventurer now, but he was still a Field Knight at heart.

"Now that's the right of it," Kinthross replied with a broad smile and a hearty tap on Dennet shoulder.

"The full story will have to wait. This is going to be a long night," Dennet said, standing up. Kinthross could not think of any other pressing matters, so he remained silent. Dennet left, briefly stopping to speak with Elias regarding necessary supplies. Kinthross sat for a while longer contemplating what lay ahead. Dennet was right.

It was going to be a long night.

Chapter 9

Kel slid to a stop, kicking up a cloud of dust that obscured his view of the mage. The first blast knocked him off his feet and left his head ringing. He rolled, lining up his shot. The crack of the rifle felt dull in his ears. Kel watched in horror as a small flash of light appeared in front of the mage. The mage gestured again, forcing Kel to roll as a second explosion racked his body. The detonation had been farther away than the first. Kel took it as a good sign that the mage could not hit him accurately.

Kel pushed himself to his feet and began to sprint away. If he could get farther from the mage he hoped it would be easier to avoid being blown to bits. He ran, allowing his unsteady feet to alter his course to avoid making himself an easy target. Kel scanned the horizon for somewhere to taken cover. A small patch of rocks in the distance provided the only cover he could see. Evimikwazi were highly territorial. The odds there was another in the area was low. Kel looked back to see the mage closing on him. The mage was propelling themself at incredible speeds, leaving craters in the ground as they leaped forward.

Kel forced himself to go faster, lungs burning. It had been years since he been in a fight and more since he was forced to run any considerable distance. Whether it was luck or a conscious choice by the mage, Kel made it to the rocks without taking another hit. Kel lined up another shot just as the mage reached the apex of one of their jumps. The shot exploded before reaching the target. Kel took cover to catch his breath. It seemed the mage was willing to giving him a reprieve for long enough to close the distance. Kel was running out of options, he might have better chances with his revolver. If he put multiple shots on target in quick succession he might overwhelm the mages defenses. It was a risky plan, requiring him to give up any chance at avoiding the mages attacks.. He put down his rifle and drew his revolver. Placing his back to the rock he waited, trying to judge the distance. It proved almost impossible the ringing in his ears muffled and distorted the sound of the explosions as the mage drew closer.

Moments felt like years as he waited, back to the rock and pistol held tight in his hands. The rock behind him exploded, chunks of stone filled the air. One fist sized chunk of stone struck Kel in the head, drawing blood and turning the world black. When his vision returned, unfocused and spotty, a figure stood over him, plate armor gleaming and holding a massive two-handed sword that seemed to move like a snake. Kel tried to speak but his words were washed away by the pounding of his blood, sending waves of pain and nausea through his body. Another explosion closer than the rest range out and the sound alone nearly drove him from consciousness, but still the figure stood unmoved. Kel's last thought before everything went black was whether this was who the mages had been hunting.

***

Kel startled awake, reaching for his rifle but only finding sheets. Kel tried to get his baring, but it was a slow and painful process. His head was bandaged and everything seemed to be working. He tried to sit up and nearly blacked out.

"Ma says you shouldn't be doing that," came the voice of a child.

"Where? How?" Kel croaked, his voice dry and tinged with pain. Kel turned his head to see a young boy sitting in a chair near the bed.

"Don't know. Da just said someone needed my bed so I had to sleep by the fireplace the last two nights," the boy said, sulking.

"Guess I should tell Ma you're up," he continued. The boy dropped the match he was playing with and all but ran out of the room.

Kel was left to try to get his thoughts together. He was alive but he did not know where or who had saved him. He could not see his rifle, and he was wearing loose clothes that did not fit him. He was working up the will to sit up when a women entered. She was somewhat younger than him. Her attire told Kel that he was in the homestead of a Purifier. The red clothes with white embroidery were a dead giveaway.

"Seems Televilus has more planned for you. Best get you on your feet to face the challenges ahead," she said, walking over to the bed and placing a steaming bowl on a nearby table.

"How did I get here?" Kel asked, barely managing to prop himself up against the headboard.

"A knight dropped you off. She said, she found you out on the plains. Odd girl never took her helm off and left immediately once Proth said, he would take care of you. Look like she wasn't in the best shape either. I can't imagine carrying someone wearing so much armor and so many weapons," she answered, sitting down in the chair the boy had vacated and tutting at the pile of burnt matches on the floor.

Kel tried to remember what had happened but everything after taking cover behind the rocks was a blur.

"Where is my rifle?" Kel asked.

"Oh, don't worry, Proth took good care of it while you were out. Said it was a fine piece and he would need to get his hands on one someday. But you're in no shape for that right now," she replied, laughing.

"Thank you for your hospitality but I need to get back to the city before I cause you more trouble," Kel said, remembering his fight with the mages. He hoped no one would be looking for him for assaulting a noble.

"His will is life and progress. Stay as long as you need to move forward," she said, head down with her thumb pressed to her forehead as if in prayer.

"I should be good in another day or so, it's not my first time taking a hit to the head," Kel said, doing his best to smile. Last time there was a mishap in the workshop he been knock clear across the room. He hoped Nadia would not come looking for him. She tended to go overboard when she was worried.

"Best eat up then," she said, offering him the bowl. Kel managed to take a sip of the broth without making too much of a mess. It was hearty made from mushroom stock. There was not much that was safe to grow on the Maras Plains but if anyone would know it was the Purifiers. Once he had demonstrated he could feed himself she stood to leave.

"If you need anything just holler," she said, before closing the door.

Kel managed to finish the bowl of broth before falling back asleep. He woke again with the fading light of day streaming through the window of the small room. He still felt weak but also extremely hungry. On the table near the bed was another bowl and a cup with water. As he looked around the room he noted his rifle leaning on the wall near the door. It had been cleaned recently the metal barrel reflecting the ruby light in geometric patterns on the floor. Kel felt foggy but the pain in his head had subsided. He quickly finished the broth in the bowl but it barely only made him hungrier. He considered calling to ask for more but he wanted to test if he could stand. He slid to the edge of the bed and bracing himself against the table tried to stand. His legs felt rubbery, but he did not fall over.

It took him a painfully long time to make his way over to his rifle and gear. He decided against grabbing his rifle. He had to slump to the floor to get his belt on with his holstered revolver. He regretted the decision as he tried and failed to stand back up. He spent several minutes trying to rise before a man entered wearing a red shirt embroidered with white swirls in the vague shape of flames.

"Might be a little soon for that, friend," the man said, and small plumes of smoke rose from his pipe as chuckled. The man offered Kel a hand covered in callouses and scars.

"Proth, I assume. I was hoping to eat something more than broth," Kel said, finally getting to his feet with the man's help.

"Aye, that's me. Welcome to my homestead, Mister…" Proth replied.

"Rickart Kel. It's a pleasure to meet you and your family," Kel said.

"Well, Mr. Kel, I think Hestia got something cooking for dinner if you think you can make it that far," Proth said.

"Why are we standing around here then?" Kel said.

The dining room was not far but the stairs proved a substantial obstacle. After a few minutes Kel had managed to get down the stairs on his own much to Proth's amusement.

"Stubborn and well armed. It's got me wondering what got the drop on you?" Proth asked while Kel was catching his breath at the base of the stairs.

"Tried to help the wrong people," Kel answered.

"Sounds like quite the story. You'll have to tell it over dinner if we ever make it there," Proth said with a chuckle. As they walked through the house Kel began to feel a better. It seemed odd. Kel had taken blows to the head before and he knew the recovery was long and slow. If he had been unconscious for two days he should be in much worse shape not up and walking. Even if the process of walking to the kitchen was slow and tortuous it was doable.

They entered the dining room where Hestia was pulling skewers of meat off the metal stove. The table in the center of the room was set for four though one set of dishes consisted of a pan and a hastily carved wooded fork.

"Talia really is a miracle worker. I did not expect to see you up and about for at least a week," Hestia said, watching Kel take a seat at the table in front of the makeshift tableware.

"Talia Stoledock?" Kel asked.

"Yes. Few years ago, when Proth was laid up after a bad cleansing. She gave me some herbs to help him get back on his feet. I had some left over, so I put them in the broth," Hestia answered.

Kel knew the homesteads near Khaldra had their own community, but it still surprised him to hear Dets's mother's name. He had only met her once when he was showing Dets how to disassemble and clean her rifle. Kel remembered Talia as a tall, thin women who wore a considerable amount of jewelry, mostly composed of shells of various colors that stood out against her dark skin. Kel was surprised to learn she had a talent for healing though it did explain why Dets always seemed to be in good health despite her many misadventures.

"Next time Dets stops by the shop I'll have her send my thanks to her mother," Kel said. Kel figured he could give Dets some more rounds for her rifle as thanks. Her family relied on her hunting to eat during the winter, and ammunition could be expensive.

"The Stoledocks are good folks. The young lass has tipped us off to some problems on the plains. Saved us the trouble of doing a full cleansing," Proth chimed in.

As they spoke the boy came in, running to the table.

"Does this mean I get my bed back?" the boy asked, interrupting the conversation.

"Alaz, don't be rude to our guest. Now go clean up before dinner," Hestia chastised. As the boy ran off Kel noted he smelled faintly of lamp oil.

While they waited, Kel began relaying the story of what had happened out on the plains. Proth seemed interested but once Alaz returned everyone began eating and the conversation ceased. Kel ate far more than he would have expected and the lack of conversation let him focus on filling his painfully empty stomach. Once everyone had finished Kel began telling his story again. He didn't get far before the fog had returned. His stomach full weariness began to set in, and he found it hard to organize his thoughts.

"You ain't much of a storyteller but I think I get your point. If that had happened to me I could spin a yarn that have you glued to your seat," Proth said as Kel finished.

"Think my head's still scrambled. Might be best if I get back to bed before you need to carry me up those gods damn stairs," Kel said.

The trip back upstairs was not as harrowing as the journey down, but it left his head spinning. He fell asleep almost immediately when he reached the bed.

Kel woke up with his side aching where he had slept on his revolver. Normally that would be a major source of aggravation, but present circumstances made it almost a relief. Kel was able to stand and walk with only the normal discomfort age had brought him. He might not be able to run or fight but he felt strong enough to make the walk back to the city. He collected what remained of his gear. It was a blessing that he had not lost his rifle. It represented years of effort and had saved his life more than once. He had a lot of explaining to do when he got back. Not only had he disappeared for a few days, he had lost Nadia's prototype..

Kel headed down the stairs to the dining room. The process was considerably easier, and he marveled at the efficacy of Talia's medicine. The dining room was empty but there was a canteen and some jerky on the table. Kel took the gifts and found his way to the door. The morning light was almost blinding after days spent inside. When he could see clearly he found himself in the fenced yard of the homestead. Hestia was working in the small garden if it could be called that. The patch of ground was filled with an odd variety of mushrooms. Kel had no clue, which of them was edible but Hestia seemed to be picking the largest and sorting them into several baskets.

"Leaving already? You must have pressing business in the city," Hestia said, looking up from her work.

"Nothing pressing but I've found it best not to leave my assistant unattended If I want somewhere to return to," Kel answered with a small smile.

"Proth took Azal on his mourning patrol. I'll let them know you left in good health. Walk forward toward life and progress," she said. Kel knew it was a call and response prayer, but he had never been a man of faith. It left a sour taste in his mouth to leave on a bad note, but Hestia returned to her work without comment.

***

Kel's journey back to Khaldra was uneventful, though it took him longer than his trip out to the plains. Kel noted a group of mages standing guard at the entrance to the city. He doubted they were waiting for him but risking another confrontation seemed unwise. Kel had to assume he would bespotted approaching the city unless he took percautions. Most of Khaldra's outskirts were sparse, having been cleared to provide room for the growing city. His options to disappear were significantly limited. The few rocks or fenced paddocks provided very limited cover and the distance between them would leave him exposed for a considerable amount of time.

Kel subtly detached the scope from his rifle and began walking toward the closest boulder that had been too heavy to clear without considerable effort. It only protruded out of the ground up to his knees, so he sat and waited for an opportunity to drop out of site. The jerky he had been given provided a good cover. It was not long before a small cart pulled by a farmer was stopped by the guards. Kel took his opportunity and slid to the ground. Crawling half a kilometer would be a slow and arduous process but one he felt was necessary.

The sun was past its zenith when he reached the first buildings. He had checked on the guards multiple times and they had not appeared to notice him. Hopping a fence into the garden of a house he began moving between yards and alleys until he was far enough into the city to feel safe. Before he walked into the open streets he stole a pair of trousers drying on a line and wrapped it around his rifle. He could return it later but for now it should obfuscate the weapon. The final leg of his journey was brief and uneventful.

Kel entered his shop locking the door behind him. He normally never locked the door but whether it was paranoia or exhaustion he couldn't say. When he entered the workshop he found Nadia sleeping at her workbench. It was a bad habit they shared though Nadia rarely made it to her workbench usually falling asleep on whatever part of the floor was closest. Out of habit he took a quick walk around. Nothing seemed out of place or left in a perilous position. Kel considered using the chemical shower they had hooked up to the cistern on the roof to wash off, but he did not want to wake Nadia. If she had fallen asleep then she clearly needed it more than he needed to get clean. With nothing better to do he laid his rifle on his workbench and began disassembling it and meticulously cleaning each part. Once done he assembled the rifle then began the process again.

He let his mind wander as he went through the motions. He did not dwell on the events of the last few days instead he thought through the current projects he had taken on. Most were custom pieces for the various hunters and merchants who traveled Expera but one stood out. It was the first time he had accepted a job that required mass production. Normally he would leave that work for the gunsmith with more apprentices but the man who had made the request was insistent. Kel knew the man by reputation and the fortune he offered was well above market rate. Regardless, a thousand rifles was more than he had made in ten years and seemed and excessive number. Even for Peter Dennet and his expedition teams. When asked Dennet had explained he was planning on establishing a new settlement closer to the Promise than Khaldra. It was a plausible explanation, but something felt off. In the end it had been the stories his father had told him about the founding of Khaldra that finally convinced Kel to take on the project. Whether Dennet was serious in his endeavor Kel wanted his work to play a role in shaping the future of the region.

He had made considerable progress in the last few months, producing almost a hundred rifles that met his exacting standards. Nadia had enthusiastically devised new methods to produce the necessary components at speed. They were still behind schedule mostly due to his insistence on perfection. Kel doubted he could get back on the original schedule but with work and Nadia's help he could complete the project in a reasonable amount of time. Kel laid out the timeline in his head, trying to work out what the best course of action was, given his recent misadventure. It took some time but finally he felt satisfied enough with the concept to stop and write it down. He was not sure how long he had been disassembling and reassembling his rifle, but Nadia was still fast asleep.

Having decided on a plan Kel set to work organizing the workshop and pulling out materials. He avoided the heavier steel components and did not start up the forge that could wait till he and Nadia were rested. Kel was moving unfinished stocks when one slipped out of his hands and thudded into the ground. Kel cursed under his breath as Nadia stirred.

"Keep it down. I'm trying to work," Nadia mumbled. She slowly raised her head and looked around. Kel chuckled at the word FRONT indented on her face. "Kel, why are you making a racket? Wait, weren't you missing? I remember planning to go send Dets to find you. Did she find you?"

"Haven't seen her. I ran into some trouble on the plains. Got my head scrambled for a bit. When did you send Dets out?" Kel replied. He hoped Dets wouldn't run into too much trouble looking for him when he was already back in the city.

"Well, she was here when I came in but then left to go answer some mage's question. After that she didn't stick around to help me test this," Nadia said, holding up the small metal box she had been using as a pillow.

"A mage? Were they wearing a uniform," Kel interrupted before she could continue. Nadia looked at him puzzled.

"I don't think so. If it was a uniform he clearly didn't know how to put it on properly. Apparently, he wanted to know about something Dets saw after walking me home," Nadia answered. "Oh yeah, you didn't disappear till a while after that. I was ready to go get Dets, but I had an idea to shorten the delay without making the trigger mechanism too sensitive. By the way, we need a new test target preferable one that won't fall apart this time,"

If the timeline Nadia had set out was correct Dets should be fine. Kel was relived that his actions hadn't dragged her into trouble. And how Nadia had managed to destroy the target dummy they used for rifles with that small box was a question that could wait. Preferably till he was retired.

"Well, if you're up you should eat. We have work to do starting tomorrow. I need to clean up and sleep in my own bed," Kel said, changing the subject to avoid any questions.

"Up?" Nadia said, confused. She felt her face where the letter was slowly fading. "Guess I dozed off for a bit. What are we working on?"

Kel explained the plan he had outlined. As he did Nadia's enthusiasm faded. She preferred working on her own projects instead of the tedious work required for mass production. It had been easy getting her to help design the process but actually implementing it was another matter. After some arguing and him promising to get her some field tests for her projects she agreed. Nadia went to grab something to eat, leaving Kel to climb the stairs to his room above the workshop. He spent some time cleaning himself up before falling asleep.

Chapter 10

Delos sat, his hands resting on the large map of the city carved into the table before him. He and Kelen had been discussing for some time as they read through the mountain of papers generated by the management of a city. The reports coming in from the guards were promising and the local nobility seemed to be falling in line. Their work was interrupted when Kardol the captain of Delos guards entered escorting the arcanist Rem. Disheveled and wide eyed the arcanist had returned alone. It took hours of questions to get anything out of the terrified arcanist and most of it was completely useless. From the few answers they received it seemed the hunting party had not only failed to locate their quarry but had been ambushed by a beast while traversing the plains outside the city. Iresel had slain the beast but the other guards, two men handpicked by Iresel, had fallen to the creature's talons. Losing two of his personal guards with nothing to show would have been bad enough but Rem's story continued. It seemed that a local had become involved in the confrontation. Whether it was to come to the aid of the guards or to ensure they died was unclear from Rem's traumatized recollection. Regardless Iresel had chased the man across the plains never to return. By the time Delos and Kelen had run out of question the arcanist was shaking tears streaking down her face.

"Kardol, we are done here. Take this wretch and string her up over the gate. I want everyone to know the price of failure." Delos growled. He would have killed her himself but there would not be enough left to send a proper message. Kardol saluted and hand resting on his sword stepped forward to take the arcanist. Lost in her own world Rem did not even flinch. As Kardol reached for her.

The wood floor cracked as Kardol fell to his knee's eyes wide with shock. Delos turned to Kelen. Kelen sat with his hand outstretched fingers pointing down. A scowl of disapproval on his face as he stared at Kardol.

"What game are you playing Kelen." Delos said, his face contorted with rage.

"I'm doing my best to keep this disastrous project running. We are making progress but if every setback is accompanied by an execution, we won't have enough people to staff the keep never mind the city." Kelen replied, his face impassive. His words were spoken with a chill strong enough to match the heat of Delos' fury.

"You dare to challenge me." Delos bellowed, magic amplifying his word enough to echo through the keep.

Kelen's fingers snapped forward and Kardol flew back into the wall with enough force to crack the stone. He turned to Delos, no hint of anger or fear on his face. Rem and Kardol were forgotten as the two lords faced off. The air crackled with undirected magic. A contest between the two could leave the keep a ruin and Delos was unsure who would be left standing. That tiny seed of uncertainty bloomed into fear as Delos turned away.

"This is our failure, Lord Delos. We lead because we have the power to do so. If we do not use that power when it is necessary, then what right have we to order others. I will personally see to this hunt even if that means searching every house in the accursed city." Kelen said, slowly rising to his feet. Delos watched as he brushed past Rem and stepped over Kardol's unconscious body.

Delos remained seated to gripping the table hard enough to leave dents in the wood. He would need to deal with Kelen eventually but Delos still needed him to hold this mess together. It seemed as if High Lord Ironsong had orchestrated this entire thing to drive Delos to madness. He breathed deeply to calm himself. A few minutes later he had regained his composer. He looked over to Kardol who was slowly rising to his feet.

"Find somewhere out of site to take the Arcanist. I'll need some time to think of an appropriate punishment." Delos said.

Kardol obey immediately though he was still unsteady on his feet. Whatever the guard captain's opinion on the confrontation between the lords he had enough sense to keep his mouth shut. Even as Kardol took them away the arcanist seemed oblivious to the events that had transpired.

Once Delos was alone he tried to turn his attention to his work. He made it through a single page before giving up. Delos rose, if he could not concentrate, he would need to find something else productive to do. Perhaps Kelen had the right of things, he could be doing so much more than reading reports and giving orders. Delos went to his room and retrieved his armor and blade. The enchanted plate was an artifact that had been in his family for generations. The plate provided substantial protection against attacks both magical and mundane. More importantly through a series of clever enchantments it relieved the burden placed on the mind of a mage allowing them to use their magic without risking burning out. His guards might be doing an adequate job in restoring order but as the Governor of Expera it was long past time he took a more personal role in that endeavor.

When Delos entered the bailey Lord Merrel was dismounting a carriage. Delos was in no mood to deal with the foppish lord, but it seemed Merrel had other ideas. He immediately moved to intercept Delos. Delos picked up his pace. Whatever report Merrel felt pressing could wait until Delos had a chance to blow off his frustrations.

"Lord Delos, you seem in quite the hurry. Has something happened that requires your attention?" Merrel said between deep breaths. Delos scoffed at how weak the man was.

"I have wasted enough time on papers and conversations. I intend to see for myself what is happening in my city." Delos said as he strode through the gate and onto the streets.

"I only need a moment; I have a rather intriguing letter you should look at. It presents a—" Merrel said still following Delos.

"You seem perfectly capable of walking and talking at the same time. Say your piece while I work if you wish." Delos said. He did not care whether Merrel followed or not. Delos headed towards the southern boarder of the city where most of the caravans entered.

"Of course, Lord Delos, it would be an honor. If there is anywhere in particular, you wish to go I have studied the maps extensively." Merrel said from a way behind Delos. Delos continued without acknowledging the man. Delos had his goal in mind and if Merrel choose to follow then he had best keep up.

The streets were emptier than Delos would have guessed. The few people he encountered hurried out of his way or fled into stores. They should be awed that their Lord had chosen to grace the streets, but fear was an acceptable substitute. After a few blocks Merrel caught up with Delos. It was a laughable use of enhancement magic but at least Merrel had the sense to augment his personal failing with magic.

"If we continue this way we will be passing the market square. If you wish to see what is really happening in Khaldra the market would be a perfect destination." Merrel said.

"I will go where I please." Delos replied, his tone showed exactly what he thought of Merrel offering suggestions.

"Of course, but perhaps the news I bring could persuade you. I had just returned from a conversation in the market with a merchant by the name of Zal Al-Zetel. He sought me out to deliver an invitation. Normally I would decline but he was persistent. He wished to offer you a seat at an auction with only one item of considerable value. He was vague on the details saying only that 'the man who rules these land should have a crown to match'. I nearly turned him away it was an outlandish claim. Before I could he offered to show me the box he kept the item in. I am not particularly sensitive to magic but the sheer amount of power coming off that box was enough set my hair on end." Merrel said pausing at various points to allow Delos a chance to respond.

Delos stopped for the first time since leaving the keep. He turned to Merrel who flinched as Delos looked him over.

"Waste my time with such inane stories again and I will cut your tongue out. If this merchant truly had an artifact worthy of my time he would be in Arabas not this magicless wasteland." Delos growled. Merrel stepped back and took a moment to compose himself as Delos walked away.

"But Lord Delos, I assure you whatever that merchant had was worth at least some consideration." Merrel said hurrying to catch up. Delos turned and pointed his hand at Merrel light shining from the crystals formed in his palm. Merrel squeaked but continued hesitantly. "Please allow me to make arrangements for this auction. If it proves a wasted effort I will cut my own tongue out."

"I will hold you to that Lord Merrel." Delos said lowering his hand. If a coward like Merrel was willing to risk his wrath, then Delos would humor the man.

They walked in silence for a time. His message delivered Delos expected Lord Merrel to return to the keep but the man insisted on following. They had made it halfway through the city when Delos heard hooves thundering down the road behind them. He smiled as he turned hoping to find someone to take his frustrations out on. Kardol rounded a nearby corner at a breakneck pace. Delos waited hands clench as Kardol brough the horse to a stop.

"Lord Delos, the guards at the eastern boarder were attacked." Kardol said. Delos could still see the dents in Kardol's armor from Kelen tossing him into the wall. If Kardol had not had time to change out of the damaged armor the report must be recent.

"Follow" Delos roared. He could feel his senses sharpen as magic flooded his body. He tore through the city streets fast enough that he left Kardol and his horse behind. Anyone unfortunate enough to get in his way was thrust aside. Minutes later he arrived at the eastern border. He crossed a line of ash as he approached. The bodies of four of his guards lay in the street wrapped in cloth stained with blood. A small group had begun cleaning the street.

Delos rushed forward and grabbed the older man who seemed to be leading the group of citizens. If he could not have vengeance than he would have answers.

"Explain!" Delos bellowed as he lifted the man into the air despite his bulk. Some fool rushed over to help. Delos stamped his foot and spears of light erupted from the ground, pinning the fool in place.

"We were just cleaning up. It didn't seem proper to leave them like that, My—" Delos tighten his grip as the man stammered.

"Worthless wretch. What happened to my men?" Delos growled.

"Lisensi, my Lord. Men that are not men. They come from the Promise, turn to ash when slain. Your men saved us." The man said his voice trembling.

Delos threw the man to the ground. There were a hundred legends about the creatures which emerged from the Promise and Delos had no way to know which were true. Something about the man's story seemed off. Delos hummed and closed his right hand a cage of light formed around the man.

"Don't move" Delos ordered as he strode over to one of the fallen guards.

He unwrapped the body. The corpse was mangled but even upon close examination Delos could not say whether it had been blade or claw that had torn it asunder. Delos moved to the next body. He unwrapped the body to reveal the face of Tinser Remas. Delos had recruited the promising young mage before his campaign in Krais. As Delos surveyed the body he could see no obvious wounds though the mans shirt was soaked with blood. Delos removed the bloody shirt and found a single gaping wound over the mans heart where something had burst from his chest. Delos turned the body over to find a small hole exactly opposite the larger one.

Before coming to Expera Delos had never heard of a gun but he could think of no other weapon which left such a wound. This had not been the work of monsters out of legend. Delos twisted his right hand and the cage of light collapse inward. The man screamed as the light seared flesh and bone. When the screaming finally cut off Delos turned light pouring off him to find the street empty. Delos stormed down the road searching.

"Lord Delos, how can we be of assistance." Lord Merrel said through gasping breaths. Blood leaked from his nose and mouth overusing magic had its price. Delos stopped he briefly considered ridding himself of the insufferable courtier, but the man look so frail that Delos would take no pleasure in killing him. With nothing around to attack Delos found his rage calming replaced with cold certainty. This city would not burn not until he brought it's people to their knees.

Chapter II

Dets loved walking through the forest. It suited her far better than the city. She had grown up hunting the woods around her family's homestead. As she grew she had wandered farther from home, discovering new wonders in the strange land so close to the Promise. Recently she had needed to spend most of her free time hunting and had less time to explore. After her conversation with the strange mage she had needed to clear her head and with the family larder full she had set off. She had brought her rifle and her normal pack loaded with supplies in case she got lost and had to camp out longer than expected.

Farther to the northwest the terrain became rockier and she occasionally needed to drop down off outcrops. Every time she did, she flinched, remembering she had taken the devices Nadia had made. Nadia had assured her they were safe to travel with, but Dets was not sure Nadia understood the word. Despite all her faults Dets view Nadia like an older sister.

Dets had never explored this stretch of forest. It was poor hunting ground. The terrain made it difficult to line up a clean shot and no matter how quiet she was there was not good way to cover the sound of boots striking stone as she jumped down the many ledges. For this trip none of that mattered she was just enjoying the freedom of traveling without a specific purpose. When she came across a small stream, she bent down to fill her canteen. The water seemed off not murky but tinged a reddish-brown color. When she dipped her hand in the water smelled foul. Something must have died upstream. Curiosity got the best of her, and she began following the stream looking for whatever was polluting the normally clean water.

The water grew more tinged as Dets moved along the stream. Only something like a deer or bear could so significantly pollute the stream.

Climbing over a moss-covered rock Dets spied the corpse of a twelve-point buck laying accross the stream. It was sad to see such a majestic animal rotting away. Dets scanned the horizon for any predators attracted by the smell of blood. Nothing seemed amiss but some things that hunted in the woods near Khaldra were patient enough to hide and take the opportunity for a fresh kill. Dets cautiously moved closer keeping her rifle at the ready. As she got closer the smell of blood and putrid flesh grew nauseating. The presence of flies and putrescence indicated it was not a fresh corpse.

Dets gagged as she surveyed the corpse. The hide had been torn to shreds obfuscating the cause of death. The horns and hooves were distorted cracked and pitted unlike anything she had ever seen. What she had originally attributed to birds feeding on the body took on a new light. She knew there were things in the Promise that could do unspeakable things to a body but this far away it seemed impossible. The stark reality before her said otherwise. If something from the

Promise had made it this far then she would need to alert someone. The homesteads that dotted the land between Khaldra and Senrena occasionally banded together to deal with threats or clear land. Perhaps her father could arrange a hunt for this creature but without a clear idea where the threat was it would be difficult to convince them to abandon their livelihoods. She had scouted threats for the Purifiers on the Maras Plains before but so far from home trying to track the creature would be suicide.

. Dets scrambled up to higher ground. If whatever had done that was still in the area, she wanted to spot it before it found her. Heading off without a clear understanding of her surroundings could end in disaster. From her vantage point a trail through the underbrush stood out. The plants had been distorted in a two clear line radiating from the corpse. The distortions made it impossible for her to determine in what direction the creature was moving. Even where the creature had passed over rocks it cracked and distorted them. Dets briefly considered getting a closer look at the effect in the hope she could determine where it had gone but it seemed too risky.

Her nerves were on fire as she headed back toward home. Every one of her senses were on high alert as she scanned the path ahead. In a few minutes she lost sight of the trail the creature had made. She picked her path carefully climbing up outcrops to keep her line of sight clear. As she climbed up the next outcrop she had to stop to catch her breath. The area seemed clear, so she leaned against a moss-covered rock and sipped from her canteen.

"Might want to run," a voice said, startling Dets.

. She bolted to her feet and began sweeping her surroundings with her rifle. She could not locate the source of the voice but kept her rifle at the ready.

"That's a plan, I guess, but I wouldn't recommend it," the voice said with a tinge of humor.

Dets spotted the speaker moving through the thick brush perhaps twenty meters away. The sound of rocks falling behind her spurred Dets to move toward the man. Dets hit the ground at a sprint, briefly turning to look behind her. Where she had been seated moments ago the rock was writhing. There was a clear area moving and twisting but its shape was constantly shifting. Dets could not see any creature causing the disturbance. She was slowed by the thick underbrush, which oddly seemed to have no effect on the man. He walked at a brisk pace, completely unimpeded.

"Promises, what is that thing?" Dets asked, not really expecting an answer.

"Dangerous" the man responded sounding almost bored.

Dets had to alter her path or risk getting caught up in a bramble. As she turned, she raised her rifle and fired at the shape. Stone shattered where the shot hit home. The shape seemed completely unaffected. The shifting stone began to vibrate creating a sound somewhere between a screech and a rockslide.

"If you're planning on fighting you're going to need something a lot bigger," the man said with a wry smile.

He was still heading directly for the creature or at least where the creature was. Dets was not sure what the man was planning but she did not intend to stick around and find out. Dets kept moving, trying to get away but the underbrush grew thicker, and she was forced to slow even further. She glanced back to watch what was unfolding.

The creature had descended from the outcrop, and the man had closed the distance to within a few meters. For the first time Dets noticed that the man's right arms lay limp and his side, and the sleeve of his long coat seemed tattered, and the color faded.

"Well this is going to be unpleasant," the man said, looking over at her with a slight smile. His eyes were a bright blue in sharp contrast to his weather face. He could have been twenty or fifty it was hard to tell.

Taking one more step the man collided with the area of distortion. The man's skin began to writhe and tear, blood pouring out from wounds opening all over his body. His clothes tore and moved, dyed red with fresh blood. The man grabbed his right wrist and held the clenched fist blacked and unmoving to his chest. There was a sound like a thousand blades slicing flesh, combined with a rushing river and the distortion jumped to the ground near the man.

The man fell to one knee, still holding his wrist. Blood pooling around him as the distortion circled. Dets could not watch the scene any further. Disgust and sorrow driving her on, she wondered who the man was and why he was willing to face that thing without a hope of surviving. Distracted, she tripped on the exposed root of a tree. As she fell sprawling to the ground a metal orb marked with a green line rolled from her bag.

Dets didn't think, she acted. Jumping to her feet she grabbed the orb and twisting the top half as Nadia had instructed. She threw the orb at the man and the creature. Realizing to late she would probably kill the man and leave the creature unharmed.

It fell short by about a meter, but the distortion moved to cover the disturbance. As the creature covered the orb, Dets could see it warp and twist causing a brief moment of panic. As Dets watched, the orb exploded less than a second later a wave of pressure passed over her. By reflex she shut her eyes. When she opened them again the distortion was gone. Only a divot remained in the ground where it had been. She scanned the area but could not see any evidence that the creature remained.

"Promises, at least warn someone before you do something like that," the man said.

He was leaning against a tree nearly ten meters from where he had been kneeling. Blood still flowed freely from a dozen patches of distorted flesh. Dets watched the man rise to his feet and pick something up off the ground, placing it in his right hand which still remained limp at his side.

"What are you?" Dets asked. She was shocked. Between the creature and the explosion the man should be dead. Yet he was already up and walking.

"Just a Field Knight," the man said, wiping blood from his eyes.

Dets had heard the title before she knew them as an explorers who entered the Promise. Dets had never met a Field Knight but stories of their actions heroic or tragic were told throughout Khaldra=. She had always felt those stories were greatly exaggerated—until today. If she replaced the heroism with a reckless disregard for personal safety many of the stories seemed almost plausible. The man had already begun walking, putting more distance between them.

"Where are you going? You need medical attention," Dets said. Even if the creature was gone she wanted to get home but she would not leave the Field Knight to die of his wounds.

The man turned, his coat clinging to his body where the fabric had fused to his skin. His expression was hard to read, distorted flesh and blood mixed with debris blocked his features, but his eyes were still bright and clear.

"Doc should be able to patch me up once I'm back in Khaldra. If you're ever in the city stop by the hall. We are always looking for people good in a crisis. If anyone asks tell them Drake sent you," he said, calmly no evidence of pain in his voice.

Dets was stunned as the man continued walking away. She began to follow him as she tried to figure out how to convince him that he needed medical attention immediately. She quickly realized that the gap between them was growing despite her pace. If she couldn't keep up with the man's pace than perhaps he did not need her help.

Dets turned toward home with renewed speed. She had a ways to go but hopefully she could get there before nightfall. As she traveled Dets thought on the encounter. It was the first time she had fought something truly from the Promise. There were many odd creatures that lived near Khaldra, but most could be found in other areas of the empire. Even those that were native only to Expera were far less alien. If venturing into the Promise meant facing horrors like that on a regular basis she could not see herself ever entering that place. Even testing Nadia's projects seemed less suicidal. She was grateful that she still had another of Nadia's devices. The other had worked with terrifying efficiency and if she ran into anything else she would not hesitate to use it.

It had felt like something out of a children's tale. The bruises from her fall and the leaden weight of her legs as the adrenaline faded told her it had been real. She had nearly died alone in the woods far from home. Worse with a reckless decision she had almost killed the man who had saved her life. The journey passed in a haze.

Tired and still shaken Dets arrived home as the sun set. The homestead was small, tucked into a clearing a few kilometer from the main road into Khaldra. A stock fence encircled the house and small garden. Dets had always wondered why her father maintained the fence so meticulously. It did not keep out any of the wildlife that often wandered through their homestead. As Dets opened the gate Freyja peeked their head out from the side of the house to greet her. The old hound spent most of their time torturing the chickens or lazing around in the yard. Dets had tried to take Freyja hunting a few time but the sound of the rifle firing spooked them too much. Dets had seen other people hunting with dogs but most of those had been raised around rifles. As a puppy Freyja had traveled to Expera with them nearly ten years ago. Dets waved to Freyja who trotted over expecting a snack. Dets pulled a piece of sausage from her bag and tossed it to Freyja, who took it and disappeared into the garden. That small bit of normalcy helped her center her thoughts.

Dets opened the door to find her parents sitting at the small table in the kitchen. Plates sat empty between them as they conversed. The room smelled strongly of spices, which meant her father had been the one to cook dinner. As she entered, their conversation stopped.

"And so the grand explorer returns, but with treasure or dark secrets? Who's to say," her father said in his usual singsong cadence. Dets could almost hear her mother's eyes roll at the overly prosaic greeting.

"Anything left to eat?" Dets asked, unslinging her rifle and leaning on the wall near the door. She did not want to just jump into describing the events of the day. With the creature dead or at least no longer a threat, that conversation could wait.

"Depends. If you don't mind tasting the same thing for the next week, I think there's something left," her mother answered, gesturing over to the pot on the stove.

Dets laughed to herself as she walked over to grab a plate. Her mother had never gotten use to food from Sera-Met, even after living in the city for years.

"What brings you back so soon? Seemed like you had packed for a few days at least," her father asked.

The question was lighthearted and expected but it made Dets uncomfortable. She paused for a while before answering, "Something from the Promise was hunting in the woods. It had killed a deer then came after me. I managed to kill it with one of Nadia's projects, at least I think it's dead," she said, speaking quickly. She had wanted to warn them of the creature when it had been a threat but now she worried how they would take her confronting it.

"That's a dark tale indeed. Best keep close till we can be sure its truly gone," her father said, his tone serious.

Her mother sat silently but Dets knew it was simply the calm before the storm. Whether that storm was directed at her or at whatever dared to threaten them only time would tell. There was a long pause as everyone processed the information. Her mother spoke first.

"Going off and acting like a damn Reefwalker. It's no wonder your always finding trouble. Leave it to other folk to deal with those horrors you're needed here," her mother said. It was harsh, but Dets knew something of her mother's home. Despite the constant internal fights all the clans of the Miralocke respected the Reefwalkers. Dets took pride in the comparison but knew better than to let it show on her face.

"I promise I'll stay close," Dets said quietly. It was all she could say if she wanted to avoid an argument. For once she actually meant it. That thing had scared her enough to keep her home for a few days at least.

"That you will," her mother said, with finality.

Her father seemed lost in thought normally he was the one pushing to give her more freedom. His silence spoke volumes.

Dets filled a plate with the thick curry in the pot and sat at the table. When she sat down her father turned the conversation to other things though the specter of her misadventure hovered over everything. They talked of simple things. Her father needed to fix a leak in the roof of the chicken coop. Her mother needed help processing some of the herbs growing in the garden. It felt good to talk about the simple things that need to be done to maintain the homestead and the conversation lasted late into the night.

***

Dets woke just before dawn the next morning. As usual she was the first one up though her parents were rarely far behind. She had planned to be out in the forest today but there was always work to do. She collected the morning eggs and let the chickens out to roam under Freyja's watchful eye. By the time she returned to the house her mother was already cooking breakfast and her father seemed to be preparing for some kind of trip. Dets wanted to ask if she could join him but thought better of it. When her mother was done everyone sat to eat a quick breakfast.

"I'm going to head over to the Marstons. They needed some help fixing up their well head," her father said as he ate. Her father did not particularly like the Marstons. If he was going to help them it was probably to get the word out about the creature. The Marstons had sevenchildren all of them older than Dets. They tended to be the go-to for dealing with dangerous beast that found their way into the area around Khaldra. Dets had her own opinions about their competence having encountered some of them while hunting.

Once the food was finished her father got up to leave. Dets sat with her mother discussing what needed to be done that day.

Not long after her father had left they heard voices arguing outside. Dets heard her father's raised voice but could not make out anything that was being said. They were not expecting visitors and from the tone Dets expected trouble. She went to the door and grabbed her rifle. Her mother remained seated, but Dets could hear her speaking quietly to herself.

"Leave it by the door. Its best to be hospitable to our guests," her mother said.

Dets was confused but did as she was asked. Her mother seemed to know something about what was happening, but Dets did not know how. Moments later Dets heard the argument approaching the door. She heard her father cursing in his native tongue. She new a few of the phrases and those were incredibly colorful. Several involved inserting camel dung into various orifices. It was far more concise in Meti and hopefully whoever had arrived at the homestead did not understand him.

Dets almost panicked as the door was opened by a man wearing a uniform similar to the ones she had seen fighting in Khaldra days ago. A house crest was displayed prominently on the man's breast. Dets did not recongize the crossed shooting stars but it did not match any of the Great Houses, or the houses with a stake in Khaldra. The man entered followed by three others all wearing similar uniforms. The others wore the crest of House Ironsong embroidered on their uniforms. Dets knew enough of Imperial culture to know they were only affiliated with the house and not actual members.

Her father followed behind, still cursing under his breath.

"Drazin, Teset, commence the search" the first man ordered. Two of the men began searching through the small house.

Dets moved to stand near her mother, who seemed unbothered by the intrusion.

"It's rude to intrude upon someone's home without proper introduction," her mother said speaking directly to the man with the shooting star crest as if he was another homesteader come to pay a visit.

"Marius Kelen, Scion of House Kelen, executing the lawful orders of Governor Delos," the leader replied with a self-assured smile.

"Well, Lord Kelen, what business does the governor have searching the house of a citizen?" her mother asked. Dets had never heard her mother speak so formally.

"Maintaining the order of this forsaken hole of a city," Marius replied, vitriol dripping from his words. The unknown man who had not gone to search the house whispered something to Marius.

Dets flinched as Marius picked up her rifle. He examined it before turning to her mother,

"Now this is interesting. Why would a law abiding citizen need such a weapon?" he asked, sneering.

Before Det could respond her father step forward. "Winters can be rough out here. A man needs to feed and protect his family," her father replied.

Dets wanted to speak up but one look from her mother stayed her. It felt wrong to see this bastard handle her rifle so carelessly.

"I'm sure you can make do," Marius said, ignoring her father's words entirely.

Dets lunged forward as her rifle warped in the man's hands. Metal screeching in protest as it twisted and snaped. Her mothers hand caught her wrist with surprising strength stopping her. She wrenched her hand free in time to see her father barreling at Marius, shouting further obscenities.

Marius raised his hand and brought it down in a swift motion.

Her father fell to the ground with a crash. Dets watched as he struggled to move, his voice silenced mid word by the magic Marius had brought to bare.

"Don't." her mother whispered. Dets heard real panic in her voice.

Unarmed against a mage, Dets knew she did not have a chance. Reluctantly, she sat down, still glaring at Marius, who simply sneered as her father writhed on the floor.

"Not a trace of them here," one of the men who

had left to search shouted from the other room. Even as he spoke Dets heard something heavy crashing to the floor.

"Then we are done, we have a dozen more flea infested hovels to check," Marius replied with a tinge of iritation. He tossed the twisted remains of her rifle on the floor inches from her father's face.

Dets heard more crashes as the two men returned. Marius released whatever force held her father pinned. He rolled over, groaning, and did not rise as the four men left in an orderly fashion. She felt like their was something she was missing but her mind refused to connect the dots.

Once they were gone her mother rushed over to check on her father. Dets sat stunned as her mind pulled her in a hundred different directions. With help her father got to his feet and made his way over to the table. He sat down and began speaking to her, but she couldn't bring herself to process his words. Instead, she stared at what was left of her rifle.

After some time, he stood, leaving her to her thoughts. Dets watched numbly as her parents cleaned up the mess that had been made of their home. Hours passed as she sat trying to put together what she could do. Dark times had come to Khaldra and she was not ready to face them.

Chapter 12

Dennet kept his head down as he made his way to the market square. It irked him that he could not openly walk the streets he had called home his entire life. But when there was a job to do he could be eminently practical. He needed to find a caravanner willing to make the journey to his settlement on short notice. There were always traders arriving and departing Khaldra but few of them would be willing to waste several days just to transport supplies. He could pull together the funds to make it worthwhile, but it would be tight. He had spread himself thin gaining influence in various sectors of Khaldra's economy but few of those would turn a profit any time soon.

As he walked, Dennet considered his situation. Whatever the expedition teams had brought back would take time to catalog and longer to find appropriate buyers. He desperately needed the funds. Not only to get his Knights out of the city but to set the stage for the coming conflict. Perhaps he could have the arcanist take a look. The man was a bit odd, but he knew magic far better than any appraiser in the city.

He would need to speak to Alex about the expedited timeline. Alex had spent years building connections and gaining support for House Hyde amongst the nobility of Khaldra. They would need to push the limits of those connection to meet the new timeline. There was significant risk in trying to speed things along where the nobility was concerned, and all that work could go to waste if they played this wrong.

Dennet had other outstanding problems to resolve but as he approached the market square it was time to get to work. Dennet noted that Delos's guards were thick around the market, but few seemed keen to enter it. Dennet slipped into a crowd entering the market. Dennet took pride in how Khaldra had grown. He remembered when the market had only had a few hundred visitors a day. Now even on a slow day there were thousands of people moving between stalls or simply passing through. He headed for the main tent at the center of the market. The massive tent was normally used for major auctions and Dennet knew the caravanners watched it closely. There were five entrances to the massive tent. Three of them were always crowded with people one was reserved for wagons and the last was for merchants. Dennet chose the merchants' entrance. The wagon entrance would certainly have caravans entering but most would not be ready to leave any time soon. The merchants' entrance was less crowded and there were usually a few caravanners trying to find clients. The merchants' entrance was tuck away between a spice stall and a pewter stall. It was intentionally hard to spot if you did not know where it was. Dennet waved to the guard as he approached.

"Owen, where's Ren? Doesn't she normally take the day shift?" Dennet asked.

"Got into it with some arrogant prick acting like

he owned the place. Boss put me on the day shift," Owen said. Dennet laughed, imagining the scene. The burly young man tossing some prim noble on their ass. Khaldra's market had its own hierarchy and the backing of enough nobles to enforce its own justice.

"Thought you were done with the street brawling," Dennet said.

"Been trying, but some folk are just asking for a solid punch in the face," Owen replied flippantly. Dennet had helped Owen get this job after one of the Field Knights had knocked the young man around in a barroom brawl. Owen had deserved it, but Dennet took the opportunity to make an ally rather than an enemy.

"Might have some work for you soon if you're interested," Dennet said.

"Not a chance, Mr. Dennet. Ain't enough money in the world to get me into the Promise," Owen replied, opening the flap for Dennet to enter.

"Just keep it in mind," Dennet said, as he entered. Owen was a good brawler, but he wouldn't last a week as a Field Knight. Dennet had other plans but now was not the time to be recruiting.

The merchants' entrance led into a sealed off area of the tent. Small, curtained rooms filled the area. Some were filled with wares usually with a guard posted others had tables and chairs where deals could be struck.

As he strolled, Dennet checked to see if any of the rooms were full but not closed. It did not take long for Dennet to find such a room. Sitting around the table were three men and a woman.

Dennet sauntered in and sat down, facing all four. "Emara, did they finally run you out of Vesrin?" he asked.

Emara was one of his main competitors though she spent most of her time in Vesrin on the edge of the Expera region. He only recognized one of the men at the table: a wine merchant by the name of Manel. The other two were dressed more like merchants than caravanners but that was not a sure thing. It was worth a shot, and Dennet could not overlook a chance to needle Emara.

"Peter, when was the last time you set foot in civilized lands? You've clearly forgotten your manners," Emara retorted.

"If I wanted a lecture on manners I would go to church. Not that a viper like you would know much about faith," Dennet replied, leaning back in his chair. He watched the other men at the table, gauging their reactions. Manel was taken aback but the other two simple watched waiting to see how this would play out.

"Speaking of churches, was House Silram satisfied with their recent delivery?" Emara responded her tone casual but her eyes focused on him knowingly. Dennet kept the shock off his face but just barely. He had bought the crest of House Silram off an unscrupulous caravanner a few years back. It was a stark reminder that Emara Morel deserved her reputation.

"Quality control was never your specialty, but to your credit I haven't heard too much complaining," Dennet said. It was a weak response and they both knew it. The question was whether the others at the table caught on.

"So you're Peter Dennet. I hear you pull delightful things out of the abominable Promise," one of two men Dennet didn't recognize interjected. Emara scoffed but the man ignored her.

"That I am. It seems you have the better of me sir," Dennet replied with a broad smile..

"Thomas Resal. Caravan master of Renmarsh Trading Conglomerate," the man said, extending a hand adorned with various gold and silver rings.

Dennet smiled and shook the man's hand. Renmarsh was the region just south of the Miralocke, known for its wines. If his caravan had unloaded its wares Dennet had a good chance to solve his predicament. He would need to be careful in how he broached the subject, especially with Emara at the table.

"I've never had the pleasure of visiting Renmarsh, but if you have a few bottles of Renmarsh red left after your long journey. I would be very interested," Dennet said.

"Good wine would be wasted on you, Dennet," Emara said, clearly annoyed at being interrupted when she had the edge. "Stick to whatever swill your men drink. It suits you better."

Dennet smiled. Emara was quick witted, but she was too quick to press her advantage.

"Of course, but one must observe propriety when they dine with nobility. Lady Hyde is known for her discerning palate," Dennet retorted. Thomas might not know anything about House Hyde but dropping the name of a noble house, even a small one, would certainly boost the man's opinion of Dennet.

"Unfortunately, Mr. Dennet, you are a little late. I just sold off my last batch to this gentleman," Thomas said, gesturing to Manel.

"Another time then," Dennet said, feigning disappointment.

After a brief pause he continued as if the idea had

just struck him, "If you have sold all your cargo then you must be looking for something to return with."

Thomas beamed at that. "Indeed I am. If you have something worthwhile it would be a pleasure to do business," Thomas said.

Dennet smiled congenially as Thomas took the bait. Dennet could see the man calculating his profits already. Now Dennet just needed to land the deal.

"In fact, my expedition teams have recently returned with many treasures. Of course, it may take some time to assess and process," Dennet said. Thomas's expression darkened at that. Time was money and any significant delay would heavily cut into the man's profits. "I understand your hesitance, but it is in both our interests to ensure everything is safe to transport."

Thomas rapped his fingers on the table as he scowled. Emara smiled, clearly amused by Dennet's apparent failure. Dennet subtly glanced at Manel and the other man seemed disinclined to involve himself.

Dennet knew exactly what he needed to do but it required either Thomas or Emara to give him something to work with. He leaned back in his chair, feigning boredom. Emara glared at him, clearly trying to figure out what game he was playing. Dennet just smiled back and shrugged coyly. The simple gesture had the desired effect.

"Never thought much of anything you pull out of the Promise. It's all as likely to kill everyone involved as turn a profit. If you're looking for something worth your while come to Vesrin with me and I'll send you off with a tidy profit," Emara said, ignoring Dennet and speaking to Thomas. Dennet knew she could probably pull together enough to make it worth it, but it was clearly an attempt to one up him.

"So close, Emara. The bounty of the Promise can be dangerous but great risk brings great reward. Of course, Thomas, you could go with Emara and return to Vesrin with mundanities enough to fund your next journey or you could wait and return with wonders enough to never need to leave again," Dennet proclaimed. It was hyperbole but it sold the point perfectly. Dennet could see Thomas weighing his options. One last subtle suggestion and Dennet would have him.

"Idleness can be costly. I understand that. Perhaps I could, but it would be a bit too early and not everything is ready…" Dennet continued, letting his last words trail off as if thinking on something.

"It would be a pleasure to do business with you, Mr. Dennet, but unless you have something in mind I can't afford such a delay," Thomas said.

Dennet kept the smile off his face. Emara eyed him knowingly but did not interrupt. She knew he had gotten exactly what he wanted and he knew she would make him pay for it later.

Or at least try.

"Well, you see I am working on a small project. A small settlement a few days from here. I was planning on sending supplies and some more people there once my current stock had sold. But perhaps I could get enough together to send on short notice. By tomorrow even. If you would be willing to make such a trip. At a reasonable rate of course. Once you've returned everything I've recently acquired will be catalogued and ready for transport," Dennet said, laying it out as if it was a spur of the moment decision.

"Depending on your idea of 'reasonable' we may

have a deal," Thomas said, smiling.

After a bit of half-hearted haggling on Dennet's part they agreed to terms. The sum was only slightly above market rate, which Dennet took as a win. He would be taking a small loss overall shipping everything off to Renmarsh but not having to worry about a standing inventory could be useful in the coming weeks.

Dennet would need to pull something together to send along with the Field Knights. Food and building supplies would be easy enough but not particularly helpful to his people in the settlement. He had commissioned arms for the settlement months ago, but it was unlikely they were all ready. Whatever was available would have to do. His men needed to train and even a few rifles would be helpful. In order to arrange that Dennet headed for the gunsmith shop.

***

The shop was not far from the market, but Dennet always had trouble finding the place. The shop was small and its signage was understated. When Dennet had originally formed his plan, he was looking for quality over quantity and Rickart Kel was known as the best. Dennet's plan had changed as he found far more support than he had expected. It had taken some work to convince Kel to agree to the larger project but if he delivered Dennet's men would be the best equipped in all of Expera. They would need to be to face Delos and his mages.

When Dennet found his way to Gunpowder Street he noticed that there were far more guards in the area then seemed necessary. The street was mostly empty, which meant Dennet had little opportunity to hide in a crowd. Dennet pulled his flask out and spilled some on his clothes. It seemed a waste, but it would sell the illusion.

Affecting a drunken stumble, Dennet began walking down the street. He closely watched the guards as he walked. He found the storefront after passing it once. It was not hard to pretend as if he was simply to drunk to remember where he was going. He slumped against the wall near the door to wait for an opportunity to slip in. When three men turned onto the street and saw the guards, Dennet took the chance to slip in while the guards were distracted.

Dennet entered the shop and stood up straight, adjusting his suit slightly. Rickart Kel was in the atrium dusting off the rack of rifles on the right wall. Kel turned to greet whoever had entered. Once he saw Dennet his expression changed to confusion. It was a comical expression with his head bandaged.

Dennet wondered how Kel had received the wound, but before he could ask, Kel interjected, "Mr. Dennet, why are you here? I'm still months aways from completing your order."

Dennet knew Kel was not someone to play games with. Kel's stoic nature had been difficult to deal with initially but after a few minor problems Dennet had come to find it refreshing.

"I have a caravan heading to the settlement tomorrow. I want everything you have completed so far to be on that caravan," Dennet said without preamble.

"I won't waste my breath asking why. I have ninety-six rifles ready and a little under a thousand rounds of ammunition. Do you have a plan to get that many weapons out of the city? It seems like the new guards are not too keen on allowing easy travel," Kel responded.

Dennet was surprised. He had already considered the difficulty Delos's guards posed but he had not expected Kel to have much of an opinion on the current state of politics in Khaldra.

"It should not be a problem. I will send someone over tonight to collect everything if someone will be available," Dennet said.

He could arrange for the rifles to be stored in the market until they were loaded unto the caravan. Funeral rights for the fallen knights would probably draw the attention of Delos's guards providing the opportunity to move everything.

"I'll let Nadia know to expect someone, and Mr. Dennet, I hope you know what you're doing. It seems to me you're playing with fire," Kel said, calmly gesturing at the sign on the workshop door before returning to tidying up the shop. It seemed Kel had come to some conclusions about Dennet's plan. Whether that was a good thing or not, Dennet would have to wait and see.

It was lucky that the door to the shop opened inward, allowing Dennet to peek outside without being spotted. The guards were still watching the street closely. Dennet quietly closed the door and turned back to Kel.

Kel scoffed and gestured to the door to the workshop. "Go out the back if you need. We have the furnace going so don't come whining to me about your clothes," Kel said before returning to work.

Dennet made his way through the workshop. He had toured the place when he and Alex had first visited. As he passed he saw Kel's assistant Nadia working on something. Dennet tried his best not to disturb her.

He thought he understood Kel. The man was

straightforward and meticulous. Dennet could not make heads or tails of Nadia. The few conversations he had had with her always ended up on tangents. She seemed enthusiastic about the project but always strayed toward suggesting more experimental additions. Dennet had enough problems getting his people trained. Adding devices no one had ever used would only complicate the situation.

Dennet made his way to the next street over where no guards were posted. Stained with soot and reeking of booze, Dennet headed back to the hall. He had a solid plan to get his knights out of the city. He just needed to send a few runners out to finalize the preparations.

Kinthross would not be happy having to move out with less than a days rest, but Dennet could deal with that. He still had a few hours before sundown, so he took a more round about path to reach the hall. He wanted to get a feel for the city and where Delos had posted guards. He knew they would not be able to avoid catching their attention during the funeral rights but it would be good to know just how much resistance to expect. Most of the guards seemed posted around the outskirts of the city with small pockets at key locations.Even as he walked more guards arrived to reinforce the already considered display. Clearly Delos had taken the deaths of his men earlier as a challenge.. It seemed that most of the people of Khaldra were avoiding the guards when they could, but daily life went on. Dennet saw some altercations, mostly started by the overly enthusiastic guards. For now the people of Khaldra seemed to afraid to fight back but it was only a matter of time.. He hoped nothing tipped the balance over the edge before Dennet was ready.

Khaldra was becoming a powder keg there was nothing he could do about that. What he could do was control who lit the fuse and when.

Chapter 13

Kinthross had spent most of the afternoon gauging the response of the expedition teams to the idea of leaving the city. Not that there had been many of the Knights around to speak to. Many had gone to sleep almost immediately and those who had stayed up were too busy tending to the wounded or beginning the process of securing what they had brought back from the Promise. He had only had a chance to speak to ten people and the response had been mixed. All were aware of the danger of staying in the city after the incident earlier but those who had been born in Khaldra seem to want to stay come what may. Those like him who had come from elsewhere in the empire were more amenable to the idea of avoiding conflict. Kinthross was use making a plan and seeing it implemented but without more details he needed more than just orders to convince the knights. . Nico may be young, but she could sell a story like no one else. She could inspire the knights to action but she seemed distracted helping the wounded.

Kinthross was not worried about their ability to move out on a moment's notice. It was a matter of getting them to agree to the plan. Having exhausted his option on that front Kinthross turned his attention to planning the funeral rights. The two fallen were from his team so it fell to him to pick the two who would act as psychopomps. It was an honorary position in the ceremony usually assigned to those closest to the fallen or those who felt the most guilt. The choice for Anis was obvious. Nico had been close with the medic. Though it had been Nico's first expedition as his second she understood the responsibility of command. It would be good for her to find ways to deal with the loss besides working herself to the point of collapse.

Mattus was another matter, a recent recruit on their first expedition. It would normally fall to Kinthross to serve when no one else was appropriate. He could not take up the responsibility with the disposition of the new guards so uncertain. He needed to keep his eyes open in case things went to shit..

Zed might be a good option, even if Elias cleared him Kinthross was hesitant to force him to fight if conflict occured. As a veteran he would know his part and it would be a good way to show respect to the next generation of knights. The decision made Kinthross head to the main part of the hall to ask Nico and Zed if they would take on the roles. When he arrived he found a rather disheveled and reeking Dennet speaking with Elias.

"I know you're trying Elias but their still Field Knights trying to keep them from joining is a fool's errand," Dennet said, as Kinthross approached.

"It's on your head Dennet I expect them all back to continue treatment. I still have work to do, and I haven't even begun to figure out what's wrong with Thomas," Elias said before turning back to cleaning his implements.

Kinthross waved Dennet over. "What was that about" Kinthross asked.

"Elias was advising against the wounded joining the funeral tonight. I informed him he was welcome to try. Everyone who can travel will be joining a caravan headed to the settlement tomorrow," Dennet said, by way of explanation.

"Tomorrow. Now I know we might be in the shit here but that's madness. Half the teams are sleeping off the expedition and half are not keen on leaving as it is," Kinthross said, exasperated. He had expected Dennet to move fast but this was insane.

"And why, pray tell, do they want to stay?" Dennet asked.

"Most seemed keen to fight it out. Bit mad if you ask me, but blood's still hot this soon after an expedition," Kinthross said.

"But not you," Dennet said. "Well, they'll get their chance when the time is right. I won't ask anything of you that you're unwilling to do." A worrying response, but one Kinthross might be able to work with.

"I thought sending us out was mad. If I'm hearing you right, you've got a truly batshit plan cooking," Kinthross said. He knew Dennet had strong view on the fate of Khaldra but an all-out fight wouldn't go in their favor.

"I've heard that before. Look where we are standing, what the Field Knights have become. We do the impossible with every expedition. For now, we just keep moving forward," Dennet said.

"Aye, but the cost has been steep. If we keep pushin' we'll find ourselves paying a price we can't afford," Kinthross replied somberly. He could appreciate the success of the expeditions but all of that had been paid for in blood. Perhaps Dennet's goals were good, but Kinthross feared the lengths the man would go to achieve them.

"Someone will pay the cost eventually. The question is who and when. Can you think of anyone better suited than us? We built ourselves to be heroes. We aren't, but that does not mean we shouldn't try," Dennet replied with a fire in his eyes. With Dennet it rarely mattered when he was being sincere and when he was playing a part. He always followed through. Kinthross resigned himself to seeing this through for the sake of those he worked with. He was a Field Knight, and that meant facing the impossible with resolve if only to protect each other.

"Got to finish up arrangements then. Any idea what to do about the crazy bastards patrolling the streets?" Kinthross asked. Tradition was important to the Field Knights. Everyone would be ready for the funeral, even on this timeframe.

"Don't know enough about how they'll respond to say. The hope is the display will shake them up enough to get us through till tomorrow. By the time they sort out what to do you'll be out of the city," Dennet said.

It was plausible, but Kinthross would need to keep his eyes open for trouble.

Dennet left Kinthross to his work and moved on to giving orders to some of the non-team staff.

Kinthross headed over to where Nico was talking with Kari. Something had gotten in Kari's head and Kinthross doubted there was anything Elias could do to set her straight. From their conversation Kari seemed sedated slurring her words and ending sentences abruptly. Nico was patiently talking about nothing to soothe the injured knight.

"Got something to ask you," Kinthross interjected.

Nico glared at him but waved him over regardless.

"We are gonna be holding the rites tonight. I know you were close with Anis. Might be right for youto take the part. Ain't much time to think on it but that's just how things are," Kinthross said.

Nico sat stunned for a second. A dozen emotions flashed across her face before settling on a stern resolve.

"I'll do it. Might be others who know the part better, but she was my friend," Nico replied, sadness and resolve mixing in her tone. It was not often the word "friend" was used among the Field Knights. They were a tight group, but attrition played havoc with the kinds of ties people formed. It was not that Kinthross regretted his choice but it sparked a new worry for his second. She would be faced with hard choices and being too close to any member might cloud her judgment.

Perceptive as always, Nico seemed to read his thoughts. "Don't worry, Boss. I know when to move on. Been doing it my entire life. It's about showing I can move forward while honoring the past. Never cared much for the past till I joined up. I think it'll be good to show everyone I know what matters," Nico said, placating some of Kinthross's concerned.

He knew so little about her past but whatever drove someone to join up at such a young age was not to be taken lightly.

"Then the job's yours. Do right by your friend cause there's a whole heap of shit coming our way and I'm gonna need you ready to go," Kinthross said.

He left Nico to continue working with Kari. No one was perfect for this job but being a leader meant overcoming those shortfalls. She might make a better commander than him some day if any of them lived that long.

Kinthross headed over to where Zed was cleaning his rifle. Brushes and oil were strewn across the cot and Zed had his rifle in his lap while he sat cross-legged at the head of the cot. Zed looked up as Kinthross made his way through the labyrinth of beds.

"Answers, yes. No need fer the pep talk. Head's still killing me, and if there was somewhere quieter to work I would be tucked up there," Zed said before Kinthross could speak. Zed had sharp ears and probably had overheard his conversation with Nico.

Kinthross had taken a few blows to the head over his life. If the man wanted quiet Kinthross would leave him be. Kinthross nodded and left the man to his work.

Kinthross informed those who were awake about the plan. Observing the state of the teams as he went. Most were tired but they seemed ready enough. He would wake the rest up after sundown. They need their rest and so did he. He posted himself up near the bar and closed his eyes.

***

Nico woke him some time later by kicking out his stool. Kinthross barely caught himself before he hit the ground.

"Good reflexes, but I'll never understand how you manage to sleep like the dead," Nico said, laughing.

"Best learn the trick of it. You got long days and nights ahead of you if you're planning to take my job," Kinthross retorted.

"Oh, I can sleep anywhere but it doesn't take an earthquake to wake me," she shot back. It was true enough. Kinthross had found her sleeping in places he couldn't even reach without a full climbing harness.

"Don't make a habit of knocking people around to wake them. It's a good way to get gutted," Kinthross joked.

"I'll be dead and buried before I'm slow enough to get stuck," Nico retorted.

"Now we best be moving on to business fore I get it in mind to test you on that. What time is it?" Kinthross said, stretching out to get feeling back in his limbs.

"Bit after sundown. Still got some time but I figured you'd want to get everyone together," Nico answered.

It was a bit later than Kinthross would have liked but everyone needed rest, and a small delay would not hurt much.

"Alright I'll get everyone together. We'll muster in half an hour. Go talk to Zed. You can figure out whose gonna carry the lantern," Kinthross said.

"On it, Boss," Nico replied with an informal salute.

Kinthross went around waking everyone. There were a few grumbles, but everyone got up and gathered whatever gear they had. It was part of the tradition to carry their full gear as if they were going on an expedition. There were no hard rules and some simply wore their packs, others would load the pack with junk to give it real weight. Everyone carried whatever weapons they preferred. It was an odd assortment ranging from standard side swords and rifles to tools of the trade augmented for a more lethal purpose.

Without Kinthross's direction the main area of the hall was haphazardly cleared. While Kinthross was waiting for everyone to gather, Dennet came over having changed into new clothes. It had been a while since Kinthross had seen Dennet carrying a pack and wearing clothes more suited for travel than a ball. Dennet carried a small sword and pistol on his belt, each simple and well maintained. Kinthross smiled to see Dennet looking more like the adventurer he had been.

"Not half bad. We actually look competent," Dennet joked.

"Not having to drag anyone out of a bar or brothel helps," Kinthross responded.

It did not take long for everyone to gather. Murmured conversation filled the hall as they waited for Kinthross or Dennet to address the crowd. The last to arrive were Nico and Zed. Neither carried packs, but Zed held a intricately crafted metal lantern on a pole with a thick black cloth covering it.

"Tonight we send off our own on their last journey. Let us show Khaldra that we do not forget. Let us show that we can move forward. Who will stand for those who cannot?" Dennet intoned.

"I will walk with Mattus," Zed responded, holding the pole up high.

"I will walk with Anis," Nico said, eyes down cast and voice filled with sorrow. She pulled the Black cloth off the lantern. and the dimly lit room was filled with light. Strange shadows flickered off the few candles that had lit the room.

The lantern held a small black stone with points of moving lights reminiscent of stars. The strange stone had been taken from the Promise on one of the first expeditions. The first expedition had always held on to something to remember their fallen, and as time went on the stone had become part of the ceremony. The stone seemed to invert light beyond even the range of a standard lantern . Kinthross had never understood much of how it worked but the effect was incredible and served to make a statement. With the lantern uncovered the room grew silent.

Zed and Nico led the way, followed by Kinthross and Dennet. Once outside, the stone's effect grew substantially. Turning the darkness of night to the light of day in an area covering nearly two blocks. Strange shadows grew from various light sources and the moon appeared as a black spot on a brilliant white sky. The group began their march to the outskirts of the city. Even the wounded were present, though only Thomas needed to be carried on a stretcher. There were some surprised shouts as they passed by houses whose windows were suddenly flooded with light. The residents of Khaldra had seen this display many times before but it was not an effect one could ignore. People in nightwear gathered in doorways to watch the spectacle or pay respects.

The group only made it a few blocks before Kinthross noticed the first group of guards gathering. He looked over to Dennet, who simply shrugged. Dennet's hand rested on the hilt of his small sword but he seemed content to let the guards make the first move.

Kinthross did not like the idea of waiting but he kept walking. The guards seemed to avoid entering the area of light and where they gathered to block the precession's path people gathering to watch forced them out of the way. Kinthross would have expected more conflicts to erupt as they went but word spread fast in Khaldra and the number of people gathering was more than the guards were willing to deal with. Kinthross could here the guards shouting for reinforcements but the calls were filled with fear and awe. When they reached the outskirts of the city without incident Dennet turned to Kinthross with a sly smile.

"That's the easy part done. Once they get organized things will get interesting," Dennet whispered.

Kinthross simply nodded, not wanting to break the silence of the somber precession.

Once they left the city the group traveled about two kilometers. It was a shorter trip than Kinthross would have liked but Nico found a clearing that would serve in short order. The group spread out in the clearing, leaving the center for Kinthross, Dennet, Nico, and Zed. Zed placed the pole holding the lantern in the ground and everyone looked to Dennet.

"A long road behind us but the challenges have been met and now we are here. Before we face the road ahead let us rest and eat," Dennet intoned.

Noah and Ral, two veteran knights, stepped forward and each offered a small bowl to Nico and Zed, who took them reverently.

"A long road ahead and a good meal made in honor of those who can no longer walk with us," Nico and Zed said in unison.

They both put the bowls to their lips and drank. Zed's faced contorted as he drank then placed the bowl on the ground in front of him. Nico remained stoic, drinking for a longer time. Kinthross smirked as her face turned dark in the strange light. Nico went to place the bowl down but doubled over, heaving up everything she had ingested. Though it was expected, many in the gathered crowd couldn't help but chuckle.

The food was made to be horrendous, harkening back to how the tradition began. It was on one of the first expeditions, before Kinthross had joined. The team had suffered heavy losses, supplies were running low and morale was all but non-existent. In an attempt to raise morale Dennet had tried to cook a meal for everyone. Dennet had failed spectacularly, and the food had been completely inedible. But watching their leader try to stomach the vile concoction had broken the malaise that had fallen over the team. When the team finally made it back it had become a story told again and again. Later the story had been incorporated into the traditions of the Field Knights.

"Ral and Noah, really, I can't tell if you're trying to teach her a lesson or hoping to find a new second," Dennet said to Kinthross.

Kinthross smirked. He hadn't put much thought into it but judging from Nico's reaction whatever those two had cooked up had been truly vile.

"I wasn't gonna deprive her of the full experience," Kinthross responded. He went over to help Nico, who was still doubled over.

With the ceremony complete people began talking, exchanging stories about the fallen or their own close calls. The lantern was covered and the clearing fell into darkness. A few people had brought normal light sources, so a mix of candles and enchanted stones began lighting the space. Once Nico was done, Kinthross sent her off to go speak with the other knights.

"Now what? By the time we get back we'll have to deal with whatever reception Delos has planned," Kinthross asked once he had returned to where Dennet was standing.

"Let's give them some time to say their piece then I'll make some announcements," Dennet responded cryptically.

Kinthross scowled but went to join the

conversations. He had his own stories to share about the fallen knights and now was the best time to tell them. The conversations went on for some time before Dennet called everyone together.

"Tomorrow both active teams will be departing to a homestead I'm constructing. Consider it a reprieve from the current events. Things will be changing in Khaldra, and the Field Knights have a part to play, but for now leave it to me. Each of you will need to choose what you want to do in the coming months and that choice will be easier to make where things are calmer," Dennet said, addressing the crowd.

Kinthross expected someone to speak up but Dennet preempted any questions by continuing, "I'll be joining you in a few weeks with a clearer picture of what's to come. If you have questions they can wait till then. For now we need to get everyone back into the city and prepare to leave. Now, if I worked this out correctly we should have a perfect distraction coming."

There were murmurs in the crowd as Dennet simply stood, checking his watch. Less than a minute later a pillar of fire appeared just over the trees, far in the distance. Seconds later a loud *crack* could be heard.

"That's our cue. Split into small teams and make your way back to the hall before the guards get that under control," Dennet said with a smile.

Kinthross remained with Dennet as the Field Knights began to move. The reaction was ingrained in all of them. When things get chaotic, follow orders and act. A simple idea but one that had kept them all alive through the challenges of the Promise.

"What was that?" Kinthross asked once everyone else had departed.

"Grain silo. I bought it a few years ago to ease the

cost of storing supplies. Did you know dust can create an explosion? Farmers are typically careful not to let it happen, so you rarely see siloes explode. Never thought I would need that little bit of trivia, but here we are," Dennet explained.

"Hope your little stunt doesn't burn the city down," Kinthross said. The plan might work but it was incredibly risky and Kinthross couldn't figure out how Dennet had gotten the timing right.

"Doubtful. Its far enough from anything flammable not to spread much before our friends in the guard can get it under control," Dennet answered confidently.

"Best get back before they get things under control," Kinthross said, beginning to head back to Khaldra.

Dennet's plan had worked, and they were not stopped as they made their way back to the hall.

"I want them all in the market by noon. Send them out in small groups to keep a low profile, " Dennet said when they were back inside the hall.

Kinthross was pleased to see everyone seemed to have made it back without incident.

"What, no more conveniently timed explosions?" Kinthross jibed.

"Two miracles in one day aren't enough for you?" Dennet retorted. Dennet began to walk away heading toward the door.

"Where you off too?" Kinthross asked.

"Works never done. Best get some rest I'll need you to keep everything on schedule," Dennet replied without turning around. The teams were organized to operate quickly but Kinthross knew he would have trouble getting everyone moving in the morning.

Kinthross managed to get some sleep before the sun rose, but not much. With Nico's help he had set up small two or three person groups that should be capable of getting to the market unnoticed. It felt wrong to leave the wounded, but Kinthross was not sure what to expect once they arrived. Between Brandish and Zed they should be relatively secure in the hall. Even wounded Kinthross trusted those two to handle any trouble. He began sending groups out an hour after sunrise.

"Your really sending everyone. I haven't even had a chance to check them all properly," Elias said, as Kinthross was sending out the third group.

"All but the most seriously wounded," Kinthross replied.

"And you're to be the judge of that," Elias said. Kinthross understood the man's hesitation. It was not common but some injuries from the Promise could take weeks to manifest in all their horror.

"Not my choice. But I'm not sure staying here is gonna be much better," Kinthross replied. Whatever Dennet had planned would shake things up even more than there actions the previous day. Whatever they would be doing at the mysterious homestead might be safer but it seemed like a setup for something far riskier.

"Lovely, now I'm some kind of guard in addition to a doctor," Elias replied. Kinthross chuckled at the thought of Elias fighting off a mage. The man was a deft hand with a scalpel but in combat the fine line between harm and healing widened substantially..

"Leave that to Brandish and Zed. Even wounded they're worth more in a fight than half the team," Kinthross said.

Elias rolled his eyes before heading off to his workstation.

Kinthross and Nico were the last to leave. They hadn't received any reports of trouble from the other groups. It was not necessarily a good sign but he chose to take it that way.Nico had spent most of the morning talking with the wounded and Elias. It was good to see her taking an interest in Elias's work. Leading a team required the ability to take on a variety of roles, or at least to understand who best fit those roles. Kinthross had learned some of the basics from the Dredgers back when he lived in the Miralocke but there was a massive gap between that and what they saw on a regular basis in the Promise.

"We're off," Kinthross said, once long enough had passed since the last group had departed.

"Ready, Boss. Let's see how this goes wrong," Nico said, shouldering her pack.

***

The trip to the market was short and uneventful. Kinthross noted the crowd in the market seemed larger than normal, as were the number of guards surrounding it. Nico seemed to slip through the crowd with ease despite the pack on her back. While Kinthross had to shoulder his way through as they made their way to the main tent where the rest of the team was gathering. It did not take long to find Dennet near the wagon entrance. Dennet was speaking with a merchant. Kinthross vaguely recognized him but could not recall his name.

"Well, I'll be there. Should be a good chance to get a feel for the new governor at least," Dennet was saying as they approached.

"Very good. I expect it to be quite the event. It seems the last of your people have arrived so I will take my leave. Best of luck on your travels, Knights of Khaldra," the man said, in a singsong voice. As Dennet turned to Kinthross and Nico the man disappeared into the crowd.

"What was that about?" Kinthross asked.

"Probably nothing but we might have a chance at something interesting in the future. That's a ways off and there are more pressing matters at hand. Like introducing you to the caravanner," Dennet said, leading them over to a group of wagons.

Thomas Resal was a corpulent man with an ostentatious amount of jewelry. Kinthross immediately disliked the man's affect. Even if the roads of Expera and the rest of the empire were safe Kinthross understood the challenges of moving so many people over such distances . It spoke poorly of the man as a leader that he seemed to value appearance over functionality. Dennet noted Kinthross's discomfort with the man and managed the introductions himself rather than leaving it to Kinthross.

"This is the last of them. Kinthross is my expedition leader and should be able to manage the team easily enough. They are quite experienced at traveling," Dennet said.

"Quite a few men and not a lot of cargo. And the cargo is largely sealed up tight. Seems a bit odd," Thomas said.

Kinthross could tell the man found the circumstances suspicious. He wondered what kind of deal Dennet had struck with the caravanner.

"I ran into some trouble collecting an order in time. If I couldn't send the proper supplies, it seemed prudent to send more hands to make the work of gathering easier," Dennet replied, completely ignoring the issue of the sealed cargo. Kinthross did not know what Dennet would be sending that needed to be sealed away. If Dennet wanted it hidden Kinthross would keep it that way.

"Very well. As long as no one causes any problems, I can't complain," Thomas replied, dropping the issue.

"With that settled. I believe I'd best take my leave," Dennet said, bowing out.

Kinthross called everyone together to speak with the caravanner and his crew. The expedition team outnumbered them two to one, which pleased Kinthross but clearly worried Thomas. Regardless they made good time loading everything up and were on the road within two hours. The efficiency of the expedition team eased the tensions somewhat.

When they cleared the guards stationed at the outskirts of Khaldra without issue Kinthross's opinion of the caravan master improved slightly. The man could wield arrogance and indignation like a master swordsman leaving the guards stunned and off kilter.

With Khaldra fading into the distance Kinthross's thoughts turned to the future. The Field Knights were veterans of the chaos of the Promise but how would they fair in the chaos to come?

Chapter 14

Marcus Velen had hit a dead end in his search for the mysterious mage. It was quite annoying. Even with the information he had gained speaking with the young woman, none of his attempts to track the mage had borne fruit. Lord Hyde had graciously granted him a workspace in the manse and had quickly acquired the numerous components Velen had requested. Some of the attempts had appeared to work but the connection had cut off abruptly. All Velen had managed to learn was that the mage clearly had an incredible internal source. If it were anywhere else in the empire Velen would have suspected a scion of one of the Great Houses. The use of blades still confused Velen. With that much power the mage should be able to overcome even the best Governor Delos sent after them without difficulty.

He had taken to pacing the halls of the manse trying to work out new spells to pinpoint the mage.

"You're nearly as bad as my brother. Spending all your time working. How many days has it been since you've left the grounds?" Lady Hyde asked as Velen paced the halls.

"I don't know. I'm sure it hasn't been too long. I've only tried a dozen spells or so. I'm sure I'll have more success in the next few hundred," Velen answered. He had only spoken to the Lady Hyde a few times since arriving and she seemed largely disinterested in his work.

"Well, I do, and it's been far too long. I already have to deal with one work obsessed fool haunting the halls and bringing the mood down," Alexandra continued.

"Um, well, I don't really… I could stay in my workshop if that helps," Velen managed to reply. He did not really know what she wanted him to do. His work was necessary, and more importantly, interesting. He did not particularly want to return to the confusing streets until he actually needed to.

"No, that simply won't do. Perhaps Peter has something in that madhouse of his that can assist you. At least it would get you out of my hair for a while," Alexandra said with finality.

Velen was not sure what she was referring to regarding Dennet's "madhouse."

"I don't know. I have—" Velen began.

"For an arcanist you don't seem to know much. Luckily, you have me. Eris should be able to take you. I'm sure she'll love another chance to show you the city," Alexandra interrupted with a mischievous smile.

Before Velen could respond she was off, striding down the hall to arrange another trip into the city. Velen was rather confused but it wouldn't do to deny his sponsor's request. Velen returned to his workshop to try to put together supplies. If he was being forced to go into the city, he could at least continue his work. He was still packing when Eris arrived. Velen had not noticed her until she tossed a flask of water into his bag while he was choosing what books might be helpful.

"Oh, when did you? I guess it doesn't really

matter. I still need a few things," Velen said. He hurriedly put both books into the bag.

"If anything you've packed looked useful I would think you're preparing to go all the way back to the Arcanum," Eris replied with a bored expression. She picked up a small vial filled with green liquid, swirled it around, then placed it back down.

"I haven't even gotten through the necessities. I still need…" Velen said, trailing off as he considered what else would be necessary.

Eris just watched, bemused, continuing to examine the various components Velen had laying around.

"Yes, I'm sure some moth ridden tomes and a jar of dirt will be most helpful," she said. She walked over and closed the bag before Velen could add anything else.

"It was a jar of sage ash and… What are you *doing?*" he exclaimed as she shouldered the pack.

"Getting us moving. If there is anything you need, I'm sure Mr. Dennet will be able to acquire it. He's at least good at that," she replied, heading for the door.

"But… But I should certainly bring…" Velen stammered, grabbing an armful of things from his workstation and rushing to follow.

Eris did not slow down as she headed for the city, forcing Velen to struggle to keep up while carrying an armful of rather fragile equipment. He received rather confused glances as he struggled through the city streets. After nearly tripping he was forced to stop or risk what he carried.

"Would I be able to put these in the pack? It's rather difficult to carry everything while trying to follow," Velen shouted to Eris, who was about to turn a corner.

She stopped and rolled her eyes at him. "As you

wish, but this is your problem now," she said, walking over to him.

It took some maneuvering to fit the equipment into the bag, but Velen managed it without incident. Velen shouldered the pack and began walking again. Within minutes the weight of the pack was slowing him considerably. Next time, perhaps, a cart would be in order, he thought as he took a break to catch his breath. Eris waited impatiently but did not leave him behind. After a few more breaks on Velen's part they finally reached their destination. The building looked mostly abandoned to Velen, but Eris confidently walked into an alley between the building and some kind of workshop.

When they entered the building Velen found himself in a open room filled with cots. There were only a few people Velen could see many of whom were laying on the cots with bandages. A man in fine clothes was walking between the cots stopping briefly to speak with different people. Eris was scanning the room carefully looking for someone or something.

"What's yer business 'ere," a man said from beside the door. The man had badges around his waist, a wicked looking hook hanging lazily from his belt.

"Brandish, right? I'm looking for your Boss," Eris replied calmly.

"Which one? Actually, never mind Drake's off gods only know where. Dennet's probably still at the market seeing everyone off," Brandish replied, relaxing back into the the chair behind him. Eris stopped contemplating where to go from here. Velen was simply relieved to be able to put the pack down and sit for a minute. Velen jumped as a small piece of wood whizzed past his head.

"Well, now we know you still have some degree of control in that state. For all the good that does. How am I supposed to build a brace to respond to movements that may as well not exist?" a man said from across the room.

Velen turned to look, wary of more flying debris. The man in fine clothes was pulling splinters out of his clothes. There was another man sitting with his legs hanging over the edge of the cot. One leg had some sort of contraption on his right leg. Pieces of broken wood hung from taut straps that might at one time have resembled a brace. Curious, Velen made his way over to the two men. As he got closer Velen began inspecting what remained, trying to determine what had caused the device to shatter so violently.

"Kindly step away from my patient," the man in fine clothes said, mustache bristling. Velen had not realized how close he had gotten while examining the puzzle.

"What can it hurt, Doc? Not like you've had much luck," the man on the cot said.

"As you wish, Thomas, but don't get your hopes up. Without someone from the Medicarum to work some magic I suspect we'll have to amputate," the doctor said sounding defeated.

"Wasteful bunch of unskilled hacks," Velen muttered. He had spent a year working in the library in the Medicarum. It had not been a pleasant experience. The magics employed for healing had proven rather simple but the requisite energy was extremely high. He had lost interest in the study quickly especially after several heated arguments over what he considered to be far more practical applications of spellcraft.

"I agree entirely, but there are limits to the

surgeon's art and even I can acknowledge the practical benefits of magic when circumstance dictates," the doctor said, looking curiously at Velen.

"I can't speak to their skill at surgery, but I knew more about magic when I was six than the entirety of the Medicarum," Velen said a small jolt of magic running through his hands.

"Your a mage then. Perhaps you would be able to offer your assistance in this particular matter," the doctor entreated.

"I'll need to know more about the problem. But perhaps it's best for me to start examining without bias. It would be an interesting problem, but I'm supposed to be assisting Lord Hyde in locating someone," Velen said, somewhat disheartened.

"Oh, just help the man. You've gotten nowhere since we spoke to that girl Dets," Eris interjected from over by the door. She returned to her conversation with Brandish without waiting for Velen's response.

"I did make some progress, just nothing concrete. But I'm sure I could spare some time," Velen said, mostly to convince himself. He did not like working on more than one puzzle at a time, but he had to admit his progress had been less than anticipated. It did not hurt that if the doctor's words were any indication this was an issue only solvable with the clever application of magic.

He began by examining the leg with mage sight. Immediately he noticed some kind of magic effecting the area, but it was far to disorganized to be the work of a mage. More akin to the natural magic that was pervasive throughout the world but that did not make sense. Naturally occurring magic rarely generated noticeable effects. Some creatures other than humans could utilize natural magic as a source, but the process of spellcraft required organization that did not occur without an agent present.

"Describe in as much detail as possible what caused you to be effected," Velen asked.

"Not really sure what. We were about ten days into the Promise, marching through a field of grass. Well, it was more like hair than grass, but I don't think that matters much. Everyone was traversing it and it seemed mostly harmless if a bit disconcerting. I take one step and my entire leg simply disappears. No pain except my wrists when I caught myself. I rolled over and with the help of the others managed to get back on the trail. Only thing that seemed out of place was a puddle of silver water about where my foot would have fallen had my leg not disappeared. It came back a few hours later but it's kept vanishing ever since," the man on the cot said.

Velen considered the man's story. Alethia's Promise could certainly produce naturally occurring spells impossible anywhere else. At least if everything he had read on it was accurate.

"I can confirm some of Thomas's story. His leg completely disappears at seemingly random intervals. I have not been able to find any inciting stimulus for the disappearances. Objects affixed to the leg detach upon disappearance and any damage to the leg itself remains once it returns," the doctor said, adding details that could be useful before Velen had to ask.

Without magic the man clearly was not a doctor in the common use of the term but his attention to detail was better than most Imperial doctors Velen had dealt with.

"I may be able to induce a disappearance, but

tampering with anomalous magic may have unexpected outcomes," Velen said. He had already decided to try as it seemed the only way to gather more useful information. The warning was simply to let Thomas and the doctor know to be ready for whatever might happen.

No one stopped him as he reached out and touched the man's leg. Utilizing the same basic cantrip he had with the melet sap he attempted to interact with the tangled mess of natural magic. The results were nearly instantaneous. Thomas's leg vanished, leaving a somewhat odd-looking stump with a hazy and indistinct area where his leg should have met his body. Though the action of the spell had been brief, Velen could make out the method of action at least vaguely.

The method of action had all the hallmarks of temporal magic. It was an extremely dangerous field of study, which Velen only knew about through his house. House Velen was a branch house of House Temprus, which was the only Great House to deal in chronomancy. If some form of natural magic was displacing Thomas's leg along the temporal plane it would explain the observation made by the doctor. It fit the information Velen had access to but his knowledge of temporal magic was severely limited. He did not have access to the kind of power needed to test any of the theories he had developed from the limited works on the subject available. Velen had a few options available. He could try to unravel the natural magic, which could have devastating results should he fail. He could attempt to syphon off the considerable amount of natural energy powering the spell but that would take a long time and might fail, leaving the man's leg displaced permanently. Lastly, he could affix a secondary enchantment to constantly keep the spell activated while he researched a more permanent solution. Velen favored the last option not only because it would allow him to study the strange magic generated in the Promise but also because it was the safest for all involved.

"I think I have some idea what is happening, however, it will take some time to come up with a long-term solution that does not risk complete temporal displacement or some other equally catastrophic consequence," Velen said after some consideration.

"I think I understood some of that. 'Complete temporal displacement' doesn't sound good. So maybe we avoid that," Thomas said, confused.

"I'll need a more detailed explanation before administering any treatment that could risk the life of a stable patient," the doctor said.

"Well, think of time as a…" Velen began.

"Just stick to solutions, Marcus. Elias doesn't have time to listen to you explain the underpinnings of the universe," Eris interrupted.

Velen sagged somewhat at the admonishment.

"Though I would love to hear your full explanation, she is correct. I have other patients, and it would be poor practice to indulge my curiosity at their determent," Elias said.

"Well, given the circumstances the simplest solution would be to keep the leg temporally displaced. That should allow you to construct a prosthetic without risking it being destroyed like the brace," Velen said.

"I take it you can manage to keep the leg disappeared. Not the best outcome but it's better than the alternatives," Elias replied.

"I just need something to keep the spell active. It shouldn't be too much trouble. I'll just need… Well, leave figuring that out to me," Velen replied, thinking through the list of equipment he had available.

"Don't know much about that magic shite. But if you're looking for something might be we got it in the wagon we dragged back. Whole bunch a magic junk in there," Brandish said from over in his seat.

Velen's eyes lit up at the thought of a wagon full of strange magics from the Promise.

"Now you've done it. I'll never be able to get him out of here," Eris said to Brandish.

Velen excitedly looked around for a wagon but did not see anything. It shouldn't have surprised him not to find it in the main room where there was very limited space with all the cots. He began walking toward one of the doors farther into the building.

"Come on, I'll show you," a man who had been sleeping on a nearby cot said, standing up somewhat unsteadily.

"You're supposed to be resting, Zed," Elias chastised.

"Leave off, Doc, I can handle a bit of walking," Zed replied.

Elias shrugged defeatedly and went back to his workstation. Zed led Velen through a labyrinthine series of rooms, some filled with supplies, others with weapons. They finally arrived at an unassuming door on the far side of the building. Zed opened the door with a key Velen had not seen the man pick up.

"Can't speak to anything the other team packed, but avoid the saplings. They bite," Zed said as they entered the room.

"Thanks for the warning. I'll be careful. Can't be

worse than some of the more dangerous books in the Arcanum," Velen replied. He had never really dealt with those books but there were always stories circulating.

"Best of luck. I'm not paid enough to sort through that stuff," Zed said, laughing.

Velen was left in a back room with double doors big enough to fit two carriges through at once. The wagon was filled with carefully packaged objects secured haphazardly in what Velen could only describe as complete disarray. He wanted to organize everything but without knowing what was in the wagon, forming a plan would be impossible. He would need to open an identify everything, which was an amusing project in and of itself, but the sheer disorganization would bother him the entire time. He climbed up into the wagon carefully avoiding the saplings, which seemed scattered throughout. He found smaller boxes that could be moved and opened.

Velen spent the next few hours opening boxes and using a combination of mage sight and more mundane analysis to identify the various items in the cart. It was mentally exhausting work maintaining the concentration required for mage sight, but the strange array of objects and substances had Velen transfixed. At some point he had found a notebook, which had quickly filled with observations. Much of what he found were rare components used in the creation of artifacts. The sheer quantity and quality of those items astounded him. What really caught his attention were those unusually small items, packed with extreme caution, that defied identification. Some carried spells like what had afflicted Thomas, an odd blend of natural and highly complex magic but others simply defied Velen's understanding of the natural world, bending or ignoring fundamental concepts like gravity without any apparent magic.

His work was interrupted while he was examining one such object, a small sample of moss that seemed to have encased itself in what Velen could only describe as solidified light.

"Well, I'm glad someone is working on this. But I thought you had a more pressing task," Dennet said from the doorway.

"Oh, Mr. Dennet. I was assisting Dr. Elias in treating a patient. I may have gotten carried away," Velen said sheepishly. He placed the sample of moss back in its container and added it to the pile he had simply labeled "anomalous."

"I'm aware. Feel free to inspect whatever you would like once we've found whoever is causing the disturbances," Dennet replied.

"We'll, I've run into some difficulties on that. Lady Hyde suggested you might have something to help," Velen explained.

"Of course she did. I don't know what assistance I can provide, but if you have any requests I should be able to make something work," Dennet said, looking around the room at what Velen had managed to unload.

About half of the wagon's contents had been arrayed across the floor in various piles of small boxes and jars. Most of the larger crates Velen had been unable to remove without assistance though he had taken a peek in some of them.

"Some of this could be useful, though I've only begun to get a picture of what's here. The main thing I need to find the mage causing the disturbance is time and space to work," Velen replied. There were some components he had found that might be useful in the task, but he was still days away from testing any of those ideas.

"Time and space. I suspect that's exactly why Alexandra sent you here," Dennet said.

Velen looked at him, confused.

"I already had a workspace set up at the Hydes' manse," Velen said, trying to understand what Dennet meant.

"Of course you did. Alex understands that providing a quality environment is helpful. Alexandra has her own ideas. But regardless, you're here now. I'll arrange for somewhere for you to stay until you've finished your work. Zed said you've been at this for some time. I would be a poor host if I did not offer you a meal," Dennet said.

"I couldn't stop now. I've only just gotten the outline of a system together. I might need some help unloading the larger crates," Velen said, wanting to get back to work.

"Come on. Elias doesn't need more patients and you're already drenched in sweat. Nothing is going to run away while you eat. Well, something might, but I'm not sure there's much either of us can do about that," Dennet insisted.

For the first time Velen noticed just how hot it was in the room. He could feel the headache coming on from prolonged use of magic. It might be a good idea to eat and take a break, at least until he was better able to continue his work.

Dennet led Velen back through the building to the main room. There were six people sitting around a table that had been set up in the main room. Velen did not see Eris among them, and he assumed she had returned to the Hydes' manse. If he wanted to return to his workspace, he would need to ask Dennet to show him the way.

Velen had not spoken to two of the people sat at the table, but both had been laying on cots in the room when he had arrived hours ago. One was a thin man wrapped head to toe in clean bandages sitting upright and smiling at the conversation. The other was a woman with long black hair and mixed features. She seemed to be sitting and staring off into space.

"Well, its not much but it's better than nothing," Dennet said, offering Velen a seat at the table.

"Maybe don't send the cook off next time," Zed said.

"If you're gonna feckin complain, do it yorself next time," Brandish retorted.

Zed handed out the food, a fairly bland looking stew with small pieces of meat and a lot of vegetables. Velen was not enthusiastic about the food but once it was placed in front of him, he realized he was hungry enough to eat it anyway. Even so he picked out the chucks of unknown meat and avoided the vegetables, which were far too soggy. Everyone except Velen and the woman spoke as they ate. Talking largely about the expedition and the various problems they encountered with Dennet and Elias, interjecting stories of their own. The woman ate slowly and stared off the entire time.

Before Velen could leave the door to the outside opened. A man pushed his way in, his clothes tattered and stained with dried blood. Velen gagged on his food as he looked the newcomer over. The man's right arm lay limp at his side blackened skin cracking and oozing blood was partially covered by the faded and tattered sleeve of his coat. The coat, if it could still be called that, appeared fused to the man's skin. The only part not completely disfigured was the man's face, dried blood streaking weatherworn features that masked a series of freshly healed wounds.

"Feckin' 'ell Drake what got its claws into you," Brandish exclaimed as the man entered.

"Don't think it had claws. More a moving blob of destruction. Might need some help getting my coat off," Drake replied with a shrug.

Elias rose, leaving his half-eaten stew on the table. Velen couldn't understand how Drake was still standing with the severity of his injuries. It was intriguing enough that he cast mage sight to better evaluate. He immediately regretted it as his head flared with pain. Clearly, he had overdone it, but the results were worth it. Drake did not appear to be a mage or at least not a powerful one, however, thousands of spells reminiscent of what Velen had seen in the objects from the Promise were affixed to the man's body. The only area not covered by the dense, almost living mass of spells was Drake's right arm. Velen tried to look closer, but his headache flared and he lost concentration.

"Well, sit down. I need to see what I'm working with," Elias said, showing Drake to a cot.

"Think I'll keep standing. It's easier if I keep moving," Drake replied as he began to pace.

"I can't help you if you're moving. Sit down, unless you want that coat permanently affixed," Elias said, reaching out to grab Drake's arm.

Drake sidestepped Elias and put his left hand up. "Probably best not to. At least till I put this thing down," he said.

Drake walked over to the table and used his left hand to place his right down. He pried open the fingers of his right hand and Velen heard something drop onto the table. Whatever Drake had put down appeared as a blank spot distorting Velen's vision. There were simply a few square centimeters of the table that Velen could not see. What he could see was the effect it had on the table. The wood began to turn grey and crack as Velen watched.

"And how do you expect us to deal with this?" Dennet asked, eyeing the table.

"Without touching it," Drake replied, shrugging. He held his right arm up for emphasis. Velen noticed his hand was reaching for the blank spot and quickly pulled it back.

"Is this thing why you abandoned your team?" Dennet said, irritated.

Drake was already returning to the cot where Elias had spread out his surgical implements.

"No, I left because I had a bad feeling about where we were headed and wanted to scout ahead. Something shifted and I got separated, found that when I was making my way back," Drake replied, ignoring Dennet's tone.

"Shifted my arse. You got lost and left me to sort things out. Lucky enough we met up with Kinthross and his team," Brandish said.

"Well done. Knew you were the right man for the job. Speaking of, where is everyone?" Drake asked, standing in front of the cot.

Elias rolled his eyes and began working, cutting away whatever pieces of fabric he could to get a better view. Zed stood up and put a kettle of water on the wood stove tucked in a corner.

"Velen, any ideas how to secure that thing before

it disintegrates the table?" Dennet asked, turning to Velen.

Velen looked up from staring at the blank spot. "Well, clearly wood is not a good idea. Perhaps metal, but I suspect it would break that down too. Some kind of enchantment might prevent the breakdown but it might destroy that too and it would take a lot of power to put together that enchantment.

"Wait, I might have found just the thing," Velen said, standing up. He remembered a strange flat stone that had been packed in the wagon. Despite an apparent lack of magic, the stone remained suspended above whatever surface it was placed on and he could not make direct contact with it despite several attempts to strike it with various objects.

Velen made it into the next room before realizing he had no idea how to get to the back room with the wagon. He needed to turn around and walk back to the main room. Dennet was already up and walking over.

Dennet led the way and waited for Dennet to retrieve the stone. It should be flat enough to place whatever Drake had brought back without risk of it falling off. Dennet looked quizzically at Velen as he picked up the stone and began walking back. When they returned, Elias was already beginning to cut out pieces of fabric twisted into Drake's flesh. Zed was assisting Elias by providing clean clothes to staunch the bleeding.

"Stop fidgeting or I'll have to put you under," Elias said.

Drake was still standing in the same spot, but he was constantly shifting his weight from foot to foot.

"That'll be a first. Haven't seen the bastard stay still for more than a few minutes," Brandish said, taking a drink from a oversized mug. When he put it down the table cracked beneath it, spilling it and the contents of that corner of the table onto the floor.

"Feckin 'ell. Now you owe me a drink. Bringing back some magic death spot," Brandish grumbled.

Velen hurried over and placed the rock on the bar before going over to examine the table.

"Do we have gloves, or some kind of tongs?" Velen asked, trying to figure out the best way to move whatever it was without touching it. He looked around the room but couldn't find anything.

Dennet strolled over and scooped the spot up in Brandish's spilled mug. Dumping the mug and its remaining contents onto the stone, Velen had placed on the bar. Beer splashed off the stone without wetting it and the spot sat neatly atop the stone, floating centimeters above the surface.

"Impressive, Velen. Now we just need to figure out what to do with a floating spot that destroys everything it touches," Dennet said, sitting down at the mostly crumbled table.

Velen would have liked to examine the strange object, but he knew his limits. Over utilizing magic, especially repeated use of the same spell, would eventually result in brain damage. It was one of the main reasons he preferred ritual casting. Instead, he sat and watched Elias work.

Despite Drake's almost constant movement Elias's cuts were precise never cutting deeper than necessary. The process took several hours but despite that Elias worked steadily and without error. From the sheer number of bloody rags accumulating Velen would have imagined Drake collapsing from blood loss long ago, however, he remained standing and even commented on the progress of the work.

Velen wondered how he had gotten here. Most of his life he had studied magic and in the span of a few days he had encountered more mysteries than he had uncovered digging through the tomes of the Arcanum in all his years of studying. Things might be far more perilous here but for the moment it seemed worth it.

Chapter 15

Dets sat down to eat breakfast. She had spent the last two days sulking around the homestead. She still got her work done but it was hard to get motivated. The house was back in order and without further intrusions things had gotten back to normal. She felt like a part of her life was still missing, a part which had been a guiding light. It wasn't so much the loss of her rifle but the loss of the freedom she had when she went out hunting. Even with the almost constant haze she had been living with she was getting restless but there was nothing she could do. Her parents had been giving her space and only asked questions when she interjected into their conversations.

"I think I need a few herbs from the city. Would you be able to get them?" her mother asked, startling Dets. It was an odd request. Her mother grew herbs in the garden with far greater success than most in the region.

"I can, but I have not finished—" Dets began.

"Don't worry your father can handle things around here," her mother interrupted.

Her father nodded his agreement while shoveling eggs into his mouth.

Dets finished her food and went to her room to

pack a bag for the trip into Khaldra. The routine of packing for a trip, even a short one, improved her mood slightly. As she was going to leave, she noticed the twisted remains of her rifle sitting on a chair near the door. It was clearly broken beyond repair, and she did not have nearly enough money to afford a new one. She would not ask Kel for more charity but maybe he would have some use for what was left. Solemnly, she packed the rifle as well. With everything packed she headed back to the kitchen.

"Get back before dinner. We still have that trout you father hooked yesterday, and I won't let him ruin it with all those spices," her mother said as Dets walked to the door. Her mother handed Dets a list with a variety of herbs to purchase.

Dets folded the list and placed it in the front pocket of her pants.

The trip to Khaldra was only about an hour but Dets was not in a hurry. She rarely made the trip in the morning when many of the farmers brought their crops to market. As she approached the city she saw a long line of carts trying to enter the city. If not for the grumbling of the farmers she passed it would have seemed normal. Dets nearly turned around when she got to the edge of the city. It was a shock seeing multiple groups of guards wearing similar uniforms to those who had visited her home. She did not want to let her mother down, so she kept going. She was stopped before entering by one of the guards. A young man in a pristine uniform without any crest.

"State your business," the man said in a bored tone.

Dets flinched at the words. She had never been stopped entering Khaldra but times were changing.

She was worried, but the sheer number of people being checked entering the city put her somewhat at ease.

"Heading to the market to buy herbs," Dets responded meekly.

"Open the bag for inspection," the man ordered.

Det took off her bag and began opening it. She worried what the guard would do when he saw the broken rifle. She tried to come up with an explanation, but she couldn't think of anything.

"Hurry it up, Mark, we don't have time to worry about a slip of a girl," another man said, gesturing for Mark to join him checking a cart.

Dets found the dismissal infuriating but starting a fight with the guards wouldn't go well. Dets stood with her bag half open waiting for Mark to make up his mind.

"Get going. I've got work to do," Mark grumbled, gesturing for Dets to enter.

Dets picked up her bag and hurried into Khaldra.

She headed for the market square. She would prefer to go to a shop and avoid the market entirely, but she never learned where any shops except Kel's were in Khaldra. It was early enough that most of the people on the streets were setting up their shops for the day or merchants heading to the market square. She could find her way to the market square on her own, but it was easier to follow a small group of merchants through the twisting streets. In a few minutes she made it to the outskirts of the market where several groups of guards were patrolling.

Dets kept her head down as she entered. She felt lost in the crowd even at this hour the market was packed, and some merchants were already hawking their wares. It was so chaotic, and she had trouble finding any specific merchants to fill her order.

"Bren shen mari telos," a sing-song voice cut through the crowd. The Meti phrase caught her attention immediately. It roughly translated to "Can I offer you a place in the storm?" and seemed distinctly directed at her. Glancing around she spotted an older man dressed like the merchants her father worked for, calling her over. The man's stall was sparse, filled with an odd assortment of things. Without a better plan Dets made her way over to the man.

"Marasi sek nara telos imen," Dets responded. Her Meti was poor, but she remembered enough to get her point across. She had tried to say "Only a fool refuses succor in the storm," but she may have misspoken.

The man smiled, ignoring her poor phrasing. "It is good to see a young daughter who knows of home. Let me know what troubles you. There is little of the market that I do not know," Zal said, fluently switching to Imperial.

"Just a bit lost. I haven't spent much time in the market," Dets admitted.

"Ah, a wanderer than. This market is nothing compared go the Grand Bazar, you could get lost for a week and never pass the same stall twice," Zal said, smiling.

"My father was a guard for merchant caravans I only ever saw the Grand Bazar from outside the city. We left years ago, and I have not been back," Dets said. She wasn't sure why she was explaining all this to the man, but he seemed a congenial sort.

"Well, you must go one day their are wonders aplenty to see. And most are far safer than what lies beyond the horizon. Now what is it you seek wandering daughter," Zal said, gesturing toward the Promise.

"My mother sent me to get some herbs, but I haven't found any apothecaries yet. But if its as you say and this is but a small market. It shouldn't be too hard," Dets said. She doubted it would be an easy task on her own. She learned from a young age not to show need to a merchant from Sera-Met, so she downplayed her situation.

"Indeed I did, but if you seek an apothecary the need must be pressing," Zal said.

"Not so much. It's just a simple chore," Dets retorted, remembering watching her mother negotiate back when they lived in Sera-met.

"Ah, then it would only be a small favor. A favor for a favor. A fine deal," Zal replied.

"A very small favor," Dets said. She needed the help, but paying debts meant a lot in Sera-Met. She was wary of owing anyone, especially when the terms were so vague.

"Indeed. I rarely have need for small things but wariness especially from the young is rare and worthy of respect. A deal then on your terms, wandering daughter," Zal said, offering his hand.

Dets grabbed the man's wrist and shook. Dets felt like the man was coddling her. It was annoying but she suspected if he had pushed then Dets would have agreed to a much worse deal. Whether Zal intended it as a lesson or he was simply amusing himself on a slow day Dets could not say.

"Here's the list. It would be best to get everything in one place and save us both time," Dets said, handing Zal the list. He held the note at arm's length with two fingers as he looked it over. .

"A daughter of sand and water. Very interesting. When the deal is done, I would have your story. Consider it payment, if that is agreeable," Zal said raising one eyebrow as he carefully handed the list back.

"A fine trade should you deliver on your end," Dets said.

"I shall show you the way. Your mother clearly knows her craft. You would have spent quite some time finding all this. The Miralocke holds a bounty, but it takes a keen mind to tell what works best," Zal said, smiling. Dets wondered how he had deduced her mother's heritage from a simple list of herbs.

Following Zal through the market proved far easier than traveling on her own. He seemed to know exactly where to go to avoid the worst of the crowd. Even with Zal occasionally stopping to speak with various people they arrived at a small apothecary stall extremely quickly. Dets expected Zal to leave or at least wait nearby to hear her story instead Zal took the note straight to the apothecary.

"Elinda's fortune smiles on you," Zal said with a slight bow. The apothecary was an older woman, clearly from the Miralocke.

"Zal, been a while. What brings you here?" Elinda replied, glancing at Dets. "You got the look of the water 'bout you. Who's your kin,"

"Ma was a Dredger fore she met Da," Dets answered, adopting the same accent as her mother. Dets found it was easier than Meti despite spending far less time in the Miralocke.

"You'd be Talia's girl then. Should've known. How's the Witch of the Green Tide?" Elinda asked. Zal took a step back, allowing them to talk.

"Wait, ma's not a witch," Dets said, confused. No one in her family was. It was part of the reason they had settled in Khaldra.

Elinda looked at Dets skeptically. "You sure we talkin' 'bout the same woman? Talia was the best witch in the Locke no lie 'bout that. Was a right shame when that boy Ves stole her away. Nothing against him, mind, just a right shame," Elida replied.

They were definitely speaking of the same people. Dets had heard the story of her parents' meeting a hundred times. Especially the trouble her parents had when her mother chose to leave.

"Never seen my ma use magic. She's right good with herbs but that's it," Dets said, hesitantly.

"Best not tell her I blew her secret. Wouldn't want to be on her bad side. Might have said too much so if ya'll forgive me let's see that list," Elinda said.

"Mistakes are costly in business, but anything can be forgiven with enough coin," Zal interjected.

Dets wanted to know more but Elinda clearly did not want to speak about it and Zal just wanted to make a deal.

"Nothing but calm waters, Miss Elinda. Let's get to business," Dets said.

Zal scoffed, probably upset that Dets so easily forgave Elinda. He clearly wanted to press the breach of etiquette for a better deal. *Typical merchant always looking for a bargain,* Dets thought. Dets handed Elinda the list. Elinda went around gathering the items, leaving Dets and Zal time to speak.

"Elinda might not be comfortable dragging up the past, but a deal stuck is a promise made," Zal said.

While they waited Dets told her story. It was not much, but Zal seemed interested in the strangest things. He cared more for the small things, all the little conversations one had when traveling. Dets struggled to remember much but Zal seemed satisfied. They paused briefly for Zal to haggle with Elinda over the price. Dets would have been happy with the first offer. It was less than she had expected. Zal had other ideas, and it was a wonder to watch him work. He argued like he knew the apothecaries are better than Elinda, and even when he was clearly wrong he sidestepped the issue and pressed elsewhere. All that and the price only dropped slightly. Even still Zal seemed pleased with himself. Dets finished her story on the way back to Zal's stall.

"Watch the skies. I've never met someone more suited for storms, daughter of water and sand, but it would be a shame for you to be consumed in the flames," Zal said as Dets departed. An ominous warning, and one Dets knew she wouldn't fully understand until it was too late. Even so she did not want to back down from a challenge. Somewhere along the line she had remembered why she had first picked up her rifle.

With renewed vigor Dets made her way to Kel's shop. It might be a waste of time, but Dets was a hunter and knew how to be patient. She'd find a way to get back her freedom. The first step would be speaking with Kel, assuming he was back.

As she exited the market she noticed guards arguing with a group of people trying to enter the market. From the look of them Dets guessed they were a hunting party from farther south, perhaps near Senrena. They all carried rifles, mostly cheaper bolt action pieces common in Expera. Dets kept her distance so she couldn't hear what was said, but the conflict seemed to be escalating quickly. Dets understood the men's hesitation after the destruction of her own rifle.

It was the hunters who struck the first blow. The crack of a rifle shot rang out, silencing the dull roar of the market in an instant. Dets took cover instinctively. She should have run but curiosity kept her watching.

The shot had only stuck a glancing hit against one of the guards—not fatal, but it might keep the man out of the fight. Dets knew the hunters were doomed when they stayed together raising their rifles warningly. Dets would have put space between herself and others and immediately followed up. Once a shot had been fired the fight was on, no use holding back. Standing clumped up just made them easy targets for the mages.

A gust of wind picked up, turning to a gale. Wind whipped the stalls blowing the merchants wares onto the ground. The hunters were knocked from their feet in an instant the few shots they managed went into the sky.

The next gust shredded the men, leaving streaks of blood on the cobblestones. It had taken seconds and only a single mage to dispatch the five hunters. A testament to the raw power of magic and the foolishness of taking it head on. It felt odd thinking through the brief battle. Dets had never fought another person, only the beasts that roamed the land around Khaldra. Still, she saw the hunters' mistakes and thought she could have done better. The biggest challenge was picking the most dangerous targets to remove first. It was a dark thought, but a coming storm brought dark times.

Her mood fouled, Dets continued on her way, and a short while later she arrived on Gunpowder

Street. More mages guarded this area, which distressed her. Nothing on the street seemed disturbed but some of the stores were posted closed. Dets could not see any signs on Kel's door, but it would be hard to tell from a distance. She knew a back way into the shop, but it would require some climbing. Dets did not want to disturb anyone, so she moved quickly and quietly, hopping a series of fences to get to the alley behind Kel's shop. There was another entrance past the shop and behind, but Dets wasn't in the mood for conversation and trying to explain to a shopkeeper why she needed to use their back door seemed like too much work.

Nadia was working the forge in the back when Dets arrived. Covered in soot, Nadia whistled to herself as she worked. stoking the fire

"Hey, Nadia, what did you do this time to get stuck on forge duty?" Dets asked.

"Kel's just been surly lately. Figure it probably has to do with getting knocked around. I'm just trying to get work done without having to watch him sulk. You're not usually here so early or so soon since your last visit," Nadia responded.

Nadia's words worried Dets but the cavalier way she said it meant it wasn't too serious. Nadia might be blasé about a lot of things, but she did care about Kel.

"What happened to Kel?" Dets asked cautiously.

Nadia paused her work and shrugged. "Don't know didn't ask. But he came back late from his trip all bandaged up. Seemed a lot more determined to get to work on the big project," Nadia said.

"Big project?" Dets replied.

"It's so boring. Just a lot of rifles for some rich

guy. Think his name was Peter Dennet. Wouldn't even consider any of my suggestions," Nadia said, sulking.

"His loss. Your stuff works great most of the time," Dets said.

"It's not like anything important has burned down in years. I don't get why people are so worried," Nadia replied.

"I'm gonna go see Kel. If you need anything tested let me know. Seems like I'll have more time now," Dets said. Testing Nadia's inventions was harrowing but Dets would feel a lot safer with something now that her rifle was scrap.

"Good luck. I'm sure I have something laying around that needs a real test," Nadia replied, getting back to loading the furnace.

"If it's all loaded up you can get to work on the barrels," Kel said as Dets entered the workshop. Kel was working on smoothing and polishing the small components that went into the loading and trigger mechanism. His workbench was covered with hundreds of small pieces organized into neat piles. Dets had never seen him work on so many components at one time.

"Nadia's still working on it. How's your head feeling?" Dets said. Kel's head was still bandaged but there were no signs of blood and he seemed to be handling the small components easily.

"Not too bad. I guess I have your mother to thank for that. Bastards got me pretty good, but some Purifiers patched me up and gave me some medicine they got from Talia," Kel replied before he turned around.

"Good folks when they aren't obsessing about their calling. Who managed to get the drop on you?" Dets asked, genuinely curious. Kel might be old, but he was incredibly careful, and the best marksman Dets had ever seen.

"Tried to help some mages who got attacked by an evimikwazi. It was a bad call. The arrogant prick tried to kill me and probably would have pulled it off. Not sure how but a wandering knight managed to get me out," Kel said, darkly.

"Ouch. Seems like those mages are making trouble all over the place. That's actually what I wanted to talk to you about," Dets said. Putting down her pack and opening it. She pulled the twisted remains of her rifle out and presented it to Kel.

"*Bratvensha*," Kel cursed as he looked over the rifle. Dets could not help but chuckle.

"It's *Bratvena* not *Bratvensha*. Not to mention you're using it wrong," Dets said, smiling. *Bratvena* translates to something like "go piss sand," and was used to tell someone to get lost in the most offensive way possible. Kel probably had forgotten the meaning, but it amused Dets that he used the word anyway.

"Still got the point across. What happened?" Kel replied, brushing aside the correction.

"Guards showed up at the homestead looking for something. They trashed the place, and some noble bastard took issue with citizens having weapons," Dets explained. She did not like recalling the events.

"The group I had a run in with were looking for someone. If they're putting this much work into it I wouldn't want to be in their crosshairs," Kel said, agitated.

He cleared a space on his workbench and took a minute to look over her rifle. Dets waited while Kel worked but she did not have much hope he could do anything.

"Seems like these new guards are causing trouble all over the place. They killed some hunters just outside the market earlier today," Dets said. People died in Khaldra all the time, but it was rare to see fights between guards and civilians that escalated that much. Kel did not seem surprised by the story but he began muttering darkly under his breath as he worked. It seemed he could not even disassemble the rifle with its frame so twisted.

"I'm sorry. There's nothing I can do to fix this," Kel said his voice distant and sorrowful.

"Didn't think you could, but I know how much you put into your work, so I figured you'd want to know," Dets replied her heart sinking. She had known it was a long shot but hearing Kel confirm it made it real. Kel was looking around the shop with a contemplative look on his face.

"If Dennet hadn't picked up everything we had ready I'd have something for you, but we are cleared out at the moment. It'll be a while before this batch is ready," Kel said.

"I couldn't afford one even if you had any I still owe you," Dets said, defeated.

"Knew that when I sold it to you. You've been good about trying to pay. When I sell someone a rifle I expect them to have it for life. If I can't fix it then that means I'll need to replace it," Kel said, giving Dets a small smile.

"That's too much, Kel. I'll manage till I can pull together enough for a new one," Dets said. It might be foolish, but she had her pride. It would be hard, but her family had managed without her hunting for meat, and they could do so again.

Kel's hands were going through the motions of

disassembling a rifle. Dets knew it was something he did when he was trying to deal with a complicated problem.

"Dets, your feedback's been a big help, and I know how much your family needs you out hunting. Promises, it might be that Talia's medicine save my life. With Khaldra becoming less stable than one of Nadia's projects. I'm not gonna leave you unable to fend for yourself," Kel said.

Dets could tell he had made a decision when his hand stopped moving. She watched, confused, as he walked calmly across the workshop. He stopped in front of one of the rifle racks, which were completely empty except for one rifle with a scope affixed on top. Dets was stunned as Kel picked up his rifle and walked over to her.

"Wait… What… Why…?" she stammered as Kel presented her his rifle with small smile.

"It'll be heavier than you're used to, so you'll need to adjust how you move. Rounds are bigger too so you'll need to compensate more for drop off," Kel said.

"I couldn't," Dets said. She held the rifle reverently.

"Nonsense, you had a Kel rifle. Wouldn't be proper to give you a lower quality replacement. You'll need some ammo too but that should be easy enough. Keep yourself safe out there," Kel said, gesturing to the boxes of munitions near the back door.

"Thank you," Dets said, hugging him. She only let go when the rifle got to heavy to hold in one hand. She did not know what to do. With a single act Kel had given her back her freedom.

"Best keep it out of sight if you don't want trouble. Tell Nadia to hurry up with the furnace. We have work to do," Kel said.

Dets just stood there, shocked. She needed to get home but it felt wrong to just leave. She wanted to help out somehow but Kel seemed intent on his project, and she did not know much about gunsmithing.

"If you need anything, just ask. I can't begin to explain how much this means to me," Dets said.

"Just stay out of trouble. If the scope gives you any trouble let me know," Kel said, returning to his work. Sometimes Kel could be far too stoic but it was his actions that showed what mattered to him. Dets loaded Kel's rifle and grabbed about forty extra rounds before she left. Nadia had just finished when Dets got to the forge.

"Seems like Kel's got more work for you. I'll be back soon so whatever you want me to test have it ready then," Dets said.

"Will do, unless Kel bores me to death with this project," Nadia said, noticing Kel's rifle slung over Dets's shoulder, even wrapped as it was. "Maybe things will get interesting around here if Kel's giving you his rifle. I might even get to try out something."

"Don't go overboard. I don't want to come back to a pile of ashes," Dets said, smiling. When Nadia sounded giddy it was best to take cover.

Dets made her way through the streets carefully, choosing to take back alleys and hop over fences to keep herself out of view. She did not think it would be too hard to avoid any guards on the outskirts, but she would need to be careful. She was watching the guards, waiting for an opportunity to sneak out. Her best chance came when the guards were checking a farmer's cart who was coming late to market. She was about to when the shouting began. Dets did not want to watch another conflict, but she could not look away. Much like they had her house the guards were tossing the contents of the wagon around haphazardly. Dets caught herself before she unwrapped Kel's rifle. Kel had said to stay out of trouble but it was hard to watch when she could act.

While Dets was considering her options an elegant women sauntered up to the guards. "Whose responsible for this mess," the woman said. Her voice carried far more than Dets would have expected.

"Move along. This is official business," one of the guards ordered.

"Unacceptable. I am Lady Alexandra Hyde. You will address me properly. Now explain yourselves," Lady Hyde replied with a mix of scorn and indignation.

"No offence, Lady Hyde. The governor has ordered everyone entering the city searched for contraband," a different guard explained unable to look at the noblewoman.

"Well, your work is disturbing my stroll. Keep down the racket and clean up this mess," Lady Hyde ordered.

"Of course, Lady Hyde," the guard replied. They began refilling the wagon while Lady Hyde stood watching disapprovingly. Dets began to move. She was happy the situation had been resolved without bloodshed. Dets did not know who Lady Hyde was, but it was good to know at least some of the nobility were against the rampant cruelty. Dets took one last look before she entered the trail back to her homestead. As she did Lady Hyde locked eyes with her. A small tilt of the head and a knowing smile told Dets that the noble had known she was there the entire time.

Chapter 16

Kel made his way down to the workshop just after dawn. He had finally managed to get a good night's sleep. The last week or so had been chaotic and Kel was sure it would only get worse. He would need to make a new rifle for himself but with the workshop outfitted for mass production that would need to wait. He could get a serviceable piece from one of the other gunsmiths in the meantime. A few of them owed him favors so it wouldn't be too costly. Kel found the door to the workshop jammed as he tried to enter. He pushed harder and the door cracked open.

"Oww," came Nadia's voice from the other side of the door.

"Promises, Nadia. I thought you went home last night," Kel said through the door.

"I had an idea," Nadia said, sleepily.

"Can I open the door now?" Kel asked. He wasn't entirely sure he wanted to, but the work needed doing. When Nadia got an idea she worked like a whirlwind and left the workshop looking like one had passed through.

"Five more minutes," came the reply.

"Nadia!" Kel shouted.

"Fine, but you're filling the forge today," Nadia

said, grumpily. Kel heard her standing up and opened the door.

Nadia was wearing the same soot-stained clothes from yesterday and her hair and face were a mess. She was rubbing her head where the door had hit her, but she had a broad smile on her face. The workshop was a mess with papers everywhere and a massive pile of sand strewn across the floor.

"Nadia, what have you been working on?" Kel asked. He would need to get the workshop back in order before he could get anything done.

"That scope you built got me thinking about how to improve the effective range of a rifle. Rifling makes helps a lot with accuracy but without a bigger charge behind it range is severely limited. It seemed like the only real answer was to make it bigger. Of course, it would need to be mounted on something, but theoretically it should work. So, I made a the biggest barrel I could with what we had," Nadia answered speaking rapidly and gesturing wildly

Kel could only stare slack jawed. Another glance around the workshop revealed a massive metal tube nearly two meters long and wider than Kel's leg. It was resting against the barrels of powder where it had rolled when Nadia had released it from the mold.

"Nadia, just how much iron did you use on that?" Kel asked, exasperated.

"Whatever we had left. I might have underestimated the weight, but I'll figure out how to mount it later," Nadia said with a broad smile as she looked over her work.

"What would you use something like that for?" Kel asked, sighing. He would need to get more supplies if they were going to continue their work. It was not all bad. He could pick up a new rifle while he was out.

"I don't know, but if my math checks out. I should be able to hit a target the size of a cart from at least five kilometers away," Nadia replied cheerily.

Kel wasn't surprised. Nadia like solving problems, and she rarely considered whether those problems needed to be solved.

"Clean up the mess. I need to go get us more iron to work with," Kel said, resigned.

"Okay, but I'm gonna keep working on this after. It would be such a waste to leave it unfinished," Nadia replied.

Kel doubted she would get much cleaning done but hopefully the mess wouldn't get worse. Kel would probably be working on his own till Nadia completed her project. Trying to stop her would be futile and just leave her sulking and unproductive.

Kel would have to head to the market square to get supplies. He should be able to get a delivery arranged to arrive by the end of the day. The guards posted at the ends of the street might be a problem, but Kel would have to deal with that if it became a problem. The streets seemed emptier than usual as Kel made his way to the market square. Dets had mentioned trouble at the market yesterday, which could be the reason. When Kel arrived at the market it became clear why the streets were empty. The market was filled to the brim. Kel had only seen this many people gathered together during festivals, and even then it was rarely confined to just the market square.

Kel noted a clear delineation between the gather crowd and the guards stationed around the market. The tension was palpable but still confined to insults and curses. Kel considered turning back but he needed iron to continue his work. Kel made his way around the market trying to find a break in the crowd where he could slip through into the market. He circled half the market before he found an area where the crowd was less dense. Unfortunately, the crowd was heaviest near where the ironmonger Kel knew was located. Some shouldering and a few crushed toes later Kel arrived at his destination.

"Mark, if you have a minute. I've got an order for you," Kel shouted. It was hard to be heard over the crowd, but Mark turned and waved Kel over.

"I got all the time in the world. You'd think with crowds like this business would be good but it's been dead all morning," Mark said. Even in the stall they need to shout to be heard over the crowd.

"Can't say I blame them. Heard there was some bad business here yesterday," Kel replied.

"That it was. Can't speak to what started it but made a mess of a good chunk of the market. Not much here that can blow away though," Mark said.

"I'm gonna need a bit over a fifty kilos. If you can manage to get it delivered. Sooner would be better," Kel said. It wasn't the biggest order he could afford, but he doubted it would be possible to get more through this crowd on short notice.

"Think I can manage that. Unless things go to shit around here. How did you get through the last order so fast?" Mark asked.

"Nadia," Kel replied.

"Fair enough. Total comes to two majors. Assuming you want delivery today," Mark said. It was a fair price, all things considered. Kel paid half up front. He considered warning Mark about the guards watching the street but that would only jack up the price. Kel figured he could handle any issues that arose on delivery.

"Got any suggestions how to get out of here?" Kel asked.

"Don't think my methods would work for you," Mark said, chuckling. Mark was nearly a foot taller than Kel and maybe twenty kilos heavier. Moving around hundreds of kilos of iron a day didn't leave much room for fat.

"Mind if I use your tables to get a better look?" Kel asked. He hoped if he could see over the crowd he could find an easy path out.

"Suit yourself. Just don't fall. It won't be a soft landing," Mark replied.

Kel stood on top of one of the tables, precariously leaning over to let his head clear the canvas overhang. His view was not perfect, but he could see the extent of the crowd. It seemed to have grown larger since Kel had arrived. More worrying was that people were now throwing various refuse at the guards. Kel was still looking for his way out when the guards decided they had enough. A wall of blue flames erupted between the guards and the crowd. A block long and three meters tall, the inferno began creeping forward toward the crowd. Kel was nearly toppled from his perch as the panicked crowd tried to retreat from the flames.

It was complete chaos as people pushed and shoved others out of the way in their attempt to escape. Kel held on to one of the stall's supports as the crowd passed. The wall of fire seemed to stop just before contacting the first stalls. The first few rows of stalls were emptied in minutes, leaving behind those unfortunate enough to be trampled. The glint of flames off steel caught Kel's eye. A single figure remained standing in the first row, a massive two-handed sword, its wavy edge reflecting the flames, held in front of them. The hazy image of a knight holding a sword writhing like a snake flashed through Kel's mind.

The crowd below him was still far to dense and panicked for him to risk trying to reach the figure. Kel watched as they charged through the wall of fire. As they passed, the flames dispersed splitting the wall, which dissipated in moments. One of the guards, hands raised toward the sky, was run through by the greatsword as the figure barreled through. With the flames dispersed those gathered charged forward, overwhelming the guards. Kel lost sight of the knight amidst the chaos. Sorcery in a dozen forms flew, dealing death and grievous wounds to swathes of the crowd. Despite the cost the weight of numbers proved sufficient to overwhelm the might of Imperial magic, and the guards were forced to retreat. Kel grimaced as he watched, unable to help. The fray lasted only a few minutes, leaving scores dead and the edge of the market in shambles.

Kel made his way to the front as the crowd that had fled turned to help the wounded. Kel was not a doctor, but he knew how to organize. Some of the stalls had caught fire in the chaos and whatever aid the crowd could manage would be meaningless if half the market was a flame. If he wanted to be heard he needed someone who could shout over the crowd. As he looked around he saw Mark following him.

"Think you can get their attention?" Kel shouted to Mark.

"As long as you got a plan. I can manage," Mark replied. Kel hopped up on a nearby stall, knocking over some pottery as he did. The merchant had already fled so Kel wasn't accosted for his carelessness.

"Listen up," Mark bellowed, turning the heads of a few hundred people. The immediate area grew quiet enough that Kel could be heard.

With Mark's help Kel broke the crowd before him into groups. Some he sent to fetch water or sand, others to move those wounded still breathing out of the way. By the time he was done his voice was sore and he was exhausted. With a guiding hand the crowd had managed to put out the flames and treatments were beginning on those who could be saved. Once word got around that someone was giving orders the number of people helping swelled. It was still a mess but there was enough structure in place that Kel felt he could begin assessing the situation up close.

Kel made his way to the edge of the market with Mark following. He was stopped a few times by people looking for directions. Kel did not know much about managing a disaster, but he gave orders anyway. Most simply followed his directions and went to work. Some argued or suggested alternatives. If Kel thought their idea was better, he agreed and adjusted his plans. By staying calm and offering a coherent plan Kel had become the de facto leader of the mob. It was not a position he particularly wanted but he didn't have a way out until things calmed down.

He found the knight when he finally reached the edge of the market. Sitting against the wall of a shop just outside the market. Their greatsword resting against the wall beside them and the bodies of seven guards lay strewn before them. Kel wonder why everyone seemed to be avoiding them.

"Are you hurt?" Kel asked as he approached.

The knight was not wearing full plate rather hardened leather armor streaked with blood. A cloth was rapped around their head, obscuring their features. When the knight looked up their eyes glowed a bright purple.

"Been worse," the knight replied. The voice was rough but feminine with a hint of an Imperial accent.

"I have reason to thank you, but I don't know about anyone else here," Kel said. Even without the plate armor a female knight wielding a unique two handed greatsword was too unlikely a coincidence.

"Noble bastards deserved it and if anyone's got a problem they can take it up with me," she replied.

"Even if they did, once things settle down it might be best for you to disappear. The least I can do is offer you somewhere to hide out," Kel said.

He noticed a glint of recognition in those purple eyes.

"You were the one fighting out on the plains. Wasn't sure you would make it," she said.

"It was close thing," Kel replied.

Mark had walked away to speak with a group looking for direction. They did not seem to want to get to close to the knight.

"I could use a place to rest. Only for a few days there are still too many of those bastards running around," she said, rising to her feet. She shouldered her greatsword and walked toward Kel.

"Then it's settled. Once I get things under control here we can leave," Kel said.

As they spoke it seemed a crowd had gathered. At least a hundred people had formed a semicircle around Kel and the knight. Mark was doing his best to keep them at bay, but he was only one person.

"Get back to work. This isn't the time to be slacking off," Kel shouted at the crowd.

Kel could not tell if they all heard him, but the crowd grew quiet. The knight stood calmly staring down the crowd, her purple eyes flaring.

The tension broke in a way Kel would not have expected.

"Magebreaker!" the crowd cheered.

Kel let out a sigh of relief as the crowd cheered. His hand returned to his side as he released the handle of his pistol.

Mark tried to get the crowd back to work and even though his booming voice was drowned out, order was restored after a few minutes. Kel gave his final set of orders, appointing a few of the more competent people to keep everything organized. The knight seemed content to wait patiently while Kel got things handled.

"Time to get out of here. The guards will probably have regrouped by now and the Magebreaker will be their primary target," Kel said.

"Not a bad title, but I think I've heard enough of it. Just call me Aria," she replied following Kel through the ruins of the street.

***

It felt odd to sneak into his own shop, but with Aria in tow avoiding the guards was paramount. When he entered the workshop Nadia was busy affixing primer to a massive brass casing. the round was massive nearly a hundred centimeters long and as wide as Kel's arm. Most of the sand had been swept into a corner but there were still pages of notes strewn across the workshop and the massive barrel had not moved. Aria followed Kel into the workshop and scanned the room hand resting on the hilt of her side sword.

214

"Nadia, meet Aria. She'll be around for a few days," Kel said.

"Thought you were getting supplies. I've got the receiver worked out but I'll need a lot more iron than she's carrying," Nadia said, still focused on her work.

"There was a bit of a mishap at the market. It might be a while before we can get a delivery," Kel replied.

Aria began wandering around the workshop, looking over the various half-finished projects and papers strewn about.

"But I need it to finish. Maybe I can go ask around. It seems like everyone is closing up," Nadia said, dejected.

"What do you mean closing up?" Kel asked.

Some of the stores on Gunpowder Street had closed for a bit till things blew over. The largest operations had stayed open and weren't likely to be intimidated by some guards and a few slow days. The riot in the market might change things, but Nadia wasn't likely to have picked up on that news. Kel would be surprised if Nadia even new there was a new governor.

"Oh yeah, you were out. A bunch of oddly dress men were going around telling everyone to close up," Nadia said.

"Did you speak with them? What did you say?" Kel asked, frantic. He was more worried about what Nadia might have done than the guards shutting down the shop.

"They barged in and were looking around. I told them we were out of stock and probably wouldn't have anything ready for a while. They said a bunch more things but they weren't very interesting so I didn't pay attention. One tried to move my project but gave up after he nearly crushed his toes. There was some shouting as they left but the casting had cooled so I got to polishing that," Nadia said, in her typical meandering fashion.

"Fantastic, now I need to worry about bastards barging in. So much for a safe place to rest," Aria said. She was examining Nadia's project curiously.

"Oh, I wouldn't worry about that. They'll have a fun little surprise if they try that again," Nadia replied. The wicked little glint in her eyes was extremely worrying.

"What would have happened if we had come through the front door?" Kel asked. He was not sure he wanted to know but it was his shop, and he couldn't risk any customers getting hurt.

"Well, if you ignored the closed sign and the warning underneath then you'd both be shredded by a couple hundred ball bearings," Nadia replied matter-of-factly.

"I feel safer already," Aria said, sarcastically.

"You'll get used to it. Nadia, go disable the death trap," Kel said, exasperated.

"All of them?" Nadia asked, disappointed.

"Yes," Kel said.

Nadia immediately went to work, grumbling to herself.

"Remind me not to piss her off. Magic I can handle, but she's clearly not a mage," Aria said as Nadia began dismantling a series of trip lines on the door to the shop.

"Just don't get in the way of her projects and you'll be fine. Oh, and avoid touching anything you are not sure is safe," Kel said.

Aria immediately dropped the end of the massive

barrel she had been holding. It crashed to the ground cracking the floorboards slightly. Aria glared at Kel, who shrugged. If it had been anything dangerous he would have warned her earlier.

"Perfect, you can help me with that later," Nadia said. She returned to her workbench with an armful of metal squares and dropped them unceremoniously on the floor nearby.

"See? You'll be fine. I am curious how you know Nadia's not a mage," Kel said.

"I can see magic. Mages always have the residue of spells floating around them," Aria explained.

"So you're a mage…" Kel began. Before he could finish Aria had crossed the room and had her side sword pressed to Kel's throat.

"Never call me that," Aria snarled, her purple eyes flashing with light.

"Didn't mean to offend. But you need to work on that temper," Kel said. He pressed his revolver harder into Aria's side to emphasize the point. Aria stepped back and sheathed her sword. Kel holstered his revolver at the same time.

"No harm done," Aria said after a few moments.

Kel was not sure what to make of her. She clearly hated mages, but he could not explain her ability to see magic or those glowing eyes. He decided it was none of his business.

Nadia returned from the store carrying more of those metal squares. She glanced between Kel and Aria before shrugging and dropping the devices into the pile by her workbench. With the shop entrance no longer rigged to explode, Kel went around cleaning up the mess Nadia had made of the workshop. Aria seemed to content to sit quietly and sharpen her swords. Nadia returned to her project. The evening passed without further incident , which gave Kel time to consider what was coming. He needed a plan. The riots and crackdowns would continue, and Kel was not sure what role he wanted to play. He shared Aria's antagonism to the nobility, but he doubted they shared the same motivations. He wanted to preserve the city his father had help build. Aria seemed intent on killing as many mages as she could get her hands on.

He was no closer to a plan when he went to sleep.

Chapter 17

Dennet sat in Alex's study sipping brandy while he waited for his host. With his Field Knights sent on their way and Velen working on categorizing the expedition's spoils, Dennet had finally found the time to speak with Alex. He had been in the middle of a business meeting when Dennet arrived, so he was forced to wait. Dennet did not mind the wait. He needed a chance to relax. He had been fielding reports on events in Khaldra and doing his best to stay ahead of Delos's guards. A task that had proven incredibly taxing.

"So how is the arcanist doing?" Alex asked when he finally entered the study.

"I'll have to thank your sister for sending him over. He's tearing through everything the expedition team brought back. I understand less than half of what he says but the results speak for themselves," Dennet replied.

Alex took a seat across from Dennet and poured himself a glass of brandy. "I'm more concerned about developing counter measures than inventorying trinkets," He said.

"I think the time for caution has passed. The city is resting on a knife's edge. We'll be seeing riots soon enough," Dennet answered.

"Perhaps, but we are far from ready to make any moves. Alexandra ran into some guards tearing apart a wagon. They did not seem too pleased with her intervention. But the farmers thanked her at least," Alex said, removing his hat and running his hand through his short auburn hair.

"It good to hear she's willing to help. Even if the citizens are highly suspicious of the nobility a show of good faith will make them more willing to work with us. I was concerned I would need to hide your family's involvement for as long as possible," Dennet said.

He had trusted Alex enough to bring him in on this endeavor but it had been a risk. Alexandra's capricious nature had been the main reason Dennet had kept her out of the more delicate of their plans.

"You are far too comfortable. Even if the citizens are likely to side with us, we haven't even begun to make inroads with the local nobility. Even getting them to take a neutral stance will prove difficult if these riots continue," Alex said.

"Actually, I have a plan for that. Governor Delos will be hosting an auction in the keep in a two days. I have it on good authority that a rather special item will be on offer and should attract a substantial portion of the nobility," Dennet said, with a sly smile.

"Odd that I haven't heard anything, but unlike you I prefer to trade in the necessities. So, you plan to attend this auction and what? Attempt to convince the nobility to ignore recent events?" Alex said.

"I planned on simply getting a better sense of the governor. We may be able to delay the inevitable but a conflict is coming. I need to know how my opponent thinks in order to win. I was hoping you could deal with the nobility. Even if you can't keep them out of things we need to know how they'll react and whether any can be pulled away should things go in our favor," Dennet replied. The plan wasn't perfect but with events unfolding rapidly they needed the information to take advantage of the chaos.

"It would be completely improper for me to arrive to such an event uninvited," Alex said, hesitantly.

Dennet had been worried that would be the case. If he was forced to go on his own he would be relegated to dealing with Zal and the staff. Not a complete waste but far less useful than if he had a noble with him.

"Perhaps, but I'm sure I can convince Zal to invite you," Dennet said, hopeful.

"Even if your merchant friend wanted me there it would be a breach of etiquette. But perhaps Alexandra could pull it off. She is always finding new parties to attend so it wouldn't be suspicious for her to ask around about such an event," Alex replied.

Dennet groaned. Alexandra was a political genius but only when the mood suited her.

"If you're sure. We'll be stepping into the lion's den without an easy out," Dennet said.

"She'll love it. Any chance to dress up and mess with the other nobility. I'm sure you can manage to keep her on task," Alex said.

Dennet rolled his eyes but could not offer a better alternative.

"Then it's settled," Dennet said, raising his glass to Alex.

There was a quiet knock on the door and one of the staff entered with a bow. Dennet recognized the young woman. She had brought Velen to the hall a few days ago.

"Lord Hyde, you're needed," Eris said, without elaboration.

"I'll show myself out. Probably best not to leave Velen alone for too long. But more importantly I need time to prepare if I'm to accompany Alexandra," Dennet said.

Dennet would have preferred to continue planning with Alex but waiting around was not an option. With his expedition teams once again outside of the city Dennet was forced to handle sensitive preparations himself. Though most of the wounded who had remained were doing better under Elias's care. Dennet needed them at the hall in case Delos's guards made a move. His only remaining asset was Drake, who was poorly suited for subtle work. So Dennet spent most of his time traveling across Khaldra getting a sense of where tensions were highest. All he could do was talk with the people and make vague assurances that help was coming. He did not want to be specific until it was time to act. The response seemed mostly positive. People were fed up with the constant surveillance. The overwhelming force displayed by the noble guards was enough to quell further riots, but nearly a hundred citizens had died in the market square, and less than ten guards had fallen. Dennet wanted to avoid further such catastrophe , which for now meant playing politics.

***

Two days passed in a rapid flurry of activity and Dennet found himself rushing to meet Alexandra at the Hydes' manse. He had been trying to see what arms he could get on short notice. He would have preferred more of Kel's rifles the lever action significantly improved fire rate over the common bolt action and the overall quality would be lower. He had to cut short the meeting with a few gunsmiths in order to get his attire in order. Dennet preferred subtlety in his attire but he needed a display on par with the nobility. He chose a black shirt embroidered with gold thread and a silver-grey suit. It was far too flashy but at least he did not feel a complete fool wearing it. He briefly considered affixing his small sword but even if it were up to the standards of the nobility, he doubted he would be able to keep it. He had no intention of going unarmed, regardless of the consequence. Luckily, the suit had a small hidden pocket specifically for his pistol. It was not much in the way of protection but even a single small caliber round could do the job in a pinch.

He arrived at the Hydes' manse on foot only somewhat late. Alexandra was already waiting by the carriage. She clearly was prepared to put on a show. Her auburn hair hung in waves matching her flowing emerald green dress. She wore a few pieces of jewelry, mostly gold and ruby but all of it incredibly tasteful. The Hyde family crest was prominently displayed on the pin she wore in her hair. Dennet always found the half-masked face disconcerting but it fit House Hyde perfectly. Dennet hoped she was as prepared to bring the nobility over to their side as she was to impress everyone.

"Alexandra, you look… okay," Dennet jibed.

"You'd be far more convincing if you weren't drooling. But I'm impressed you managed to string a sentence together," Alexandra replied.

"My inability to speak shouldn't be a problem. Clearly you plan to speak for both of us," Dennet said.

"Of course, it would be a waste to let you fumble your way through this," Alexandra retorted.

Dennet was pleased that she seemed interested in assisting. A disinterested Alexandra would have been disastrous.

"If everyone knows their roles, I suggest we depart," Dennet said. The journey to the governor's keep was short, but Dennet wanted to arrive early and get a feel for the place.

"Showing up late then trying to rush. I should make you wait but my brother insisted this was important," Alexandra replied.

Alexandra entered the carriage without assistance, snubbing Dennet's offer of help. Dennet signaled the driver then hopped in himself. He sat across from Alexandra as the carriage began to roll. Dennet hated riding in carriages, not only was it a waste of money, but he preferred the freedom of action afforded on horseback. It was probably a carryover from his time exploring the Promise. Even if you could get a carriage to traverse the terrain being trapped in a box would be a death sentence.

"So how did you manage to get an invite?" Dennet asked.

"It was easy. Lord Rolos's daughter was looking for a chance to debut, and it was a simple matter of convincing her that such a prestigious auction would be a perfect opportunity. She pressured Lord Rolos to allow her to debut at the event and once word got around, with a little help, far more invitations were sent out. Your silly little auction had become the social event of the year," Alexandra said.

"And you did all that in two days," Dennet said.

"Only one. If it had taken two, I wouldn't have had time to plan my outfit," Alexandra said.

Dennet had to concede that it was an impressive bit of maneuvering.

"With so many nobles present hopefully I'll have a chance to speak with Governor Delos," Dennet said. If Alexandra could be trusted to speak with the nobility on their behalf, then Dennet would focus on the governor.

"And I thought this was just going to be a pleasant stroll through the lion's den. But you seem insistent on going around poking all the lions," Alexandra replied. She seemed more hesitant about the idea of speaking with Delos than anything else.

"I doubt he'll try anything in such a public setting. I want a chance to look him in the eyes," Dennet said, resolutely.

"Before you what, shoot him with that little toy?" Alexandra replied.

"I'm not suicidal, I just want a better idea of who I'm up against," Dennet replied, somewhat shocked. He knew Alexandra was observant, but his pistol was hidden away without leaving an imprint on his suit.

"Good, I'm not dressed for a daring escape," Alexandra joked.

The carriage came to a halt and a few moments later Dennet heard the sound of the keep's gate opening. This would be Dennet's third time in the keep. The first had been during a major renovation. He had been young and construction had been a good way to make the funds he needed to fund his first foray into the Promise. The second had been to receive recognition for the Field Knights' assistance in repelling a swarm of shadar that had emerged from the

Promise. Nasty little bipedal monsters that hated lights. The shadar had made a mess of multiple homesteads before they turned their insectile eyes on Khaldra.

The carriage stopped and Dennet rose to open the door.

"Last chance. We could always go find a real lion's den," Dennet said.

Alexandra just rolled her eyes.

Dennet assisted Alexandra from the carriage. It was all part of the performance and Alexandra knew how to play her part. There were only two other carriages in the baily of the keep. Dennet tried to determine who they belonged to but neither bore house crests.

"House Kelen and House Lanris. Lord Lanris is a bootlickto whoever's in power not really important but he's always early, trying to ingratiate himself with the host. I've only seen Lord Kelen back when I was at court but apparently the heir came with the new governor," Alexandra whispered.

Dennet smiled. At least one of them could identify the myriad of houses involved in Khaldra's politics.

He escorted Alexandra over to the entrance. Two guards were stationed at the door. Both bore the crest of House Ironsong and were armed with poleaxes. The guards eyed Dennet suspiciously. Regardless of how fancy his dress, his lack of house crest marked him as just a citizen.

"Lady Alexandra, I'll see you inside," Dennet said.

"Running away already?" Alexandra whispered as she entered. The guards allowed her to pass but watched Dennet cautiously as he waited for the door to close.

"I have business with the auctioneer. Would

either of you fine gentlemen care to show me the way?" Dennet said, addressing the guards.

When neither responded Dennet produced the letter Zal had written to serve as an invitation. It had been a chore to convince Zal to write it. His aversion toward books extended to letters as well. Dennet could not comprehend how the man ran a business without proper notes, but Zal seemed to make do.

"Follow me," one of the guards said, gruffly. The man had only glanced over the letter, but Dennet doubted anyone would be foolish enough to forge such a thing and the guards seemed to share that doubt.

Dennet followed the man through a servants' entrance. He could have blustered his way through the front door, but this was easier and afforded him a chance to speak with Zal before the event. There were a few servants milling about who jumped to work as the guard passed. Dennet did his best to remember the layout as they traveled. He hoped he would not need to use the information but better safe than sorry. Zal was waiting in a lavish sitting room. The guard left without a word once Zal turned to greet Dennet.

"Dennet, my friend, come sit. Our host has certainly prepared well. Perhaps a bit much for a humble merchant," Zal said.

"You can blame Lady Hyde for that. So, what do you expect to get from all this?" Dennet asked.

"That would be giving the game away. But perhaps a trade. I am curious what game you are playing. So much money spent in such a short time… how do you expect to compete?" Zal responded.

"A hard bargain but one I must refuse. This is not the place to speak of such things. As for the auction it matters not who wins. Any attempt will fail without my

Field Knights at the helm," Dennet replied. He would prefer for the map to fall into his hands but from the little he had gleamed the Dreamer's Crown was deep in the Promise. It would be hard for even the strongest Imperial mages to make that journey without significant experience. There was also the simple fact that the map could lead nowhere.

"To those who know how to listen saying nothing speaks volumes," Zal said. It annoyed Dennet that Zal always seemed to know far more than he should.

"And yet you're here. What does that say of your own plans?" Dennet said.

"Anything for a good deal. Nothing more. But perhaps you wish to speak of lighter things," Zal said.

"A simple question then. Who do you expect to take part?" Dennet asked.

"Yourself and Governor Delos are the main contenders. The other nobles may via for position but will bow to the governor should they win. There are few others with the funds or inclination to participate. The only merchant who accepted my invitation was Emara," Zal said.

If Emara was here things were bound to get messy. Dennet had gotten the better of her at their last meeting, but she could hold a grudge. If she saw an opportunity to screw him over she would.

"Lovely, now I'll need to watch out for a knife in the back instead of a sword to the chest," Dennet replied.

"Still feuding then. A shame. Fury should be saved for the *Temarisal*," Zal said.

Dennet had dealt with Zal long enough to recognize the Meti word for open market or negotiating table.

"Perhaps you're right but that's more a question for Emara," Dennet replied. Zal looked at him skeptically.

A servant entered bearing a tray of drinks. Zal took a glass for himself filled with red wine. Dennet choose to refuse the offered beverage with a wave of his hand.

"A first to see you refusing a drink," Zal said.

"I'll need my wits about me tonight," Dennet replied.

"Interesting. A bold move to place yourself in the heart of the storm. Should you need a respite come a rest here. I offer you my word that no harm shall befall you here," Zal said.

"It's unlike you to make promises you can't keep, my friend. I think I've given Alexandra enough time to set the field. Enjoy yourself while you can things are bound to get interesting," Dennet said.

Zal smiled and pointed Dennet toward a door farther into the keep. Dennet made his way through the servants' hallways until he found himself in the main ballroom. The massive room was bedecked in finery and crystal lamps lined the wall providing the room with far more light than was strictly necessary. It was early enough that there were far more servants than nobles milling about. Dennet quickly spotted Alexandra, speaking to a young lord with a crest of crossed shooting stars displayed prominently on his dress uniform.

Dennet chose to avoid Alexandra for the moment. He did not want to be embroiled with a member of Delos's contingent just yet. He found a small table tucked in the corner that provided a reasonable view of the main doors. He watched and waited until the room filled with nobility. Dennet heard the names of twenty different houses announced representing most of the nobility of Khaldra. Only two of the announced parties were foreign to Dennet. The nobility began congregating in their various social circles. Alexandra flitted between the groups, always greeted warmly. After she had spent a few minutes talking to one particular group she subtly waved Dennet over.

"Lord Pell, Lord Rylan this is the merchant I was speaking about," Alexandra said, once Dennet had made his way over to the group. Dennet recognized them as minor lords whose interests were centered around agriculture.

"A pleasure, Mr. Dennet. I've heard stories of your Field Knights. Its good to finally meet the man behind such a renowned organization," Lord Rylan said.

"My thanks, Lord Rylan. It's a pleasure to make you acquaintance. If there are are any problems on your land do not hesitate to ask. My men are at your service," Dennet said.

"Always looking for handouts. This is a time for leisure, not business," Lord Pell interjected. Lord Pell was known to hate his status as an outcast in Khaldra. The rumors were that he had had an affair with a member of one of the Great Houses and had been ostracized to Expera as a consequence. The details were murky and looking at the man Dennet doubted the veracity of the claim.

"If I have to listen to you complain about slowdowns due to the new inspections… I think its entirely appropriate for Peter to offer a valuable service in deference," Alexandra scolded.

"Lady Alexandra, even if you speak well of this man, matters of such importance are far above his place," Lord Pell said.

Dennet bit his tongue to keep from offending the arrogant lord.

"Richard, there is no need to disparage the man. His Field Knights have assisted this city greatly in matters of far more import than minor trade. Mr. Dennet, as a merchant perhaps you have some insight into this matter," Lord Rylan said.

Dennet appreciated the diplomatic gesture. He would need to follow up with Lord Rylan when Lord Pell was not around.

"Delays are always burdensome, but they can be accounted for. The real issue is damage to product during such inspections. But it's not my place to speak on such policies," Dennet said. It wasn't a useful answer, but he wanted to plant the idea of challenging the excesses of Delos's governance.

"At least you know when it's not your place to speak," Lord Pell said.

"Lord Pell, I understand your irritation. No impertinence was intended. Your settlements to the south have been a boon to my teams and it would be a shame to sour that relationship," Dennet said. It had been his teams who had saved Lord Pell's fledgling settlements, but he hoped to win the man over by framing it in the lord's favor.

"Keep to your place and perhaps," Lord Pell said. He turned and left to speak with others in the vicinity.

"Don't take it poorly. Lord Pell can be a bit formal. It was a pleasure," Lord Rylan said, leaving Dennet and Alexandra.

"Could have gone worse. Lord Rylan seemed

willing to hear you out, and Lord Pell did not burn you alive," Alexandra said, with a laugh.

"Was that on the table?" Dennet asked.

"Probably not but I'll still count it as a win," Alexandra replied.

Dennet followed Alexandra as she made the rounds looking for more of the nobility who might be amenable to speaking with them. A young man approached them. His clothes were an eye-catching mix of red, white, and black. He had a crest displaying a falcon holding a sword in its beak.

"Lady Hyde, a pleasure to make your acquaintance. It's been a while since your family has been to court," the young man said, mostly ignoring Dennet.

"Lord Merrel, what brings you so far from the capital?" Alexandra asked.

"Impressive. Few around here know of House Merrel. House Vertus did not wish to send anyone of import with Lord Delos, so here I am. It has been quite a change from the capital," Lord Merrel replied.

Dennet hoped this would be a brief exchange. He wanted to speak with Delos's retinue, but a court fop was unlikely to know anything of value.

"Well, that is quite unacceptable. I must show you to the fine lords and ladies of Khaldra," Alexandra replied, far too excitedly for Dennet's liking. It might be a good cover to meet other nobles, but he would have to watch his words far more carefully.

"I would be honored Lady Hyde," Lord Merrel said with a bow.

Alexandra resumed her rounds with Dennet and Lord Merrel in tow. Before they could strike up a conversation Governor Delos appeared on the balcony above. A hush fell over the room as everyone waited for him to speak. He wore the same uniform as he had when addressing Khaldra for the first time.

"I thank you all for coming. I had not expected such a response when I agreed to this event. I am pleased to have the chance to speak with all of you regarding what we have accomplished in the short time since my arrival and what needs to be done. Before my arrival Khaldra was a disorganized mess, but my men have taken to the streets to ensure proper order is observed. The work is far from done, but rest assured I will see order restored. Some of you may feel I am being too harsh, but we have only acted in response to those who violate the laws of the empire. The gravity of my charge here weighs heavily on me but for tonight I ask you all to enjoy yourselves and feel free to speak candidly on any concerns," Delos said, his voice projecting perfectly across the room.

His speech finished, Delos descended from the balcony accompanied by a few other lords in similar uniforms. Dennet took note of the lords that immediately went to speak with the governor.

Dennet broke away from Alexandra and Lord Merrel. He might not have a good opportunity to speak with Delos without Alexandra present but listening in on his conversations would be a better use of Dennet's time. Alexandra noted his departure but said nothing. He made his way to the gathering crowd of nobles around the governor. He grabbed a drink from the tray of a passing servant. He hoped it would make him less conspicuous while he lurked around the edges of the crowd. Most of what Dennet managed to overhear was pointless pleasantries. It was good to get names to associate with the faces of the lords seeking Delos's favor.

"Who might you be?" said the young lord Alexandra had been speaking to when Dennet entered.

"Peter Dennet, a merchant with some interest in tonight's main event," Dennet said.

The man looked Dennet over before responding. "Dennet. I've heard that name before. Some of the local nobility mentioned you as the best person to follow the map into the Promise. I'm skeptical how a citizen would be better than a contingent of Imperial mages," the young lord said.

Dennet needed to be very careful with his answer. Whoever this young lord was he was clearly looking for an excuse to move against Dennet.

"I trade primarily in items retrieved from the Promise. A contingent of Imperial mages would be more than capable of traveling deep into the Promise but why risk such losses when others could do the job," Dennet said. It was not a complete lie, Imperial mages might be able to travel far into the Promise but he highly doubted any would make it back alive.

"A clever answer. But what would prevent whoever we send from running away with the prize?" the young man said.

"If the map is real then I suspect it would be a trivial matter to track such an artifact anywhere outside the Promise. Running away would be futile," Dennet said. He needed to listen in on Delos's conversations but dealing with this lord required his full attention.

"Perhaps, if you really wish to offer your services, we may be able to strike a deal. It would save us the trouble of competing, which would only enrich the auctioneer," the lord replied.

"Would I be making this deal with you, Lord…?" Delos said.

"Kelen. You would do well to learn the names of your betters," Kelen replied irritation clear in his tone though his face remained impassive.

"I beg your pardon, Lord Kelen. A humble merchant rarely has the honor of dealing with nobility," Dennet said. He felt like gagging as he spoke.

"Better, but you best watch your tongue. Lord Delos is the one you need to convince of your usefulness," Kelen said. It was a perfect opportunity, but Dennet was wary of a trap. Not that he could do anything if it was. Running away now would be risky at best, so he followed Lord Kelen through the gathered nobility.

"Lord Kelen, who have you brought me," Delos said when he saw their approach.

"A merchant who believes himself useful," Kelen replied.

Delos turned his eyes on Dennet. The man's eyes were cold and flat as he surveyed Dennet. Dennet did not feel any contempt in that stare. Dennet was too far beneath Delos to warrant any emotion. Dennet wanted to kill the man on the spot for the insult. He held his rage and bowed low.

"And what is your assessment, Lord Kelen? If you are wasting my time there will be consequences," Delos said, glaring at the younger lord.

"I think there is no need to pay more for what is rightfully ours. Removing someone from the auction only serves our interest, Lord Delos," Kelen said, his previous bravado gone.

Dennet did not like the talk of removal but speaking out of turn would be a death sentence. Delos rubbed his beard for a moment before turning to Dennet.

"Speak your piece, merchant. I have little time for prattle," Delos said.

"Lord Delos, I humbly offer my services in retrieving the item the map leads to. The Promise can be dangerous and there is no need to risk your nobles on a quest that may not bear fruit," Dennet said.

"Is that all? Lord Kelen, we shall speak on this later. You've wasted enough of my time," Delos growled.

Kelen tensed as if ready to fight before taking a breath and looking away.. Dennet was a bit surprised at the terse response. Delos was either far too confident in his own people, or he had some information Dennet was unaware of.

Delos turned away, leaving Dennet standing surrounded by the nobles. Lord Kelen wheeled on Dennet with barely suppressed fury.It was an understandable response, but Dennet had no intention of being the man's punching bag. He slipped his way into the crowd putting space between himself and the lord. Dennet did not have time to look back as he did his best to avoid shoving anyone out of the way who looked too important.

The crowd fell silent as Dennet heard the muted thump of a body hitting the floor.

"Governor Delos!" Someone shouted over the crowd. Murmurs of "murder" and "assassin" began rumbling through the crowd.

"Shit, shit, shit," Dennet cursed as he began pushing people out of the way.

Dennet broke free from the crowd, searching around for Alexandra. She, like everyone else in the room, was fixated on where Delos had been standing moments ago. Dennet began walking quickly toward her. Running would mark him as guilty and he hoped to escape while everyone was distracted. He made it only a few feet before an unseen force drove him to the floor.

"Seize him!" Lord Kelen shouted over the crowd.

Dennet could not breathe under the crushing weight. He watched helplessly as Lord Kelen emerged from the crowd with several armed guards. The world went black. Dennet could still feel the crushing weight, but the shouts of surprise indicated that he was not the only person unable to see. He struggled, futilely, trying to rise.

"Get up. I can only hold this for so long," Alexandra whispered in Dennet's ear. The weight lifted off him and Dennet shot to his feet.

"Follow me. We can leave through the servants' entrance," Dennet said through gasping breaths.

"Not exactly an option," Alexandra said, her voice strained.

"Alexandra, we need to run," Dennet said, doing his best to orient himself in the total darkness.

"They won't kill me. But if they catch you you're dead," Alexandra said, breathing heavily.

Dennet doubted her but there was nothing he could do against a room full of mages. Dennet ran through the darkness hoping he had picked the right direction. He crashed into several people as he went but he had never been more please to run headfirst into a wall. He felt his way along the wall looking for the door to the servants' hallway. As Dennet found the door the light returned. Whatever magic had cloaked the room in darkness had been dispelled. Dennet hazarded a glance back as he slipped through the door. The nobles were scrambling, trying to retreat or capture the assassin. Most concerning was the nobles gathering around a body laying in a pool of blood where Dennet had been moments ago. He could not tell for sure but it could only have been Alexandra. He did not have time to mourn but he would make them pay.

Dennet sprinted his way through the hallways barging through doors. He needed to get to the outer baily before word spread to the guards there. It would be hard enough to convince them to let him pass. He could attempt to scale the wall, but he did not have proper gear for that and a ten-meter fall onto cobble stone would leave him incapacitated if not kill him outright. Dennet entered the room he had met Zal in. The merchant was nowhere to be seen but a single guard stood sentry at the door on the far side. Dennet did his best to slow his breathing as he approached the guard. The man seemed bored, which was a good sign.

"If you would kindly move aside, I need to retrieve something from my carriage," Dennet said.

"Can't. Orders," the guard said.

"It is a matter of some import. Is there any way I can persuade you?" Dennet pleaded.

"Get…" the man began, his voice trailing off as he fell to the ground. The guard was still breathing, apparently fast asleep.

Dennet took the opportunity and headed for the door. He was not sure what had happened but for the moment it did not matter. Dennet opened the door, pushing the sleeping guard out of the way as he did.

"Don't know why you wasted time with conversation," Alex said, standing in the hallway on the other side of the door.

"Alex, what are you doing here?" Dennet asked.

"Still wasting time," Alex replied. As he began

running down the hallway. Dennet followed Alex, who seemed to know exactly where he was going.

"Go help your sister. I can make it out on my own," Dennet said through heavy breaths. Alex kept running. Dennet was surprised at the man's disregard for his family.

"Promises, Alex, I think she's dead!" Dennet shouted. He stopped, waiting for Alex to respond.

"Your concern is sweet but if you keep blathering on you might actually get me killed," Alex said, slowing. As he spoke his voice changed from Alex's deep calm to Alexandra's lighthearted sarcasm.

"Wait, what?" Dennet exclaimed as he began moving again. The air shimmered and now Alexandra was running ahead of him.

"You really aren't as clever as you look," Alexandra teased.

He had known that Alexandra was a mage, but he had never seen her work such a convincing illusion. He had never seen either Alexandra or Alex work a spell beyond the basic activation of some artifacts. From what he knew they were far weaker mages than most in the Imperial court. That had been a major reason why the house had moved to Khaldra where magic was far less important to social status.

"Can you cover us both like that?" Dennet asked. If they were disguised it would be far easier to convince the guards to let them leave.

"Too easy to spot. Even these half-wits will be looking out for illusions. The trick is timing it so they don't think to look," Alexandra said. They reached the door to the baily and stopped to catch their breath.

"Then what's the plan? If word hasn't reached the guard post yet we might be able to talk our way out.

Even if you can pull off that sleeping spell again, I don't like our chances in a stand-up fight," Dennet said.

"You're really going to make me think of everything? Fine, give me thirty seconds then make for the exit. I hope you're clever enough to come up with a good excuse," Alexandra said.

She did not immediately leave, instead she placed here hand on Dennet's chest. With a whispered word his clothes began to change. In seconds it appeared as if he was wearing a guard's uniform. It was odd to see a longsword hanging from his hip but not to feel the familiar weight.

"I can work with this. But how do you plan to get out?" Dennet said.

"Easy, I don't. I plan to play the damsel in distress, and it would look poorly on my house if I was caught running away from such an incident," Alexandra said, with a wicked smile.

Dennet hoped she knew what she was doing. "Very well see, you on the other side," he said.

Alexandra opened the door and ran out, sobbing. Dennet waited thirty seconds then emerged at a run. He was surprised how well the illusion mimicked the actual motions of a sword as he ran. Alexandra was being consoled by two guards near the gate. A third stood guard near the door.

"Assassin in the keep. Get on the wall! We can't have them escape," Dennet bellowed as he approached the guard by the door.

The guard looked between Dennet and Alexandra before saluting and running up the stairs to the top of the wall. The two guards helping Alexandra to her feet looked at Dennet, confused.

"Escort the lady into the keep" Dennet ordered.

The two men helped Alexandra to the door who glanced back at Dennet with a smirk.

Once the guards were clear Dennet examined the door. It was locked with a heavy steel padlock over the bar holding it in place. He reached into his pocket and pulled out his pistol. It was odd seeing his hand pass through his clothes without moving them. Dennet placed the barrel of his pistol against the lock and pulled the trigger. The sharp *crack* rang through the baily hopefully distorting the direction of the shot. The barrel of his pistol had ruptured but the lock fell open. Dennet scrambled to pull the bar and ran into the city. As he moved away from the keep the guard uniformed faded away. Dennet moved quickly until he was far enough away to feel safe. Then he cautiously made his way through the city toward the hall.

With Delos dead the fuse had been lit. His troops were a weeks travel outside the city even if he could order them to move out immediately.. Dennet would have to move fast to galvanize the city behind his cause while he got word to Kinthross. Otherwise, he would lose any chance at victory.

Chapter 18

Kelen smiled to himself as he waited for Lord Merrel to bring in the next guest for questioning. Over the last week Delos had been growing more erratic. Kelen and Merrel had done their best to temper his rage. Locking down entire swaths of the city had been necessary to ensure order but Delos had ordered his troops to use lethal force at the slightest provocation. Kelen felt it was unnecessarily wasteful. Even the citizens of Khaldra could be made useful with proper governance. With Delos dead Kelen now controlled the city and by extension all of Expera. He would need to make some changes to the cities guard. Some of them were extremely loyal to Delos and they would prove difficult to control.

For now he needed to catch Peter Dennet. Kelen had his doubts about whether Dennet was the killer, but it did not really matter. Whoever had aided Dennet's escape clearly wanted to pin the blame on the citizen. Powerful illusion magic had played a part in the man's escape. Between the sudden darkness and the fake corpse only a noble could have assisted the Dennet. If Kelen was seen pursuing Dennet whoever had aided him would believe their ruse had worked. Kelen could peruse the real culprit once his rule was stabilized. Painting Dennet as the culprit also suited Kelen's purposes as well. It would resolve the matter of the assassination in the public's eye and remove a potential obstacle to Kelen's rule.

As Lord Merrel escorted Lady Alexandra Hyde into the room Kelen wiped the smile from his face. Lady Hyde had been the one to accompany Dennet to the auction making her a suspect. She might also have information on Dennet's current whereabouts. Lord Merrel left once Alexandra sat down. Kelen suspected Merrel did not have the stomach for this kind of interrogation. Lady Alexandra sat watching Kelen while she fixed her disheveled hair. It was not the reaction Kelen expected.

"Lady Alexandra, your choices are simple. Cooperate and perhaps there will be mercy or resist, and I will see justice served no matter how long that takes." Kelen began giving no hint which he would prefer.

"Lord Kelen, all you offer me is death. Quick or slow. What have I done except partake of the late governor's hospitality?" Alexandra replied still fixing her hair. She met Kelen's gaze. Kelen saw no fear in her eyes-only confusion.

"Not only did you accompany the assassin, but you were introducing him as a friend. Such evidence is more than sufficient to bring imperial justice upon you. If you confess and aid us in capturing Dennet your house may in time recover from your treachery." Kelen said raising his hand and pressing his magic against her just enough to show he was serious. Alexandra gasped but kept her head raised against the pressing weight.

"Dennet was a known figure in Khaldra half the nobility would speak to the aid he has offered this city. Perhaps in Arabas it would be uncouth to accompany a citizen to such an event but I was not the only noble to accompany a citizen tonight. Lord Rennar accompanied Emara Morel, a merchant from Vesrin. Lord Lanris may have been here with his wife, but she was not the only person who accompanied him. I can keep going if you wish?" Alexandra said, raising her voice and glaring at Kelen. He had to admit she had a point. Though his new authority would allow him to pass judgement it would not go unquestioned. If he wanted to avoid provoking the local nobility, he would need more than just suspicious circumstances.

"Well, let us say I believe you. If you are innocent then there is no reason for you not to tell me everything you know about Dennet." Kelen said releasing her.

"Dennet had the wealth and arrogance of a noble if not for his place of birth he might have been a peer. Beyond that his Field Knights have been a boon to the city when they aren't causing trouble. I could tell you where his home is but unless you think someone who could orchestrate an assassination such as this and escape would be foolish enough to run home. I doubt it would be much use," Alexandra said relaxing into her seat with a smile.

"And would you know where these Field Knights reside?" Kelen asked. Alexandra seemed rather confident, but he saw no indication she was lying.

"You really know nothing about Khaldra. Finding their residence is the first step in joining the Field Knights. As I am not mad enough to have considered that particular line of work I have no idea," Alexandra said.

"Rest assured, I intend to learn everything I need to. You may go Lady Alexandra. I know where to find you if I have any further questions." Kelen said waving towards the door which opened at his will. The conversation was going nowhere but Alexandra had let slip one piece of information that might prove useful. If none of the nobility knew much of Dennet perhaps a rival would.

"Was that wise Lord Kelen?" Merrel asked eyebrows raised from the doorway.

"We shall deal with her in time. For now, bring the merchant Emara." Kelen replied.

Lord Merrel left with a bow. Kelen could hear him mummering something but could not make it out. Delos had underestimated lord Merrel, but Kelen could tell the man was cleverer than he appeared. A weak mage who had wormed his way into a position of power was a useful ally. Kelen would watch the man closely. As he waited Kelen pondered whether threats or bribes would serve him better.

"How may I be of service Lord Kelen?" Emara said with a bow, her sapphire blue dress adding a flourish worthy of nobility. Except for the jagged scar, running from her nose across to her right ear, she would have fit in well at court.

"At least you understand your place. Your presence here is a stain on this court but I will overlook it if you prove useful. What do you know of Peter Dennet." Kelen said watching her closely.

"Straight to the point. He is an arrogant, ambitious, scoundrel. I could go on but let us get to business. I can tell you everything you want to know but this information has come at great personal cost." Emara said with just a hint of confidence.

"This is not a negotiation. Tell me everything and should it prove worthwhile your service will be rewarded as I see fit." Kelen said his tone sharp.

"I will humbly accept your benevolence, Lord Kelen." Emara replied, her tone not matching the look in her eyes.

It took time for Emara to explain Dennet's expansive connections in the city. It was solid information, but Kelen was focused on the location of the Field Knights. Emara explained how to find their hall and what to expect inside. Kelen took note of how numerous and well equipped these so-called knights were. Emara seemed genuinely afraid of them but from what Kelen could gather it seemed a pittance. He dismissed the merchant without ceremony before going to find Lord Merrel.

"Let everyone return home. Make sure they are properly accompanied. I will deal with the assassin myself." Kelen ordered when he found Merrel.

"Apologies, I am needed." Merrel said to the collection of lords he had been speaking to. He turned and walked over to Kelen and continued in a hushed voice. "Do you wish me to keep an eye on anyone in particular?"

"Use your judgement." Kelen said.

"Of course, Lord Kelen, may I offer a suggestion." Merrel said, unable to meet Kelen's gaze.

"Out with it. I have business to attend to." Kelen snapped in reply.

"Take Lord Pell's men with you they know the city better and can be trusted." Merrel said. Kelen considered for a moment before nodding and heading off to gather a party to capture Dennet.

Kelen led the party of fifteen of lord Pell's best men through the streets of Khaldra. Mercius Rekor, the captain of lord Pell's guards, walked just behind in full plate armor. The man may have lost to Iresel on the dueling ground, but Kelen needed competence and control not chaos. Following Emara's directions, they found the hidden entrance to the Field Knights hall. Mercius ordered seven of the guards to secure the area. Once they had disappeared around the sides of the building Kelen nodded for Mercius to proceed.

Mercius walked up to the door and ran his hand down it. The wood twisted and cracked. As the door erupted into a series of snaking vines Kelen strode through the breach. There was a series of cracks and he could feel something striking the magic he had placed around himself. Kelen surveyed the scene secure in the protection of his power.

Peter Dennet and another man stood facing the door. Kelen noted figures scrambling to leave out a door on the far side of the room. With his quarry in front of him Kelen left those fleeing to the guards. Dennet held a smoking pistol in one hand and was striking at the vines with a sword held in the other. Kelen smiled at Dennet struggling to keep the vines at bay. The other man seemed unconcerned as the vines failed to find purchase. The guards rushed around Kelen surrounding the other man while Mercius continued his assault.

Kelen raised his hand to crush Dennet but a wave of heat washed over him strong enough to break his focus. He turned to see the other man standing in a sea of molten stone flames licking up his boots as the guards who had surrounded him burst into flames and fell. It was a strange form of magic unlike any Kelen had seen. Dennet raised his pistol in a vain attempt to take advantage of Kelen's distraction. Three shots fired in rapid succession failing to even strike Kelen's defenses. Kelen focused on his magic once again bringing his hand down to drive Dennet into the ground.

The strange field of molten stone vanished as the other man strode forward over the charred corpses to aid Dennet. Kelen's other hand shot forward and he snapped his hand into a fist. Kelen could hear bones crack as the man's body collapsed in on itself, and yet he kept moving forward. Blood leaked from his mouth as he closed the distance in a few strides. Mercius's vines wrapped around the mans legs forming into solid blocks of wood fused to the floor. The man smiled at Kelen showing blood stained teeth.

"Sorry Dennet it might get a bit cold" The man said.

Kelen threw his fist to the side sending the man flying but not before the air shimmered. Even in the brief instant that the man's magic engulfed him Kelen felt his body begin to freeze. His magic surged struggling to keep his blood from turning to ice in his veins as the air itself began to crack a sound like a thousand panes of glass shattering at once filled the air. A rain of tiny shards fell to the ground around the man even as he slammed into the wall denting it. Arcs of blood frozen mid flight stuck from the mans gaping mouth. Kelen's body shook with the cold but he kept his magic in place holding the two in place.

The man pinned to the wall struggled to move even as his skin began to crack like a sheet of ice. The floor of the room looked like a field of snow reflecting light without a source. Mercius stepped forward gesturing as if pulling something towards him. Vines erupted from the man's chest, pinning him in place. The field of snow faded aways.

Kelen released his hold on the man and turned to Dennet. Dennet raised his head eyes filled with defiance but with his lungs crushed under their own weight no words passed his lips. Kelen strode over and let his boot fall on Dennet's head.

Mercius and the three remaining guards secured Dennet as Kelen examined the room. Four of the guards had been incinerated and one had been unfortunate enough to be half caught in the field of snow. Half the guard's body was a shattered mess of gore returned to its normal state after the effect had faded. With Dennet secured Kelen ordered the guards to return to the keep. Mercius balked at leaving the bodies of his men behind, but Kelen's words were law.

****

Kelen waited just outside the cell for Dennet to wake up. Finding a cell in the keep had proven more difficult than expected. The keeps dungeon had been sealed after an incident regarding something Mercius called a tolemor, a vaguely canine creature whose body was a rippling distortion of light with a somewhat crystalline structure. In the end Dennet was shackled and locked in a room in the guard house.

Growing impatient, Kelen strode over to Dennet unconscious from and placed his hand over the man's heart. Healing magic was not particularly complicated on its face, however a minor misstep could leave permeant injuries or outright kill the patient. Dennet was a dead man anyway, so Kelen found the risks inconsequential. Kelen ran his hand through the half-remembered pattern while chanting. It was irritating to have to use such primitive methods, but Kelen had never internalized the mental pathways necessary to cast healing magic. Dennet awoke screaming as Kelen's magic brought him to consciousness.

"I plan to use your death as a warning. No one will remember who you were or what you did only that crossing the empire means agony and death. So consider this a last mercy, a chance to explain yourself if only to your executioner." Kelen said when Dennet stopped screaming.

"I have nothing to explain to an arrogant prick like you but whoever killed Delos will come for you in time. It's a shame I won't get to see that." Dennet said, defiance burning in his eyes despite the pain writ large on his face.

"Arrogance is wasting the benevolence of your betters." Kelen said voice as cold as ice.

"You really believe that don't you. Everything I have I built through my own strength and cunning. Can you say the same lord Kelen" Dennet said spitting blood as he spoke Kelen's title.

"I've wasted enough time on idle curiosity. Enjoy your last hours nameless cur." Kelen said. He twisted his hand slamming the prisoner into the wall hard enough for the shackles to crack the stone.

"Though I may die alone and forgotten, I will change history." Echoed the dead man's words as Kelen walked out of the cell.

Chapter 19

After several days Velen had finally managed to organize everything in the wagon. Understanding it all could be a lifetime worth of work. He was pleased with his progress and already had identified some of the most useful components he could incorporate into his spellcraft. But Elias had dragged him away from his experiments to assist with the wounded.

Kari, the quiet woman who had eaten with them the first night, had been afflicted with some kind of living curse. Velen had been initially hesitant to dispel it fearing damage to the brain. But when Kari had a fit and nearly burned the building to the ground around them Elias had insisted. Thomas was getting used to his new prosthetic, but Velen had yet to come up with a way to dispel the temporal displacement. Both of these problems required him to unravel the mysteries of the natural spells occurring in the Promise. Which was why Velen was currently examining Ryan Drake, commander of the first expedition team.

"You've been staring at me for hours now. Is this really going to be useful," Drake said, as he paced back and forth in front of Velen. Drake was nearly fully healed from his injuries after only a few days. Whatever magic suffused his body seemed to have a powerful effect. Even his right arm was starting to regain feeling, which Velen would have thought impossible.

"You're being affected by multiple natural spells. If I am to help others so afflicted I need to understand how they affix and how they interact. If you would stop moving it would be easier. The sheer complexity of this is far beyond even the greatest constructions of the Artifactory," Velen said. He had been trying identify each of the individual spells but had given up on that quickly. There was a level of integration in the knots of magic that Velen would have thought impossible.

"You're lucky Dennet ordered me to stick around, otherwise I'd be on the road again. There is so much to see and wasting time here just feels wrong," Drake replied.

"Lots to see my ass, most of it's shite that'll burn you from the inside," Brandish chimed in. The burly knight was sitting in his usual chair by the door, twirling his grappling hook in sweeping arcs in front of him.

"That's what makes it fun. If the world tries to stop me then I'll keep going out of spite," Drake said, smiling broadly and stretching his arms. The movement made Velens work more difficult but getting the man to stay still had proven impossible.

Velen continued writing in his notebook as Brandish and Drake began exchanging stories. At another time Velen would have paid more attention, hoping to glean some insight. He was too focused on watching the spell work as it inexorably spread over Drake's right arm. It was a slow process but over the last few hours there had been a clear change in the density and intricacy. The process was fascinating. Normally, spells only grew at the moment they were cast then faded over time. But the natural magic of the Promise seemed to be a combination of casting and manifestation. If Velen could replicate the effect, he could revolutionize magic in a way that had not been seen since Imisaras Vertus discovered the neural components of magic.

The hall door slammed open and Velen's hand slipped slightly, tearing the page where he had been sketching the spells on Drake's arm.

A haggard Dennet entered wearing finery Velen had only seen at court. All the knights except Drake had instinctively gone for their weapons when the door opened. Once they saw Dennet they all relaxed.

"Dennet, you look like shit. Did Alex finally kick your ass for trying to court his sister?" Drake said.

"Shut up, Drake. We have bigger problems than your asinine interpretation of my personal life," Dennet said. Velen had not known Dennet long but the man hadn't seemed like the kind of person to snap at his subordinates.

"What's the plan?" Brandish asked. He held his grappling hook at the ready, his eyes scanning for threats as he moved to close the door.

"Lock us down for now I. need time to think," Dennet ordered.

Velen closed his notebook and dropped mage sight.

"Perhaps it would be good to know what the problem is. There seem to be a few problems at present but I don't know how locking the building would help with any of them," Velen said.

Dennet glared at Velen before taking a deep breath. "Governor Delos is dead, and it seems like I'm to blame. Every mage in Khaldra will be coming for my head shortly—if they're not already," Dennet said.

"Well, I have no intention of trying to fight you. I would rather avoid getting myself killed. So, not *every* mage," Velen said.

"Fair enough, Velen. I doubt Lord and Lady Hyde will be trying to kill me either. But if not all enough that it makes no difference," Dennet said with a slight laugh.

"Um, It might be important to know if you did kill the governor," Velen said.

"Doesn't make a difference. The reaction will be the same," Dennet replied.

"At least things are finally getting interesting. Where do you need me?" Drake said, a smile growing across his weathered face.

The air around Velen grew suddenly cold and Velen could see Drake's breath as the man spoke. Velen would have liked to see which of the spells affixed to the man had produced this effect. But the air returned to normal before he could cast mage sight.

"Drake, you're with me. Brandish, get everyone ready to move out should we run into trouble," Dennet said.

"Feckin 'ell, guess everything was bound to go to shite at some point," Brandish said.

Velen was not entirely sure what he should be doing so he sat and watched. Dennet went over to the bar and sat down. Drake grabbed his coat from a nearby cot and began pacing the entire room in wide circles. Brandish went over to his cot and started throwing what he could in a pack. The other knights began doing the same, with Zed packing for Kari. The process took only a few minutes and once all the knights were ready all eyes turned to Dennet.

"You'll just get caught in whatever net they're dragging through the city if you leave now. Your best chance to make a break for it will be once they arrive. Head to the Hydes' manse. It should be safe enough," Dennet said.

"That means we are leaving you to the wolves, Boss," Zed said.

"Once you're all in the clear Drake and I can make our own way out. If I don't meet up with you at the Hydes' manse by tomorrow tell Alex to make it count," Dennet said. Velen liked the idea of running. It was a shame to lose access to the contents of the wagon, but he did not stand a chance in a stand-up fight.

"It'll be war whether you make it or not, no doubt about that," Brandish said. The other knights all nodded agreement. Elias simply twirled his mustache contemplatively.

"Came sooner than I would like but here we are. Hopefully Kinthross can put together the plan and get the boys out there ready," Dennet said.

"So, you had this planned all along. And I'm the one they call crazy," Drake replied with a smirk.

"Your madder than a hatter but Dennet might 'ave you beat on this one. Not sure we are the best lot to pull off something like this," Brandish said, wrapping the rope around his arms and back so the hook rested on his chest in easy reach.

"You won't be alone. You'll have all of Khaldra behind you. They just need a push in the right direction," Dennet said. He reached behind the bar and drew out his small sword and a revolver.

"So much for my new coat. But at least it'll be interesting. Haven't had a chance to hit back at most of the things that try to kill me," Drake said.

The group sat in silence for a few tense minutes. Everyone except Velen seemed to know their roles. Velen considered asking what he should do but he got lost in thought thinking about what he could do. He could use mage sight to determine if the guards were outside but without a timeframe keeping the spell up for too long would be draining. He could ward the building but that would require going outside. Most of his other options would take far too long to implement. In the end the decision was made for him.

The door erupted into a series of snaking vines twisting and growing into the room. In an instant Dennet was on his feet, pistol leveled at the door. Drake strode to the center of the room, hands in the pockets of his long coat. Dennet fired as the first guard entered, the shot crashing into the ground at the man's feet.

The vines began choking the room as guards poured in through the hole where the door had been. Dennet, who had moved to stand with Drake, was forced to focus on cutting away the vines attempting to ensnare him. Drake simply ignored them and no matter how many constricted around him they seemed unable to hold him in places as he marched inexorably forward to meet the guards.

"Move it, Velen," Brandish shouted from the door near the bar.

Velen jumped to his feet and ran to the door. The other knights having already exited.

Velen glanced back one final time as he reached the door.

Drake stood apart from Dennet with four guards around him. There was a shimmer in the air around him as the floor of the room vanished into a sea of molten rock in a three-meter radius around him. The guards screamed as they caught fire, their bodies melting into the floor below. Drake simply stood there, the edges of his clothes blackening as the air writhed with a haze from the heat.

Dennet fired three times before being driven to the floor by an unseen force. The haze of heat and floor of molten stone vanished, leaving the charred corpses of the guards laying on the floor, as Drake rushed to assist Dennet.

Velen was violently pulled through the door.

Velen followed Brandish through the back rooms of the hall. They caught up with the rest of the knights and Elias in the room where the wagon was stored. Velen considered grabbing what he could carry but he already doubted his ability to keep up with the others after his short sprint through the building.

"Ready," Zed said, raising his rifle.

Brandish unwrapped the rope around his shoulder in a single smooth motion. Thomas moved to the double doors with a pistol in hand. With a kick from his prosthetic leg the doors crashed open. Velen was pleased that the contraption he had devised with Elias held up to such abuse. Only two guards were waiting outside. They turned when the doors crashed open and one fell with a hole in his head as the crack of Zed's rifle nearly deafened Velen. The other managed to draw his sword before Brandish's grappling hook snapped forward and impaled itself in the man's forehead. Brandish snapped the hook back to him and began spinning it as he advanced into the alley. Brandish moved with Zed covering him once the he was satisfied he waved for the group to move forward.

As they ran through the city Brandish took point

with Zed covering their rear. Though he spent most of his time keeping Velen moving.

Velen was panting and his sides ached as he struggled to keep up with the group. Kari seemed content to follow the group, but Thomas watched her closely in case she strayed. Even with his prosthetic Thomas was more than capable of keeping pace, unlike Velen. When Velen finally gave up the group stopped. Zed directed him to an alley and whistled for Brandish to turn around. Velen leaned against the wall with his hands on his knees.

"We'll make a knight of you yet, Velen," Zed said with a chuckle. He was barely breathing hard and the only indication they had run several blocks was the few beads of sweat on his brow.

"I… don't… think…" Velen panted.

"Don't worry about it. We're all in the shite now. Save your breath for more running," Brandish said. He offered Velen a canteen of cold water. Velen drank it between gasps.

"I'll take my leave. As much fun as running for my life is I think my time would be better spent preparing to treat the wounded," Elias said. The man's suit was drenched in sweat, but he seemed in better shape than Velen would have expected.

"Keep yourself safe, Doc. Think we'll be needin you soon enough," Brandish replied.

Elias fixed his bowler and with a bow began walking away.

After a few minutes, Velen felt able to keep going. Zed took point this time and he kept the pace to just barely tolerable. As they drew closer to the nobles quarter Zed led the group through alleys instead of down the main streets. It slowed the group's progress but climbing over walls and fences proved even more difficult than the straight run. Velen needed to rest two more times, but Brandish only allowed short breaks. A journey that had taken Velen two hours of straight walking was complete in less than one at the demanding pace of the Field Knights. Had Velen not been with them he suspected the trip would have taken only half an hour.

Velen's legs felt like jelly as he hobbled his way down the drive to the Hydes' manse. There was a carriage stopped in front bearing the crest of House Hyde. The driver was still tending to the horses when the group approached. Ignoring the driver, Zed strode up to the door and began knocking with the butt of his rifle. Seconds later the door swung open.

"Perhaps you'd like a ram. It would make knocking the door down easier," Eris said snidely.

"More courteous than those bastard," Brandish muttered.

Eris looked over the group, and stepping back she opened the door fully. "Get inside before anyone notices. I suspect you have a story to relate to Lord Hyde," she said.

"Not a pleasant one," Zed said as the group filed into the manse.

"I would expect not. Lady Alexandra returned moments ago from the keep. Lord Hyde will see you once his business had been concluded," Eris said, leading them to the study where Velen had first met Dennet.

"If you understand the situation then you know we need to speak to him as soon as possible," Brandish said, impatient.

"Take that up with him if you wish. I just work here," Eris said, leaving the group in the study.

Velen collapsed into a chair while the others stood around impatiently. Without the imminent risk of death Velen began to consider his situation. There seemed to be a consensus among the knights that war was coming to Khaldra. Velen wasn't sure what that meant exactly but if the fight in the hall was any indication it would be brutal. He was fond of the Field Knights and Lord and Lady Hyde had been good patrons, but direct conflict with the Imperial forces in Khaldra seemed suicidal. Velen had never involved himself in Imperial politics, preferring to stick to his studies, but it seemed he had stumbled into a conflict he could not avoid. He would help how he could as long as it did not involve more running.

***

Thirty minutes later Lord Hyde entered the study. By then the knights had settled down, resigning themselves to wait. Zed had his rifle disassembled in front of him on the floor. Brandish stood looking over the bookcase. Thomas and Kari were sitting in the other two chairs conversing quietly though it was mostly Thomas speaking. Velen noted that Lord Hyde was wiping blood from his nose as he entered. A clear sign the man had been using a considerable amount of magic recently.

"Where's Dennet?" Alex said.

"Don't know. He was duking it out with the guards when we fled." Zed said, pausing for a moment before adding, "On his orders."

"Well then he's either captured, dead, or on his

way to make my life significantly more difficult," Alex replied.

"Don't think they were planning to take 'im alive. Drake might be able to get 'im out but there were a lot of the bastards," Brandish said.

"Then you don't know the nobility. They'll want to put on a show to crush any thought or revolt," Alex said.

"If they want a show I think we can make that happen," Zed said, slamming the bolt home on his rifle to emphasize the point.

"Shouldn't count them out just yet. Dennet's a tough old bastard even if he looks like a fop, and Drake is something else entirely," Brandish said.

"Until we know one way or the other we assume the worst," Alex said.

"I might be able to find out but I'll need access to my workshop," Velen said, hesitating.

"Easily done. We'll plan while you work," Alex said with a slight smile.

Velen headed through the manse to his workshop. It was still in the same disheveled state from his abrupt exit. He had to fight the urge to put everything back in order. Time was of the essence, so he struggled through. He found a ceramic mixing bowl and some candles and set them on the table, knocking aside other pieces of equipment. It took him longer to find the salt. Technically, any powdered crystal would do, but sugar tended to make him sticky and other crystals got into his eyes as they did not dissolve. He filled the bowl and lit the candles, placing them just on the edges of his vision. The flickering lights painted strange shadows across his vision. He said a few words as he added the salt to the bowl then, picturing the hall, he dipped his fingers in the water and dabbed his eyelids. The picture in his head clarified.

The spell cast, Velen could see the hall as it was at that moment. The main room was a wreck. Shattered and burned cots littered the floor. Unmoving roots covered the floor and walls. There was no sign of the guard except charred corpses, uniforms melted to their skin. Dennet was nowhere to be seen, though his sword lay impaled in the floor. Pinned to the wall by roots impaled through his chest was Drake. The man's clothes had mostly crumbled to ash and where his skin was not burned it was black with frostbite. Despite his wounds, Drake was breathing and a smile rested across his face. Whatever magics the Promise imprinted on him they seemed to keep him alive far beyond human limits. Velen suspected the guards had assumed he was dead or dying and had left him as a warning to any who stumbled on the scene.

Velen opened his eyes and the scene faded from his vision. If he had something of Dennet's he could have viewed him specifically. He had never been to the keep or anywhere else the guards would have taken a prisoner or corpse so he could not gather more information by scrying. Velen headed back to the study.

The room fell silent as he entered. Alex had taken the seat Velen had been using and was sipping from a glass of brandy.

"They took Dennet when they left. I can't determine if he's alive without more to work with. Drake appears to be alive but stuck to the wall. I don't know how bad his condition is, but it looks rough," Velen said.

"Then we assume Dennet has been captured. We

can retrieve Drake once night falls if he is still alive," Alex said.

"Don't worry 'bout Drake. Let the bastard hang for bit. It'll do him some good to stay in one place. He'll show up when its most inconvenient," Brandish said.

"He seemed to be quite injured. It might be best to send someone sooner," Velen said. "Even magic had its limits, and Drake should be dead several times over."

"He'll surprise you. It'll take more than those prissy nobles can throw around to keep him down for long. Now we just gotta make this shite count for something. Boss's orders," Brandish replied with certainty.

Chapter 20

Kel woke to the a rhythmic thumping from below. The night before he had managed to get the workshop back in order and even started on construction of a new rifle for himself. Without more iron he would only be able to get so far. From the lack of light through his window, it was before sunrise. The thumping continued as he got dressed and made his way downstairs. If Nadia had spent another night destroying the workshop he would need to have words with her

When he entered the workshop he found Aria dancing across the floor, blade and dagger cutting wicked arcs through the air. She wore pants and a loose, stained shirt. Without the cloth wrapped around her head Kel could make out her features for the first time. Without the scars and close cropped hair she would have fit in among any group of nobles Kel had ever seen. He had little experience with nobility, but he suspected she hailed from the Dracic Coast, which was about as far from Khaldra as one could get. Kel judged her to be in her early twenties though it was hard to judge with all the scars.

Aria stopped shortly after Kel entered. Her blades ceasing their deadly movements and rested in a guard position as she turned to Kel.

"Don't worry about me, I just wanted to make sure Nadia wasn't doing something excessive," Kel said.

"Just getting through my morning routine," Aria replied, taking deep, heavy breaths.

"A bit early for my tastes. But if you expect to get far in Khaldra with only those swords you'll need all the practice you can get," Kel said.

"Can't cut magic with a bullet. I don't deny firearms could be useful in certain circumstances. It's hard to deal with someone who can kill you from a hundred meters away. But I'll stick to what I know," Aria said.

"Cutting magic? Not sure what that means, but you can certainly handle yourself in a fight," Kel said, walking over to his workbench.

"Iffel would scoff at that. She could always find flaws in how I fought," Aria replied.

Kel was apprehensive about inquiring further, considering how Aria had reacted when he called her a mage.

Aria resumed her practice, flowing through a series of strikes and blocks at a snail's pace. Kel did not know much about sword fighting but Aria seemed extremely skilled. Her movements were precise, and she changed stances easily without compromising her balance. Kel would be dead in an instant if he ever tried to cross blades with her.

Kel turned to his desk and began working on the inner working of his new rifle.

Aria continued her practice for nearly an hour while Kel worked. When she finished, her clothes were soaked with sweat and she was breathing heavily.

"Does this place have a bath?" Aria said, after she had sheathed her swords.

"Depends what you need. I've got a shower upstairs, but it'll be cold as ice till at least midday then it'll be barely tolerable," Kel replied.

"Better than staying in this for another day," Aria said, gesturing at her clothes.

"Not sure how much I can help you there. I might have an extra set of clothes but they might be a bit loose and you're not fitting in anything Nadia might have laying around," Kel said. Aria was a few inches shorter than him and despite her considerable amount of muscle Kel was broader in stature.

"I'll make do. Shouldn't be a problem unless I need to fight," Aria said, heading up the stairs to Kel's room.

Kel went back to his work but quickly ran into a dead end. He put down the half-finished receiver and walked over to Nadia's project. It was ridiculously excessive for any practical use, but he had to admire her ingenuity. Even unfinished he could see what she had planned. The receiver was designed as an oversized bolt action capable of holding the enormous rounds she had devised. It could be loaded and fired nearly as quickly as a standard rifle with a team working together. She had not finished the mounting but if she placed it on wheels the piece would be mobile enough to adjust between shots while retaining the stability necessary to handle the immense recoil . He had questions about accuracy but if Nadia had run the numbers he trusted her math. The sheer destructive force such a weapon could direct was astounding but Kel wondered what Nadia had been thinking designing such a thing.

"How did you find her anyway," Aria said. She had returned while Kel was examining Nadia's project.

She had wrapped cloth around the cuffs of one of Kel's shirt and rolled up the pant legs and tied them in place with a length of twine. The baggy clothes hung off her body, but she seemed able to move easily enough.

"She found me. She had a bit of a problem with starting fires and her parents needed to find work for her outside of the family farm. Normally I try to keep kids from playing with the stock, but I was speaking with a customer at the time. When I finally noticed she had managed to break down the rifle completely and was struggling to put it back together. After some negotiations with her parents, she became my apprentice and she's been causing me trouble ever since," Kel explained.

"Trouble sounds like an understatement," Aria replied.

"True enough. But she is a better gunsmith than anyone in the city except myself," Kel said. It was not far from the truth even if Kel had to admit Nadia was far more inventive.

"If you say so. But the real question is can you use the guns you make," Aria replied.

"How about I show you," Kel said with a smile.

Nadia arrived an hour after dawn. Kel had begun showing Aria how to use a pistol. Even if Aria preferred her blades, learning how to handle a firearm was nearly a necessity in Khaldra. Once Kel had explained the basics Aria had taken to it quickly. Even if she could only hit the mark once out of six shots she was attentive to the minor details of grip and stance. Given a week Kel could make a fair marksman of her.

Nadia had waited quietly for Kel to finish his critique of her last shot before interrupting. "Seems like something big is being set up near the market."

"What did you see?" Kel asked.

"Not much. Too many of those guys in uniforms. There were at least sixty all standing around while a few men built some kind of stage at the center of the amphitheater. Seems like they pulled them from all over cause there wasn't anyone watching the street when I came in," Nadia replied with a dismissive gesture.

Aria tensed as Nadia spoke. Kel took the revolver from her before she shot herself in the foot. He was rewarded with a glare from Aria for his efforts.

"Sounds like something worth checking out. But we can't be looking for a fight," Kel said, meeting Aria's gaze. The flare of light in her eyes told him exactly what she thought of that plan.

"I can keep the peace as long as they do," Aria said, glowering.

"Well, try not to get clonked in the head again. I still need you to do all the boring stuff around here," Nadia said, with a smile as she fiddled with her hair.

"Don't worry about that. It'll be easier to save his ass this time. Won't have to wait till he brings the fight to me" Aria replied.

Kel had to admit he would rather have Aria along if things went south. "Fair enough. Let's go see what kind of show they're putting on," he said.

It took some time to convince Aria to not bring her greatsword. It was far too identifiable and they wanted to go unnoticed. There was not much they could do about her eyes but hopefully she could keep them from flaring with that purple light. Nadia had suggested they take some of her spheres, but Kel felt the risk of collateral damage was too high. In the end Aria brought her side sword and dagger and Kel pulled an old sword his father had used from a chest in his room. He hadn't spent much time practicing with it but if all he had was his revolver he would be easily overwhelmed.

A crowd had already gathered in the market just in front of the amphitheater. Nadia had either been off in her count or more guards had arrived. Nearly two hundred guards were stationed around the platform at the center.

The platform only had two features: a lectern and a solid wooden pole with chains hanging from it. Kel and Aria pushed their way to the front of the crowd of citizens. They stopped just before they reached the front row to avoid being seen by the guards.

"No matter how brutal this gets don't get any ideas," Kel whispered to Aria.

"I'm not a child, I'll only intervene if the crowd turns," Aria replied crossing her arms.

"I hope they don't. It looks like the governor pulled half the garrison for this event. What happened yesterday in the market was bad, but this would be catastrophic," Kel said. He would do his best to intervene if things turned violent, but he doubted he could make a significant difference.

The crowd only grew as the morning progressed. Kel let himself be pushed farther from the front, much to Aria's annoyance. He wanted a clear exit and did not like the idea of being boxed in by the crowd. He had a worse view of the stage, but Kel wasn't sure he wanted a clear view of whatever the governor had planned. There were considerable grumblings from the crowd but nothing on par with what had happened in the market yesterday. They waited for two hours before a young lord took the stage without fanfare and stood behind the lectern. He was followed by an old scribe carrying a long parchment.

"I am Lord Marius Kelen, my purpose here is two-fold. To address the growing discontent in the city and to bring the justice of the empire. It seems that the minor alterations needed to restore order in this city have been met with disproportionate resistance. This will no longer be tolerated. Any attempt to disrupt the lawful actions of the empire shall be met with overwhelming force. Anyone found to be fomenting such actions shall meet the same fate as this traitor," Lord Kelen intoned, gesturing for a hooded figure to be brought on stage.

Kel expected a far more aggressive response from the crowd to such a speech, but the crowd remained quiet. Aria turned to Kel her eyes glowing.

"They are calming the crowd with magic. If I was closer I could break the spell," Aria whispered. Once Aria had brought it to his attention Kel could feel something suppressing his emotions.

"Best not, we'd be putting all our cards on the table if you did and I don't think we have a winning hand," Kel replied.

Aria placed her hand on Kel's shoulder and the light in her eyes flared brighter.

"Still think it's a bad idea?" she asked. Kel felt his thoughts clear up.

"Yes, but it's good to know you can break the effect," Kel said.

Aria accepted his answer but seemed disappointed. He could feel the tension in her hand as her nails dug in.

When the hooded man was brought to the center of the platform he was chained to the pole. The man seemed to struggle futilely as he was bound but Kel could tell he was severely injured. Blood stained the rags they had placed the man in, and the stains grew as he struggled. Kel watched Aria closely, but she seemed to be watching dispassionately.

"Perhaps you expect a reading of charges but this man's crimes deserve no recognition. Nothing of his past matters. He is simply an example. Those who act against the lawful authority of the empire shall be erased. Their names forgotten. Only the memory of their fate shall remain. Remember this well lest temper or arrogance drive you to violate the peace," Lord Kelen shouted, rage clear in his voice.

The bespelled crowd simply watched with only the slightest of grumbling.

Kel wondered who the poor bastard chained to the pole was, but it seemed he would not have a chance to learn. Whoever they were they had clearly shaken the nobility and Kel suspected no matter how hard the nobility tried to quell the population it would inevitably fail.

Lord Kelen strode over to the the chained man. He took a second to gloat before the execution began. The snap of bones was audible, even from where Kel was standing. As the lord gestured the man's body shifted and broke in horrible, unnatural ways. His chest caved in only to expand nearly to the point of bursting. His arms hung limp, twisted and broken at a dozen points, but Kel could still see the faintest signs of life in the man. The impassive crowd made the scene seem unreal and Kel felt his hand going for his gun if only to end the man's suffering.

Aria stopped him before he drew. "We wait. This Lord Kelen will pay the price in time," she said, her voice filled with barely suppressed rage.

Kel's hand fell to his side. If this was something Aria had seen before he could understand her hate for the nobility.

The execution was dragged on for minutes before the chained man finally died. The crowd seemed to stir, perhaps pushed beyond even the limits of whatever magic had infected their minds. Kel waited for an eruption of violence, but none came. Aria's eyes flared again as the growing tension cut off. Whoever had cast the spell had redoubled their efforts to keep the crowd pacified. Lord Kelen returned to the lectern to give his final remarks when a voice rang out over the crowd.

"Perhaps I will die forgotten. But that doesn't matter. I don't matter. But this city and its people matter, so I prepared to bring about real change. I wasn't fast enough to save everyone but if my life meant anything I will save this city. A city built by fire and steel, not sorcery. If they think magic can rule this city. Then they will learn just what fire and steel can do," the voice said, ringing over the crowd.

Kel recognized the voice and knew exactly who had died on that stage. He had wondered what Peter Dennet had been planning with all those rifles, and now the pieces came together. Khaldra was going to war and Dennet's death would be the spark that started the fire.

"I can see where that spell was cast from. Whoever they are are their doing their best to hide, but its not good enough," Aria said as she began pushing through the stunned crowd.

Dennet's words had startled the guards and broken the spell over the crowd. Even as Kel moved to follow Aria the crowd began to surge toward the platform. Kel did not know whether it was the lesson they had learned in the market or simply the sheer size of the crowd but the guards moved to retreat the second the spell broke. Kel was surprised Aria was more interested in finding whoever had relayed Dennet's last words than fighting with the crowd. Regardless, it seemed the guards were more inclined to let the crowd burn itself out than feed the flames.

Aria stopped in front of a small general store the faded sign barely hanging on above the door. The store seemed closed its windows boarded up with sun bleached wood, Aria tried the door. It was locked which only stopped her for a second. She kicked the door open, her heavy boats shattering the frame. Kel followed, his pistol drawn, as she rushed inside blades drawn.

Four people stood in the room. Kel trained his pistol on the man with a rifle aimed at Aria. Aria was facing off against a burly man spinning a wicked looking hook on a rope. Behind those two were a woman in a gown, hands raised toward the stage, and a somewhat chubby man sitting cross-legged in a circle of candles.

"We were expecting company, but this is a pleasant surprise. Close the door… if you can. It would be better to talk away from prying eyes," the woman said her tone amused.

Aria glanced back at Kel.

"Think we should hear her out. They're not with the guards and she looks somewhat familiar," Kel said, lowering his pistol.

Aria kept her sword trained on the man in front of her but did not move to attack.

"Alexandra Hyde, you must be Rickart Kel. My brother has mentioned you before. And you must be the mysterious Magebreaker. I hope my status won't be an impediment to what I think will be a fruitful conversation," Alexandra said, bowing to Kel and Aria in turn. The bow was polite and graceful but the sly smirk on her face made it more playful than anything else.

Kel recognized the name Hyde. He had dealt with a nobleman by the name of Alex Hyde when he first began dealing with Dennet.

"Depends on what this is all about," Aria said, glancing around the room.

The man in the circle seemed to be staring intently at Aria with wide eyes.

"Velen, it's rude to stare. Our new friends are jumpy enough as is. I assume you saw my little message. I felt it was fairly self explanatory but if there is anything you need me to clarify now is your chance. At least until the guards find us, now that you've distracted our arcanist," Alexandra said.

Aria seemed skeptical but she lowered her sword in time with the man in front of her stopping the spinning of his hook.

"So, you expect to fight. With, what, four people? That is not gonna turn the tide. It seems like you've put the city into revolt without a real chance at victory," Kel said.

"On that we agree, which is why Dennet gathered a thousand men to fight. They are far enough from the city not to be discovered until we are ready to move. The last piece is finding the right person to lead them," Alexandra said, staring directly into Kel's eyes. Her green eyes seemed to draw him in making it hard to think.

"Kel, are you really gonna trust this witch," Aria

said, the air around her shimmering with a purple haze as she stared down Alexandra.

"Dennet trusted her enough to clue her in on the plan before his own knights. Might not mean much to you but if you get any funny ideas I'll put you in the ground," the burly man said, stepping between Aria and Alexandra.

"No need for that, Brandish. We all have the same goal here," Alexandra said, stepping closer to Aria.

Aria seemed hesitant but she shifted her feet from a fighting stance. Once Alexandra was within arm's reach, Aria struck. Her blade flashed across Alexandra's chest. The air shimmered as Alexandra vanished, reappearing back where she had been standing moments ago.

"Playing games won't win you any friends, witch," Aria growled. The exchange had happened so fast no one had time to react.

"Perhaps not, but I don't need friends I need fighters. The people of Khaldra would never accpet my brother and I at the head of this. Which is why I need people like you and Kel. People who can stand with them and give them the strength to win," Alexandra said. Even with Aria ready to kill her, Alexandra seemed intent on pushing Kel to the forefront of this conflict.

Kel knew this war was coming whether he was involved or not. If he could save lives by taking on the mantle of a soldier then could he really refuse? All eyes turned to Kel, waiting to hear his response.

"Don't know why an old gunsmith should stand for the people of Khaldra, but I've lived my entire life in this city, and I won't let it burn to the ground without a fight. If that means I need to lead, then I'll do it." A moment passed with all eyes on him before he continued

"Let's show them what fire and steel can really do," Kel said, with a certainty he did not really feel.

Chapter 21

Dets was returning to Khaldra for the third time in less than two weeks. Even as isolated as it was word from the city reached her family's homestead in short order. She had been worried when she heard about the riot in the market. Then when she heard of the brutal execution carried out by the guards, she needed to check on Kel and Nadia. It had not taken much to convince her parents to let her go but her mother had warned her not to bring her rifle. It still felt odd to think of it as hers but after days of practicing with it she had begun to think of it that way. The road to Khaldra was completely empty, which only served to worry her further.

There were even more guards watching the entrances to Khaldra than on her last visit. She chose to sneak in rather than undergo whatever inspection they would subject her to. It was tricky but years of hunting had taught her how to move unseen. It took longer than she would have liked to gain entrance to the city, but she slipped in without being noticed. She took a series of back alleys and side streets as she made her way to Kel's shop.

From what she could tell the city was on full lockdown with squads of guards patrolling the streets in full armor. The only other people she saw were glimpsed through windows as she passed through their yards and gardens. She could see sickening terror on their faces.

Det made her way past Kel's forge, which lay cold, but stopped before opening the door. She heard Kel arguing with someone. It sounded like a woman, but it was definitely not Nadia. She tried to listen in, but the door was designed to cut down on the sound of Kel's work so all she could hear was bits and pieces. She was so focused on the conversation she did not hear the handle of the door being turned. Dets jumped back as the door pressed against her face.

"Hey, Dets, might want to wait a bit. Those two have been going at it for the last hour and it's getting in the way of my work," Nadia said when she saw Dets.

Dets recognized the woman immediately. Those bright purple eyes were hard to forget. Dets could not begin to guess why Kel was arguing with the swordswoman who had killed three mages.

"Who is she?" Dets asked quietly.

"Oh, Aria. She showed up a few days ago. Apparently, she saved Kel when he ran into trouble on the plains. Not really sure why she's still hanging around but she doesn't get in the way too much. Seems a bit touchy about all that magic stuff but other than that she's fine" Nadia replied at her usual rapid pace.

"If you say so. I'm sure that's the same person I saw killing guards a while ago," Dets said. Dets was torn whether that was a good thing or a bad thing. Her recent experiences with the guards tainted her view, but it mattered why Aria had been fighting them.

"Well, it seems like the guards really want to kill her so I wouldn't think too much about it. It's not like she can block bullets, so you'll be fine" Nadia said as if shoting someone was a simple everyday thing.

Even when she was trying to be helpful Nadia could be terrifying. Dets appreciated the honesty and even if Nadia's judgement could be questionable on some thing Dets trusted her.

"Moving off the topic of potential murder, do know what they're arguing about?" Dets asked.

"Kel agreed to lead an army or something. Bad enough he wants to leave me with all the work around here, but he wants to leave Aria here. Other than lifting stuff, I don't know what to do with her," Nadia replied brushing metallic dust from her trousers.

"Wait, what army? Leading them where? To do what?" Dets asked, rushing through all the questions in a flurry.

"Don't know, didn't ask. Seems like a waste of time unless I can get him to test the Renat gun once it's done," Nadia replied. Dets was frustrated but she expected as much from Nadia.

"I need to talk to Kel," Dets said, moving to the door.

"Good luck. I've got work to do anyway," Nadia said walking away with a smile and a wave.

Dets slipped her way into the workshop hoping not to disturb Kel or Aria. She hoped to be able to listen in to get a better sense of what Kel was planning. Her plan did not work too well as Kel noticed her almost immediately, despite his back being turned to her.

"Dets, you should probably head home. Khaldra is not safe right now and it's only going to get worse," he said. He meant well but it annoyed her that he was trying to send her home when he was planning to do something stupid.

"Not a chance. Nadia said you're planning to lead an army. I need some answers before I go anywhere," Dets replied.

"Promises, I don't need more problems right now. The nobility has pushed things too far and now there will be war in the streets. If I can keep the bloodshed to a minimum that's what I need to do. Which means I need to go collect this mysterious army hiding out in the wilderness and show them how to actually fight. Any more questions?" Kel said, struggling to keep the frustration from his voice.

Dets had never seen him so pressed. Kel was always cold and calculated when it came to problems, but this seemed to be more than he could handle.

"Then I'll go with you," Dets said. She knew it was crazy, but it felt like the right thing to do.

"No," Kel and Aria said in unison.

The immediate rejection made Dets want to dig in. Kel could be a stubborn old bastard, but Dets could play that game too.

"The guards destroyed my home and threatened my family. I have as much right to be pissed at the nobility as anyone. Not to mention I'm a better marksman than anyone else you know, and I know the area around Khaldra better than you. If you're going to get this army of yours and bring them back trained and in one piece. Then you'll need help and I'm the best option you have," Dets said.

Kel did not seem moved by her little speech. His expression just grew darker.

"You know what? I like her. Dets was it? Think you can keep the old bastard alive while I keep the city together?" Aria replied before Kel could.

Kel's expression went from dark to defeated.

"Now you're willing to stay," Kel said rubbing his eyes and taking a deep breath Dets just stared at them in surprise.

"What, didn't your just spend the last hour trying to convince me to keep things together? If I want my chance at that bastard Kelen then I need you and your army here and ready to go. You going alone could mean I don't get that chance, but Dets here seems up for it," Aria explained.

"Dets, do you really think you're ready to fight a war. You're a great hunter but this will be different," Kel said.

"I'm not, but since when has that stopped me? Not like the worlds gonna wait for me to be ready," Dets replied. It was a bad negotiating tactic to admit she wasn't ready, but it was true. Kel seemed stunned for a second then smiled.

"That might have been the best answer you could have given. Promises, I guess I'll take all the help I can get," Kel said.

"Well, now that's settled you better get your ass moving. I can only hold this place together so long. Not to mention I'll throttle that witch Alexandra if I have to put up with her any longer than necessary," Aria said hand taping on the hilt of her sword.

"I'd have been on the road already if you hadn't kept fighting to come along," Kel retorted.

"I'll need to grab my bag on the way out, but it shouldn't take long. Where are we going?" Dets interjected.

"About four days west on foot. Might be closer but the terrain gets rough about two days out. Alexandra gave me a map, but I don't know how accurate it is," Kel said, handing Dets a hastily scrawled map.

She looked it over quickly before pocketing it. Kel eyed her curiously.

"We can do it in three assuming you can keep up," Dets said.

"Knew I was right about her. Now I need to go speak to our new friends about what to do while you're gone," Aria said. She left, grabbing her greatsword from where it rested by the door.

"Good luck, Magebreaker. Leave some alive so I'm not traipsing across half of Expera for nothing," Kel joked. Dets was glad to see Kel was no longer in a foul mood.

"I'll see what I can do," Aria retorted with a wicked smile as she closed the door behind her.

"Is it safe yet?" Nadia shouted through the door.

Dets opened the door to a rather soot stained Nadia. The forge was still cold.

"What were you doing?" Dets asked.

"Dug through the slag to see if I could get anything useful out of there. It hard to work without proper supplies," Nadia replied, smiling.

"Looks like Dets will be accompanying me. Keep the shop together and don't go rigging the entrance to explode," Kel said. He was already packing his bag with supplies he had laid out on his workbench.

"Fine, but I 'reserve the right to blow up anyone who barges in unannounced," Nadia replied crossing her arms and staring at Kel.

Kel rolled his eyes but kept packing. Nadia disappeared to her portion of the workshop, leaving Kel and Dets to their preparations.

Kel took less than twenty minutes to pack

everything he needed. The last thing he grabbed was a bolt action rifle he had tucked behind his desk. Dets could tell it was not one he had made. The finish was poor and the woodworking seemed bare and somewhat lopsided.

"Where did you get that?" Dets asked, gesturing to the rifle.

"Called in a marker. Won't be half as good as yours but I can swap it out for one I sold to Dennet when we get there. Even if we don't run into trouble on the way out of the city, I don't want to face off against any of the beasts out there with just a pistol," Kel said.

"Are you sure you don't want yours back?" Dets said. She didn't want to give up Kel's rifle, but it was his.

"It's yours now, and if we're gonna make it through this shit you'll need it. I can manage till I have time to make another. Not that I'll have time for that till this is done," Kel replied.

"Catch," Nadia said, tossing a satchel to Dets. Dets barely caught it before it hit the floor. She looked inside to see five of those metal orbs she had used before, and two metal squares with the word FRONT imprinted on them.

"Made some improvements so they should be more stable for travel. Hook up something to the metal loop on the bottom of the squares and when it's pulled anything in front should go away. I'd keep back. They're decent at directing the blast, but things happen," Nadia explained while Dets looked through the bag.

"Um, thanks, I think," Dets replied, shouldering the bag.

Kel was already heading for the back door.

***

Kel took point as they made their way through the deserted streets of Khaldra. They made good time through the city with two sets of eyes watching for guards. They only had to duck behind a building once as a group of five guards rode past on horseback. Dets climbed the building to get a better view before moving forward. She kept to the rooftops as they reached the edges of the city. It was easy enough to signal Kel when to move out of the city from her vantage point. She then climbed down and waited for Kel to signal her to move.

Once they were out of the city Dets took the lead. The road to her family's homestead was still empty but that meant less chances to run into guards. Kel hung back as Dets approached her house. She looked back and waved for him to hurry up. Kel just sat down against the fence and took a sip from his canteen.

"Come on, might as well rest inside while I get packed," Dets said.

"Of course. I'm sure your parents would love to talk about how I'm dragging their daughter off to war," Kel replied sarcastically.

"Suit yourself but don't whine when your back starts hurting," Dets said, opening the door. She hadn't really considered what her parents would think when she had agreed.

"Back already? I haven't even started on dinner," her mother said. Dets hesitated for a second before deciding she might as well just say it.

"I'm gonna be gone for at least a week or two," Dets blurted out.

"And why is that?" her mother replied raising an eyebrow.

"I don't think the guards are gonna leave us alone

and I intend to do something about that, or at least help those who can," Dets answered with more conviction than she felt.

Her mother glared at her.

"Had a feeling it would be some foolishness like that," her mother replied. Her eyes softened as she continued, "You might be my child but that don't mean you're a child. Your brother left cause he thought the same back in Sera-met. I tried to stop him but all it did was hurt everyone,"

"I won't be gone forever. Just till all this is sorted out," Dets replied. She remembered her mother arguing with her brother. He'd been sixteen when he left to fight in one of the many clan wars that erupted in Sera-Met. It had not been an easy parting and Dets had been too young at the time to understand just why her mother had cried for days after.

"I know you'll try but the tides aren't ours to control. Stay safe and keep your bracelet with you. I'll deal with your father," her mother said somberly.

Dets had expected more of a fight but in some ways this was harder. She hugged her mother for a long time before she even began packing. She was always half ready for a trip, but this would be longer than most. Even if she expected it to only take three days it was better to prepare for twice that in case they ran into trouble. She did not have enough food on hand for six days. When she came back to the kitchen to see what she could scrounge up, Kel was sitting at the table, and her mother had laid out what supplies they had on hand.

"Where're your manners, girl? Ain't right to leave your companion outside in the cold," her mother said as Dets entered.

"He didn't want to get involved if there was a fight," Dets replied. It was odd to see Kel act so respectfully to someone his own age. Her mother just had the kind of presence that made everyone feel like a child.

"Age ain't a cure for foolishness. Better not run from a fight you're planning to start," her mother said, looking at Kel.

"Can't argue with that. But just cause it's foolish doesn't mean it doesn't need to be done. Honestly, I was hoping you'd keep Dets out of this," Kel said.

Dets's heart sank a bit. She knew he just wanted to protect her, but it still hurt to be treated like a child.

"Thought there might be something in that head, but guess I was wrong. Can't keep the young from actin' the fool. Just gotta show them how to do things right and hope it sticks. Think you can do that?" her mother said.

"Who knows? I know this needs to be done and that no one else is going to step up. Doesn't leave me much choice," Kel replied.

"Now that might be the first thing you said worth its salt. Best keep my girl safe or you'll find out what a real fight is," her mother said with finality.

Kel stood, bowed to Talia, then headed out of the house.

Dets threw everything her mother had laid out into her pack, shouldered her rifle, and headed out. They circled to the west and began the trek toward Dennet's settlement. Dets led the way, doing her best to follow the map and adjusting course as needed. They walked in silence till the sun began to set. Dets picked out a good spot to make camp for the night. It would be the first night on the road, so they started a fire to cook the more perishable food.

"So, how are we looking on time?" Kel asked as they sat around the cookfire.

"Not bad, but things will get rougher from here. I have us taking the shortest route, but we'll have to ford some small rivers and the banks are steep," Dets replied.

"Sooner we get there the sooner I can assess just how much of a mess Dennet left me with," Kel said.

"You want the first watch? Doubt we'll run into anyone but waking up to a bear in your tent is never fun," Dets asked.

"You take the first watch. It's been a while since I've traveled this far from the city," Kel said. He looked tired.

"Fine. Help me set up those devices Nadia gave us," Dets said, reaching for the satchel.

"Let's save those. I don't want to wander into one when I need to take a piss," Kel said, laughing.

***

Kel was asleep an hour later. Dets sat alone by the fire and thought about what she had really agreed to. This was not just a hike through the woods or teaching some people how to really use a rifle. She was going to war and that meant she would need to be ready to kill people. She remembered watching Aria fight and how she had hesitated to intervene. Could she really pull the trigger knowing it would end someone's life. Maybe in the heat of battle it would be easy, but she suspected she would need to shoot first if she wanted to survive. That meant looking down the sight and choosing to kill someone who did not even know she was there.

Something felt wrong about that. It was a question she would need to answer before her hesitation got people killed.

Chapter 22

"Think we're only a few hours away. Don't see much use wastin' time starting fires when it's just around the bend," Kinthross said.

It wasn't the first time he'd started an argument with the caravan master about picking up the pace. The man seemed content to take his sweet time and Kinthross had needed to push them to keep moving. The Field Knights could have made the trip almost a day faster if they were on their own. That would have required leaving the wagons full of whatever supplies Dennet had sent them with. It would almost be worth it to not have to deal with the caravanners.

"You're too hasty. We are making good time and arriving exhausted and hungry for no reason is just silly," Thomas replied. He was eating a bowl of warm porridge with a side of bacon as he spoke.

"Ain't been pushing at all since we left. Maybe your people ain't used to a hard road but Field Knights won't be tired from a little walk like this," Kinthross said.

"Perhaps, but this is my caravan, and I will decide when we move. If you have a problem with that you can make your own way," Thomas said, mildly irritated. This was not the first time this conversation has been had. Thomas knew Kinthross did not trust him and would not be willing to leave the wagons unguarded.

"Just get moving when you're done indulging. Think I'll go see what's ahead," Kinthross said.

"Suit yourself. If you don't get lost get them ready to unload the wagons. I have business back in Khaldra with Mr. Dennet," Thomas replied.

Kinthross scoffed as he walked away. The arrogant bastard seemed content to force everyone to hurry up when it suited him. If it meant Kinthross would not have to deal with Thomas a day longer then he would make sure the wagons got unloaded the second they arrived.

Kinthross walked past the wagons to where the Field Knights had set camp. Their camp was far more organized than the rest of the caravan. The first night on the road Kinthross had been shocked to see the caravanners setting up camp in such a haphazard way. The issue only grew worse when he had sought to work out the lookout rotation with Thomas. The caravan master had laughed, saying they only set watches when they were in areas with bandits. Expera was not nearly rich enough to make banditry a viable lifestyle. It had been the first of many conflicts between himself and the caravan master.

"Boss, you get them to start rolling. Everyone's been ready to get moving for an hour," Nico said, hopping down from the one wagon the Field Knights had kept in their camp. It was the wagon containing the sealed packages Dennet had sent. Kinthross had not opened them yet, mostly because he did not want to deal with any issues their contents might create.

"Not just yet. But I think we should go prepare

the reception. Jorn can handle the team while we are gone," Kinthross replied.

"Sounds good. Should be interesting to see what Dennet has been up to all the way out here," Nico said. She grabbed her pack off the back of the wagon and slung it on.

"Not sure I want to know. Got a guess but I'm hoping it's wrong," Kinthross said.

Once they let Jorn know he was in charge, Kinthross collected his pack and harpoon. Xec was perched on Kinthross's pack trying to get at the trail rations inside. Kinthross called the bird to him, and they headed out. The caravanners glared at Nico and Kinthross as they walked to the front of the caravan. Nico choose to antagonize them further by jeering back and showing off. Showing off was Nico's specialty. She walked alongside Kinthross playing her violin through a fast-paced song, drowning out any comments. When she knew the caravanners were watching she broke into a series of flips and one-handed cartwheels all the while playing her violin. Kinthross had never bothered to ask where she learned all that but clearly she had some performance training.

Nico continued to play until they were well out of sight of the caravan. Kinthross had to gesture for her to stop. She did, pouting as she put away her violin. Kinthross wanted to get a look at this settlement without alerting everyone there. It was still a few hours walk but Nico would play the whole time given the chance. It wasn't so much a road they were traveling on, more of a marked area of relatively flat ground with some evidence of human passage. The road became more pronounced as they got closer to the settlement.

"Let's move off the road. Think you can take the lead?" Kinthross said.

"Got it, Boss. Think you can keep up?" Nico said, heading off into the underbrush.

"Slow and quiet. I want to see what's up before we go in," Kinthross said, following Nico. Xec launched into the air when they entered the trees. Kinthross knew she would follow them from above till they were out of the trees.

"Quiet is easy but I thought we were trying to avoid slow," Nico said. They entered a copse of trees along the road. Nico ran up a tree enough to grab the lowest branches. She swung up and began running through the canopy. Kinthross had to jog to keep up. He was making more noise crushing the underbrush than Nico was as she moved through the canopy. Kinthross could not really complain about the pace. Nico seemed intent on her way of doing things and as long as he did not alert anyone it would work. The view from above was also an advantage he could not ignore. After twenty minutes Nico stopped and signaled Kinthross to wait. He crouched down as best he could and waited. Nico disappeared for a few minutes before dropping down next to him.

"Found it. No one seems to be watching the perimeter, but the ground's cleared a good fifty meters from the tree line," Nico whispered.

"We stick to the trees and watch for a bit. Then I'll head in with you watching my back," Kinthross replied quietly.

Kinthross did his best to stay out of sight as he surveyed the settlement. It was not the easiest thing considering his size, but his clothes broke up his outline sufficiently that a passing glance would not immediately alert anyone. The settlement was set like a small town with an open square at the center. There were few real buildings but numerous temporary shelters and tents were packed in haphazardly over the area. Kinthross could see people moving between the tents, but nothing stood out about them. Most were men between the ages of twenty and thirty, with a small number of women and children. No one was over thirty, which fit the idea of a settlement.

"Looks normal enough to me. It's a bit odd that there aren't any market stalls in the square," Nico whispered from above.

Kinthross gave Nico the sign to watch his back and stepped out into the cleared area. He walked slowly, keeping his harpoon slung across his back but in easy reach. He made it up to the tents on the outer perimeter before anyone noticed. Even for a settlement the security was terrible. He should have been spotted before he got three meters from the tree line. Xec was circling above but whistled for her to stay aloft. The sound also alerted someone passing between two of the tents. A young man strolled over to Kinthross with a rifle leaning on his shoulder.

"Don't get many visitors out here. What's your business stranger?" the young man said.

Kinthross took a step forward and the young man just stood his ground, unconcerned. Kinthross knew just how dangerous Expera could be, and the carefree attitude of the settlement was irritating. It might be a bit harsh, but Kinthross decided to teach the young man a lesson on how harsh reality could be. Kinthross closed the gap in an instant. He knocked the young man to the ground by placing his leg behind the man's and striking with his palm. Before the man hit the ground Kinthross had his harpoon pointed at the man's throat. When the man opened his mouth to shout, Kinthross pressed the tip of his harpoon into the man's throat hard enough to draw blood.

"Gun doesn't mean much if it ain't pointed in the right direction. Now, what's your name? And don't get any ideas 'bout calling out," Kinthross said.

"Tren Stoll," the young man whimpered.

"Well, Tren, let's get you up. Think I need a tour round here if I'm gonna be staying for a while," Kinthross said.

Tren just looked up, shocked, as Kinthross removed the harpoon and offered his hand.

Tren took Kinthross's hand tentatively.

"Who are you?" Tren asked when he finally got to his feet.

Kinthross signaled Nico to circle around before he responded, "Kinthross Reefwalker, Field Knight of Khaldra. Think I might be taking over here till Dennet comes around and makes a mess of everything."

Tren stared, wide-eyed.

"Sorry, sir, didn't expect anyone. Especially not coming out of nowhere alone," Tren stammered.

"Ain't a sir. Might be a knight but not that kind," Kinthross said. The Field Knights might function like a military unit, but rank was rarely considered. When the job was survival, capacity was all that mattered.

"You should speak to Coras. He's in charge of the whole army, not just my unit," Tren said, beginning to walk into the settlement.

"Army?" Kinthross said, halting.

"Um, sir, did Dennet not explain? Figured from how you fight you were here to help train us," Tren replied.

"Promises, the bastard is really planning on fightin' it out. Said your boss's name was Coras, right? Might be good to speak with him," Kinthross replied. He was cursing Dennet for sending them here, but he would deal with Dennet later. Kinthross understood why Dennet would want to fight, he just was not so inclined himself.

Tren led the way through the settlement. Kinthross noted that though the settlement was ostensibly a military camp few people were armed and the work being done was far more mundane than military. At least it seemed like there would be work for the Field Knights who were unwilling to fight. Kinthross didn't know how many would choose not to join up but he suspected there would be a few. A few men were drilling with wooden rifles, moving through positions and pretending to fire on distant targets. Kinthross was not an expert on firearms, but they seemed amateurish compared to Zed or the other knights who routinely used them.

"Commander Coras, sir. Field Knight here to speak with you, sir," Tren shouted to a man watching over the drilling group.

Coras was nearly as tall as Kinthross with features typical of Krais. He had cold blue eyes and a serious expression that matched the typical hard leather attire of a Krais mercenary. Kinthross wondered why this operation was so sloppy with a Krais mercenary heading it. Krais was located between the Miralocke and the uninhabitable regions of the far north. It was infamous in the Miralocke for its mercenaries, who often skirmished with the Dredgers when they were searching the shore.

"Your weapon marks you as a Reefwalker. What

could bring you so far from home? But then you are also a Field Knight so perhaps there is an answer to be found. It matters not. I have little time to concern myself with such oddities. So, Reefwalker, what is it you need of me?" Coras said, his hand resting on head of the hand ax on his belt.

"That's to be seen. Dennet sent a caravan with supplies and all the operational knights. He didn't tell me about all this," Kinthross replied.

"This is good. At least he listened. Hard enough to make soldiers, harder still to do so with enemies at your door. But which are you, Reefwalker, enemy or ally?" Coras asked.

Kinthross choose his words carefully. He did not want to fight the Krais mercenary. It was not a fight he was certain to win.

"Neither, least till I get a chance to speak with the rest of the knights. Some will want to fight alongside you, others not so much. Don't need to worry 'bout us coming at you even if it be easy," Kinthross said.

Coras laughed while he took his hand from his ax and approached.

"I respect this. Each man's war is his own. But if any wish to join, this is good. Few here are capable, and I am but one man. So, I must choose what risks are acceptable. With help perhaps a real war camp can be made of this place," Coras responded, extending his hand to Kinthross.

Kinthross shook the man's hand and was surprised by the strength of the man's grip.

"Caravan should be here in a few hours if they actually get moving. Think you can get some people together to help unload? Then we can talk about what's happening here," Kinthross said.

"Easily done. We can speak as we walk," Coras said. He handed control of the drills over to a woman carrying a real rifle and began heading toward the center of the settlement. Kinthross followed, wondering when Nico would show up. Even if the settlement was secure Nico would find a way in eventually.

As they walked Coras explained his role in the settlement. Dennet had hired him off a caravan months ago to train his recruits. Coras had found the task far more difficult than he had originally thought. Firearms were non-existent outside of Expera and Coras had no experience in their use. He had needed to learn himself while trying to organize the haphazard group into a coherent fighting force. Dennet had clearly planned to have the Field Knights assist in that training. It was a task Kinthross was ill-suited for, but others among the knights would certainly take to with enthusiasm. Coras called together a small group and told them to make space in one of the tents. Once the wagon arrived there would be more than enough people to unload it quickly.

"So, Reefwalker, why do you hesitate to fight? I have seen few of your people, but all have been capable warriors," Coras asked while they waited in the square for the caravan.

"Never thought much of the squabbles between clans back home. Hoped to avoid the same here. Doesn't mean I won't, just that I ain't looking to," Kinthross replied honestly.

"Boss might not, but I think the mages deserve a good thrashing. Most of the Expera born agree," Nico said, emerging from a nearby tent with Xec perched on her pack eating a piece of jerky.

"Thought I told you to look around, not raid the pantry," Kinthross said.

Coras did not seem to mind the intrusion and simply looked Nico over with a bored expression.

"Got bored and they seem harmless enough. Not exactly a good sign if they're supposed to be an army," Nico replied, pulling a loaf of bread from her pocket and sitting down with them.

"I take it she's one of yours," Corus said. "Sneaky is good. Maybe the only way these boys can handle Wirala."

"Wirala?" Nico asked.

"Wirala, like this. Makes men dangerous but still men." Corus said, holding his had out as frost covered it and formed into the shape of a dagger. "Unprepared men die no matter how dangerous they are. This I think is Dennet's plan. Wirala do not respect your weapons, but they should as I have come to,"

"You're a mage. Why then would you fight the nobility?" Kinthross asked.

"I am Krais first, Wirala second. I fight those I am paid to. Is simple," Corus replied with a smile.

Kinthross was wary of the man but what he knew of the Krais told him that he spoke honestly.

They sat discussing the layout of the camp and where the Field Knights would stay for the next few hours. The caravan arrived about an hour after noon. Thomas led the train of wagons into the center of the settlement where they waited. The opulently dressed merchant hopped down from the lead wagon and waved for Kinthross to come over. Corus followed but he seemed more interested in the contents of the wagon at the end of the train surrounded by the Field Knights.

"You see we have arrived just in time for lunch.

We can eat while you unload the wagons then return to Khaldra and collect our reward. Good planning without the need for haste," Thomas said.

Kinthross wondered what kind of deal Dennet had struck with the caravan master. The cost of such a trip would be high enough that even Dennet would be stretched thin with all the other expenses he had accrued with this little project.

"Might have been longer than I would've liked but you got us here without trouble. I'll give you that," Kinthross said.

"Of course, it is what we do. Your lot may be impatient but that is better than dead weight," Thomas replied.

The wagons were unloaded within the hour, and the caravan was on the road shortly after. Kinthross asked Corus to gather his men while he spoke to the Field Knights. Regardless of what they decided the teams would remain in the settlement until Dennet arrived, so everyone needed to know what was happening. Nico stood next to him as he addressed the assembled knights.

"Might be some of you already figured out what's up. But I'll make it clear, Dennet got it in his head to build an army. Don't know if he expects us to fight or just train this lot. Ain't gonna ask either of you less you want to," Kinthross said.

"Boss won't force anyone, and I agree with that. But we are a team. If some of us are gonna go to war than we all need to be ready to fight. So, I say we take a vote. Whether we choose to fight or not we do it as one group. No one is left on their own. That's the way it should be," Nico said, to Kinthross's surprise. He had expected that the group would split, with each acting as individuals. From the response of the crowd of assembled knights they agreed with her.

"Guess it gets the choice made. Unless anyone's got a reason to disagree then we'll vote," Kinthross said. No one spoke up against the idea though Kinthross somewhat hoped they would.

The vote went quick and easy. With all the knights assembled it was a simple matter of counting hands. Once it was clear that the majority favored joining up with the fledgling army even some of the knights Kinthross would have expected to be opposed voted in favor. By the end it was a unanimous decision of sorts. Nico seemed surprisingly pleased with the outcome despite Kinthross's obvious reservations.

"Well, its decided then. Ain't gonna be easy but we got shit to work with. It'll take a lot just to make something worth calling an army out of this lot. But that's exactly what we are good at. We deal with the impossible and come out on top. Guess we just need to do that outside of the Promise," Kinthross said, to cheers from the knights. The Field Knights had faced horror unlike anything else in the world, but Kinthross knew war was a different thing. Only time would tell whether they could succeed, but when the Field Knights set a goal it would take more than the magics of the empire to stop them.

Chapter 23

Kel had left the city a few days ago and Aria was already tired of dealing with the Hydes and their arcanist. The few Field Knights seemed like decent people but most of Aria's time had been spent planning with Alex. Alex Hyde was more tolerable than his sister, but Aria distrusted him more. Highly analytical and soft spoken the man seemed to play a much larger game than his sister. His methods were straightforward but still reeked of manipulation. The arcanist Velen seemed like a strange case. It was hard to hate the man. He seemed entirely genuine, though often incoherent. It was Velen's near obsession with Aria and her abilities that annoyed her most. Even if it was simple curiosity, she disproved of the scrutiny.

"So, what do you see now?" Velen asked. He had been casting variations of the same cantrip for the last hour.

Aria had obliged to the tests while she waited for Alexandra to return with the knights.

"You delayed some part. I can see the gap, but I have no idea why that matters. I don't need to know what's coming to know I need to destroy it. There is not time to be considering the intricacies of someone's magic in the heat of battle," Aria answered. She had begun pacing the study, only glancing over at the arcanist when he asked questions.

"Fascinating, and there is no strain from continuous use. Perhaps its a by-product of the sheer quantity of magic your source contains. That would explain the near constant activation, but how you survived long enough to develop any kind of tolerance should be impossible," Velen said, scribbling down more notes. He cast again but before he could ask anything Aria interrupted. She cut the spell from the man's hand with a swift cut from the draw. She did not hit him, but he nearly fell out of the chair as he shifted his weight back.

"Enough. You said, you could help me fight. I don't need anyone digging into my life story. So, unless you can explain how I'm supposed to use this in battle we are done here," Aria shouted.

"Oh, umm… I thought it might… Well, perhaps its not directly applicable, but without a comprehensive understanding I can't evaluate the limits of your magic," Velen stammered.

Aria glared at him, but she had been unable to get the man to refer to her abilities in another way. Despite many threats and not a few direct attacks Velen seemed attached to his specific terminology. The only reason she had not already killed the irritating mage was that the knights seemed fond of him.

"Keep away from my past and maybe we can try this again later," Aria said, scowling.

Velen seemed more disappointed than scared as he listened.

"The foundations would be important without a comprehensive…" Velen said, trailing off as Aria pressed her sword closer.

After that Velen quietly went back to looking through his notes and the several books he had laid out around his chair.

Aria sheathed her sword and resumed her pacing. It would not be long before Velen began asking questions again. Aria hoped that the others would return before he did. As it happened Alexandra, Zed, and Brandish entered the study a few minutes later. Alexandra was dressed for a party as always while Zed and Brandish wore limited leather armor and carried their weapons openly.

"Seem on edge. Can't say I blame you but it's been getting crazy out there," Brandish said.

"I don't appreciate being stuck in here all day," Aria replied. She understood the basic plan. Until Kel got back with the rest of the troops they needed to keep tensions down in the city. That meant Aria couldn't keep starting conflicts even if she could do considerable damage on her own.

"Trust me, the Magebreaker is still the talk of the town. Love to have you out there, but it would be hard to keep that a secret," Zed said.

"Just another few days, Aria. Once the stage is set it'll be time to give the city a symbol to rally around. I expect you'll find yourself wishing for a break once things really get going," Alexandra chimed in.

"Not trying to play hero. I just want my chance at those bastards," Aria replied.

"None of us are. But people need a hero and the mysterious knight charging headfirst into the full might of the empire is a perfect symbol. A bullet to the head or a knife in the back gets the job done but it doesn't have the same panache," Alexandra said, as she wandered over to where Velen was scribbling away.

"Any big conflicts?" Aria asked, ignoring Alexandra. Even if she wanted to help the resistance, she wanted no part of the Lady Hyde's plans.

"Been putting out fires all over the place. Mostly just talking people down fore they do something stupid but there 'ave been a few dustups," Brandish replied resting his head against the bookcase he had slumped against.

"Pain in my ass. Alexandra has the right of it. It's too early to play all our cards, which means I have to hold fire unless it's absolutely necessary," Zed added.

"Oh, quit whining. I'm the one whose had to get his hands dirty," Brandish retorted. Both the knights were competent fighters. Aria had only sparred with Brandish as there was not safe way to train against a rifle. Brandish had managed to score more than a few points on her. The advantage conferred by the reach and unpredictability of his unique fighting style made him incredibly dangerous.

"Lady Hyde, I have news," Eris said, entering the study. The Hydes' servant was a common sight around the manse and Aria had grown to like the young woman. She was capable and unafraid to speak her mind, even to her employers. Aria found her sharp wit amusing, especially when it was directed toward the lord and lady.

"I was hoping for an easy afternoon but there is no rest for the weary," Alexandra replied.

"Perhaps if you weren't still hosting parties it would be easier. But I think that will be easier after today. It seems like there is a rather irate crowd gathering just outside of the noble quarter. I'm honestly surprised it took this long. People rarely draw a distinction between members of the nobility and with the increase in tensions, well, we may have rioters at our doors in short order," Eris explained.

"This could be tricky. I can't be seen acting openly this close to home. I would make the next phase considerably more difficult. Brandish, Zed, do you think you can handle this on your own?" Alexandra replied.

"Depends on how big the crowd is already. If they're turning on the noble quarter then the response will be extreme," Zed said.

"Unknown at the moment. But from the reports I have at least a few hundred people," Eris said.

"Shite, this'll get messy. Be a damn good time for that bastard to show up," Brandish said. Drake had been missing since Dennet's arrest but even when they searched the remains of the hall they could not find him. None of the knights seemed overly concerned about his disappearance, which Aria found odd for such a tight knit group. Velen had nearly cried when the scouting party had returned without the wagon of oddities pulled from the promise. Some of those items might have been useful but with the city on lockdown it was to much of a risk.

"I can go. If the response is as big as Zed expects then it'll be a massacre," Aria said, glaring at Alexandra defiantly.

Alexandra seemed unconvinced but did not immediately reject the suggestion.

"Holding our cards ain't worth shite if the game's over before we can play 'em. Think Aria's got a point. We'll need her to keep those bastards off our backs while we get everyone out," Brandish said.

"Unfortunately, you're correct. Keep the destruction to a minimum. I plan to take Velen to visit the local nobility over the next few days and they will be rather less receptive if their houses are burned to the ground," Alexandra said with a nonchalant wave of agreement.

Velen looked up worriedly at the mention of his name. "What am I going to be doing?" he asked. He had been uninterested in the conversation up to this point.

"Don't worry, it won't be too much trouble. Just a few minor lunches and some boring conversations," Alexandra replied a mischievous smile dance across her lips.

"I don't think…" Velen began.

Aria was out the door before he finished speaking. She needed to put on her armor and get out there. Whatever intrigue Alexandra had planned was not her concern.

***

Zed and Brandish were waiting outside when Aria finished donning her plate armor. It was not technically full plate. She had modified or removed some pieces to make it possible to don without assistance. It was still a tedious process, but the protection offered was worth it. She could shrug off most magic, but a blade or rubble still posed a real threat. Her greatsword rested on her shoulder. She expected to need it, and wasting time drawing it off her back would be a problem.

"So much for subtlety then. Though let's keep out of sight till we get there. Best not to blow our base of operations this early," Zed said.

"Just lead the way. We can worry about spooking the nobles when things are under control," Aria shot back.

"We go fast. Ain't enough time to worry about

getting spotted. But if you think we can keep a good pace then I ain't gonna complain 'bout where you lead," Brandish said.

Zed nodded and began running. He led the way through the noble quarter, keeping them close to walls and out of sight as much as possible. The Field Knights were impressive, covering ground at a rapid pace with no sign of fatigue. Aria, with her heavy armor, was slower but not enough to fall behind. Zed called a halt as they reached the edge of the noble quarter. They did not have to waste time looking for the crowd. Shouting from a few blocks over gave them a decent idea where to head next.

"What's the plan?" Zed asked.

"Hit them hard," Aria responded as she began heading toward the shouting.

"Hold up. We ain't trying to start a fight. Zed, take overwatch. Keep the bastards' heads down. I'll deal with getting the crowd to turn their asses around and go home. Aria, once I get them moving we'll need you to cover the retreat. Can't do much if we got fire shooting up our arses," Brandish said.

Aria stopped to glare at him but with her helm in place the effect was more comical than terrifying.

"Why are we gonna let the bastards off the hook when we can bloody their noses?" Aria replied with mild irritation.

"Oh, we'll bloody their noses. Just ain't trying to get a bunch of random people killed in the process. Trust me, you'll get your chance to hit 'em. We just need to keep to the mission," Brandish said. He had a point. As much as she wanted to fight the number of dead in the market had been horrific.

"Fine, take point. I'll cover your ass while you go try to talk them down," Aria said.

Brandish scoffed at her tone but began running.

It took them about a minute to begin seeing the gathered crowd. Once she and Brandish began pushing through the crowd Zed disappeared. Aria tried looking for him, but Brandish gestured for her to focus forward. Aria had not worked as part of a team, but it seemed the two knights trusted each other enough to focus on their individual tasks.

Tensions were high but Brandish was big enough to knock people out of his way and once they got a look at him no one bothered to complain. Aria, with her plate armor and greatsword, was given a wide berth. She could hear murmurs of "Magebreaker" pass through the crowd, but she was focused on the guards arrayed about ten meters from the front of the crowd. Nearly forty guards had formed a line across the street, shining great shields and nasty looking spears backed by a dozen robed nobles' hands crackling with magic. Aria was more concerned with the spear wall than the mages. Whatever magics were in place on the shields wouldn't be a problem, but she would struggle to break the spear wall without help.

Brandish and Aria pushed through the front of the crowd and stood about halfway into the dead man's land between the two groups. Brandish turned toward the crowd while Aria kept her focus on the guards. As Brandish began shouting at the crowd the mages began launching spells at them. Aria was too focused on keeping the knight alive to hear exactly what he was shouting. She spared a brief glance behind her when he had finally stopped talking. The crowd was hesitant, but it seemed to be backing away from the wall of guards. One of the mages got the bright idea to launch a sphere of fire high over her head. She couldn't disrupt the magic and the sphere crashed down into the crowd. The crowd roared, and Brandish cursed behind her. She could see magic coalesced around the same mage as he prepared to fire off another blast. A sharp *crack* rang out and the mage fell. The spear wall began advancing as the mages broke for cover. She could see a few still standing in the open walls of force covering them as they launched more magic at the crowd.

Aria hoped Zed would understand her plan as she charged forward. Her greatsword held in guard, ready to turn the points of the spears she was sure would come. She got within a meter of the shield wall when the guard directly in front of her fell dead. Blood and brains splashed over the glimmering shields of his allies. Aria crushed the man under foot as she blocked the spears. She felt a few glancing blows deflected by her armor as she passed through the line. With Zed providing cover and an entire mob of angry people in front of them none of the guards could risk turning around to face her. She broke through the line and headed straight for the mages still standing in the street.

Most were too focused on their magic to notice Aria closing the gap. One older woman in a gold trim black robe turned to face her. Lightning crackled around the mage's hands. Aria was too far to stop the casting but that did not matter. As the blinding light shot forth Aria braced her feet and skidded for half a second. The bolt struck home and once she could see again Aria continued her charge. The last thing the mage saw was Aria's armor smoking and glowing with heat, shrugging off the attack and bringing the blade of her sword down. Aria turned with the swing, moving toward her next target. She was sweating and the steam was beginning to obstruct her vision. Only the cloth lining of her armor protecting her from the scalding metal.

Aria struck out on instinct as the hazy figure before her turned. She felt the small jolt of energy as her blade cleaved through whatever spell had been cast in her direction. She followed up with a thrust, burying her blade in the mage's chest. She let the blade fall with the man as she carefully removed her helmet. Her short hair was only slightly singed as she pulled the catch free, tossing the helmet aside.

Three mages remained and were advancing on her, their bodies thrumming with enhancement magic. She could see the other mages fleeing further into the nobles quarter. The advancing spear wall had managed to push the crowd back across the street but the crack of rifle fire from the crowd had them cowering behind their shields. She did not have time to think about where Brandish had found enough men with rifles to hold back the guards. Instead of retrieving her greatsword she drew her other blades and waited to meet the mages. Unlike the last enhanced mages, they advanced slowly waiting for an opening to exploit with their incredible speed. Three on one would be possible even against enhanced opponents. Her armor gave her a significant advantage. The heat was finally seeping through the cloth lining and her entire body felt like it was on fire.

She held her guard hoping one of them would make a mistake she could exploit. She did not hear the *crack* of Zed's rifle but one of her opponents fell forward, blood spurting through a hole in their robes.

One of the other turned to launch a flurry of ice blades in the direction of the shot. Aria took the opportunity to charge the third, taking his attack on the side of her torso and wrapping her arm around the blade to lock it in place. The man immediately released the sword and jumped back. His enhanced speed made her follow-up miss by a hair, but it was enough to sever the magic around him. He stumbled as his body tried to adjust to the change in strength and speed. Her next strike cut the man across the chest, and he fell to his knees. She drove her dagger through the man's spine as she ran past.

The last mage had called for a series of walls of ice to block the hail of bullets. With his focus on Zed he did not notice Aria's approach. Her side sword thrust through the back of his neck. As the ice wall faded she could see the guards falling back from the crowd down the road to the right. Some of the crowd moved to follow or to move into the noble quarter.

"Hold, ya shites!" Brandish bellowed.

The crowd halted and the few so lost in the madness of battle to hear the order were stopped by Aria's glare. The sight of her over the body of the fallen mage blood sizzling on her still glowing armor and eyes flaring with purple light was enough to stop even the most battle crazed.

"Enough blood's been spilled. There will be plenty more in the day to come but for now we fall back. Pressing on will only turn a victory into a defeat. Return to your homes knowing that I and others stand with you. Knowing that the nobility will fall. Be ready to answer the city's call," Aria shouted, raising her blade to the sky, its edge shining red in the afternoon light.

When the cheers of "Magebreaker!" faded the

crowd dispersed. Aria moved out of the road to avoid whatever response the guards would have.

Brandish and Zed found her a few minutes later peeling her armor from her singed skin. Zed's rifle was slung over his shoulder, and he had cloth wrapped around his right arm with blood soaking through. Brandish was unharmed, his grappling hook, dripping blood, was wrapped around his chest. He was carrying her greatsword on his shoulder and her dagger was stuck through his belt.

"Not a bad speech. Half thought you'd call them to press on. Think they would follow you if you did," Brandish said.

"That wasn't the mission," Aria replied.

"Good call. I was running low on ammo anyway. We best get back before more guards show up," Zed said wincing as his rifle sling rubbed against his injured arm.

Brandish walked over and offered Aria her blades back. She took them once all the pieces of her armor were piled in front of her. Brandish went to pick up her chest plate and jumped back as he touched it.

"Shite. The 'ell you fighting in that?" Brandish said, pouring water over his singed finger.

"Better than nothing. A few burns won't stop me but a sword to the gut certainly will," Aria said, with a smile.

Brandish poured the rest of his water over the pile of armor before tentatively going to pick it up again.

"Fair enough. Certainly didn't hurt your image none. Put on one 'ell of a show while we got things sorted," Brandish said, as they moved to leave.

"Oh, fuck off, Brandish. Zed covered me while you were off cavorting. You don't have a drop of blood on you and you're claiming you got things sorted," Aria jibed.

Zed laughed as Brandish sulked, unable to come up with a good retort.

They made their way back to the Hydes' manse at a slower pace. Aria was pleased with what they had managed to do. There had been some losses among the crowd, but it would have been much worse had they not intervened. If they could keep people from targeting the noble quarter or any area the guards seemed intent to defend, this battle should keep the guards hesitant to confront the populace. Aria hoped she would have time to let her burns heal before she needed to fight again. It irked her that when she would fight again depended on Alexandra and whatever game she had planned with the nobility.

Chapter 24

It was the third day of their trek and Kel was exhausted. Dets seemed certain they would arrive by midday, which was a relief. Kel knew Dets was accustomed to travel but she set a demanding pace and had taken them on an incredibly difficult route. She had assured him it was to save time but by the end of the second day he was convinced she just wanted to watch him struggle. Dets was already ready to go when Kel finished striking camp.

"If you're really that tired, I'll just scout ahead. Shouldn't be too hard to spot an entire army," Dets said, when Kel shouldered his pack.

"No, we stick together I don't want you running into a picket. It'll be hard enough convincing them we are allies without having to explain at gunpoint," Kel said.

Dets scoffed but did not run ahead. Kel had to admit she could probably find her way into the camp without getting spotted. Even when they were walking close together it was easy to lose track of her.

***

A few hours later, when they stopped to fill their canteens, Dets announced they were less than a kilometer away. Kel took a look at the map and agreed.

If they wanted to approach from the road, they would need to go nearly the same distance out of their way to reach the marked path on the map.

"We should just keep going. You're gonna keel over if we have to go too far out of the way," Dets jibed.

"Not that old just yet. It be better to head for the road less troubling for our new friends," Kel replied. He would prefer to take the shorter route, but it made more sense to approach from the road.

"Suit yourself. If we go this way we can split the difference. I doubt they'll have any pickets that far from camp," Dets said, drawing a line on the map. Kel nodded his agreement, and they headed out.

About ten minutes later Dets signaled Kel to stop. Kel was about to ask what was up when Dets signaled him to be silent. Kel surveyed the area and noticed a small number of broken branches littering the forest floor. Kel nodded as Dets removed her pack and slung her rifle over her shoulder. She silently climbed into the canopy and began moving toward the road. Kel watched her as best he could, moving only when she signaled him.

"I think it's time for you to get down," Dets said, pointing her rifle at another figure in a nearby tree,

"Or what, you're gonna shoot me? I doubt it," a female voice responded.

Kel could barely make out the speaker through the canopy, but he readied his rifle and moved toward the base of the tree they were in.

Dets fired the shot, thudding into the tree inches from the speaker's head. The figure yawned performatively and rose to her feet. From his new position Kel had a better view of the figure. A young woman, perhaps a few years older than Dets. Her long brown hair was tied in a ponytail that draped over a case strapped to her back.

"Next one goes through your eye," Dets said, aggressively. Kel doubted she meant it but hoped the young woman wouldn't know that.

Kel watched the young woman begin running across the branches directly at Dets. He tracked her with his rifle. Whoever she was she was moving fast and with surety through the canopy. Dets might be capable, and she moved silently, but this woman seemed completely unafraid of falling, and though she wasn't silent she made up for it with speed.

Dets held her fire but kept her rifle trained on the young woman. Kel fired a warning shot when the young woman reached the same tree as Dets and reached into her shirt. The young woman stopped and looked at Kel. She slowly drew out a pistol and without pointing it anywhere dangerous dropped it to the forest floor.

"We might be getting off on the wrong foot. I'm Rickart Kel and you've already met Dets. Now, we can all be civilized and you can show us to Dennet's army, or I can shoot you," Kel said.

"Two people getting the drop on me in one day. Kinthross will love that. Guessing you want me to come down too," the young woman replied.

Kinthross nodded, watching her closely in case she was still armed.

Spreading her arms, the young woman dropped forward, her back straight. Kel nearly rushed to catch her, but she caught a branch, swung her legs, and released, landing on the lowest branch. She jumped down from nearly three meters up and landed in a roll. Kel kept his rifle trained on her back.

"Best kick it over here or things might get messy," Kel growled.

"Can't blame me for trying," she responded with a coy smile. She kicked the pistol over to Kel.

Dets descendend at a reckless pace. Not as showy but still faster than Kel had seen her climb before. Dets tried the same jump once she reached the lowest branches rather than lowering herself. She landed with a wince and rose, favoring her right leg slightly. Once Det brought her rifle to bear, Kel reached down to retrieve the pistol.

"Lead the way," Kel ordered.

The young woman shrugged and started walking toward the camp, keeping her hands plainly visible. Dets took the rear as they made their way to the road. Kel hoped she hadn't hurt herself trying to imitate the young woman. Six figures were waiting on the road when they emerged from the trees. Five had rifles trained on them and the sixth, a tall heavily muscled man carrying a harpoon, stood behind them.

"Nico, what you manage to get yourself into?" the man with the harpoon said.

"Nothing to worry about, Boss. Just a mix up with some new friends," Nico replied.

"Think I'll do the speaking for now on. Be a lot more comfortable If my own rifles weren't pointed at me. I'm guessing you're Kinthross," Kel said. The man nodded and gestured for the others to lower their weapons.

"You ain't nobles or the guards so I think we can oblige. Now, if were done pointing guns in the wrong direction, might be we can have a conversation" Kinthross said with a smile. Kel lowered his rifle and Dets did the same.

"We have quite the story to tell. But it's been a long trip, and I could use somewhere to sit and something to drink," Kel said.

"That we can manage. If you got news from Khaldra, love to hear it," Kinthross replied.

Kinthross led the group into camp, walking alongside Kel. Dets followed behind but her ankle clearly pained her, and she was limping. Kel turned to help but Nico got to her first. Nico offered to support her but Dets refused. Kel decided to let Dets keep her pride and turned back toward the camp. He ignored the quiet argument between Dets and Nico as they made their way to camp. It was better than them trying to kill each other.

"She must be quite good. Nico rarely respects anyone unless they prove themselves," Kinthross said with a laugh.

"Seemed more flippant than respectful. But I'll admit Nico can read a situation and she is fast and clever enough that if we didn't get the drop on her she'd be the one leading us to camp," Kel said.

"Impressive, most of the knights couldn't get the drop on her even when they're trying," Kinthross replied.

"Dets takes the credit for that. She might be young but she's the best hunter I've met, and you meet a lot as a gunsmith," Kel said.

"If you're here to help. It'll be good to have someone who knows how to use them. Best marksman we got is still in the city. We been making do, but if Dennet expects us to handle things it'll take more than a few half-trained farm boys," Kinthross said.

Kel waited till they were seated to address the news. Kinthross had dismissed the rifleman, and it was just the four in, what Kel assumed was the command tent, near the parade ground. Dets splinted her ankle while glaring at Nico, who seemed to revel in irritating Dets. Kinthross seemed to be in charge of the army at the moment, which saved Kel the effort of finding the commander.

"Best to get the big details out of the way. Dennet is dead, executed by the new governor. For the moment Lord and Lady Hyde are doing their best to keep tensions down with the help of Field Knights still in Khaldra. I was tasked with leading you all back to Khaldra to put an end to all this before too many innocents get killed," Kel said, keeping his tone neutral and watching Kinthross's and Nico's reactions.

"Can't say I'm surprised. Dennet was always pushing things farther than any sane man. Bet he made the most of it to rile things up. The Field Knights will remember him for what that's worth," Kinthross said running a fist down his arm and opening his hand at the end. Dets mirrored the gesture from where she sat eyes downcast. Kel assumed it was a sign of respect for the dead but he was unfamiliar with the custom.

"You seem to have things under control here. Will a change in command be too much of a disruption? We need to move fast even if your men aren't quite ready," Kel said.

"Job's yours. I'm just here to keep my knights alive. You seem like you got your wits about you. Uless you prove otherwise, we'll follow," Kinthross said.

"Then I'll need a rundown of what I'm working with," Kel said, pulling a notepad from his pack.

"Now you're soundin' like Dennet. Jumping right in without considerin' just how impossible a task it'll be," Kinthross replied. Kel took the comparison as a sign of respect.

Kinthross spent the next hour running through the details of the army camp. They had over a thousand men and women ready for combat but only two hundred had access to rifles. Most of the remaining eight hundred were armed but it was a motley assortment of repurposed tools and old Imperial military arms. The twenty-three Field Knights all armed in a variety of ways and acted as an auxiliary force. Training had been going on for months, but with only a few capable leaders before the arrival of the Field Knights, Kinthross viewed their readiness as extremely lacking.

Dets had left to go survey the camp at some point during the explanation. Kel hoped she wouldn't cause too much trouble. She could be reckless when she felt her pride had been wounded. Nico seemed bored with the business of running the camp and was fidgeting with her pistol throughout the entire conversation. When they began the arduous task of restructuring the army for mobilization a rather tall and wiry man entered the tent.

"Corus, looks like we'll be moving out. Might be good to get your input," Kinthross said, pausing his explanation of the Field Knight's capabilities.

"This is good. Little games can only take people so far. Real battle? Now that shall show their measure. When do we march?" Corus replied, looking to Kinthross.

"Tomorrow. We'll take the long way and stop frequently. I want time to get everyone organized and used to moving in units," Kel answered. Corus looked Kel over skeptically.

"So, a new leader then. I do not know you so why should anyone follow? You do not reek of war, so what do you bring?" Corus said.

"Besides making the majority of the arms we have. I can shoot better than anyone here should the need arise. I know the limits of our weapons and how best to deploy them. Is that sufficient?" Kel replied calmly.

"A gunsmith. Interesting I have only learned of these things recently, but you may shift the face of war. I would see if you are as good as you say. It would prove the truth of your words," Corus replied.

"Might as well. It'll be a good chance to show everyone just what a rifle can really do. Kinthross, how long would it take to gather everyone at the range?" Kel said. He understood the need for people to see their leaders as capable. He could demonstrate his skill while getting his own evaluation of the skill of the army.

"Been workin' on that. Shouldn't take more than ten minutes to muster but I expect more like twenty," Kinthross replied.

"Too long. I will do this thing faster. Be ready, gunsmith, it shall be an important showing," Corus said, then he left.

"Where did Dennet find him?" Kel asked.

"A Krais mercenary. You must be Khaldra born if you've never seen one. The better question is how did he convince the man to fight for such a long-term project?" Kinthross replied.

He would need to borrow a rifle from someone. The old bolt action he had with him was serviceable but not particularly impressive.

Kinthross led the way as they went to the range. It was a makeshift line marked with ropes and colored fabric to warn people off from entering the firing line. Dets found them along the way. She had a strange hunting bird perched on her shoulder. Kinthross had never seen an all-white falcon before, but the bird seemed comfortable around people. Dets seemed to be in a better mood despite her limp.

"Xec, 'ere," Kinthross called. The bird took off and landed on his shoulder.

"I didn't mind. She's a fine bird. Seems a bit attached to pecking at my bracelet but otherwise well behaved," Dets said, a bit disappointed.

"Just don't let her see into your pack. Bit of a thief even if she can hunt 're own food," Kinthross said with a hearty laugh.

"So, what's the plan, Kel? Seems like everyone is gathering," Dets asked.

"Gonna put on a bit of a show. If you're comfortable with your rifle might be good to show them what you can do," Kel replied.

"Bet I can shoot better with this than you can with that," Dets said, with a broad smile.

"I'm planning on using one of the company's rifles. This old piece can go into circulation if it doesn't fall apart," Kel replied.

Dets kept smiling but she seemed a bit more worried. She was good but Kel had been shooting for longer than she had been alive.

It took about fifteen minutes for Corus to get everyone assembled at the range. It was Kel's first chance to survey the army he would be leading. Dennet had been discerning in who he had recruited. They were all young and in good shape. Most seemed to hold their weapons with some familiarity. There was no standard uniform, and they formed up in ragged lines.

Kel was not worried about typical order. They would need to fight dirty if they wanted a chance against real soldiers, even with the advantage of rifles.

"Seems like I need to show you all why I'm the best man for the job. Dets and I could go shot for shot here and maybe some of you would be convinced. But I think a good comparison is in order. So, who's the best marksman here?" Kel began. His voice didn't carry far but the assembled troops were quiet enough that he could be heard.

"Ren, get up here. Boy can't keep up on a march, but he can shoot. Give me some time and he'll be a real soldier. If we don't all die first," Corus said, with a macabre smile.

Ren was a thin young man with sharp eyes. Kel could tell from how he held the rifle that he'd been training longer than a few months. The range might be good enough for practice but Kel needed to put on a show. He placed a card on each of three targets, the thin side facing the firing line. He managed to do it without anyone noticing, which suited him fine.

"Let's see what we are working with. Three shots three targets. Ren, you can start us off," Kel said.

Ren fired three times, aiming carefully from a kneeling position. All three fell on the edges of the inner most circle of the target. Kel was impressed. It wasn't fast but it was accurate. Dets went next. She shot from a standing position in rapid succession each shot landed close enough to dead center if not perfect. Dets smiled at Kel challenging him to do better. Kel walked over to Ren.

"Mind if I borrow this for a second?" Kel said.

"As long as you give it back. I ain't much good without it… sir," Ren replied.

"Don't worry about it you're good enough that I plan on outfitting you properly," Kel said. He took Ren's rifle it was one of the later ones he had made after Nadia has perfected their mass production method. It was good much, better than his current piece but if he remembered correctly the trigger pull was heavier than he was used to. He turned to look at the crowd gave a slight bow before turning on his heel. He fired three times in quick succesion. He changed positions between each shot standing to kneeling then back to standing. When he finished, he returned the rifle to Ren. The crowd seemed confused they were watching the center of the targets, and each shot had missed the mark entirely.

"Showoff," Dets said, cursing. She ran down range and pulled the three cards from the targets and held them up to the crowd. Each card was cut in half with a single shot. The assembled troops cheered as they realized.

"Impressive. If we all can shoot like this than victory shall be an easy thing. But you are far too quiet it will be hard to hear you over the field of battle," Corus said, while Kel waited for the cheers to die down.

"That's what officers are for. Now shut them up so I can finish addressing them," Kel replied.

"Is good you understand this. We will work well together gunsmith," Corus said. He shouted the crowd down so Kel could speak.

"We are undertrained and under equipped. But anyone who know the history of Khaldra knows how little that matters. Our city was built by men and woman like you who did not understand the challenges they would face. Those challenges were overcome not with magic but with force of will and inspiration. The weapons you wield were made in response to one impossible task, now we shall turn them to another. I cannot promise victory, but I can promise we will show the nobles just what Khaldrans can do. Tomorrow we march not as some nameless band but as the First Khaldaran!" Kel shouted. Kel smiled raising his rifle as shouts of "First Khaldaran!" rang through the crowd.

Chapter 25

Velen had spent the last few days starting a new project. Lord Hyde had requested he construct a Sa-ren map. It was a difficult project in numerous ways, but Velen found the complexity of the magic involved interesting. His workbench was filled with numerous samples collected from throughout the city. Each was meticulously labeled with its origins. The Field Knights had been incredibly useful in obtaining samples and the current impediment was the intricate repeated spell casting. On his own it would take him months to finish but with Lord and Lady Hyde's aid he hoped to finish in less than a month.

"Velen, do you have time to speak?" Lord Hyde asked from the doorway.

"Oh, um… Give me one second. I need to… Well, now I've lost it. What is it you need?" Velen said. He had been placing another sample, but the interruption had broken his concentration, and he would need to re-cast the spell.

"Seems like you're making progress. If this works as you suggest it will be incredibly useful. But I wished to speak about the Magebreaker. She had proven a boon to our cause, but I wonder…" Alex said.

"Wonder what?" Velen asked.

"Who she was? How she gained her power? Perhaps I'm worrying for nothing, but it seems an odd coincidence that someone with just the skills we need would travel so far at exactly the right time," Alex replied.

"I have some theories, but Aria is rather touchy about her past. I can only say with certainty that she was raised around mages. A person's source grows somewhat as they come of age but not substantially. It would defy all known theories for a child to survive with that much power without some form of intervention. As for her motivations she is quite clear that she wants to kill as much of the nobility as she can. You and your sister excluded, for now," Velen explained. He was extremely interested in the Magebreaker but if he could understand her magic without knowing her history that would suit him.

"I had hoped for more, but we must work with what we have. As long as she is on our side then she can keep her secrets. I believe you were supposed to be getting dressed," Alex said.

"I am dressed," Velen said, checking to make sure he had not forgotten to put on clothes.

"True, but you are to accompany Alexandra as she speaks with the local nobility. She would have a fit if you went dressed like that," Alex said, with a sly smile.

"Wait, what? I have work to do here. Why would Alexandra want me along?" Velen asked, confused.

"Alexandra was vague on her reasons, but she assured me it was necessary. If you need better attire I will have Eris bring something. As you will be acting as one of our representatives you will need to wear your crest," Alex said.

"If I must. It might be inappropriate for me to wear the Velen crest. There are some issues between myself and the house," Velen said. He felt bad not explaining but such issues were rather sensitive, and he would prefer not to dredge up that part of his past.

"This is Khaldra, all the local nobility are from small houses or have similar issues. No one will look twice at another outcast. That alone is the main reason we have a chance to get some of the nobility to stand aside in this conflict," Alex said.

"I don't think this is a good idea. Anyone else would be better suited," Velen said, Pacing around and looking at anything other than Alex. His previous interactions with other nobility had been rather distressing and he had hoped to avoid it by coming to Khaldra.

"I'll send Eris with some proper clothes. Find your crest while you wait. Leave worrying about dealing with the nobility to Alexandra. Whatever she had planned I'm sure she's aware of your reservations," Alex replied. He left, closing the door behind him before Velen could protest further.

Velen had to dig through his bags several times before he found his family crest. The silver pin bore a complex magic sigil with small hourglasses at the four corners. It has been years since he had worn it, but he still found its intricate design intriguing. He had tried to decipher it when he was younger, but it had proven to be an artistic choice. He had been rather disappointed to learn that it was not a functional representation.

"Does he think I'm a miracle worker? Look at what I have to work with," Eris said from the door a few minutes after Velen had located the crest.

"I don't see what the problem is," Velen said.

Eris strode in and handed Velen a fine suit. "Put that on and we'll see what I can do about that mop on your head," she said.

"Mop?" Velen said, running his fingers through his hair to check nothing was on his head.

Eris rolled her eyes and went to wait in the hall.

It took Velen some time to dress. He found the suit tight and uncomfortable. He much preferred his traveling clothes, or better yet his lab clothes. Once he had figured out where all the buttons went, he pinned the crest on his chest. He told Eris he was done and she returned with a comb and scissors. After she adjusted his suit for a few minutes she began working on his hair. He sat quietly while she worked. The process took nearly thirty minutes and left the floor of his workshop a mess.

Eris stepped back to survey her work.

"It'll have to do. If Alexandra wants anything else done she can deal with it herself," Eris said, then she turned to leave.

"When will we be leaving?" Velen asked.

"Soon, I would think. Alexandra has quite the schedule planned," Eris said, and she closed the door.

Velen began cleaning up the floor while he waited. He saved some of the hair in one of his jars. It might be useful later and it seemed a waste to just throw it out. Most mages could control constructs without such a direct link, but Velen found it improved responsiveness substantially. Once he was done he began to worry about what exactly Alexandra had planned. Luckily, she entered shortly after he had finished.

"I'm really not paying her enough. If we could do something about the sulking you'd pass as a proper noble," Alexandra said, as she inspected Velen.

"What exactly are we doing? Your brother would be a far better choice to deal with the nobility," Velen said.

"It's not so much what we will be doing. I'll be doing my best to convince people, while you will be looking out for any surveillance magic. It would be improper for me or my brother to be delving into other peoples' spellcraft, but an arcanist… well, it's almost expected. You lot are nosy and obsessive," Alexandra explained with a smile.

"I'm not really nosy. Honestly, people are far less interesting than magic.".

"Maybe, maybe not. It's how people see you. So, we'll give them exactly what they expect. It really is an elegant lie," Alexandra said.

"What are we lying about?" Velen asked. He hated lying, mostly because he couldn't do it convincingly and never understood why people bothered.

"Again with the we. I'll be lying, you will simply be telling me exactly what you see. Subtly, of course. It would be rude to just blurt out in civil conversation," Alexandra said.

Velen didn't really understand but he nodded along. If he didn't need to say much, this trip would be a lot easier. Watching out for magical surveillance was a simple task and he was interested in the kinds of magic the nobility of Khaldra employed in their homes. The Hydes seemed far less inclined to use magic in their daily lives than most mages he had met.

They took the Hydes' carriage, which seemed a waste considering they stopped less than five minutes after entering. Velen stumbled a bit as he exited though Eris's adjustments had made the suit more tolerable, the tight clothes and new shoes were uncomfortable to move in. Alexandra practically glided out of the carriage despite the rather precarious heels she was wearing.

"Shouldn't be more than an hour. So, no need to untie the horses," Alexandra said to the driver.

Velen cast mage sight as they approached the manse. Nothing seemed particularly amiss just a simple series of enchantments against fire and a simple alarm spell. Velen shook his head when Alexandra looked his way. She smiled and walked up to the ornate double doors. She rapped on the door once and waited until an older man in servant's clothes opened the door.

"Alexandra Hyde and Lord Velen to see Lord Rylan," Alexandra said.

The old man nodded and gestured for them to enter. They were led to an opulent study and the servant left with a deep bow. Velen began perusing the books to see if Lord Rylan had anything worthwhile.

"Sit down. We are here on business," Alexandra said.

Velen found a seat where he was comfortable and cast mage sight again. Before he could get a look around Lord Rylan entered.

"And what business would that be?" Lord Rylan asked.

"Nothing of import. Lord Velen is an arcanist who has recently come to Khaldra. It would be in poor taste if I did not introduce him," Alexandra replied.

"The last person you introduced me to turned out to be a traitor. Forgive me if I'm somewhat wary. These are trying times," Lord Rylan said.

All the magic in place was more of the same, though one of the books seemed to be heavily enchanted. From what Velen could tell it was an obscuring enchantment making the text completely unreadable unless it was dispelled. Velen wasn't sure how Alexandra wanted him to tell her that he saw nothing amiss. She was too focused on Lord Rylan to notice any subtle signs. Velen preferred to remain silent, so he did. If Alexandra wanted him to say anything she would ask.

"A rather unfortunate mishap. But I find recent events far more concerning. Riots all over and what is the new governor doing? Nothing. Just sending guards completely incapable of resolving anything without violence," Alexandra said.

"How else would you expect them to deal with traitors?" Lord Rylan asked.

"Oh, that's far beyond me. It just seems like such a waste. So many dead and it's only served to fan the flames. It seems as more nobility get involved the problem only gets worse. My brother is concerned for his interests in the city. I know you have considerable interests as well, so perhaps we can align ourselves to better protect them," Alexandra replied.

"You're not wrong, but what can we do except support Lord Kelen? With the nobility united, order will be restored quickly. I hope," Lord Rylan said, looking away.

"Unity is certainly needed but perhaps it should be a more passive unity. Lord Kelen is backed by the Great Houses. We have no such luxury. If we simply stand back and let him deal with things, what have we to lose? If we throw our weight behind him we may lose what little support we have with the local merchants. It seems doing nothing would be the best course of action," Alexandra said.

Velen had lost track of the conversation but that

was fine. He was simply there to inform Alexandra of any magics at play.

"A dangerous prospect should Lord Kelen demand action," Lord Rylan retorted.

"Not nearly as dangerous as you might think. The Great Houses expect competence and if Lord Kelen needs us to solve such a simple problem he would lose favor quickly. We can simply wait it out and make some token apologies once it is all over," Alexandra said.

"Perhaps you're right. My house had little to add to the strength already at the governor's disposal. I expect it would be easier to make excuses than send my people to their deaths," Lord Rylan replied.

"Then we are in agreement. Lord Velen, you have been awfully quiet. Is something amiss? I understand such trivial matters are of little concern to an arcanist, but we are here to introduce you," Alexandra said.

"Oh no, it's nothing. I was just admiring Lord Rylan's collection. *To Call the Dawn* is Telom Solaris's seminal work. An almost poetic approach to chants and incantations. A few others are interesting, but that is by far the best among those I can make out from here," Velen said. He was more interested in the obscured text, but Alexandra had warned him about exposing peoples' secrets.

"It was a gift. I haven't had time to read it, but if you are recommending it then I will find the time," Lord Rylan replied . He seemed eager to move off the topic of recent events.

The conversation continued on mundane things for another few minutes. Velen did his best to comment but Alexandra took over the conversation. They parted with pleasantries and an invitation for Velen to look over more of Lord Rylan's collection.

The carriage took them to the next location in short order. The conversation at the next several noble residences followed much the same pattern. Alexandra would guide the conversation and occasionally check with Velen that nothing was out of place. All of the nobles seemed to come to the decision to stay out of whatever conflict might erupt. Alexandra paused before they moved to the last noble residence.

"Lord Lanris is going to require a bit more effort. He's a spineless coward. I saved him for last because he's likely to follow the crowd. If Lord Kelen has not gotten his hooks in the man, then this will be tricky if not outright dangerous," Alexandra said.

"Does this effect what you want me to do?" Velen asked. He had been getting more comfortable with the simple task. Some of the nobility had even had interesting variations of spells in place. One he had discovered when using the restroom. The faucet was enchanted to heat the water using ambient magic collected from the property. It was a simple spell but the mechanisms in place to transfer ambient energy were ingenious.

"No, you have been doing a fine job. Though I wonder why you have needed to use the restroom at nearly every house we have visited. I simply wanted to make you aware that of all the locations we have visited this is the most likely to have hostile surveillance," Alexandra replied.

"Oh, I was just interested in some of the systems in place, Lord—" Velen began.

"I don't need to know all the details. Just be ready. Actually, here return this to me if you notice something amiss," Alexandra interrupted. She handed him a small silver flask engraved with the crest of House Hyde.

Velen was confused where she had kept it before or where she expected to keep it if he needed to return it. Her dress did not have pockets or anywhere it might fit.

"I can do that," Velen replied.

Alexandra rapped on the wall of the carriage signaling the driver to begin the journey, which was considerably longer this time. It seemed they were going to the very outskirts of the noble quarter.

Lord Lanris's estate was massive. Several times larger than the Hydes' and completely fenced in. Alexandra seemed bored as they made their way down the drive despite the various sculptures and water features that caught Velen's attention.

"Don't gawk. It's all a show. Lord Lanris tries to compensate for his lack of status with displays of opulence. His house is nearly bankrupt attempting to maintain just this property," Alexandra chided.

Once they arrived at the main house Velen surveyed it with mage sight as soon as he exited the carriage. The house had a distinct lack of spell work. Nothing protecting it from fire or other damage. Some of the water features and the plants were enchanted to preserve their appearance. Nothing was amiss so Velen shook his head, and Alexandra went to the door. A middle-aged man with a full beard, neatly trimmed, wearing a fine suit answered the door.

"Lord Lanris, your estate is looking wonderful. I nearly had to drag Lord Velen away from the window when we arrived," Alexandra said.

"Lady Hyde, what business do you have with me, and who is this Lord Velen?" Lanris replied curtly.

Velen looked up to meet eyes with Lord Lanris and quickly looked away. Mage sight had some visual indicators when it was employed, and he did not want to have to answer questions already.

"Lord Velen is an arcanist of the Shin-Rhi Arcanum. He is new to the city and needs help introducing himself to civilized society," Alexandra replied.

"I have met most of Lord Kelen's arcanists, why would another be needed? And why would he be traveling in your company?" Lanris asked.

"That is a bit of a story. Perhaps we can enjoy your hospitality while we speak," Alexandra replied, largely ignoring the implied question.

"Very well. Come in," Lanris said.

Lord Lanris led them through the mostly empty house to a extensive if poorly furnished study study. Unlike most of the others Velen had seen there were few books, and the room was generally in poor repair. Dust had built up on empty shelves and the upholstery was fading. Velen took the opportunity while Lanris was looking for glasses to survey the room. There was only one spell present on anything in the room: a small crystal lamp was enchanted not only for light but with a full scrying. With little effort whoever had cast the spell could see everything that happened in the room and even see events that happened in the past. Technically it would only showed events that occurred after the spell was cast. Velen knew some variations that could look farther back but those would require an incredible amount of power.

"So, Lord Velen, what business do you have in this retched city?" Lord Lanris asked. It had been the first time he had been addressed directly in all their conversations. Velen looked to Alexandra for help, but she simply smiled.

"Just assisting the lord and lady in what ways I can. The Promise has always been a region of great interest among arcanists, but few have practical experience in the area," Velen answered. He took a drink from Alexandra's flask to calm his nerves. The liquor inside had a considerable bite.

Velen rarely drank. He preferred to focus on his work, but social situations were irritatingly stressful. Alexandra eyed him skeptically. Velen remembered he was supposed to return the flask if there was a problem he wondered if it would be a problem that he had drank from it first.

"And what exactly are you assisting the good lord and lady with?" Lanris asked.

Alexandra put her hand out as if to ask for the flask. Velen was worried that if he handed it over he would send the wrong signal, but he did need to offer it. Alexandra coughed to get his attention, which knocked him out of his confused state. He handed the flask to Alexandra, who disappeared it with a spell. The flask was on her hip but cloaked by magic.

"Oh, nothing that would interest you. Alex was hoping Velen could assist in keeping the vermin away from our grain and a few other similar projects," Alexandra lied.

Velen winced at the obvious lie, but Lanris seemed to lose interest quickly.

"Is that really all you came to speak about? Introducing a glorified exterminator?" Lanris said

"If this is the hospitality of house Lanris then we shall take our leave," Alexandra replied indignantly.

The conversation deteriorated after that, but Velen lost interest quickly as insults were exchanged. The meeting ended shortly after with Alexandra and

Velen practically fleeing an irate lord. Once they were in the carriage Alexandra signaled the driver and sat down. All her indignation faded and she broke out laughing.

"Well done. I haven't had that much fun since all this began. I wish I could have fully told the bastard what I thought of his house, but I still need to pretend," Alexandra said.

"I don't understand. We did not get Lord Lanris to agree to withhold aid to Lord Kelen," Velen said.

"Doesn't matter it seems that was a lost cause. We did good work today. I deserve a break and another drink," Alexandra replied taking a long drink from her flask.

Chapter 26

The march back to Khaldra had taken six days. With a bit under a thousand men, that was decent timing. Kel had spent less time than he would have liked training the troops, but he would need to make do. Between Corus and the Field Knights they managed to move like a true army. They made camp on the sixth day, approximately three kilometers from the outskirts of the city. Corus wanted to push closer, but Kel overruled him. They were far enough that the risk of discovery was small, and Kel wanted a chance to arrange his forces before they attempted to enter the city. As the sun set he called a meeting to discuss their strategy.

It was a long an arduous process but Kel felt it necessary to their success. They would attempt to make a foothold in the market square. The bulk of the troops would be moving under Corus' direction with the scouts clearing the way. Dets and Nico nearly came to blows arguing over who would be leading the scouts during this operation. Both were eminently capable but Kel would need to intervene if their squabbles threatened the mission. When the meeting closed Kel returned to his tent to find that Jack, the armies quartermaster had somehow fashioned Kel a proper uniform.

The jacket, a subdued mix of grey and black with brass trim was in a standard military cut with a pair of crossed rifles and the words First Khaldaran embroidered where the nobility typically wore their family crests. It was far finer than anything Kel owned and would stand out among the motley attire of the regular soldiers.

***

Kel emerged from his tent into the dim light. The camp was silent and seemed almost empty. The few people moving around were coming off the last watch. It had been a risk to take their best troops off guard duty, but Kel needed them ready. As he walked through the camp, checking to see if any of the other unit leaders were up, Corus joined him. The mercenary slipped in beside Kel without a word. Kel had been skeptical of the man, but Corus had proven a competent leader and the amount of effort he had dedicated to training the men was praiseworthy.

"We move out in two hours. The scouts could use the sun at their backs, and we'll be in the city before the real fighting starts," Kel said.

"You think like a solider, gunsmith. A bit naive but battle will fix that. Plans are good but this is what wins war," Corus said, placing his hand over his heart.

"The hope is that *this* wins the war," Kel replied, patting the rifle slung over his shoulder.

"Yes and no. One does not work without the other. Today we learn if this army has both. That will determine who wins the day," Corus replied.

"We follow the plan and hope for the best. Not exactly the best advice. I know how to organize and plan. But if that's only half of the problem then I have to learn the other half fast."

"You will understand. It is not something to learn, but you will see this. But enough of talking about victory or defeat. It is time to fight," Corus said, with a broad grin.

Orders were given and the camp was struck.

Kel and Kinthross led their units through the woods. Kel would have like to ensure the main force was ready to move but he needed to be on the front so it was left to Corus, Dets, and Nico. Moving fast it took them over an hour to circle the city to where they planned to approach. They crossed the main road far enough from the city that they would not be spotted. Kel called a halt just on the edge of the forest. He allowed them to rest for a time while he surveyed the city.

The number of guards had increased substantially on the outskirts and the patrols he saw were ten strong. He had estimated the garrison at under three hundred based on what he had seen during the execution. Now he needed to revise the estimate if they were covering the majority of the outskirts in this fashion the garrison would need to be double that. His thousand were still likely to outnumber the garrison but without substantially more arms they would struggle against the well-equipped garrison and their access to magic. Kinthross came over while Kel was considering how best to begin.

"Could sit here all day trying to think. In the Promise lots of problems require just jumping in. Seems to me this is one of those," Kinthross said.

"Fair enough. We don't have much time before the scouts move anyway. Take the knights in, make some noise, and get them to come out after you. We'll hit them when they move then follow you in," Kel replied.

"Decoy for the decoy. Not a role any sane man would volunteer for. But we are Field Knights, so nothing new there," Kinthross said, with a smile.

"I'm gonna order my sharpshooters to shoot to wound anyone not in robes. We kill their strongest mages first, but I want them scared. We need to draw as many as we can. So, when they run, let them," Kel said.

"Now that's a brutal plan. Can't say they don't deserve it. Just don't want it becoming how we operate," Kinthross replied.

"Noted," Kel said. He needed to win here. If that meant fighting brutally so be it.

***

Kel got his sharpshooters into position as the Field Knights marched out. It did not take long for the guards to take notice of the armed group approaching the city. Only two groups of guards moved totaling twenty men, two of which were mounted. Kel sighted down his rifle. He estimated the distance to the outskirts to be a bit over one hundred and twenty meters. Once the guards moved to intercept the Field Knights Kel held his right hand up. He held just long enough for the guards to cover twenty meters then he dropped his hand and a wave of thunder exploded around him. Twenty rifles fired in near perfect unison. Kel watched the effect. Half the guards fell instantly. One of the mounted men in robes fell from his horse but rose to his feet shakily. Kel snaped his rifle at the man and fired. A clean shot through the heart dropped him.

The Field Knights moved in to harass the

remaining guards. Of the remaining guards only four stood their ground while the others limped away. Two of the guards were severely wounded and clearly lacked the ability to run. Kel held his unit's fire while the Field Knights dispatched the remaining four guards. It was a quick and clean action, over in less than a minute.

"Sharpshooters, advance," Kel ordered.

Kel advanced with his unit, focusing on sweeping the flanks in case other units emerged to meet the advancing force. The Field Knights had already entered the city before his sharpshooters had crossed the gap. Kel saw signs of fighting up ahead. Flashes of light and shouts of pain emerged from the city. He picked up the pace, and his unit followed suit. It left their flanks exposed but with the Field Knights drawing the majority of the attention Kel was less concerned. Kel gestured for his men to spread out as they entered the city proper. Most took cover in alleys or behind stalls and barrels that lined storefronts. Kel moved down the center of the street keeping his eyes on the Field Knights.

Kinthross had led them as a single unit, pushing a few blocks straight into the city proper. A guard patrol had come to assist but had arrived to late to aid in the initial encounter. Kinthross and his knights were pinned down by a near continuous stream of magic. Lighting and fire set shops alight all around the knights. Ice and wind carved cover to bits, forcing the knights to fall back or into the nearby buildings. Kel watched Kinthross toss one of the knights through a window seconds before a blast of blue flame landed where the knight had stood. Kinthross batted aside a spear of ice as he followed the man through the shattered window. The few knights armed with rifles returned fire halting the guards advance but they were unable to provide a chance for the knights to close the distance.

The knights were pinned down about two hundred meters away, and Kel needed them moving forward. He signaled for his men to break into three groups, two would flank the guard patrol while the third would advance down the center with Kel. The guards began attacking his unit as they drew closer, but it seemed they were just outside the effective range of these mages. Kel knelt down and his men followed suit. A small volley drove the mages to cover, wounding a few.

With the mages in cover Kinthross rose to his feet and charged, Kinthross crashed through the door of the building he had taken cover in. . One foolish mage broke from cover and unleashed a blast of dark energy. The beam tore through one of knights who had joined Kinthross. One of Kel's sharpshooters dropped the mage and once the distance was closed the knights made short work of the guards. Kinthross turned and ordered two knights to move the wounded man into a nearby building. Kel arrived in time to see a family take the man into their home. Kel wondered if it was worth the risk. If they were discovered harboring one of his soldiers it would mean death. Kel did not have time to think it over. He heard a ragged volley fire from his right.

Kinthross turned to Kel questioningly. Kel pointed forward even as he moved down an alley to the right. He hoped Kinthross would understand. The plan was to capture and hole a building just outside the noble quarter. The map did not specify what the building was, but it was suffcient to hold their forces and seemed defensible. It was about two kilometers away and it was critical to make it there quickly. Trying to hold out on the streets was not feasible. If the response was as big as expected it would be a hard-fought operation even if they took the building.

Kel moved down the alley at a sprint. He was tailed by his unit. Seven men was not a lot, but Kel prayed it would be enough. He dived for cover as he entered the side street. Twenty guards were pressing his sharpshooters. Of the seven who had gone to the right three were already dead, vines exploding from their chests. Kel could only see two more. One, a young man named Cro, was wounded and hiding in a storefront. The other was a young woman whose name he could not remember. She was kneeling behind a stall. Both had the guards' full attention. Rounds bounced off a writhing tangle of wood that shielded the guards' advance.

Kel needed to act fast but with his limited forces he needed to break the guards' formation before they could react. Kel signaled to fan out and began a slow advance. The guards were already in range, but Kel needed his men to send off multiple volleys in quick succession. Kel held fire until Cro and the young woman broke. He watched them try to flee down the street, but the vines were faster, piercing them and nearly tearing the woman apart as they writhed.

"Leave none of them alive!" Kel bellowed, rage clouding his vision as he charged forward.

Kel fired until his rifle was empty six shots in under six seconds. His men followed shouts of "First Khaldaran!" barely audible over the thunder of gunfire.

Kel reached the line of guards as they finally realized they were under attack. He was not prepared for melee combat, but he was not thinking clearly. The first man he struck with his rifle was doubled over, blood seeping from a bullet wound in the gut. The man fell dead as the butt of Kel's rifle broke his nose and shattered the skull beneath. Kel looked around for another target but all that remained was the mage who led the guards.

Writhing vines wrapped around the man and began to unfurl, revealing a middle-aged man with blood seeping from a limp right arm. The mage's face was a rictus of pain and fury as he raised his good arm. Vines shot at Kel, who jumped back, raising his empty rifle futilely.

Kel's leg erupted in pain as the thorny vines ensnared him. Kel beat at the vines with his rifle but could not free himself from the encroaching vines. A rifled cracked and the mage's head exploded. The vines withered away as Kel looked around for who had fired. On the roof of a nearby building was Ren, the young man Kel had beaten in the shooting competition days ago. Smoke wafted from Ren's rifle as he waved to Kel.

Kel gave the young man an informal salute as he got to his feet Then reloaded his rifle and gathered what remained of the two units. With the remains of Ren's squad he only had ten men, himself included. One had died in his charge, a spear thrust through the heart from a wounded guard. Kel and two others had minor wounds but could still fight. They moved to the building alternating between sprinting between cover and creeping along alleys. Kel's injured leg slowed him but with help he managed. Ren flashed a mirror at the windows of the building as they approached. It worked, and one of the knights poked their head out and waved them over. The rest of Kel's sharpshooters were stationed in all the windows, and the Field

Knights were holding the doors and sealing those exits on the sides of the building without windows.

"Place is a warehouse. Foreman wasn't too pleased, but I got him to listen," Kinthross said, patting his harpoon. The barbs were dripping blood and pieces of flesh.

"Things get hard from here. We need to hold for as long as possible. Got some wounded that will make breaking out tricky. But that's a problem for later." Kel took a sip from his canteen. It seemed the guards were wary of approaching. Shots were fired sporadically as his sharpshooters tried to catch guards moving between cover.

"Got those mages keeping their heads down. Ain't much we can do if one gets the bright idea to light the place up," Kinthross said.

"Check the roof. Might be some cisterns up there. If we can keep the wood wet it'll take time for them to set ablaze," Kel said. He needed to sit. His ankle was still bleeding and he was sure some of the thorns were still imbedded.

Kinthross ordered two of the knights to check the roof and Kel sent Ren and another sharpshooter with them. Ren had show himself to be capable and from that vantage point the sharpshooters would be a real problem for the guards. Kel did his best to remove the thorns from his leg. It was easier than he expected, as the wood had already started rotting. Cleaning it out would have to wait. Kinthross noted Kel's limp as he made his way to a shooting position.

"Need you giving orders, not waiting to get killed. Let your men do their jobs while ya keep an eye on everything," Kinthross said, and he grabbed Kel's shoulder. The Field Knight commander was strong, and Kel was stopped in his tracks.

"Need all the guns we have on the line," Kel protested.

"Melus, you can shoot, right?" Kinthross said.

One of the Field Knights turned and nodded.

"Then take this and get on the line." Kinthross continued pulling Kel's rifle from him as easily as if Kel had handed it over. Melus took the rifle and moved to the shooting position Kel had planned to take.

"Fine. Then help me get to the roof. I need a clear picture of what we're facing," Kel said.

Kinthross helped him up the stairs and waited at the bottom of the ladder to the roof as Kel climbed up. When Kel reached the roof he saw the knights standing ready to break the cisterns if they saw a hint of fire. His sharpshooters were prone on the edge of the roof, surveying the streets. Kel kept low as he made his way to the roof's edge. Kel could see a few hundred guards scurrying around the streets. Some of the mages stood watching but any shots directed at them were stopped and Kel's sharpshooters only fired sporadically to keep them on the defensive.

The stalemate held for what seemed like an eternity, but Kel's forces only had so much ammo. If they kept firing at the current rate they would run out before long. Kel watched the sun, which had only made it halfway to its zenith. They still needed to hold for another hour at least. Two would be preferable. Their ammo wouldn't last that long, so Kel needed a new plan. Kel descended from the roof to find Kinthross. It was a hard to do with his ankle starting to swell but he made it without falling. Kinthross was giving water out to the soldiers holding the line.

"We need to shake things up. We will run out of ammo before we have bought enough time," Kel said.

"They got us locked down tight. Not sure we got much choice," Kinthross replied.

"I've got an idea. But it'll require us to take a big risk," Kel said.

"Whole thing's been a risk. Ain't sure we can push our luck any further," Kinthross replied.

Kel smiled and held up his satchel. The plan was simple. They would slow their rate of fire and make it seem like they were out of ammo. Kel would set the traps Nadia had made on the doors. They would hit whatever probe the guards sent hard enough to send a message and hopefully it would buy them the time they needed. Kinthross wasn't happy about it, but he agreed eventually.

***

Twenty minutes later Kel had the traps set and all but two of his sharpshooters had been pulled from the line. Kinthross had the Field Knights sealing the windows though they received probing attacks from the mages while they worked. Kel had set the trip lines just past where the doors would swing if they were broken down. Once the building was sealed as best they could everyone waited for the attack they knew would come. The guards obliged and in short order both doors Kel had trapped were broken in and nearly a hundred guards began to poor in. The ones at the front were moving faster than Kel though possible but they were not faster than Nadia's traps. They made it less than a meter into the building before two massive explosions shook the entire place. Kel was nearly deafened by the blast, but all the damage went forward. Two gaping holes remained where the doors had been and at least fifteen guards were dead outright. Many others had been wounded as thousands of tiny steel balls erupted from the traps. The wounded died as Kel's sharpshooters fired volley after volley into the assembled guards. The guards retreated when their momentum was shattered by the First Khaldaran counter blow. The Field Knights moved to fill the gaps in the building once the firing had stopped.

Kel had expended almost all of their remaining ammo, but he had bought them time. By the time the sun reached its zenith no further attacks came but the guards had reformed their perimeter and doubled their numbers at least. Kel had bought the time but now he needed a way out. Even if they fell here if the rest of the army accomplished their goal he would call it a win. Despite his injury Kel began pacing as he tried to find a way out that did not involve all of them dying.

"Got any more of those?" Kinthross asked as Kel limped past.

"No, I have a few other things in my bag of tricks, but I doubt it'll be enough," Kel replied trying and failing to hide the fear that crept into his voice..

"Ain't a good place to die. Think I'd rather go out with the sun on my back. What say y'all?" Kinthross shouted. All the Field Knights and even some of Kel's sharpshooters cheered in response.

I guess this is what Corus meant, Kel thought.

"Think you can break through" We can keep them off your back but only for a bit," Kel said.

"Oh, we'll break through. Get the wounded paired with my knights. You'll stick with me," Kinthross replied with a dark smile.

Kel handed two of Nadia's devices to Ren with a

quick explanation on their use. He kept two for himself. Once everyone was ready Kinthross and Kel moved to the back doors. Kinthross had the planks removed, already anticipating the plan. Kel tried to think of something to say before they made their last desperate move. Nothing came to mind but as he looked around at his men it seemed nothing needed to be said. The best of the First Khaldaran charged forward into the blinding light of the noon sun.

Chapter 27

Dets waited in one of the back rooms of the massive tent at the heart of the market. She was tired. The scouts had moved in when the guards began pulling back from their posts. Her side of the operations had gone almost flawlessly. They only encountered one patrol as they moved to clear the route to the market. Nico had led the more bloody-minded scouts in an ambush that removed the patrol without the need to fire a single shot. Dets had never seen Nico practice with the oddly curved knife, but it was clear she new exactly how to use it.

Once the route was clear Corus had marched the bulk of the army into the market without any issues. The response from the guards had been exactly what Kel had planned for. The sheer number of guards Dets had watch move into the city was far more than they had anticipated and that was what worried Dets.

"Still sulking? They aren't even late yet. Boss will get everyone out. Been in worse shit than this a hundred times before," Nico said as she entered the room.

"This isn't a game," Dets snapped. "We got off easy because Kel managed to draw the entire city guard down on his head."

"Give it time. Not like we can do anything," Nico replied.

"Promises, Nico your friends could be dead and you're just going on like it's nothing!" Dets shouted. She respected Nico's skill but her attitude was infuriating.

"Field Knights aren't friends. We move forward and remember, and that's all you can expect when any day could be your last," Nico said her face impassive. Dets could hear the pain in the other girl's voice but it did not match her expression. If that was what being a Field Knight meant, then Dets could understand why Nico seemed so flippant in the face of everything.

"Maybe that works for you, but I can't accept it. If you're not gonna help me figure out what to do then just go," Dets replied exasperated. She glared at Nico hoping to see some sign of sympathy.

Nico shrugged and turned to leave, but Dets noticed that she hesitated for a second, just as the flap closed. Dets wondered just how much Nico believed what she had said. It seemed like an impossible way to live your life, keeping everyone you knew at a distance because death lay around every corner. In a way that was the world Dets had chosen to enter when she joined Kel in this war.

Dets sat, disassembling her rifle and cleaning it meticulously, while she tried to calm her nerves. Nico was right that there was nothing they could do. If they moved too fast they would waste the chance Kel had bought them. She was so lost in thought she missed when Corus entered. She had just finished reassembling her rifle when she noticed the mercenary sitting across from her.

"You are Kenar now. Act like one," Corus said.

"Kenar?" Dets asked, glaring at the mercenary.

"Kenar is… hard to explain. Maybe you know what Sharas is. Kenar is like Sharas but smaller. Not less, but smaller," Corus explained. Sharas was the title given to a leader of a warrior clan in Sera-met.

"Kel is our Sharas, not me," Dets replied.

"Yes and no. We do not fight as one. With many moving parts we need many Sharas. You are Sharas of scouts. You must play the part. This may help you but not them. It is your job to help them, especially when it is hard," Corus said.

"What do you want me to do?" Dets asked. She understood the mercenary at least somewhat. She was so lost in her own thoughts it was hard to figure out what he wanted her to do.

"Go be seen. Speak with your people. Many will be worried like you. We did not fight but everyone knows that others are fighting for us. In time all will fight and if they are not ready they will die. You must help them be ready," Corus replied, standing up and offering his hand to her.

Dets got up on her own and slung her rifle over her shoulder. Corus smiled and gestured toward the door. Dets took a deep breath and walked out into the rest of the tent. The First Khaldaran occupied most of the space with the few disgruntled merchants clustered by the wagon entrance. It had not been too difficult to convince the merchants that hundreds of armed men were not something you could ignore, but damage control was important if they wanted to remain hidden. Zal had been useful in that regard. Dets wondered what the merchant expected to get out of it but that would be Kel's problem if he returned.

Dets looked around to see what the soldiers were

doing. Some were simply resting, others seemed to be pacing around and occasionally glancing at the entrances. Dets was surprised to find Nico playing her violin to a growing crowd of soldiers. Dets could not understand how Nico could simply ignore what was happening and play music. As she looked over the crowd of soldiers she realized Nico was doing exactly what Corus had told her to do. Nico was present, showing the men that everything was fine. Taking away their anxiety—at least for the moment. Whether it was true or not did not matter, the effect it had was real.

Dets could not play like Nico, and she had spent most of her time in the woods not speaking with people. She understood what she needed to do but she doubted her ability to do it. All she could do was try. She went over to a group of soldiers who were sitting around looking bored. When they noticed her approach, a few gave an informal salute but remained seated.

"Jack is still getting the supplies sorted but is their anything you need?" Dets asked.

The soldiers looked at each other, confused.

"Ain't much we need. Just waiting for something to happen, ma'am," an older man replied.

"I could find work for you, but we did our part. Now we get a chance to rest before the real trouble starts," Dets said, as convincingly as she could manage.

"Aye that we did. Just doesn't seem right. Can't shake the feeling that we got off easy," the man replied.

"Just because we executed the plan doesn't mean the work's done. When Kel and the others get back the real work starts. I expect you all to be ready when that happens," Dets replied. She had her own doubts about whether Kel would return but she needed to present it as a certainty.

"We'll be ready, ma'am," the man said, and the others nodded in agreement.

***

Hours passed as Dets repeated variations of the same conversation. It felt good to get to know the people working with her and it seemed to help even if she couldn't solve their problems. Her presence bolstered the soldiers in a way she had not expected. She noticed Corus watching her, a smile on his scarred face, as she moved between groups of soldiers. She had managed to speak with most of the troops by the time members of the decoy force began filtering in. It was mostly Field Knights arriving in ones and twos, but Dets was able to get some picture of what had happened.

None knew the fate of the others as they had separated to give everyone the best chance to move unseen. What interested Dets most was the story of how Kinthross and Kel had led the breakout. The reports were various and often hyperbolic but there were a few consistent threads. The guards had completely encircled the troops, and it had taken Kel's and Kinthross's units working together to break out. It seemed Kel had used some kind of weapon to break the guards' lines. From the description Dets recognized it as one of Nadia's devices. Kinthross had followed up, charging straight into the enemy lines and holding the gap. Stories varied from there with some saying the two commanders had fought to keep the breach open until everyone had escaped and others saying that they had drawn the enemy away from the escaping troops. No one could confirm if either had survived the battle.

Over the next two hours Dets grew more

concerned. Most of the troops had returned, some injured, but there was no sign of Kel or Kinthross. At some point Nico had stopped playing and joined Dets in questioning the arrivals on the state of the operation. From what they could gather of the forty-three soldiers who had been part of the decoy force thirty had returned so far. Eight were reported killed in action and five were missing in action including Kel and Kinthross. In every way the operation had been a success. They had accomplished the goal and suffered only minor losses compared to what they reportedly inflicted, but if they lost the majority of their leadership in a single action the chaos that would ensue would destroy any chance of success.

"We'll need to move out when night falls. We need to know if anyone was captured," Dets said when they had finished speaking with the last arrivals.

"Giving orders already? Looks like you're learning fast," Nico replied with only a hint of sarcasm.

"Someone needs to do it, and I don't see anyone else stepping up," Dets retorted.

"It's a good plan. Boss would say the same thing. One change, though. We only take three of the scouts with us. We'll cover less ground but there's a lot less chance of us getting caught," Nico said.

"Now what would I be sayin'? Kinthross said from somewhere behind them.

Dets and Nico both turned to stare.

Kinthross and Kel stood at the entrance to the tent. Kel was being helped by a Field Knight Dets did not recognize. The burly man had a grappling hook wrapped around his chest. The man's clothes were clean, unlike all the returning troops had been. Dets ran over to check on Kel. He seemed tired and his right ankle was swelling and covered in blood.

"Sorry for the delay. We needed to make contact with our allies in the city," Kel said, wincing as Dets hugged him.

"Promises, Kel you look like death," Dets said when she finally let go.

"Feel like it too. But the day isn't over yet. Still need to get everything organized here and get a feel for the city," Kel replied with a small smile.

Once they moved away from the entrance two more people arrived. Aria and a man carrying a rifle. Aria was not in armor and Dets could see patches of red skin all over her exposed skin. Nico walked over as the other two entered and eyed Aria suspiciously. Dets was curious about the two men but assumed they were the Field Knights who had remained in Khaldra.

"Brandish, Zed, how have things been in the city? Looks like Dennet left us in the shit. Figures he would pull some stunt and leave us to clean up the mess," Nico said, addressing the two men. Dets watched their reactions and guessed which was Brandish and which was Zed.

"Got it in one. Been a whole world of shite but Aria here's been helping out," Brandish said.

"There will be time for everyone to catch up. For now, I need to sit down and get something to eat," Kel interrupted.

Dets led everyone to the back portion of the tent, and they set up enough chairs around the table for everyone to sit. While Kel was explaining the events of the day Corus joined the impromptu meeting. The mercenary entered quietly with his own chair. He dropped the chair when he saw Aria sitting at the table.

"Aria, is good to see you. Is surprising, but good. What brings you to this place?" Corus said. Dets had never heard the mercenary sound surprised but his shock was clear.

"I could ask you the same. Last time I saw you we were fighting off bandits while trying not to freeze to death in that Promises damned place you call home," Aria replied.

"A man must eat and that requires money. Where there is war there is money, so I find myself wherever there is war. But this is not your way so is odd to find you here," Corus replied, righting his chair and bringing it to the table.

"I was just passing through trying to get away from the fighting, but I found a chance to fight the right people. So, here I am," Aria said. Dets found the answer cryptic but as long as Aria was on their side it did not really matter.

"Sorry to cut the reunion short but we have business to discuss. It's been a long day and I for one need to sleep," Kel interrupted.

"Actually, Nico and I were planning to scout things out when it gets dark," Dets said.

"Both are good ideas. The day has been won and those who fought need to rest. But the war goes on," Corus said with a laugh.

"Ain't a bad plan. If ya think your scouts are up to it," Kinthross said.

"We'll get the job done, Boss. It'll be easier now that we don't have to hunt you two down," Nico replied.

"If you're going to head out it would be good to check in on Nadia. Those devices she made saved our asses back there and I want more. Might be able to convince some of the other gunsmiths to send arms while you're over there, too," Kel said.

The meeting continued for another two hours. With Kel and Kinthross present they were able to confirm the casualty figures. It seemed none of those missing in action were still alive and they had managed to bring all the wounded to the market during the retreat. Kel laid out the beginnings of a plan. Over the next few days the scouts would evaluate where in the city the guards were operating. Once they had a decent understanding of the enemy's disposition they could begin operations. Kel grew more tried throughout the meeting, but he managed to make it through without passing out. Once the meeting closed Dets and Nico went to go get the scouts they planned to take. It was an easy choice: Taran, Relt, and Kevin were the three most capable of the scouts. They were all Khaldra born hunters and knew how to move unseen. All were eager to join in the operation and were ready to go before the sun had set.

Once the sun set Nico and Dets gathered their unit in one of the back rooms.

"So, whose Nadia and will she be able to keep up if we have to move fast?" Nico asked.

"She's Kel's business partner. The shop isn't far so we shouldn't run into trouble. The biggest problem will be if Nadia's actually in the shop and we surprise her. She might overreact," Dets replied.

"What kind of overreaction are we talking about? I don't need to get shot by one of our allies," Nico said.

"Nadia isn't a good shot. I'm more worried about the whole place being rigged to blow," Dets said.

"You know some strange people. But from what

the knights were saying she could be a real asset if she has more of those devices," Nico responded.

"Oh, Nadia's great just don't let her convince you to test anything. She doesn't really understand safety features," Dets joked.

"Noted. If everyone is ready let's move out," Nico said.

The other scouts nodded their agreement. Dets would have liked more input from the scouts, but they seemed to trust their leaders enough to follow orders. It was odd all three men were older than either Nico or Dets and from her experience the hunters around Khaldra were fiercely independent. It made them good scouts but Dets would have expected more trouble issuing orders. She had to assume it had something to do with Nico showing them all up when they were doing combat drills.

The five moved out of the tent and into the mostly empty market. Dets had only seen the market at night from a distance but there were always many lights and customers present even late into the night. Though she had found the market overwhelming seeing it nearly empty was somehow more disturbing. They moved through the empty market using the stalls to stay out of sight. They only saw one patrol as they made their way to Kel's shop. The patrol was too far away to spot them and it wasn't worth it to engage unless they were sure they could eliminate the patrol without raising an alarm.

Dets signaled for everyone to watch the road as she made her way to the back of Kel's shop. She didn't risk trying the front door though there was a light on inside that she could see. Dets made her way through an alley of a nearby shop then around the back to the forge. The forge was warm, which meant Nadia had been working recently. Dets knocked lightly on the back door.

"Unless you're bringing the iron go away," Nadia shouted through the door.

"It's Dets. Is the door safe to open?"

There was a series of thumps and clangs followed by Nadia opening the door.

"Why's it still dark?" Nadia asked sleepily.

"What have you been doing?" Dets asked.

"Well, I went out and got some supplies to finish my project. It was hard to find anyone open that early, but I managed. The sun was just coming up when I got in. Wait, was that yesterday or this morning? Guess it doesn't really matter. It's finished," Nadia said, with a sleepy smile.

Det looked into the workshop to see a massive gun mounted on a set of wheels. It was aimed at the door into the shop proper.

"Is that loaded? Actually, never mind, we need to get going. Kel is back and we're trying to gather everyone in the market. If it helps, you'll get a chance to test some of your projects," Dets said.

"Oh, that seems fun. Let me get everything packed up. But I'm gonna need help with the Renat gun. It took me over an hour to get it set up like that, and I only needed to move it a few meters," Nadia said her normal energy returning.

The Renat gun could be useful but moving something that heavy would require all the scouts. She wasn't sure if Kel would approve of the risk, but Nadia probably wouldn't leave without it.

"Okay. I'm gonna go get the rest of my allies. Is their anything I need to worry about if I bring them through the front?" Dets asked.

"No, Kel said I couldn't set anything up, which I why I aimed the Renat gun at the door. Haven't had a chance to test it but there's enough powder in those shells that even if it just explodes in place it'll do enough damage," Nadia replied completely ignoring the fact she would be caught in such a blast.

"Okay, get everything packed. We can figure out how we'll fit the Renat gun through the door once we're ready to go," Dets said.

"We could just use it. I think it will make a big enough hole," Nadia said.

"We are not blowing a hole in Kel's shop," Dets said, exasperated.

Nadia just shrugged in response.

Dets circled the building and looked around. She couldn't see any of the scouts. She whistled, imitating a bird call. The response call came a second later from the roof of a building down the street. Once the scouts had gathered again appearing from their various hiding spots. Dets led them through the front of Kel's shop and into the workshop. Nico took one look at the Renat gun and smiled wide.

"Now that is something. We could level the keep in minutes with a few of those," Nico said.

"It would probably take ten but now I've put one together more shouldn't take that long. Assuming it doesn't explode on the first shot," Nadia replied.

Nico took a careful step back from the weapon.

"Don't worry about that for now. The big problem will be getting this thing out of here and to the market unnoticed," Dets said, trying to get the unit back on mission.

"I still say we just blow the door but if you want it does come apart. Looks like some of you can lift the pieces then we reassemble it outside," Nadia interjected, looking at the three other scouts.

It took nearly ten minutes to move the Renat gun into the street. Nico and Dets watched the road for guards while the others worked at Nadia's direction. Once it was reassembled it only took two people to roll the contraption down the road. It was slow going and tensions were high as they crept through the open streets toward the market. They ducked into an alley, doing their best to fit the weapon in with them when Dets spotted a patrol moving several blocks away. Once the patrol passed they resumed their trip.

The attack manifested from nowhere. Ten guards, four in robes, led by a man in a flashy suit of red, white, and black appeared around the scouts between one second and the next. Nico reacted first ducking between the wheels of the Renat gun. Dets had to duck a spear thrust at her head and lost track of the others as she dashed forward to escape the encirclement.

When she rose, Kevin was locked in combat with a guard moving at enhanced speed. He wasn't able to bring his rifle to bear before he was run through. Relt managed to get a shot off, but it phased through the flamboyant noble and crashed into the wall behind.

One of the robed guards raised their hand and Relt crumbled to the ground, body writhing as if something was moving beneath his skin. Taran was the next to fire, hitting the guard facing him point blank and spraying blood and brains high into the air.

"Leave one alive," the leader said, voice echoing through the street.

Nadia pulled one of her devices from her bag and threw it at the cluster of mages. The explosion took out the four robed guards but knocked Taran off his feet. While he rose one of the guards drove their spear through his heart. The guard's left arm was tattered but whatever magic he was using was enough to keep the man standing.

Nico was ducking blows from three of the remaining guards weaving in and out of the Renat gun. Two of the guards advanced on Nadia, who was reaching into her satchel.

Det raised her rifle and aimed it at the advancing guards. Her hands shook as she tried to aim down the sight. She was scared, not of her own death but of losing Nadia. Her fear made it impossible for her to get a clear shot. Part of her knew it was because despite everything she had never taken another person's life and faced with the choice of killing someone or losing a friend she froze.

The *crack* of small arms broke her out of her shock. Nico had risen with her pistol aimed at the two guards advancing on Nadia. With two clean shots she had dropped the advancing guards, but it had exposed her to her opponents. Nico took a spear in the shoulder and her pistol fell from her hand. She managed to dodge the next two strikes but took two shallow cuts to her torso.

Dets's hands steadied, and she took a deep breath. If she did nothing everyone would die. There were only four opponents left. If she could pull some off Nico she could take Nadia and retreat. Dets just needed to pull the trigger. She looked to the leader of the guards. The young noble looked out of place in his finery. The look of pure elation on his face was what drove her to act. This was a man who reveled in the deaths of others, and he needed to die, even if it broke something in her. She raised her rifle.

"Nico, take Nadia and fall back. I'll hold them here," Dets shouted just before her rifle thundered. The bullet hit nothing but air as the noble vanished only to reappear a few feet to the right.

It did not matter she had pulled the trigger with the intent to kill, and she could do so again. She fired three times in quick succession, dropping one of the guards attacking Nico and wounding the other. Nico took the opportunity to run, grabbing Nadia's hand and practically dragging her down the street.

Det fired again at the unwounded guard, hitting him dead center but not stopping his charge. The man barreled into her as she tried to reload. She bounced off the ground, jumping to her feet and attempting to take cover as she reloaded. The now wounded guard was still propelled by his magic and shrugged off the gaping hole in his stomach as he advanced, spear raised.

Dets managed to get one round loaded through the side gate but was forced to block with her rifle as the man thrust forward. Her side flared with pain as the rifle knocked the spear off course. She worked the lever and brought the gun to bear just as the man thrust again. Her left hand was cut deeply but she brought the barrel in line with the man's chest in time to fire.

Blood spattered her face as the rifle thundered. She tried to reload, but her left hand would not follow her instructions. Unable to fight further she turned to run.

As she sprinted down the road, only the laughter of the leader echoing through the street followed her.

Chapter 28

Kel was awakened by the sound of distant gunfire. He had only managed to rest for a few hours on his rather uncomfortable sleeping pad. The gunfire was far enough away that he knew they were not under attack but the only people outside of the camp were Dets and her scouts. Kel was up and ready in seconds. His rifle sat loaded next to where he was sleeping. He hobbled into the main area of the tent.

Kinthross was speaking quietly with Aria and Corus in one corner of the room. Many of the soldiers were waking up but others were undisturbed by the sound.

"Who is available to send out?" Kel asked. Whatever trouble the scouts has gotten into he needed to send a response force quickly.

"Too big a risk. You must learn to trust your people. They will return or they won't," Corus replied.

"To the Promise with that. I'll go myself before I leave them out there," Kel retorted.

"Now, I don't like the idea of leaving people behind either. Nico will get them out or they'll all be dead before we get to them. Best thing for us to do is get ready to treat the wounded or hold the line if they come in with guards on their asses," Kinthross said.

Kel knew they were right, but he turned to Aria, hoping for support.

"They're half right. We can't do much without taking unacceptable risks, but I can. I've been avoiding the bastards for a while and I can handle whatever trouble they send my way without putting all this at risk," Aria said, gesturing to the camp.

"Fine. I'll get things ready here, but you best get moving," Kel said.

Aria gave a silent salute as she turned to go. She already had her black leather armor on, and her weapons were leaning nearby.

"Elias and Velen showed up after you went to sleep. Seems like a good idea to let 'em know to be ready for more wounded," Kinthross said.

Kel had met the arcanist Velen briefly, but he had only heard of Elias from the Field Knights. Apparently, the man was an accomplished surgeon who had assisted the Field Knights after their expeditions. Kel found the two men in one of the back rooms working with the few wounded. The area had been immaculately cleaned in short order and filled with cots. Velen was off in one corner working with what Kel assumed was alchemical equipment. Though the creation of gunpowder was an alchemical process it did not require the same elaborate setup the arcanist was working with. Elias was writing notes while speaking with one of the wounded sharpshooters. Kel decided it would be better to speak with Elias than disturb the arcanist's work.

"My name is Rickart Kel, Commander of the First Khaldaran. I understand you are to be our medical officer," Kel said.

"Don't expect me to salute you. I'm a doctor first

and foremost. I'll treat those who need it, but I have no interest in fighting. Now, unless you need me to treat that leg, I have work to do," Elias replied twirling his mustache as he survey Kel's leg.

"Keep my people alive and you can act however you wish. We may have more wounded coming in so be ready. Once things settle down I can worry about my own injuries," Kel replied.

"I intend to save everyone I can. That includes you. So, sit down on that cot and let me have a look at that leg," Elias ordered, as he unrolled a set of medical insturments.

"No time for that," Kel responded, moving to the door.

"It wasn't a request. If you expect to lead this army you'll need to have that treated. It's difficult to give orders if infection turns your brain to soup. Now sit," Elias said, leaving no room for disagreement.

Kel sat on the cot while Elias cleaned and rebandaged the wound. The man worked quickly and with precision. Whatever concoction Elias applied burned but seemed more effective at cleaning out the rotten wood than simple water. Once he had finished Elias made a note in his book and went back to his other patients. Kel rose to his feet with significantly less pain than before though he still had a slight limp. Elias eyed him as he moved to leave but said nothing.

When Kel reached the door out of the infirmary he was met by a rather sweaty and disheveled Nadia, half carrying Nico. Nico was covered in blood from several wounds and seemed to be only slightly conscious.

"Elias, wounded incoming!" Kel shouted.

Elias turned calmly and walked over to take Nico form Nadia.

"Velen, unless you're about to finish with that I need you over here," Elias said, ignoring Kel.

Kel felt somewhat useless as Elias began his work. Nadia seemed uninjured and simply took a seat on one of the cots. It was odd to see her so quiet, and Kel went over to see what had happened.

"Nadia, where is Dets?" Kel asked, keeping his voice as quiet and calm as possible.

"Oh, umm… I think… She was with us until… Then things got crazy and Nico was dragging me down the street. We got a block or so away then she collapsed," Nadia said, slowly struggling to put words together. Kel could see she was afraid and that was terrifying.

"Well, you made it. Elias will patch her up while you rest. I'll go find Dets," Kel said.

"They just appeared. I got some of them, but they were everywhere. Dets…" Nadia continued.

"Just rest. We can talk later," Kel said.

He let Nadia lay down and headed to the find Kinthross. The Field Knight would want to know about his second if he did not already.

It took Kel a few minutes to find Kinthross who was moving between the pickets, warning them. Kinthross had been the one to spot Nico and Nadia's approach. Kel wondered just what kind of work the Field Knights did if Kinthross could leave his subordinate in such a state and continue working.

Kel scanned the horizon while he spoke with Kinthross hoping to spot Dets.

"Any idea what happened out there?" Kinthross asked once Kel informed him that Elias had begun treatment.

"Not much. Nadia seemed shaken up, which is

surprising. All I know is the guards somehow got the drop on them and things went south," Kel replied.

"More to worry about. Hopefully, Aria can catch whoever got the drop on them," Kinthross said.

"Hopefully. Once Nico is up we can get a clearer picture. If we have already been discovered then we need to change the plan," Kel replied. He was still worried about Dets, but he needed to keep everyone else alive.

Kel heard shouting from one of the pickets to the east of his current location. Kinthross was already moving through the market, ducking between stalls at a run. Kel struggled to keep up but he doubted he could keep up, even uninjured. Despite his size Kinthross was fast and he seemed to know exactly when he could barge through something or needed to go around. By the time Kinthross arrived at the pickets' location Kel was a dozen meters behind. Kel saw the picket fire out into the market the flash of their rifle lit up the post and Kel could make out another figure ducked down in the stall. Kel could not identify the person until they fired as well. Dets had her rifle resting on the edge of the stall and was firing with only her right hand on the gun.

"Hold fire! They are just illusions," Aria shouted from somewhere down range.

The picket and Dets stopped firing just as Kel reached the stall the picket was using. He saw multiple approaching figures that all seemed armed. They moved through the market like real people avoiding objects and following paths. The only indications that they were not real was the fact their clothes did not move in the slight breeze. If Aria was wrong or it wasn't really her then they would be in trouble.

Kel chose to trust the pickets' judgement and

instead turned to look at Dets. "Are you wounded?" Kel asked her, breathing hard.

"Nothing life threatening, but my left hand is useless," Dets responded, holding up her hand, which dripped with blood. Kel could see white bone through the lacerated skin.

"Kinthross, get Dets to the infirmary. I'll handle things here," Kel said. The camp was his responsibility, so he needed to stay and see whatever was happening through.

The advancing force stopped just outside their perimeter, standing motionless and unblinking. It was eerie to see faces so still but that held so much detail. It was as if they were real people frozen in time. The illusions broke as Aria approached, swinging her greatsword with clinical efficiency. Once they were all dispatched Aria walked over to the post.

"Not enough time to track down whoever sent these. All I know is they're extremely powerful. Alexandra is an illusionist, but this would take ten of her to pull off and even then she would risk burning herself out. We have a big problem now that the nobility knows where we are," Aria said.

"After the beating we gave them today we'll have some time. We need a new plan, but first let's find out what happened out there," Kel said, turning to head back to the main tent.

The picket seemed shaken but kept his post. Kel would need to double the watch even if he did not anticipate a major assault that did not rule out some of the guards trying to gain favor by striking at them.

"From what traces I saw the illusionist cloaked a patrol and stumbled on the scouts while they were transporting that giant gun Nadia made. Looks like the scouts put up a fight despite the ambush but three of them died. I don't know where Nico is or if they had Nadia with them," Aria replied as they walked.

"Nadia and Nico are in the infirmary. Nico was severely wounded, and Nadia seems to be in shock. If they were bringing something that big it means Nadia finished the damned thing. If it's still intact we should recover it. I think I know just what we can use it on," Kel said, new plans running through his head. He would need Nadia's help to operate the thing, but it could prove a decisive advantage.

They headed straight to the infirmary. Kel needed Kinthross and perhaps the arcanist would have some ideas of how to deal with illusions. When they arrived they found Corus and Kinthross waiting outside. It seemed that the presence of so many people not actively assisting in the process had annoyed Elias enough to kick the two ranking officers out. Kel wanted to check on Dets and Nico but one look from Kinthross told him it would only cause problems.

"Fine, we'll leave Elias to his work. We have our own problems to deal with. I have a plan, but we need to work out the details. Corus, can you take a squad and retrieve something from where the scouts were ambushed?" Kel said.

"I can do this. It is good you ask this of others. Perhaps you are learning. But I will take more than one squad. Small numbers are good for scouts, but if the enemy also seeks this thing, perhaps I will need more force. I must ask, though ,where did this happen?" Corus replied with a grin. His hand rested on the haft of his ax.

"Aria can show you. Once you're back come to the meeting room," Kel said.

***

Kinthross and Kel spent the next hour or so in the meeting room pouring over the map and trying to come up with somewhere they could hide the army. It seemed to be a futile effort. Perhaps they could spilt the force up into small enough units to hide amongst the population. That had its own problems. Communication would be risky and difficult and most of their forces would not do well in open combat without the weight of numbers to make up for their lack of accuracy. Aria and Corus returned when they had finally given up on finding a new location.

"Well, I see why you sent me. That is quite the device. What do you call it?" Corus asked.

"Its Nadia's creation. She called it the Renat gun. Though why you would want your name attached to something like that I don't know," Kel said, putting down the papers he had been looking over.

"Might be time for whatever plan you were talkin' about," Kinthross said.

"Plan might be a strong word. We can't run and we can't hold out here. That really only leaves us one option. We take the fight to them. If we can get the Renat gun working then we might have a chance. We blow a hole in the keep's walls and march in with everything we have. Cut the head off the snake and put ourselves in a defensible position if anyone else wants to try their luck," Kel said.

"Defensible minus the big whopping hole we just put in the damn wall. But anything that gives me a chance to hit those bastards is fine by me," Aria replied with a laugh.

"Better than cloth walls and civilians. Might be all

we can do is push through," Kinthross said.

"I'm not hearing a no. Its a half-baked plan but I don't have anything better. All I know is we can't sit around here and do nothing," Kel said.

"I like it. Is simple. Less room for things to go wrong," Corus added.

"Except the whole damn plan going to shit," Kel replied.

"Parts of any plan go to shit," Corus replied. "This has the benefit that if it goes wrong none of us will be alive to care. When do you want to move?"

"Two days. We need time to prepare, and I want to press them a bit to see if we can get enough of the guards into the castle to make cleanup easier," Kel said.

They spent the rest of the night working out the exact disposition of troops. Despite Corus' warnings about the ever changing nature of battle Kel insisted on a complete accounting of everyone's positions and duties.

It was hard to tell time in the confined room, but everyone was exhausted by the time they concluded planning. They would not have much time to rest if they wanted to get moving on Kel's timetable. It would have to do even a few hours of sleep were better than none and the longer they waited the more likely it was that an attack would come. Kel stopped by the infirmary before he went to sleep. He doubted Elias would still be operating and even if they were asleep at least he could check on every one's condition. When he entered he was surprised to find Nico awake and mostly healed. Nadia and Dets were both asleep. Dets's left hand was wrapped tightly in clean bandages but from how it was raised above her on thin ropes it was still in poor condition. Kel walked over to where

Elias sitting half asleep in his chair. Before he spoke Nico signaled him to be quiet. She rose off her cot and silently walked over to Kel.

"Seems you're doing better. I had heard Elias was good but…" Kel whispered.

"Doc's good but this was mostly Velen and… well, Dets, kind of. If you want to waste an hour, ask Velen how it worked. All I know is Velen used Dets's bracelet to heal me a lot faster. Apparently, he could only fix one of us with it and Dets told him to use it on me. Elias said she might lose her hand because of it but she insisted," Nico whispered.

"At least you're both alive. I will need to adjust the plan somewhat. Assuming Elias clears you, I could really use the scouts in this operation. We will need to go over the plan before things kick off," Kel replied.

"You'll need to take that up with Dets. She's the scouts' commanding officer," Nico replied.

Kel was a bit shocked. Something had clearly changed between Nico and Dets.

"Very well. Have Elias send her over when she wakes. Kinthross might still be up, and he will want to know you're up and about," Kel said.

"Think I'll wait on both of those. You look like death and Kinthross has probably pushed himself too far as well. I might be up and about thanks to magic but both of you need to rest," Nico replied with a smile.

"Probably true, but that doesn't change what we need to do," Kel said.

Chapter 29

Aria stood in the doorway of a jewelry shop waiting for the signal. Over the last day and a half, the First Khaldaran had moved through Khaldra, pushing back the guards while avoiding a large-scale confrontation. It seemed the guards were confident in their defenses and had readily fallen back into the keep. Aria was worried that they were spread too thin. Even with the full thousand troops deployed their lines could be breached by a group of fifty guards moving in concert.

Nico and the scouts were on constant patrol, keeping an eye open for any attempted breeches. Dets had remained back with Nadia at the newly formed artillery unit. Nadia had chosen to steal the name it from the Imperial long range magic corps.

Kinthross, Brandish, and the rest of the vanguard were nearby, waiting patiently for the signal to begin the assault. Kel and Corus were moving constantly between the various units to maintain morale and respond to any deviations from the plan.

Aria watched the keep closely. Unlike most of the First Khaldaran she could see the spell work that reinforced the structure. She had brought the magical defenses to Kel's attention, but Nadia had assured them both that her Renat gun would overwhelm those defenses. Aria had her doubts, but no one had seen anything like that weapon deployed in battle. If it worked as intended its effect would be equal to some of the more devastating war magics and it had the benefit of being entirely physical. The other major problem were those spells set to kill anyone approaching the keep. Even if Nadia managed to create a breech those spells would make their entrance nearly impossible.

Aria had spent most of the morning working with Velen. The arcanist might be irritating but his suggestion could prove decisive. Aria might be able to resist whatever magic the keep threw at her, but she could only disrupt magic she could reach with her blades. Velen had suggested she might be able to extend the range of her ability. She had ignored most of his rather esoteric explanation, but she understood the broad strokes. Her natural resistance came from her inordinate source. If she allowed that magic to run free it would disrupt anything that entered the area. She had apparently done this in the past when she was in the heat of battle but doing so on command had been a challenge. She had needed to dredge up memories best left forgotten. The result had been a field nearly ten meters across centered on her that disrupted any magic that entered. She could only maintain it for a few minutes before the effort would burn her mind to ash.

"Worthless shites are just watching us. It's honestly a mite creepy," Brandish said, gesturing to the guards posted on the keep's wall. There had been a small exchange of blows when the First Khaldaran had taken their positions but neither side had accomplished much, and the fighting had died down.

"At least they aren't trying anything. Seems like

they are just waiting for us to try and take the keep. Arrogant bastards are in for a surprise if they think that wall is gonna keep us out," Aria said with a smile.

"Not even sure we need to blow the gate. I could get up there if I had enough covering fire," Brandish said, spinning his grappling hook.

"You wouldn't make it five feet up that wall before the defenses kicked in and killed you in any number of horrific ways," Aria replied.

"Ow the 'ell we plan to deal with that?" Brandish said with a grimace.

"That's why we have such a small vanguard unit. I'll keep us safe till we can take the wall. Nadia gave us charges to blow the sections around the breach. Should give us enough of an opening to funnel everyone through," Aria said, patting her satchel.

It was odd to carry a device capable of cracking a stone wall around, but she had been assured it was safe. She had her doubts but if it could help her fight she would accept the risk.

"Aye, that's a wonderful plan. Funnel everyone right into the bastards who can shoot fire from their arses," Brandish replied.

"Enough chirping. We got work to do," Kinthross interrupted from across the street.

Aria and Brandish both had their weapons drawn and ready in a second. They moved to their locations and waited. Kinthross raised a short barreled pistol into the sky. A bright red light shot forth and slowly fell to the ground. Even in the light of day it should be visible throughout the city. Kinthross had aimed it to fall just on the keep's main gate.

Aria held her breath as she waited. There was a thud from far in the distance. A second later the air filled with a whistling sound as she watched the sky. She couldn't see the shot until it exploded, landing perhaps ten meters from the wall of the keep. It was far closer to her than she would have liked and she felt the concussive force roll over her. Small pieces of cobblestone peppered the vanguard unit as Kel loaded another shot in his pistol. He fired another red light into the sky at the same location.

Aria flinched as she heard the second shot whistling through the air a few seconds later. It landed in the courtyard of the keep. If the first shot had not spooked the guards this one had them shouting, calling more men to the walls.

Kel fired again and this time blue light lit the sky above. Aria was aware they only had a few shells. If this missed they only had one more opportunity or they would need to scrap the operation.

Aria readied herself to charge as the third shot whistled toward them. It fell directly on the gate of the keep. Aria watched the spell work, reinforcing the structure strain and break as the immense force generated by the shell overcame the magical protections , reducing the gate to rubble.

Aria waited for Kinthross to fire the green light before she charged forward.

The Vanguard unit fell in around her and she spread her magic in an invisible field around them. Aria's vision swam and her head pounded. It took a lot to control her magic even in the simplest of ways.

Kinthross guided her through the breech as she struggled to keep her footing on the rubble. Once they were inside the firing started. Each shot sent waves of pain through her head. She could feel hundreds of spells attempting to break through, but each fizzled out sending a shock through her system. Even when they had tested the efficacy of the shield it had only been a with a fraction of the magic currently assaulting her. The plan had been for her to keep the vanguard protected until the courtyard was secure, but she was forced to drop the field as soon as they passed through the gate.

Aria dropped to her knees as she released the effect. As her vision cleared, she could only watch until her body felt like cooperating again. It was a sensation that remined her of growing up when her power threatened to overwhelm her. The riflemen of the vanguard had fanned out in the courtyard and were firing in alternating volleys to keep the guards on the wall pinned. Whenever a mage rose with a shield to block the incoming fire, one of Kel's sharpshooters on the outside would take them out from behind.

Brandish was already approaching one of the staircases leading to the top of the wall. His grappling hook spinning as he faced off against the guards pouring into the courtyard. The guard's shield might block bullets, but Brandish's hook would snap over, and with a twist he would pull the guard's shield forward. If one of the rifleman did not take a shot Brandish would whip the rope around his arm or leg and snap the limb forward, sending the point of the hook flying directly into the guard's face.

Kinthross was dancing between the guards' spears, snapping his harpoon forward into exposed limbs and rending flesh as he withdrew the viciously barbed weapon. The commander of the Field Knights was not the fastest or even the strongest fighter Aria had ever seen. Despite that he was a brutally efficient warrior. His fighting style reminded her of her first sword master. The Sword Saint Iffel Vendres was known for her complete command of the battlefield. Always a dozen steps ahead of her opponents she could move through even the fastest series of attacks without taking a single blow. Never moving more than was necessary and always ready with the perfect counter.

Kinthross was not quite on that level, but he had a command of the battlefield that Aria envied. His harpoon always found flesh while his opponents caught only air as he moved through the battlefield forcing the guards to respond with his sheer presence.

"Focus fire on the guards defending the stairs. We need to take the wall," Aria shouted over the mayhem. She rose to her feet and drew her side sword and dagger. Her greatsword would only be a hindrance in the confined space of the stairwell.

"If you want us up there then get off your arse and clear us a path!" Brandish called, pulling his hook through another series of spins before sending it sailing forward to skewer another guard's exposed leg.

The riflemen were exchanging fire with the mages on the wall and only a few were able to respond to her orders. Flashes of lightning and fire exploded all around as the mages did their best to strike down the vanguard without exposing themselves to the withering fire of the first Khaldaran.

Aria moved to fight alongside Kinthross, and together the two forced their way up to the wall. Aria took the lead as they emerged onto the wall. A dozen mages turned to face the new threat. They looked almost comical weaving their magic while crouched behind the ramparts.

Aria dropped the satchel to the floor and charged forward. She cut a dozen spells from the air to keep them from reaching Kinthross as she advanced. She cut down the guards standing between her and the middle of the wall. Her armor took a beating as she relied on it to protect her from the spear thrusts allowing her to close the gap and dispatch the guards. She had to hold the line once she reached the middle of the wall long enough for Kinthross to set the charge. She focused on fighting defensively, a feat only possible because of the narrow walkway atop the wall. Bullets whizzed past, far too close for comfort as the sharpshooters turned their fire on the mages focused on Aria.

"Fall back!" Kinthross shouted.

Aria crossed her sword and dagger above her head, signaling the sharpshooters and riflemen to cover her retreat. Aria retreated, watching as dozens of bullets slammed into the ramparts or anyone unfortunate enough to have stood to follow her.

When she reached the bottom of the stairs Kinthross and Brandish were facing off against a swarm of guards that had emerged from the keep proper. Aria took Kinthross's place as the Field Knight loaded another round in that strange pistol he had.

Aria was too busy facing off with the guards to see when he fired but the green glow from the projectile sent an eerie light over the courtyard.

A few seconds later everyone in the courtyard except a few of the mages were driven to the guard as the charges exploded with far more force than Aria would have expected. The guards rose to their feet while the soldiers of the First Khaldaran remained on the ground. Some of the riflemen were firing from prone but others were simply covering their faces. The Field Knights mostly armed with melee weapons were also covering themselves as best they could. The guards advanced on the fallen troops and the mages launched a dozen spells that Aria could do nothing to stop killing several of the rifleman.

The vanguard only had to endure a few seconds, but the toll was heavy. Aria was about to order the troops to their feet as the bulk of the First Khaldaran opened fire. Nearly one hundred fifty riflemen advanced, firing in volleys that tore the guards to pieces. The air above the vanguard was filled with hundreds of rounds as the troops advanced. Shields and spells broke under the overwhelming fire. Once the First Khaldaran advanced into the courtyard Aria and the rest of the vanguard rose to charge the keep.

"Corus, I leave taking the wall to you!" Kinthross bellowed as he charged the remains of the guard force.

Aria covered Kinthross and the Field Knights as they dispatched the remaining guards. It was bloody work, but they could not risk leaving forces behind them as they entered the keep proper.

Brandish took one part of the vanguard and advanced through the main doors to the keep. Aria and Kinthross took the smaller portion of the unit through the servants' entrance. Alexandra's information regarding the layout of the keep was critical to the success of the operation. Aria might be able to spot any hidden passages that utilized magic, but the layout was designed to disorient invaders and provide ample ambush locations.

"Kinthross, clear and hold or push for the center," Aria asked as they entered.

"Clear and hold. Need to take the keep if we want the city. Cutting the head off the snake can come once we get things under control," Kinthross replied.

Aria did not like the answer, but she was not fighting alone. The First Khaldaran was a full army, and its objectives had to come first. Aria and Kinthross led the way through the winding hallways. When they cleared a room, they left a few of their troops behind to hold the location. It was a slow process, and they heard more combat than they saw. The main body of troops led by Brandish was clearly facing heavy resistance in the ballroom. Aria would prefer to divert and assist but she needed to trust the plan. Alexandra had said there were multiple ways out of the keep and the Lord Kelen would look to escape if the tides turned against his forces. Her unit was supposed to block off the exits and tighten the noose around the governor's neck. If everything went according to plan Aria would have her chance at the noble bastard once he was forced to stand and fight.

Aria and Kinthross only faced limited resistance, and by the time they held most of the keep it was only them and two other riflemen proceeding through the last rooms. The small units of guards they had encountered were dispatched quickly either with rifle fire or blades. They entered the keeps main kitchen, which was the last area they needed to clear before Aria could join the real fight. Ten guards were in the room. Four of them wearing robes and one a fine suit with a family crest bearing a falcon holding a sword. The man in the suit was an illusion, which meant that the illusionist was nearby. Aria could hunt the coward down once the guards were dealt with.

She took the lead, doing her best to cover the riflemen from the mages. Kinthross ignored her protection, instead charging headfirst into the melee.

For such a big man he moved fast enough to catch the guards before the mages could unleash their magics.

Aria ignored the illusion and headed straight for the robed figures. Kinthross, with fire support, should be able to handle the five guards armed with spears. Even if they were enhanced they did not have the space to encircle the Field Knight, and they would be forced to hide behind their shields or risk exposing themselves to the riflemen.

Aria blocked the stream of fire shot at her from the air and parried a bolt of lighting with her dagger. She did not want a repeat of the last time she had taken one of those head on.

One of the mages forced a blood-red sword in their hands and charged her. She met the man's cut with her dagger, knocking it offline. Shock filled the man's face as her blade shattered his sword. She had seen that spell before the blade it formed could sheer through steel like butter, but with her magic pumping through her blades the spell crumbled like any other. Her side sword cut across the man's throat and she shoved him into a table as she moved past.

Dozens of knives flew through the air, driven by one of the other mages' spells. She had neither the time nor the reach to counter the spell entirely. Her armor stopped most of the hits, but she took a blade in the gap of her armor just between the cuirass and the legs. One of the riflemen screamed as a dozen knives riddled his unarmored body.

Aria ignored the two casting fire and lightning for the moment and charged the one whose magic had propelled the knives. She vaulted a table the mage propelled at her and ran the man through with her side sword.

She turned to face the other two. They had made the smart decision to focus on the remaining rifleman rather than deal with her. The rifleman fell to the ground as a charred husk as fire and lighting engulfed him.

Kinthross was locked in combat with two of the guards. The other three lay dead on the floor, bullet holes piercing their light armor. Kinthross was on the back foot against two enhanced opponents, but Aria needed to deal with the mages before she could go help.

The mages had turned to assist their allies, but it left them open for Aria. She cut down the one who could throw lightning and severed the hand of the fire mage. The mage had managed to complete his spell before Aria cut his hand and an abridged gout of flame shot forward, searing Kinthross.

Aria finished the man by driving the pommel of her side sword into his head. The mage crumbled to the ground as Aria moved to face the last two guards. The illusion had vanished at some point, but Aria could track the caster down later.

Kinthross fought valiantly against the two guards despite half his body being blistered. Aria was still too far away to assist but she threw her dagger anyway. She was not adept at throwing weapons but the blade sailing at the guard proved enough of a distraction. The man turned slightly and raised his shield to block. The dagger bounced off the shield but Kinthross's harpoon took the man in the gut. Kinthross kicked the man's corpse off the end of the harpoon, sending him into the other guard, who dodged out of the way with ease, but Aria had closed the gap. The man was trapped between the two and even his enhanced speed was not enough to overcome two experienced fighters working in concert. Aria landed the final blow with her side sword, landing a deep cut to the man's chest as he desperately tried to parry Kinthross's thrusts.

"I'll hold here. Need a minute to catch my breath," Kinthross said, leaning against one of the tables and dropping his harpoon from his blistered hand.

"Fall back to one of the other positions. You're too injured to keep fighting," Aria said as she moved to the door.

"I'll manage. Lets put an end to this, then I'll take a break," Kinthross said with a pained chuckle.

"Stay safe, Field Knight," Aria said as she left.

"Bring the storm, Magebreaker," Kinthross called from behind her.

Aria advanced through the rest of the corridors, heading too the main battle. She kept an eye out for signs of illusion magic. She stopped not far from the room she had just left when she noticed the smallest thread of magic coming from behind her. She turned around and ran back to Kinthross. As she approached, she heard Kinthross speaking through the slightly open door.

"Nico, what are you doing here?" Kinthross said.

"Kel ordered the scouts to help secure the castle. Figured I would come help," Nico replied.

Aria redoubled her pace and burst through the door into the kitchen. She was too late. A figure that looked exactly like Nico stood over Kinthross's body a knife buried through his heart and a look of shock on his face.

Aria charged the figure, which morphed into side same noble whose illusory self had stood with the guards they'd just fought. This time the man held a rapier and met Aria's thrust with a clean parry.

The man stepped back and addressed her. "What a pleasant surprise. You've fallen into such poor company, little Aria."

As Aria searched her memory for who the noble was she realized that this too was a facade.

"Show me your real face so I know who I'm killing," Aria shouted as she launched into a flurry of strikes.

The man dodged or parried each one with ease.

"Impressive. You really have grown. Such a shame I need to kill you," the man said, thrusting forward as he knocked her blade offline with a flick of the wrist.

Aria's armor turned the blow, but her counter stroke hit only air. The strike was close enough that the blade severed the magic and the illusion faded.

"Ales Dimiris? Promises, what are you doing here?" Aria said, stunned by the appearance of one of the heirs to the Great Houses.

Ales Dimiris was a completely unassuming person whose features were barely memorable, but that wicked smile was burned in her memory.

"Well, that is quite unfortunate," Ales said, still smiling. "I had hoped to remain in the shadows until this little revolt was dealt with. But it seems my cover has been blown, and the battle is lost."

"Then you die a complete failure. It's still better than you deserve!" Aria screamed.

She barreled into Ales, letting her armor protect her. She drove her helmet into Ales's face, drawing blood and sending the illusionist reeling back. Instead of following up with her side sword she used the time to draw her greatsword. Ales might seem like a pushover, but the mage was at least as well trained as Aria and even if she could see through illusions they could still be problematic. With her armor and greatsword Aria had the advantage and she intended to use it.

"Now that was rude. I suppose I should get serious," Ales said, laughing. Hundreds of illusions burst forth. A roiling mass of people some bore faces from her past carved into her mind despite her best efforts to forget. Though she could tell which were illusions the sheer density of magic blocked Aria's ability to see the mage.

Aria cut down the illusions as they fell over her. She could not advance unless she was sure Ales would not use the cover to strike from an unexpected direction.

Seconds passed as Aria faced the swarm, but no blow came. Aria decided she needed to risk it and expanded her magic, creating the same field as before but only for a second. When her vision cleared she was alone with Kinthross's body.

Ales might have fled but the illusionist would be a deadly threat until they were caught. The heir of House Dimiris was known for their cunning and ruthlessness. Backed up by the magical ability of the greatest mages in the realm, Ales was a miles above any of the nobility in Khaldra. Aria tried to follow Ales, but the mage had left a dozen false trails as they made their escape.

When Aria had finally given up on hunting down the mage, she moved to meet up with the bulk of the First Khaldaran. She did not know what awaited her, but the muffles sound of gunfire and the crackle of magic in the air told her it would be bloody. She had played her part now the rest was up to those who called Khaldra home.

Chapter 30

"Not a single one of those worthless bastards answered my call!" Kelen shouted, his normal ice calm shattered. Weeks of dealing with riots followed by a surprise attack had shattered morale and left his troops exhausted. Merrel's report that none of the local nobility sent reinforcements was a disaster.

"We can still hold the walls are strong and a prepared mage can turn aside their weapons with ease." Merrel replied in a blatant attempt to soothe Kelen.

"Then go prepare" Kelen snapped.

Merrel departed with a bow leaving Kelen to ponder his situation. He needed an opening. Sending troops through the city was simply asking for an ambush. Even if Merrel had reported the location of the enemy camp a direct assault would only cause them to scatter. The keep was secure but simply waiting for the enemy to attack the stronghold was foolish. Whoever led the rebels had shown considerable acumen feinting with a small party while the bulk of their troops entered the city unopposed.

Kelen stalked through the keep heading towards the workshop he had granted the arcanists. He had ordered them to construct an angel in the hopes the war construct could be deployed to suppress riots. It was an expensive and time-consuming project but now it might prove enough to turn the tide.

When Kelen arrived at the workshop he found Arcanist Modrel asleep at his workbench. The arcanist was the closest thing to an artificer Kelen could drag away from the arcanum. Kelen slammed his hand down on the workbench.

"Is it ready?" Kelen asked as Moldrel startled awake.

"Who...Why?" Moldrel said scrambling around for his spectacles. Once he put them on his eyes grew wide as Kelen stood arms crossed waiting for an answer. "Lord Kelen, I was just —"

"Is it ready, or do I need to find someone else?" Kelen interrupted. It was an idle threat, but Moldrel did not need to know that.

"Mostly Lord Kelen, the body is finished but we need more time to finish the control matrix. As it is operating it would require a dedicated mage of substantial power." Moldrel answered.

"It will have to do," Kelen began. He had controlled angels before but only in military drills. Normally they acted like an extension of the mage following specific orders with rudimentary intelligence. Without a control matrix it would be more like stepping into the construct's body. "Get it to the bailey, I'll take the control crystal now."

"Of course, Lord Kelen. Let me get..." Moldrel said picking through the cluttered workbench. The ground shook as the muffled sound of thunder rang through the keep. Moldrel dropped the box he had just picked up.

"No time to move it now." Kelen said grabbing

the box from the table. He smiled as he ran through the keep towards the ballroom. This was the opening he needed. The enemy might be clever but attempting to assault the keep was an impulsive move. Kelen intended to make the last move these rebels made.

The keep rocked again causing him to falter for a second. *What kind of weapon were they using,* Kelen thought to himself. If this assault continued, he would need to reinforce the keep lest it collapse. He reached the ballroom just as a third explosion detonated just outside. He could feel the spell work on the gate collapse even from here.

He barked orders to hold the ballroom as he ran. It was the only location in the keep where the majority of his forces could fight as a cohesive unit. He climbed the stairs to the balcony and entered one of the adjoining rooms. Locking the door behind him he took a deep breath, readying himself. He opened the box removing the gilded crystal within. The glyphs carved on the metal swam in his head as he poured magic into the crystal.

He felt himself fall to the ground, but it felt distant. For a time, the world was dark, and his mind felt heavy. He focused on the glyphs swirling through his mind and the world shot into focus. He stood head bowed in the workshop. He could see arcanist scrambling to remove restraints from what was now his body. Ten feet tall with steel limbs lined with glyphs and dotted with crystals the angel was built for combat. Its left arm ended in a two-meter-long curved blade, its right arm was tipped with a crystal designed to channel magic into a burst of elemental fury. Kelen rose snapping chains and sending the arcanists scrambling. He took a few uncertain steps before he got the feel for the construct's movements. The few doors that stood between him and the ballroom exploded as his new form crashed through them. The sensation of running without feeling was odd. The construct could not transmit sensations through its metal shell but provided a vague awareness of impacts through jolts of magic. The world was oddly silent despite the shattering of wood and stone. The angel was capable of hearing but only sound above and below a specific threshold. He could adjust that threshold, allowing him to hear the beating of a flies wings even in the midst of combat.

Kelen entered the ballroom to a combination of shock and cheers. His guards had arrayed a barricade in the center of the room composed of stone and steel conjured into place. It was a formidable defense though Kelen doubted it would be needed. He adjusted his hearing to listen in on Mercius giving orders to the assembled men. It was all basic positioning and responsibilities, but Kelen wanted to be sure that the men were listening after the sudden shift in leadership. There had been a few incidents of insubordination following Delos' death. It was a bitter irony that if not for the losses suffered at the hands of the 'magebreaker' Kelen might have needed to dispense justice himself. Kelen smiled to himself at the thought of crushing the 'magebreaker' once and for all. His emotions prompted the angel to let loose a discordant screech. He could see the guards covering their ears, which only served to amuse Kelen. The sheer sense of power that thrummed through the construct was intoxicating. Kelen reveled in it for a time until the sounds of battle outside caught his attention.

Kelen chastised himself for losing focus. He

adjusted his hearing listening to the sounds of struggle outside. He could hear the enemy officers giving orders as they took control of the walls. Kelen cursed himself for underestimating the enemy. The crystal arm glowed a bright red as the door exploded inwards leaving an obscuring haze of smoke. It might hinder the men behind him, but the angel was made for battle its eyes if they could be called that were attuned to more than light. His vision shifted revealing the internal magic present in all life as glowing outlines. Most of the men arrayed outside were barely visible. Their sources so feeble as to barely register. However, a massive source of magic crossed the edges of his vision for an instant. Kelen considered pursuing the magebreaker who seemed to be entering another way, but pragmatism forced him to deal with the immediate threat. There would be time enough later.

An arc of lighting shot from the crystal snuffing out the lights in front of him. He advanced ignoring the tiny jolts of magic as rifle fire raked his form. A gust of wind from behind cleared the haze of smoke as streams of magic shot forth from the barricade. The angel screeched as Kelen watched the panic grow on the faces of the traitors before him. They might not know what an angel was, but its deadly presence was enough to put fear in their hearts. Kelen waded forward arm scything out to cut them down like wheat. Some stood strong but without the physical enhancements of magic none could so much as slow his blade. He raised the crystal altering the spell to release a burst of flames. The crystal glowed black as flames wreathed it. Before he could incinerate those before him ice sprouted around the crystal turning his attention to a mage amongst the traitors. The man held an ax in each hand

and was dressed like a krais mercenary. Kelen sprung forward blade arm sweeping out to cut the man down. His arm was slowed as two men rushed forward and held on to his arm. One raised a hammer and began pounding on his joints. The ring of steel on steel thrummed through his senses. The other simple held on for dear life. Kelen brough the crystal down on the clinging man crushing him while a steel spike pierced the head of the man hammering away.

He returned to focus on the mage, but it seemed Mercius had already engaged vines snaked around the man spearing forward from every direction as the man whirled his axes cutting them away. Ice armor formed to take any blows that passed his guard. Kelen left the mage to Mercius and returned his attention to slaughtering the traitors.

"Shite, why's it always my job to handle the big ones." One of the enemy officers said, the words clear as day despite the battle raging around. Kelen turned to focus on the arrogant gnat who dared challenge him.

The man was stocky with heavy muscle clothes tattered and stained with blood. Something blurred through the air around him swinging silently on the end of a heavy rope. The man advance as Kelen raised his bladed arm in challenge. The man struck from farther then Kelen would have guess but the futile attack simply pinged the constructs legs. Kelen's blade swept out to cleave the man's head from his shoulders. The man ducked and Kelen saw the rope pull tight as the man slide across the blood slick stones under the blade. Kelen looked down to see the man at his feet.

"Wanted to shove this up your arse but this'll have to do" The man said. Thrusting something from his belt into the body of the angel where its torso met its legs. Kelen raised a leg and kicked the man away sending a satisfying jolt up the legs. Kelen wished he could hear the man's bones crack as his body flew into the ranks of the traitors. Kelen once again raised the crystal arm with the mage engaged elsewhere he could unleash upon the enemy.

Kelen felt a jolt from his torso and his vision moved against his will. He felt his body hit the ground and could no longer sense the constructs legs. Even damaged he unleased the flames in a torrent. It was difficult to aim from his current position, but dozens burned in the magical flames. Three men cloaks steaming emerged from the torrent. Kelen dropped the flames to bring his blade up to cut out their legs. One of them raised a rifle and a jolt shot through Kelen's arm as he lost control of the blade. Another of the men raised a splitting maul modified to a war pick and brought it down on the crystal arm shattering it. The last placed something just under Kelen's neck. Kelen managed to crush the man's arm with his head, but the man was dragged back before Kelen could do more.

Kelen shook his head to dislodge whatever it was but moments later a flash engulfed his vision. He brought his hands up to clear his eyes, realizing that he was back in his body lying on the floor just outside of the ballroom. The sounds of battle crashed over him, rifle fire like rolling thunder and the crackle of lightning filled the air, it was all overshadowed by the screams of the dying.

Kelen rose to his feet unsteadily, he needed time to adjust to his own body again. The battle raged on as he raised his defenses. Moments later he strode through the door armor gleaming with magic. The maelstrom of battle swirled around him as he took in the scene.

The mages more suited to ranged combat were ducked behind their barricades unable to defend and attack simultaneously in the face of the withering fire of the traitors. Even behind the barricade dozens had already fallen either riddled with holes or blown to pieces by explosions. Craters dotted the backline, but the barricade itself remained intact.

Mercius along with the melee troops were faring better. Enhanced strength and speed allowed them to overwhelm the traitors armed with makeshift weapons. Even if the rifles were proving a match for those behind the barricade there were only enough men armed with them to deal with one threat at a time.

Mercius was facing off against the officer who Kelen had thought dead. The man was clearly injured but still fought on. If Kelen had not seen the man's lack of magic, he would have assumed he was using enhancement magic. The man was snapping his hook out in a complex series of arcs and straight strikes, it forced Mercius to fight without the time to utilize more powerful magic. The vines that shot forth or writhed across the ground were intercepted by the officer's allies.

As Kelen watched one of the traitors fighting in the melee drove a blade affixed to the front of a rifle under a guard's breastplate. The man ducked a strike from another guard and jumped back. The gap filled by another traitor wielding a spear. Without hesitation the man raised his rifle and fired towards Mercius, ignoring the guards rushing him. Kelen raised his hand to stop the shot, but he was too slow. Mercius spun blood spurting from his shoulder. Kelen directed his magic to the officer who had instantly responded to press the advantage. The man was driven to the ground and Kelen pump more magic into the spell seeking to crush the man once and for all. Kelen was forced to duck as rifle fire whizzed passed him. He kept focused on crushing the man but with so much of his power focused on the spell his defenses were faltering.

As more rounds pierced his defenses Kelen was forced to focus on defense. He watched as the man blood flowing from his ears and mouth rose to one knee. Mercius had recovered and begun resuming his attack. Vines crossed paths with the officer's hook as both shot towards their target. The man's hook proved faster burying its point in Mercius's neck. Vines shriveled and died centimeters from the officer's face.

Kelen began to chant working his hands through a complex pattern of motions. He poured more magic than was wise into the spell feeling the pathways in his head burn with power. Kelen spread his own defenses across the entire barricade. Providing cover for the mages huddled behind it. His men sensed the change and rose confident in Kelen's protection. Blasts of magical energy pierced through the defense unimpeded. Dozens of riflemen fell in an instant. The others scrambled to cover some huddling behind the body of the fallen angel. Kelen smiled as his men brought death to the traitors.

Chapter 31

The sounds of battle reached Kel as he moved through the backlines where he was directing supplies and the meager reserves he had. Even over the sound of rifle fire a discordant screech reached him. He had no way to know what could make that sound, but it was concerning. He turned before reaching Jack's position and broke into a run. His rifle bouncing on its sling as he sprinted through the streets towards the keep. He knew his men could handle whatever abomination Kelen was throwing at them but Kel felt useless hiding while other's fought and died. He knew what he had been doing was important but so close to the end he could not bring himself to simply sit back and direct others. Even at a dead sprint it took him a minute or more to reach where his sharpshooters were stationed.

Kel caught up with a squad of sharpshooters moving to a better position. They only noticed him when he ran passed. Kel burst into the road directly infront of where the keep's gate had stood. No magic flared to cut him down. It was a good sign that the enemy mages were unable to return fire.

"Form up on the commander." The squad leader shouted ushering his men to cross the road and support Kel.

Kel climbed the stairs of a nearby building, taking a vantage point that allowed him to see into the open door of the keep. The battle was chaotic, and smoke and flames made it hard to differentiate friend from foe. In an instant the smoke crashed to the ground revealing Marius Kelen in glowing armor casting some kind of spell. Its effects became apparent immediately as magic burst forth from the enemy lines. Kel watched as his men were cut down. Some burned alive other's bodies were torn apart by unseen force. One small squad had ducked behind some metal construct that lay just in the doorway. Black shapes like butterflies swirled around them and where they touched down the men shriveled and died.

Kel leveled his rifle doing his best to ignore the horrors before him. He needed to do something, or his men would die. Kelen and his spell were the problem, so he focused on that. He could see rifles firing uselessly into the magic defense. He slowed his breathing focusing on the task at hand.

Kel watched the swirls of smoke around Lord Kelen. As the smoke drew close it fell to the floor like everything his men had thrown at the mage. Every so often for just a brief moment the smoke would rise subtly. Kel focused everything on those brief moments as he lined his rifle up. The screams of the dying and the roar of rifle fire fell away as he focused. Kel was alone, no soldiers facing death on his orders, no war council, no city to save, just the swirling smoke. Even Kelen in all his power, faded to nothing more than a vague idea beyond that smoke. His breathing slowed to match the odd rhythm of the smoke.

He could not say when his finger had closed on the trigger but the rifle thundered. The odd silence shattered like glass as the world returned in all its horrific glory. Even through the chaos of the battle Kel could see Kelen slump against the wall with a look of surprise across his face. Kelen slid down the wall a trail of blood marking his passage.

Without lord Kelen the imperial forces faltered and broke. The mages who had fought under Kelen's protection fell first under the withering fire of the first Khaldaran who responded immediately to the change. Blades and rifles brought low those that remained over a few bloody minutes. Some of the imperial forces attempted to flee but trapped in the keep they would be hunted down in time.

Kel watched as Brandish walked supported by Zed to stand over Kelen body. Blood dripped from Brandish adding to the growing pool on the ground. Brandish one arm limp at his side tore Kelen's crest from his armor and raised it into the air. The men of the first Khaldaran paused in their gruesome work all eyes on the field knight.

When the cheers reached his position Kel ordered his sharpshooters to march into the keep. The courtyard was a charnel house. Bodies of over a hundred guards and at least fifty of his own troops littered the ground and pools of blood splashed over boots as his men marched through. He ordered his men to man the walls then went on his own to the battlefield in the ballroom. The courtyard had only been a precursor to what he found inside. The ballroom was the site of the fiercest fighting and distance had obscured the details. Over a thousand men in total had been crammed into a space smaller than the main tent in the market. Between the vanguard force and the mainline troops, he had sent nearly five hundred men to face off against nearly six hundred guards. From what he could see all of the guards and the nobility who led them had fallen but it had cost the First Khaldaran dearly. Of his five hundred only a fraction remained.

"Corus, status report," Kel shouted, doing his best to be heard above the wails of the wounded and dying.

"It is done. The men fought with real heart. I've seen men break when faced with far fewer loses. This speaks well of the men of Khaldra. We will know in time what price was paid but this will be a story for the ages," came the reply.

The mercenary made his way over to Kel. His scarred face bore new wounds, but he moved with a calm ease. His hand axe, stained with blood, hung at his waist and his left hand was covered in an icicle stained red with blood. Corus seemed to fit the morbid tableau perfectly.

"The day isn't over yet. I have Elias coming with the artillery unit. He'll see to the wounded while we prepare for whatever response comes," Kel said. He wished the fighting was done but there were still the local nobility and any guards who were not in the keep to contend with.

"On this I must disagree. Even if others come it will not be to fight. Those here fought to the last because we gave them no choice. Others will not be so inclined. We can prepare but you should prepare to speak to the people. The city is yours whether you want it or not. This is the battle you must prepare for. I can only speak for myself, but war is simple. What comes after, not so much," Corus replied.

The mercenary's words proved true in time. No attacks came from the remaining enemies in the city. Hunting down those who feld into the keep was simple enough. When Dets and Nadia reached the keep a few hours later. Dets reported that her scouts had seen a large group of scouts and some of the nobility fleeing the city. Nadia seemed inordinately pleased with herself. Her Renat gun had worked perfectly, and she spent more time looking at the results than at the horrors laying all around. Kel could not blame her. He would look away too if he could.

The victory felt somewhat hollow as reports came in on the casualties the First Khaldaran had suffered. Of the over one thousand men Kel had led into Khaldra three days prior only four hundred remained and a third of those had suffered wounds. It was a stark number that included nearly half the Field Knights, most notably Kinthross. Kel had learned from Aria that the commander of the Field Knights had fallen. Kel did not have time to process the loss of someone who had proven crucial to their success. He dreaded having to inform Nico about Kinthross's death, but as the commander it was his duty.

***

Kel had spent the last two day planning. So much needed to be done. Khaldra was free but only as long as it stood united. To that end Kel had prepared an address to the people of Khaldra. A process which had proven far more difficult than he had anticipated. Prepared or not the time had come.

The amphitheater was even more filled than it had been on the day of Dennet's execution. Kel had ordered the First Khaldaran to come unarmed. He would not be a leader who ruled through force. He would have preferred his troops to stay at their posts but that had proven impossible. Despite their losses the men trusted him and none of them would miss him addressing the city. It was a massive security risk and but Corus, Nico and Dets had volunteered to stay and watch the keep. Some of the scouts were already on patrol so they would have some warning.

Kel took the stage exactly at noon. It was a new stage built specifically for the occasion with posts holding banners featuring the crossed rifle design matching the pin on Kel's uniform. How Jack had gotten those made was a mystery, but the quartermaster seemed even more capable now they had access to the city. As he took the stage his men cheered, and the crowd responded by cheering even louder. Kel wonder how he would be heard over the noise of thousands of people, but Alexandra had assured him she would handle it. Kel took a deep breath and began to speak.

"It is my honor to announce that Khaldra is free. Two days ago the brave men of the First Khaldaran fought and won. I do not need to tell you why we fought each of you has struggled under the empires rule. But what I need to say is that it was not the wealthiest or strongest among you who won the day. It was your neighbors and friends it was the people of Khaldra who banned together and faced the might of the empire. The First Khaldaran is not a new overlord it is the strength of the people of this city brought to bare. A city built without magic that overcame the harshness of this land. In the name of respecting that strength and the freedom it has brought the people will have their chance to choose who leads them. You have my word that none of my men will challenge the people's voice. We must move forward secure in our strength, which mean we cannot turn on those who will add their strength to ours. I understand that many of you hold great resentment for the nobility who ruled you, but we must stand united. Khaldra is free but we cannot take that for granted we must stand ready to face what may come. It was fire and steel that brought us to where we are today, but it will be Valor and Cunning that preserves what we have built."

[end]